P9-CES-065

Books by B. V. Larson:

STAR FORCE SERIES
Swarm
Extinction
Rebellion
Conquest
Battle Station
Empire
Annihilation

IMPERIUM SERIES
Mech Zero: The Dominant
Mech 1: The Parent
Mech 2: The Savant
Mech 3: The Empress
Five By Five (Mech Novella)

OTHER SF BOOKS
Technomancer
The Bone Triangle
Z-World
Velocity

Visit BVLarson.com for more information.

EMPIRE

(Star Force Series #6)
by
B. V. Larson

STAR FORCE SERIES
Swarm
Extinction
Rebellion
Conquest
Battle Station
Empire
Annihilation

Copyright © 2013 by the author.

This book is a work of fiction. Names, characters, places and incidents are either products of the author's imagination or used fictitiously. Any resemblance to actual events, locales or persons, living or dead, is entirely coincidental. All rights reserved. No part of this publication can be reproduced or transmitted in any form or by any means, without permission in writing from the author.

ISBN-13: 978-1482652765
ISBN-10: 1482652765
BISAC: Fiction / Science Fiction / Military

-1-

I stood on the bridge of my battle station, gazing into a sphere filled with photo-reactive nanites. We called this three-dimensional display system a "holotank". The unit took some getting used to, but it was definitely superior when it came to depicting space battles and had replaced our planning tables. The base of the unit was surrounded by flat screen consoles which could be manipulated by touch. I ran my fingers over the consoles, and the imagery in the holotank responded, displaying data from anywhere I wished in the Eden star system.

The Eden system was like most of the star systems we'd encountered in that there were two "rings", each of which connected the system to another. The rings were interstellar gateways. Each of these vast structures was a massive alien artifact. Most of the rings hung in space in stable orbits. They were often miles across and to the best of our knowledge they were made of collapsed star-matter. When passing through a ring a spaceship was instantly transported to another location, usually to another star system.

We didn't know who'd built these amazing structures we called "rings", but they now provided our only realistic method of travel from one star system to the next. Our ships weren't fast enough to make interstellar leaps on their own, not without many years of travel time.

Collectively, the rings connected a long chain of star systems. The chain went back to Earth and one step beyond that to Bellatrix. At our end of the chain, there was only one system we'd discovered

1

beyond Eden, which I'd named the Thor system. All told, we'd discovered six connected systems.

The battle station I was aboard now was the only one of its kind. I'd built it very close to one of the rings to protect the Eden system from invasion. Like a castle built atop a mountain pass, it guarded against intruders by focusing its defenses on a single, small entry point. The station and the ring it guarded both orbited Hel, the coldest, most distant planet in the system. On the far side of the ring was the Thor system with its population of unfriendly lobster-like inhabitants. Beyond Thor, we didn't know where the chain of rings led. It was my suspicion there were more chained-together stars out there, each circled by alien worlds. I suspected there was a *lot* more of them.

The holotank showed the local tactical situation, which was routine at the moment. I manipulated the consoles again, causing the imagery in the holotank to shift. Green slivers of light flashed into focus as I panned across the system. The green slivers floating in space represented my ships, which were scattered around Eden's star. When I located the biggest cluster of ships, I zoomed in. I'd assigned most of them to guarding the second ring, which began a path of interstellar jumps that led home to Earth.

I no longer needed ships on guard here, at the gateway to Thor. The battle station took care of that duty now. It had been a tremendous effort to build the battle station. It wasn't finished and I didn't have enough people to man it properly, but it was an amazing fortification. No one was going to pass by without having to deal with this monster I'd built on the border.

I spent an hour going over reports and adjusting a few standing patrol orders. Reassured that nothing interesting was happening, I left the command center and walked the long, echoing corridors. The battle station was as big as a sky-scraper and the exterior bristled with weaponry. It wasn't finished yet, but it would have to suffice, as I had new worries now. I'd put so many of my resources into this station, I'd neglected the fleet. This was an elementary flaw in my strategy. Ask any commander running a war: you have to have fleets, not just forts. Fortifications were cheap and powerful, but they couldn't move to meet the enemy wherever they might come. If Earth was hit next, and Crow begged for my help, this monstrous battle station might turn out to be a colossal waste of effort. If it turned out to be badly placed when the time came, it wouldn't save a single life.

I walked down an echoing shaft to a big observation window on the sunward side of the station. The blast shields had been rolled back and the stars outside were visible to my naked eyes. I stared out there in the stark beauty of open space. Outside the station, the stars around us formed a thousand points of light. This far away from the G class sun, they were intensely bright against the perfectly black void.

My boots clanged on metal floors as I approached the big window. There, almost pressed up against the frosty quartz plane, was Sandra. Her pose reminded me of a housecat watching the world go by outside.

"I knew I'd find you here," I said.

"I knew you'd come looking," she responded, and gave me a warm smile over her shoulder. Then she turned back to the darkness of space that rotated gently as we watched.

"I think this station is done for now," I said. "I think it's time we moved back to the planets, and retooled our factories. It's time to produce mobile defenses."

"Ships?"

"Yes."

I walked up to join her at the window. She didn't move, but continued staring.

"I can see them sometimes, you know," she said. "My eyes aren't like normal eyes anymore. I can see the faintest flicker of movement out there, when one of our vessels drifts between my eyes and a star."

I glanced at her, but said nothing. What she was describing should not have been possible. The ships were too far, too tiny relative to the stars. A specialized telescope might not have been up to the task. But no one, not even Sandra herself, fully understood the natural capacities of her new body. She was part human, part nanotized super-soldier—and part something else. She'd been changed by an extinct colony of Microbes. In essence, she was one of a kind now. I'd undergone similar baths administered by Marvin. But his application had been much more controlled and specific. Hers had been done by the Microbes themselves, free to experiment and edit whatever they wished in her flesh.

3

"I thought when I went through the baths we'd become closer," I said. "You know that don't you?"

Now, she did look at me. She seemed troubled. "That's why you did it? Not just so you could run off and be the first human to risk your life landing on a gas giant?"

I hadn't actually *landed* on the gas giant, if such a thing was even possible. I'd only dipped down several thousand miles into the dense atmosphere. But I'd met the Blues there, and talked to them in their own environment. Most importantly, I'd survived.

This business of her body alterations and mine was a sore point between Sandra and I, so I decided to switch the topic. I turned my attention back to the scene outside. I knew my ships were out there somewhere, dark and invisible to my naked eyes among these jewel-like stars. I'd reorganized them since we'd driven the Macros out of the system. One ship patrolled each of the habitable worlds, and the rest were out at the far ring, the one that guarded the route home to Earth.

"What do you think is happening back home?" I asked Sandra.

"Crow is taking over, of course," she said quietly.

"How can you be so sure?"

"If he was in serious trouble, he would have begged us for help. If he was in minor trouble, he would have whined and complained. Since he's being quiet—that's the worst. That's when he's up to no good. That's when things are going his way."

I nodded. "Your analysis matches my own. He's planning something. He's not talking because he wants to catch us by surprise."

"You have a history of underestimating him. Let's think bad thoughts for a moment. What is the worst move he could make?"

I shrugged. "He could send out a fleet, maybe. A force strong enough to order us to submit to his will. Or something else—something I haven't even thought of yet."

"What are we going to do about it?"

We both looked at one another. Her pose was relaxed, crouching there in the window, but I could see her eyes were troubled. I forced a thin smile.

"Don't worry. I'm building a fleet of my own."

"We only have three hundred marines. After you train every last one of them to pilot a ship, what will we do then?"

I frowned, she had a good point. My battle station was operational, and I was convinced it could stop a small Macro invasion consisting of one hundred ships or less. It couldn't be at both ends of the star system at once, however.

"We could built a second station at the Helios ring."

She shook her head. "Where would you get the raw resources?"

"That's the problem. At the other ring, we don't have a handy planetoid to mine and provide all the metals and fuels we need. Hell, we don't even have any real idea if this one can stop the Macros when they come again. How big will the next enemy flotilla be when it finally arrives? It's unnerving, having no true concept of the extent of the enemy empire or their forces."

"Intel has still produced nothing?"

"Exactly squat."

"Then we have to guess, and guess right."

I nodded, unhappy that I was the one doing the guessing. The Macros didn't keep rolled up maps or computer files on hard disks, explaining their plans. As closely as we could determine after dissecting their artificial brains, they didn't have a grand central plan. They operated like a termite mound. Each individual linked with whatever others were available. Each piece of the puzzle did its part without central command beyond the local area, which at most consisted of a star system. In a sense, they were centralized and decentralized at the same time. Whatever Macro forces were close enough to one another to coordinate did so automatically, but they had no discernible grand strategy, other than the outcome of their programming.

I'd once theorized there was another kind of Macro, a Macro-Superior. But now, I'd abandoned the idea. The enemy did appear to become smarter when there were a lot of them in close proximity. But this was apparently due to their design, not the existence of a Macro-Superior. When the machines came close to one another, they automatically linked up and each shared part of its processing time with the others. This process formed what we called "Macro Command". In a sense, when I communicated with Macro Command, I was talking to all of them in the local region at once. There was no single super-macro that held the role of leadership.

Logic dictated that smaller groups should be dumber, and that there would be a lack of grand strategy. They had no overall plan, just sets of heuristic rules to follow. Still, this disadvantage didn't seem to bother them all that much. Individual colonies were very effective at building up forces until they metastasized to the next star system along the chain of rings. They didn't need a grand strategy, which was difficult to maintain over such a vast region of space anyway. If each little soldier robot did his job, the effective end result was a steamrollering force of endless machines.

I had no way of knowing how big the next fleet would be, which left a gnawing sensation of worry in my gut. I knew the battle station could hold against the invasion fleets I'd seen in the past, but maybe they'd been scouting missions on the fringe of a vast amorphous blob of star systems.

"I'm flying out tomorrow," I said. "I'll hit the inner planets, and see how our exploration teams are doing. Will you be coming with me?"

Finally, she gave me a full-fledged smile. "Just try to stop me. I'm sick of this ghost-filled station. The air still smells canned no matter how many algae tanks you run it through."

We left, and headed back to our quarters. Sandra hadn't been too happy about my recent associations with Captain Sarin, but she'd gotten over it once Jasmine had left the system. This was a positive for me, as I had my girlfriend back and she was sharing my bed again.

As our simulated, preprogrammed nighttime fell over the station, the hull creaked and rattled in odd ways. The inner layers of the station were thick, layered metal, but the outer armor was a blanket of raw bedrock. The combination never stopped shifting, as the various metal sectors expanded and contracted in reaction to sources of radiation. To make things worse the station rotated slowly, exposing new portions of the exterior to the star's radiation then to the cold of deep space in turn.

Sandra and I had become used to the noises and weren't deterred in making some unusual sounds of our own. I think knowing we were getting off the station in the morning energized us both.

As a newly rebuilt man, I was able to keep up with Sandra in bed now. I thought to myself when we'd finished how pleasant it would be not to wake up bruised and chafed the next morning.

But our happy farewell party to the battle station didn't last all the way to morning. Long before the night shift was over, the klaxons wailed and yellow flashers went off in our bedroom. The lights bathed our sweaty bodies in a rhythmic amber glow.

-2-

The klaxons forced all thoughts of sleep from my mind. Still naked and slick with sweat, I slapped a wall with four fingers and a thumb. A channel-bump welled up in response, pressing against my forefinger as the wall's smart metal interface identified me and brought up valid options. I applied pressure to the bump, and a voice began speaking from the dim walls of my chambers.

"Sir? Colonel Riggs?"

"Go ahead, Welter," I said.

Commander Welter was my exec on the station and led the bridge team when I was off-duty. I wasn't surprised to hear his voice, but I was a little irritated. I'd just fallen asleep. I thought to myself hazily that this had better not be a minor malfunction. Welter was an excitable officer who tended to sweat the details. This trait made him an attentive exec, but he was also something of a pain.

"Scout one has returned to base, sir. They've made a sighting."

"How many ships? What type?" I asked, sitting up in bed and shoving my feet in the general direction of my boots. The boots sensed my feet, recognized their beloved owner and immediately wrapped themselves around my flesh in a perfect fit.

"I'm going over the report now," Welter said. "Give me ten seconds."

"What's going on, Kyle?" Sandra whispered behind me.

I shrugged, struggling to get my pants to activate next. My chest piece was getting frisky, and tried to grab me, but I dodged. Smart clothes were great, but a little tricky at times. I still wasn't sure the

8

design was the best. They didn't always understand when I wanted to stay nude, such as when I crossed the cabin to take a shower. They occasionally sprung traps on me, reaching out from closets or from where I'd dropped them on the floor.

"Dammit," I muttered, shaking off my jacket. I had to have my pants on first to ensure a good seal. If we were going into battle soon, I wanted the suit to work in the case of a sudden loss of pressure. My jacket didn't give up. It clung to my elbow, pulling out a few dozen arm hairs. When smart clothing went into target-acquired mode, it was like being wrapped up in packing tape.

"Colonel?" Welter asked, coming back on the channel. "We've got one ship incoming. An unknown class from the Crustacean water-moons."

"Just one ship?" I demanded. "Why the klaxons for one ship? Is it really big or something?"

"No sir, not according to the report. It's about the size of one of our cruisers."

I nodded. "That *is* big, but not panic-worthy. Are they transmitting?"

"Yes sir, they claim they're on a mission to provide 'understanding and clarity'."

I frowned. "Is this a diplomatic mission?"

"I don't know, sir. I asked for them to provide some immediate understanding and clarity before they arrived. The scouts relayed the message, and they simply repeated they're coming to 'personally enlighten' us."

"That's just great," I said, "What's this ship's ETA?"

"Six hours or so."

I grunted in disgust, finally getting my jacket under control enough to allow my pants to wrap me up first. "Six hours? You set off the all-hands alarm for a single diplomatic ship that's six hours out?"

"Just following orders sir—your orders."

I broke the connection and muttered something unpleasant about Welter's heritage.

Sandra stood beside me, naked and gorgeous. "Aren't you going to take a shower? Sounds like you have the time—and you could seriously use a shower, Kyle."

I sighed heavily. She was right. I slapped the disrobe points on my clothing, which fell back onto the floor in a trembling heap. I hopped away gingerly before the jacket could get any ideas and headed for the shower stalls.

Freshly washed but slightly sleepy, I marched through a series of nanite doors. The doors dissolved as I came near, and some of the thicker, automated bulkheads hissed open then slammed down behind me with a clang. When I reached the bridge my staff had already assembled there.

The alarm had been triggered by one of my scout ships. I'd posted two of them on the far side of the ring, in the Thor system owned by our sneering neighbors, the Crustaceans. The scouts had strict orders: upon noting any kind of anomaly, one ship was to return to our side of the ring and report it. The other was to stay on alert, observing, until such a time as they were directly threatened. Only then were they to retreat and make a follow-up report.

I'd set up this engagement policy to prevent us from being easily surprised by an ambush from the far side of the ring. If anything was starting up out there, I wanted to know about it. I'd soon figured out that one scout couldn't do the job properly. If the scout returned immediately, we'd get an early warning, but while he was making his report he'd be missing out on details. Valuable information could be potentially lost. Therefore, I'd taken to posting two watchful sets of eyes.

The Crustaceans themselves were a strange folk. As their name implied, they looked more or less like lobsters. These, however, were *intelligent*, gigantic, eight-legged lobsters. Their shells were bluish and thick, and they were definitely an aquatic species. We knew they could survive in an atmosphere like ours, or completely submerged, but preferred to be under water.

Their system consisted of three gas giants and a load of other rocky worlds circling a binary star. The stars consisted of an F class bright white star and a tiny red dwarf. For some reason, I'd named the big one Thor and the smaller sun Loki. The three gas giants themselves weren't inhabited as far as I could tell, but one of them was in the zone that supported liquid water. Circling that world were several water-moons that were the homeworlds of the Crustaceans. Being within the band of space that supported liquid water, the moons were covered in oceans.

Although their worlds seemed pleasant enough, the Crustaceans themselves were not overly friendly. They'd been suspicious and competitive with us from the start. They searched every comment we made to them for insults, and frequently found them. In turn, they liked to brag, bluster and behave in a generally snobbish fashion toward us. I found them tiresome to talk to, but I tried to maintain an open mind. After all, in this war it was the biotics against the machines, and all living things needed to stay on the same side—even if some of us were obnoxious.

I got some coffee and stirred it, looking at everyone with bleary eyes. I wasn't overly tired—marines full of nanites and Microbial edits rarely got a full night's sleep, and I was edgy. Even after all our modifications, our brains still needed to sleep and dream.

"Have we attempted further contact with the incoming ship? What exactly do they want?"

"The incoming ship still won't answer any detailed queries," Welter said. "They just say they're coming to provide us with "enlightenment", whatever that meant under these circumstances."

The Crustaceans were a snooty race that fancied themselves to be the best thinkers in the universe. They were highly competitive in this regard, and delighted in pointing out the foolishness of anyone else's statement. In this case it seemed they were being cryptic as well.

I felt confident in the military capacity of my battle station, of course. Any single ship the Crustaceans were sending would be no match for our weaponry, should they be foolish enough to attack. The Crustaceans had built themselves an impressive-looking ship and probably just wanted to brag about how much more advanced their design was when compared to ours.

So, we waited. There were only fourteen humans aboard the battle station. Most of my people were out flying a ship around somewhere or serving in a marine assault squad. Fourteen was more than enough to operate the station due to the centralized control setup I'd built. I'd purposefully designed the station to be manned by over a thousand if necessary, taking a cue from the Macros in layered control systems. But the guns could operate without gunners. They could all be targeted from the bridge. If I'd had the crew, and the bridge had been knocked out, individual batteries could also be manned at the turrets themselves.

"We're just going to let them fly in here and dock?" Commander Welter asked for the tenth time some hours later. As the alien ship kept creeping quietly closer, he seemed to be unnerved by it.

"Yeah," I said. "What else are we going to do? We've scanned the ship, and I see one lonely Lobster aboard. I'm not going to fry a diplomat for just flying here to talk."

"What if he causes trouble?"

"Then you can load a pellet in the primary railgun batteries and personally blow him to atoms, Commander."

Welter smiled at that idea. Several more staffers joined him in his amusement. No one was terribly fond of the snotty Crustaceans.

We watched and waited. Just after the six hour mark, our second scout ship flew back to our side of the ring and the pilot made his report.

"The ship is about to come through, Colonel."

I nodded at the viewscreen. "Good. Now, get back out there and watch them do it."

"Colonel," Commander Welter said, "I recommend we contact Earth and make an official report."

I thought about it. Earth hadn't bothered to even acknowledge my reports lately, but it was supposedly our job to report things like this. "We will—after we figure out what the Crustaceans want."

Commander Welter looked unhappy with this decision, but he didn't say anything further. While we waited, the fifteenth member of the battle station's crew made his appearance. Marvin snaked into the room dragging his bloated metallic body with a dozen whipping steel tentacles.

"Is the messenger here yet?" he asked.

"Any time," I said.

"Very good. Everything should be clear to us soon. I'm going below decks if you don't mind, Colonel."

I frowned at him for a moment. I noticed he had a large number of cameras on me, meaning that he was intent upon my response. Today, he'd configured himself with seven hardened military cameras. This was an unusual arrangement of eyes for him, as he preferred more sensitive scientific units. I thought about asking him why he was set up for a fight, but didn't bother. There were only a few minutes left, and I figured it could wait.

12

"All right," I said. "We don't need you right here. Choose your own ground, Marvin."

He reshaped himself into a cylindrical formation and snaked away into a circular conduit in the floor. Everyone glanced at him as he left. The crew was used to him, but he still elicited headshakes and rolled eyes wherever he went. Most of us in Star Force knew Marvin by now. He was bizarre, but in a familiar way, like the crazy uncle who lived the family attic.

"There it is," Welter said.

My eyes flew to the holographic tank in the middle of the room. The Crustacean ship appeared at the ring without fanfare. There was no explosion of radiation upon its arrival on our side of the ring. It simply slipped from another part of the galaxy into the Eden system without so much as a whisper.

We scanned it the moment it emerged, of course. I examined every reading, and everything showed green. The ship was armed, but it wasn't a flying bomb stuffed with fusion warheads. There were radioactive elements aboard, but that was to be expected. The type and amount of dangerous components wasn't out of the norm for a cruiser of this size. If it did fire a missile into our base at extremely close range, it would definitely damage us, but at the cost of having us destroy a nice ship. I was confident in the layered armor and layered systems in my battle station. We could withstand a hard blow if it came down to that. I didn't think we had any choice, we had to let him come close to talk to us. The risk of an attack was small, and was worth the chance of normalizing relations with these prickly neutrals.

The alien ship decelerated rapidly as it made its final approach. It had been slowing down for hours, as if it intended to dock when it reached our station. The design was new to me and oddly-shaped. Rather than a geometric configuration, or even a symmetrical one, the ship had humps here and there seemingly at random. It looked off-balance, but I supposed to the Crustaceans it was sleek and beautiful.

"The ship is passing through the primary minefield," Welter said, adjusting the tracking controls on the holographic tank.

I looked around at my crew with a new thought. Most of them weren't doing anything other than standing around watching. "Staff, I want everyone to scatter. Sandra and Welter, you stay here.

Lester, head down to engineering. Pramrod, get yourself to maintenance. The rest of you, choose a weapons battery and set up camp. You can sip coffee and watch the secondary screens from there."

They stared at me for a second, then picked up their things and shuffled out of their seats. No one questioned me aloud, but there were a large number of baffled looks. I frowned. They were well-trained, but too slow for my taste.

"*Move*, people!" I roared suddenly, clapping my hands together. "In ten seconds, I don't want to see so much as your suited butts walking away. I want you all *gone*."

This got their attention. Everyone rushed out of the bridge and jostled into the various corridors and elevators that led out to remote parts of the station. After they'd left, I noticed Sandra was watching me rather than the holotank. The Lobster ship was about half way between the ring and the station.

"What was all that about, Kyle?" she asked.

I shrugged. "I don't know. But when I saw Marvin take himself out of here, it occurred to me that maybe he was smarter than the rest of us. What if you only had one ship, and could only make one suicidal attack? Where would you hit us?"

She looked at me, her eyes widening. "The bridge?"

"Why not?"

"But they can't know—" Sandra began.

"Alien ship docking in ninety seconds," Welter interrupted in a loud, but calm voice. He was at the helmsman's post even though the battle station wasn't capable of independent flight. He could still adjust its tilt and yaw, swinging its massive girth in space. These controls were designed to bring fresh weaponry to bear in a serious fight, when one side of the station might be scorched and battered. I hoped to never find out if those rotational systems would operate as planned under fire.

Sandra glanced at him, then back to me. She lowered her voice to a harsh whisper. "They can't know we only have a handful of people aboard."

"No, they can't," I said. "But maybe they do anyway. Don't get me wrong, I'm all for a peaceful chat with them. Maybe they've realized it's time to start kissing human behinds for protection. I can respect that. But they attacked us before, and forgive me if I'm not willing to let them sucker-punch us twice in a row."

She nodded, and together we watched as the ship slowed to crawl in front of us and came in to dock. The external cameras cut out and regional optics in the belly section took up the feed as the ship came very close. Finally, the holotank showed the ship had merged with us, and the only camera that could pick it up was the one in the landing bay itself. Located like a drawer in the gut of the station, the bay doors yawned wide to receive it.

I signaled for Sandra to open a channel to the Crustacean ship.

"You've arrived, Ambassador," I said. "Now that you're here, perhaps you can at least tell us your name?"

The viewscreen responded with a bluish glow that grew until I could make out the outline of a Crustacean sitting in a chamber that bubbled and surged with floating debris. I knew in an instant the creature was in a tank full of seawater. Flecks like brownish snowflakes drifted in swirls around its antennae. The Ambassador was dimly lit, as was comfortable for him, I imagined. A deep sea creature would not be accustomed to bright light.

"Ambassador?" the alien said. "Yes. That title could be construed as appropriate. I am a Senior Fellow, a female of the Fifth Rank. I have bestowed great honor upon you by coming here, by allowing you to view my person. Are you capable of comprehending the magnitude of the gift my physical presence represents?"

I felt a sudden tightness in my shoulders. These arrogant shellfish really had a way of getting to you. I forced a smile, trying to see the funny side of it all. I took a breath and relaxed, deciding to play along.

"We are overwhelmed, your worship," I said. "Words can't express how pleased we are with your magnificence."

The antennae waved for a moment, then floated a trifle higher in the water around the ambassador's thorny head. I suspected the translation was just coming in, and she liked it.

"Excellent. It is best that the lesser creatures grasp the magnitude of the sacrifice they are about to witness. Anything else would be inappropriate."

My smile slipped away as I tried to decipher the creature's meaning. Oftentimes, aliens used idioms and wandering patterns of speech that didn't make sense at first, until you got to know them.

"Perhaps it's time we get down to the purpose of your mission," I said. "Please Enlighten us."

The antennae moved again, then stilled. "Agreed," said the aquatic creature.

I opened my mouth to say something else, but within an instant the thought was driven forever from my mind. From that day to this, I'm unable to recall what I'd been about to say.

Because in that fraction of a second, the Crustacean Ambassador's ship exploded.

-3-

In the first few moments after the explosion, I'd smiled grimly. The ruse had been a good one: they'd gotten in close and blown a hole in our central hold. But the attack was far from fatal. In fact, it was rather pathetic. I calculated it had to be less than a megaton warhead by the way the station only shivered, rather than swayed and shook under my feet.

"Well, we've been 'enlightened', all right," Welter said.

I nodded. "I don't see what their objective—" I began, but I didn't finish.

Every system on the bridge dimmed, and then died. My sentence died with the equipment. It took several seconds for the change to work itself through the instrumentation and power systems. Our jaws sagged and our heads swiveled this way and that. *Everything* was dying, or was already dead.

"What the hell is going on?" I demanded.

"Some kind of system virus?" Sandra offered. Her eyes were big and I saw something there I'd rarely seen in her since the battle for Andros Island: fear.

"I don't know what it is," Welter said, fighting the controls, "but I think the corruption is affecting the entire station."

As we spoke, the central holotank went dark and the nanites inside slid down into a fine gray sand at the bottom of the vessel. I stared at them. It was as if they had all suddenly been shut off. Trillions of nanites…

"EMP blast?" I asked aloud.

"Either that, or a very fast-acting virus," Welter answer.

17

"Sandra, order the systems to isolate themselves."

"I've been trying to do that, but the primary console is not responding, Kyle. We're cut off."

I nodded and slammed my fist down on the console. It dented slightly, a common side effect after being smashed by an angry officer with altered musculature. This was nothing new to me, but two details struck through as unusual. First of all, the console didn't reinflate itself like a balloon, returning to its original form. Secondly, smashing my fist down on the metal surface *hurt*.

I lifted my gauntleted hand and blinked at it. Nanites and blood trickled together down from my arm. It looked like a mix of fresh red paint and mercury. The flight suits I'd designed for comfortable service-work aboard the station were made primarily of nanite fabric. As I watched, the nanites were disintegrating. I realized that the nanites in my body were dying too, turning to waste metals in my bloodstream. I had to be careful, they could reach toxic levels. We all needed fresh nanites if only to dig the old ones out. Otherwise, they could form deadly clots.

"We should have reported the transgression to Earth when we had the chance," Welter complained. "Now, our communications have been knocked out and we can't tell anyone what hit us."

I glared at him for a moment. "Every time an alarm goes off on this station, in the back of my mind, I think of Earth first. But our relations with our homeworld have gone badly since I refused Crow's recall order. I've sent messages, loads of them. Diplomatic apologies, explanations and even full reports—but there's been no response. I requested reinforcements just last week. No answer."

Commander Welter didn't say anything. I knew the silence from Earth had everyone on my command staff tense. After all, we were supposedly Earth's border guards. What did it mean to that mission, if Earth wouldn't even talk to us? My people weren't sure what it all meant, but they knew it couldn't be good. Some had been whispering, speculating that Earth had been lost to another Macro fleet coming from the Blue giant system, via the Venus ring. I rejected this. I was sure Crow would have sent a new message in such a situation, begging for our aid if he was in real trouble.

But he hadn't. He'd stopped sending requests and reports out to us. He hadn't responded to our queries, so I'd stopped sending them myself. Now, we were in a sort of diplomatic limbo. Everyone was wondering and waiting. It was beginning to eat at my men. On this side of the war, some muttered that we'd built the battle station on the wrong end of the chain of rings, that we should have put it on the side facing Earth. I'd done my best to make sure such talk was squashed, but I'd never managed to stop the conversation in dimly lit passages. The talk had lowered to a dark murmur, but had never entirely gone away.

Sandra cursed about two minutes after the EMP blast first hit us, causing Welter and I to look at her. Her clothing unraveled before our eyes. I realized then that my own outfit was slipping away from me. Everyone's body-hugging clothing was falling apart. It was as if we we'd all been wearing strips of cloth taped to our bodies and the tape had suddenly let go all at once. The adhesion of the fabric was gone. The nanocloth unwrapped itself, billions of components relaxing in death. They fell to the floor around us and we stood in thin, sheer undergarments. I reflected it was lucky most of us still wore undergarments.

Sandra kicked at her clothing and clucked her tongue in disgust. "Treacherous little bastards. When you really need them, they shut off on you."

"They aren't the traitors here," I said. "The Crustaceans did this on purpose. They hit us with something, and we have to assume the whole station is knocked out of action. Have we got any old tech lying around? Something as simple as a transistor radio?"

A bit of scrambling went on, and Welter found it first. I'd placed primitive tech systems here and there all over the station. I'd always suspected too much nano-based tech was vulnerable to an attack that neutralized it. In the tradition of the Macros themselves, I had backup systems. They were woefully inadequate however, allowing only basic communications.

Within a minute, I had an emergency handset in my fingers. I tried to raise the rest of the crew in their remote locations but got no response. I turned the com system out toward space next. We still had two ships out there and I wanted to talk to them.

"This is P-niner, calling base, please respond."

"Pilot?" I asked, grabbing the microphone from Welter's hand. It felt strange to grasp simple molded plastic again. "Identify yourself."

"I'm Marine Lieutenant Becker, sir," said a female voice. The radio crackled, but it worked.

"Okay Becker. Good to hear your voice. What is your status?"

"My ship is fine. I seem to have been outside the range of whatever effect damaged the station."

"What did you witness, Becker? Any clue what hit us?"

"No sir, not exactly. There was an energy surge—like a small explosion. My guess is it was an electromagnetic wave generated by the Lobster ship. They suckered us, sir. Is the battle station operational?"

"Negative," I said. "We're knocked out for now."

"What can I do to help, sir? Do you need rescue operations?"

"Negative. I want you to return immediately to your primary mission. Join your wingman on the far side of the ring. Scout the Thor system and scan for any evidence of a follow-up attack. If it's coming, I need to know immediately."

"Roger that, Colonel. Becker out."

Becker left through the ring. We were left behind standing on a dark bridge lit only by glowing emergency lamps. I felt helpless and increasingly pissed-off.

"These crawdads had better know what they're doing," I muttered. "'Cause I'm not happy standing around in my skivvies in the dark."

"We should recall the rest of the local Fleet, Kyle," Sandra said.

I shook my head. "Welter, report our status to the other commanders. Do not order an emergency assistance mission—not yet. We don't know their true goals. Maybe they *want* us to pull back from the Helios ring."

Sandra frowned at me. "Are you suggesting the Lobsters are working with the Macros? Or with Crow?"

"We simply don't know."

"But Kyle, how could they have made contact? They're stuck in their own system, aren't they?"

I shook my head. "Remember Marvin's experiment with ring-to-ring communications? He was able to use the rings to transmit and relay messages. I've always suspected the Macros could do it, and I know the Blues can. Maybe the Crustaceans have this technology, too. Maybe they've been working treacherously under our noses."

Marvin had only recently discovered the technology that allowed us to use the rings to transmit interstellar messages at a speed that was effectively faster than light. It was done by creating a mini-ring, using sympathetic quantum mechanics. It operated using the principles of quantum entanglement. The important thing was the resulting communication, which was essentially instantaneous over any distance, once two objects were attuned.

Welter had been listening to us intently, and joined the conversation at this point. "But sir, what could they gain from hitting us like this? They have to know we have the strength to destroy them if we want to. We have far more ships and this station alone is more deadly than anything they could throw at us."

"Is it?" I asked grimly. "They just took it out with one simple ruse."

"Yes, but we'll get it back online within days sir, I'm sure of that."

I wasn't so confident, but I didn't argue with him. "They may be in league with our enemies. They must have a plan, something that will shock us just as much as this strike did. Something to follow up on their advantage."

They couldn't argue about that. All of us were worried, wondering what underhanded nightmare they had in store for us next.

After I'd managed to pull on some old-fashioned spare coveralls and bandage my hands, I went below decks.

"Where are you going?" Sandra asked me sharply.

"To find Marvin."

"Is he still alive?"

I shook my head. "I don't know, but I'm going to find out."

"I want to come with you."

"I need you here on the bridge. Keep Welter alive and listen for the scouts. They should come back and report soon. When they do, come find me and relay the message."

She didn't want to be left behind, but she didn't argue. I found the hatch Marvin had wriggled into and slid inside.

Without nanites, much of the battle station had been crippled. There wasn't a major system on the station that didn't depend on Nano technology. Even many of the doors, which normally operated by forming openings in the skin of nanites that formed

21

temporary walls, now resembled gaping wounds in the hull. At the base of each of these ragged holes drifted eddies of dead nanites, looking like piles of ground-up metal.

Recalling that Marvin had said he was going to the generator chambers, I followed the Jefferies tubes in that direction. As the big station was parked in orbit over Hel, there was naturally little or no gravity. Our station had zones that provided gravitational fields for convenience, but the Jefferies tubes weren't on that list. The tubes allowed access to rarely-visited regions of the vast structure that were too remote and underutilized to warrant building a full-fledged corridor.

As I passed into the generator zone, I saw massive walls of shielding which the tubes pierced. I nodded to myself and pressed ahead. Down here, the lights were dim and few, but there was enough to see by. It felt cold now, as the heating systems had failed and the freezing temperatures of the void seeped in.

I saw movement ahead of me, something dark that slid away with a rasping sound. The noise reminded me of a steel brush dragging across a concrete floor.

"Marvin?" I called as calmly as I could. "I know you're here. Talk to me."

"Why have you come, Colonel Riggs?"

"To talk to you, Marvin."

"About what?"

"About exactly how you knew what the Crustacean ship was going to do."

Marvin hesitated. I could see him now, in the dim light—or rather I could see one of his cameras peeping out. He was hiding around a corner of a tube that teed off to the right. I crept a few feet closer and gathered my feet under me, tucking my knees to my chest. There was no room to stand here, but I could squat under the low roof.

"Are you armed, Colonel?" Marvin asked.

I glanced down at the laser pistol in my hand. I'd taken it along without a thought when I'd abandoned my limp flight suit back on the bridge.

"Yes, I am."

"Might I ask why, sir?"

"I'm a Star Force marine, and we just suffered a serious attack. I'd have to be a fool to wander around the station unarmed."

There was a bit more shuffling and rasping ahead of me. I saw shadowy, tentacle-like shapes move into view, then retreat. Two cameras floated into sight, their activation lights glowing in the darkness.

"I suppose that makes sense. In answer to your original question, I didn't know what the Crustacean ship was going to do. I simply took logical precautions."

"Like hiding down here? Inside a shielded area?"

"Exactly."

"Okay, do you know what kind of attack just hit us?"

"I suspect it was an electromagnetic pulse—a powerful one. It has damaged most of the ship's systems."

I realized then the extent of Marvin's guilt. He'd known what was coming—or at least had expected it—and had said nothing to us.

"Indeed it has," I said in a surprisingly calm voice. I knew it was best not to show Marvin how angry you were when you wanted to get information out of him. He was much more likely to answer you squarely if he thought he had nothing to worry about. Right now, I was boiling inside. I wanted to dismantle him and scatter him in pieces in an orbit bound for Eden's bright yellow star. But I didn't want him to know that. He would not be able to talk about anything else if he understood my true mood.

When I could think clearly and continue in an even voice, I asked him another question that didn't directly revolve around his guilt in this matter: "Why do you think they did it? Why do you think they attacked us?"

"To destroy us, to drive us from the Eden system."

"Logical. But they can't hope to defeat us on their own. I have therefore deduced that they might have allies in this situation."

"Agreed. I've calculated the probability at higher than ninety-two percent."

My right hand twitched and tightened on my laser pistol. I had no shielding, no autoshades to protect my eyes. But if I aimed it at him at this close range and simply slapped my left hand over my eyes, I figured I could burn him down without losing my vision. It was hard to think of doing anything else. But I knew I needed information more than I needed revenge, so I pressed ahead.

"So, let's assume they have allies. They've aligned themselves with a foreign power, such as the Macros."

Marvin rustled and slid his bulk closer. I saw three cameras now. A fourth wandered, looking in various directions down the tubes. I hoped this indicated only a natural curiosity rather than a search for an escape route.

"It could be the Macros," Marvin said. "But the signal didn't travel in that direction."

I frowned. "What signal?"

"The one they sent through the rings recently. I'd been meaning to tell you about it, but I was worried you would suspect I'd caused it somehow and remove me from my passion."

"Your *passion*? You're passionately interested in fooling with the rings as communications relays now?"

"Of course. Imagine the possibilities! The rings go on and on for an unknowable distance in every direction, a chain of new worlds, peoples, cultures. I find them fascinating."

Some months ago, Marvin had figured out how to use the rings to transmit messages. It didn't seem surprising they could do so, after all, they were capable of transmitting something as bulky as a spaceship, so why not a use them as a repeater for a radio signal that could hop from system to system? The application of the technology seemed so obvious that it was staggering we hadn't seen it before.

At the time, however, I had no time for experimentation with the ring-to-ring transmissions. Every hand had been needed working on getting the battle station operational. If an enemy fleet had arrived in the meantime, everything else we'd done would have been a complete waste of time.

But facts had caught up with me. Apparently, as best I could gather from Marvin's hinting, my enemies had been using the rings to transmit messages and Marvin hadn't seen fit to tell me about it.

"So, let me see if I have this scenario hammered down in my mind," I said, changing position so my butt and back curved with the wall of the tube behind me. It wasn't as comfortable as sitting a chair, but it was better than hunkering forward or crouching on my knees. "You overheard messages between the Crustaceans and the

Macros—which you monitored but did not report. Then, when the Crustacean Ambassador came in to dock, you feared for your safety, and fled to this region of the station where an EMP blast couldn't destroy your nanite-packed brain."

Marvin's cameras studied me. "There are occasional truths in your account, but as a whole, it is peppered with falsehoods. I didn't know it was the Crustaceans and the Macros who were conversing via the rings, therefore I'm not guilty of consorting with the enemy in any way. I believed I'd detected some kind of traffic, and was performing a detailed analysis when the crisis came to a head."

"You deny that you knew this attack was coming, and the form it would take?"

"Absolutely."

"Then why did you retreat to the one area that would be immune to this form of attack and hide here, telling us nothing of your suspicions about the origins of the messages? Telling us nothing, in fact, about the existence of these messages."

"My actions were based upon concerns that were very likely false. They were merely precautions that turned out to be accurate by chance. I had no desire to trouble you, my human allies, with my idle fantasies. There was no gain in doing so for me. If I'd been wrong, you would have lowered your estimate of my usefulness as a Star Force officer."

"But you turned out to be right, and you could have prevented a lot of damage!"

"Really? What would you have done, Colonel Riggs, if I had warned you? What if I'd explained the threat as the Crustacean Ambassador approached? Would you have shot him down? Based on a hunch from a single officer?"

I thought about it and shrugged. "Probably not," I admitted. "I would have let them come in, hoping for peace."

"Exactly."

"So, that's why you're hiding down here, to avoid the blast? If so, you can come out now. The enemy ship has been destroyed."

"You misunderstand my actions. I have a cache of valuables down here. Could you help me retrieve them? I'm having difficulties."

I scooted forward warily. Part of me couldn't help but wonder if Marvin had changed sides. He'd done so in the past, and I knew I could never *fully* trust him. But what I saw him struggling with when I rounded the T section of the tube and stared downward made me smile.

"I don't believe it," I said.

There were barrels of fresh nanites down there, jammed into the tubes. There were at least two dozen large containers. The nanites were alive and well, I could tell by looking into the glittering mass of them pressed up against the tiny observation window. I grabbed a handle, and together, Marvin and I pulled the first one loose and dragged it up into the unshielded portions of the station.

As we worked together, I pondered Marvin and his alien patterns of thought. I considered lecturing him on working together with one's allies, on the necessity of honorable dealings and honesty. But would such a lecture sink in? Was it even a good idea to try? He'd always had his own way of dealing with humanity, and he'd always been invaluable in a fight.

Perhaps, I thought to myself, I would just have to accept the kind of friendship I had with him and not try to turn him into a human companion. If there was one thing the universe had taught me over the years, it was that sometimes it was best to take what you could get.

-4-

When I returned to the bridge hours later, two key elements of our strategic situation had changed. For one, the battle station was about eleven percent operational due in large part to the judicious use of Marvin's stash of living nanites. We'd poured them into every essential piece of equipment, starting with weapons, communications and power systems. The tiny robots did their duty with relentless efficiency, removing dead nanites and replacing them with new, living chains. Silvery streams of them flowed down the roof of every corridor leading from the bridge, working like bucket-brigades to take the dead nanites below decks for reprocessing. There was only one factory aboard the ship we could get running again. This single factory ate up a significant portion of Marvin's precious nanite supply, but I knew it would pay back very quickly as it generated fresh equipment. The moment we got it operating, I programmed it to churn out more nanites. After that, it was simply a matter of distributing the products. Every hour that passed, the station rebuilt itself and became increasingly viable. Like liquid metal ant trails, the nanites stretched deeper into the station's structure every hour, slowly repairing the damage.

The second critical detail that had changed was the disposition of my scout ships. Becker, the pilot of the first ship, had returned to our side of the ring. She didn't have good news to report to us.

"Colonel Riggs? We've sighted a large formation of enemy ships. We don't have much information on them yet, but they match the engine signatures of Macro ships, sir. They're crossing the Thor system toward the Eden ring. Repeat, the ships are on an attack

27

approach and appear to match enemy configurations. In addition, squadrons of small vessels are gathering in high orbit over one of the inhabited water-moons."

"Which moon is fielding a fleet?"

"Yale, sir," the pilot responded. "They're all coming up from Yale."

As the Crustaceans had an academic hierarchy for a social structure and seemed to value knowledge above all else, we'd named their water-moons after universities. Harvard was the largest, while Princeton and Yale were smaller and orbited more tightly around the gas giant.

"Is it your assessment that these squadrons are hostile to Star Force?" I asked.

"I would bet on it, sir. They could be flying the force to give the Macros a warning show, but I don't think so. The Macros are bypassing them completely. Their current course won't take them anywhere near Yale, so why launch and risk provoking them?"

"Why indeed?" I asked thoughtfully.

"Because they are working with the Macros," Sandra said angrily. "They have sold us out—their fellow biotics."

"They wouldn't be the first to do so," I said, thinking of our own truce with the Macros some years earlier. We'd worked with them and done a lot of damage on Helios, killing Worms who really hadn't deserved it.

"You think the Macros threatened them?" Sandra asked. "You think they've been forced to do this?"

I nodded. "Probably. We didn't put them inside our defensive umbrella, remember. They're sitting out there in an open system, without a significant fleet, while in the next system Star Force is busy covering our own rear ends. They watched us conquer the Eden system, and in the process we destroyed a lot of Nano ships they thought of as their navy. From their point of view, we're quite possibly worse than the Macros. Certainly, we've done them more harm than the Macros have. They don't get the big picture. They don't know that eventually, the Macros will come for them too."

Sandra frowned, nodding. "I still won't forgive them for this. They attacked us pretending they were sending a diplomatic mission, under a flag of truce. They may be fellow biotics, but that was underhanded, dirty. They have no honor."

28

I chuckled. "Apparently, you haven't been to many faculty meetings," I said. "But let's focus on what we can control. Because of Marvin's foresight, we aren't as crippled as they might think we are. Their entire plan was to sucker punch us while keeping the Macro fleet out of sight. Now that they've done that, they're racing forward to slip past this battle station, or maybe destroy it while it's weak. Then they'll have shot at retaking the Eden system."

"What are your orders, sir?" Welter asked.

"Let's get the holotank working for planning purposes."

We dumped half a barrel of nanites into it before it finally began operating properly. The big problem was the connected sensory systems. The tank had long nanite-cables that led out through the layered armor to the sensor pods on the outer hull of the station. Unfortunately, the nanites that made up those cables were all dead. Partly to save nanites, I ordered that only the passive sensors should be activated for now. When they came in on us, I wanted the station to look as dead as possible. With enough weaponry at close range, it wouldn't matter if we could see the enemy clearly or not. I only had to see their emissions; that would be enough to lock on and blow them apart with railgun fire.

I had Welter put up the projections of the approaching Macro fleet. We couldn't see it directly, of course, as it was in the Thor system. We could see the recorded data from Becker's scout ship and the brainboxes were able to project their flight pattern. If they slowed down enough to come through the rings at a cautious pace, we had about sixty hours before they were on us. If they came on faster, more recklessly, we had less time than that.

We counted the enemy ships and classified them, then I ordered another report from the scouts and another recount. The data solidified, and it wasn't good. There were better than sixty cruisers coming at us and, worse, the enemy appeared to have a dreadnaught—a supership of vast dimensions.

After frowning into the tank for several minutes. I heaved a sigh. "Sandra, could you relay a recall order to the other commanders? I want them to pull half their forces and send them to us. We'll have a skeletal defense everywhere else, but we'll have to take that chance. How long until they can join us here?"

"If they take off now, they'll all be here in forty hours," Welter said.

"That should be fast enough."

"But Kyle," Sandra said, "I've seen the numbers. You're betting the Macros will slow down and take a cautious approach. If they're smart, they'll come in on us at full throttle, taking us out before we can recover."

I stared at the situation quietly for a moment, then cursed for a while. "Clever metal bastards. They set this all up. Sandra, relay the recall. We'll need the ships, I think. Ask for a full marine squad on each of the destroyers that respond. I'm not sure how badly this is going to go."

Commander Welter stepped to my side and we gazed into the holotank together. He fiddled with the control screens, running his fingers in complex patterns.

"We're recovering faster than they can know," he said.

"Yeah. But Macros play with thick margins for error. They like three to one at a minimum. This time, they should have had a hundred to one, but they don't. The bad part is Sandra is right. Since they think they have the overwhelming advantage they will come on recklessly, at full speed. That's bad for us, as we need every second to recover."

"What can we do to delay them?"

I glanced at him. "Not much. We've only got two active ships, and I want the battle station to play dead until the last minute."

"What about the minefields?" Sandra asked me, having finished her relaying my requests for reinforcements to all the sub-commanders. "If they come in fast, they're going to lose a lot of ships to mines."

I shook my head. "I don't think so. They will fire a barrage of missiles to blow a hole in the field when they get closer. Worse, they have a dreadnaught. That thing will provide cover-fire for their ships as they come in."

Sandra looked at me. "What are we going to do then?"

"Let's go down to the pool deck."

"You're thinking of playing around now?"

"Yeah. Humor me."

She muttered something about having to humor me too often, but followed me out into the corridor. We had poured out all the nanites we could into the critical systems and they were functioning on their own now. Nanite streams had formed by themselves, crisscrossing the walls, decks and ceilings of every chamber we passed through. The streams were different than those I'd seen in the past, as there were two types. One was brighter and more silver-colored, while the other was duller and closer to the luster of lead.

Sandra was as fascinated by the nanite streams as I was. "It's like they've formed arteries and veins," she said.

"Which is which?"

"The arteries are the bright ones, bringing up fresh nanites from the factory as fast as they are produced. The veins are the leaden ones, taking away the spent dead to be recycled."

I nodded, liking her analogy. As we made our way to the pool room we were careful not to disrupt the streams with our stomping boots. The boots themselves felt odd on my feet. I'd been wearing nanocloth for months now, and good, old-fashioned leather boots seemed oddly clunky on my feet.

In the pool room, there were no nanite streams. This chamber was one of the few that existed purely for entertainment and thus was classified as nonessential. The room was only dimly lit. In the gloom, I could see the various colored balls hanging in the enclosed space. The room was one of the few chambers on the station with no gravity plates installed.

"Are we really going to play this dumb game?" she asked me.

For an answer, I reached up and took down a bat and a facemask. "It helps me think."

Sandra chuckled, shook her head, and put on her own facemask. She took a bat from where they floated, tethered to the wall nearest the entrance. She didn't love the game, but she was better at it than I was. It was a matter of accuracy and reaction time rather than brute force.

We arranged the balls into a tight cluster in the center of the room and I let Sandra have the first swing. She cracked the bat hard against the cue ball and fired it right into the clustered balls. It was a good break, and the balls scattered wide and far.

The pool room was much like any pool hall, but it was a sport that appealed to Star Force Marines more than it would normal humans. First of all, it was incredibly difficult. Instead of landing the balls in pockets on a flat surface, the balls moved in three dimensional patterns that were vastly more complex. Secondly, there were no pockets—only players.

"Sandra in three," I announced, and cracked the bat onto the cue ball.

The white ball flew true, clacked into the yellow one-ball and fired it upward, toward the ceiling. It zoomed down right into Sandra herself, who snatched it out of the air.

"That was heading right into my skull. Do you hate me today, Kyle?"

I chuckled. "You caught it, didn't you?"

In our version of pool, the *players* were the pockets. Hitting your buddy with the ball was the objective, which I thought added a good deal of spice to the game. The target player was not allowed to move once the shot was called, but they were allowed to stop the ball by catching it—if they could.

Since I'd hit my target, I took another shot, calling a difficult bankshot this time. I missed, and it was Sandra's turn.

"The two-ball into you, banking once! Take it like a man, Kyle!"

I winced as I heard the bat whistle, and the crack that followed reverberated from the walls. I was all hands, knowing what I had to cover. The ball banked and came up from the floor toward my rear. Fortunately, I had a hand in the way. The hard ball smacked into it and jarred my hand painfully. Both Sandra and I had taken a refresher injection of nanites, but they weren't one hundred percent yet. The ball hurt my palm and, embarrassingly, spun away out of my grasp.

"Ha!" she said triumphantly.

The game went on, and soon there were three of my color left, and only one of Sandra's. She confidently popped me in the chest with it.

"Game!" she shouted, breathing hard.

I smiled at her. I'd expected her to win. "Now, I'll show you why we came down here. I have an idea, and I wanted to try it out."

Her smile faded. I reached into the storage chute, snatched out three balls with each hand, and hurled them all at the wall behind her. Six balls flew with blurring speed, bounced and came at her from behind. She whirled, and gave a small screech of surprise.

"Sore loser!" she hissed as the balls flashed into her. She dodged her head to the left, her hips to the right, and grabbed two more out of the air. The last two, however, made it past her

32

defenses. She woofed as one caught her in the chest and the second thumped into her belly.

"Two hits," I said thoughtfully.

"You cheated!"

"Yes," I said. "And that's the essence of my plan."

She had a dark look in her eyes. I wondered if she was about to crack me one with the bat. I rather hoped she wouldn't do it. I suspected I would feel it if she did.

Sandra tossed the bat away and tilted her head to one side. "You're looking smart to me again," she said. "I can't kill you when you're doing that. It's not fair, really. You know my weaknesses too well."

We kissed for a few minutes, then she pulled away. "Tell me your plan. How will you screw the Macros?"

"I'm not sure it will work."

"It worked on me."

I nodded. "I got the idea from you, really. You mentioned the mines. We've largely discounted them lately, as they aren't as effective as they used to be. By firing in swarms of missiles and having dense point-defense fire, I've seen them defeated recently. Only intelligent delivery systems, such as my marines delivering nuclear grenades, have been effective in recent battles."

Sandra walked around the pool room, snatched a few balls out of the air where they floated, and rolled them between her fingers thoughtfully. When she suddenly turned around to face me, I winced, expecting the balls in her hands to smack me painfully at point-blank range. But they didn't. Apparently, she had forgotten about my little trick. I was glad.

"I think I get it. You want the mines to *move*. You want them to come flying at them, so they can't knock them out while they're sitting in space? Something like that, right? But how will you bounce them into the Macros at an unexpected angle?"

I smiled. She was catching on. I took the ball from her hand and held it up between us. It was green, and had the number six printed on it.

"I wasn't going to bounce them, not exactly. But I do want them to be flying around at high speeds. A moving target is harder to hit, harder to predict. You can't knock it down as easily as a sitting target. Just like these balls. When you serve and crack that bat into one that's stationary—that's easy. But if it is flying hard from an unexpected angle, and there are several of them, a few are bound to get through."

She nodded and came closer to look at the six-ball.

"What I want to do is set the mines up in an orbital stream around the planet below us. They need to move fast, and come in like a shower from an unexpected direction. Rather than sitting around the ring waiting for the enemy to arrive they'll be swinging in a fast orbit and will come crashing into the Macros out of the dark, pelting them like a swarm of projectiles. Unlike a missile, they'll produce no emissions and will be hard to detect and shoot down, hard to avoid."

Sandra frowned, nodding. She took the six-ball from me and rolled it around in her hand. "There's a problem. If they're going too fast they'll break orbit, won't they?"

"Yes, exactly. That's the problem I'm working on. How do I set up an environment like this room? The key difference between this room and space is the walls. Out there, there is nothing for the balls to bounce against, nothing to keep them on target. They'll fly off into the void."

She looked around the room thoughtfully. "I have an idea. What if you make a bumper for them out there?"

I snorted. "They'd smash into it and explode, or at least be disintegrated."

"No, not a physical barrier. I mean another gravity point. Something that will catch them like a hand and throw them in a different direction."

I stared at her for a second then nodded slowly. "You know," I said, "that just might work."

Sandra looked very pleased with herself. I grabbed her then, and she resisted at first, but soon relaxed. Her body was already slightly slick with sweat from our workout. We made love in the pool room, and I was as surprised about it as she was. Our passion was brief, but intense.

"I hope the cameras were off," she said when we'd finished.

"All nonessential equipment is still dead."

"What turned *you* on?" she asked—then she smiled. "Never mind, you're almost *always* on."

I shook my head. "It was more than that," I said. "I guess you looked smart to me."

She laughed, and kissed me again. I knew I'd said the right thing and scored some easy points.

-5-

The Macros reached a high cruising speed on their rush across the Thor system and did little in the way of slowing down as they approached our ring. Apparently, they wanted to give us as little time as possible for repairing the station as they could. I cursed as their tactic became increasingly clear. I was ahead of the game due to Marvin's nanite supply, but I needed every hour.

Forty hours might sound like a long time, but it really isn't. Especially when most of your systems are knocked out to begin with. Even the basics like communications and life support were sputtering. I kept luxuries like that to a minimum and kept working on weapons systems. The battle station had independent factories, of course. But only one of them was had been spared by the EMP blast. Having been sheltered near the generators, the most heavily shielded section of the structure, this single factory was critical to our strategy.

After about twenty hours of churning out replacement nanites of various types, I switched production up a notch to something slightly more complex: mines. These units and a few more nanites were all I had time to create before the enemy reached us. The only other specialty system I allowed to be built was the space-bumpers Sandra had dreamed up: large generators welded to extremely powerful gravity plates. We launched these when we had less than ten hours to go, and my two scout ships maneuvered them into position. Dark, hulking chunks of equipment, they sat parked in far orbit over Hel, waiting.

Even with Marvin's help, the math was tricky. We needed to project a new kind of orbit, one that was theoretical in our calculations but which was destined to take physical form. We had to release the tiny, sputnik-like mines in a pulsed stream pattern. They were to orbit Hel seven times before they built up too much velocity and achieved speeds capable of escaping orbit. Hel wasn't a powerful, tugging gas giant, so at about nineteen thousand miles per hour, they came loose and drifted up into high orbit. Without any further controlling influences, they would break out of the gravity well of the icy world and probably impact with the distant sun years from now.

But that wasn't my plan. Instead, I'd placed my bumpers high above Hel. Dumping repellant gravity waves they were able to drive the mines back down into orbit, where they flew with increasing speed around the planet. I fired them off in thick pulses, rather than a steady stream. When they hit, flying out of the cold darkness at blinding speed, I wanted them to hit hard.

"You've built a trap for them," Sandra said, admiring my work as she studied it with me in the holotank.

"Pretty neat, huh?"

"What are you going to call this trick—this new tactic?"

I glanced at her and smiled. "The *Sandra Special*. A flying kick in the ass when you are least expecting it."

She snorted and shook her head. "I'm not sure if I'm flattered or not."

I could tell by the curve of her lips that she *was* flattered, so I left it at that. "What have we got in the way of working weapons systems now, Welter?"

"Twelve heavy railguns arranged in three batteries. The nanite brainboxes are young on those, and need guidance. We'll have to have a human gunner in each bunker to help operate the systems. We also have three heavy beam weapons. They have extended range and hit very hard—but there are only three of them. We don't have the power to operate more."

"Okay, what else?"

"Six flocks of mines, all flying around Hel in tight groups. I've aligned them with the station itself, so they'll fly over our shoulder every half-hour and shower directly into the face of anything exiting the ring. Depending on when the enemy comes in, they should be in for a nasty surprise."

I nodded. "What about lighter lasers? Point-defense systems?"

"We don't have much in that category," he admitted. "Those systems have to be automated, and the brainboxes are so young I've been worried they're as likely to shoot each other as incoming missiles."

I shook my head. "Not good enough. You have to have a hundred small PD systems active before the Macros come in, minimum. They love missiles, and we have to knock them down. Get the software for the brainboxes from Marvin. I'm sure he has it stored in his monstrous neural chain somewhere."

Welter looked as if he were about to object, but shrugged instead and turned back to his console. I knew he didn't like Marvin much, and more importantly didn't fully trust him. I couldn't blame anyone for that. The idea of allowing Marvin to seed our defensive the brainboxes sounded crazy on the face of it. The trouble was we didn't have any choice. There simply wasn't enough time to rewrite and debug the code for gunner brainboxes now. We couldn't setup simplistic self-learning boxes, either. By the time they figured out which way was up and how to fire their weapons, the Macros would be all over us.

About ten hours later, the scout ships came in and made their final report. The enemy ships were going to arrive sooner than we'd projected. They were slowing down now, but only at the last minute, using maximum burn. I deduced from this they knew something about our fleet disposition. Our own ships would not make it to the battle in time. They'd raced toward us, crossing the Thor system as fast as they could, starting the moment the EMP blast had been delivered.

In the final hours before the attack struck us, Welter pulled me aside for a huddled conversation on this very topic. Marvin was in the control center, tweaking the holotank settings. His metal arms snaked out in a dozen directions. Some supported his central mass, while others held aloft cameras or worked tools.

"I don't like it, sir," Welter said quietly, nodding toward Marvin.

I glanced toward Marvin, who scanned us with a half-interested camera before turning back to the work at hand.

"Explain yourself, Commander," I said.

"He knew when the attack was coming. He stashed himself in the single spot aboard the station where the EMP wave wouldn't reach him. Then, he comes out full of nanites, the very substance we need. Next, we use his software to program our PD systems."

"I understand your thinking, and you make a strong case, but—"

"That's not all, sir," Welter said. "The enemy knows what we have and where it is."

"Why do you think that?"

"Because they're going to arrive less than an hour before our reinforcements do. You can't tell me that's just a coincidence."

"You think Marvin told them?"

"Didn't he just 'discover' how to use the rings to make transmissions? Isn't he the only one who really knows how to do it? Who else ratted us out to aliens in remote star systems?"

I sighed. "You have a point. But I don't see what we can do about it."

"We can pull the software on the PD systems and disconnect that self-built robot."

I shook my head. "We've got nothing to put into the PD lasers. We don't have enough human gunners and we can't train new software. We're out of time."

Commander Welter frowned at Marvin suspiciously. "Is that all you've got for a solution? We'll just have to wait until we see how this all plays out?"

I nodded. "That's right. If Marvin has ratted us out, we're all as good as dead. That's just how it is. I understand how difficult it is accepting our situation, but try to be a realist. We're out of time for second guesses."

Welter looked at me oddly, and raised his eyebrows. "I have another possible solution," he said quietly.

"Talk."

"Let's retreat from the base. We'll leave everything on automatic and evacuate."

I stared at him. "You want to bail out on this station?"

"If we are compromised, we're going to lose anyway. My way, no one dies. If we aren't compromised, I still don't like our odds.

Let the enemy chew on the station. We'll come in with the fleet and clean up afterward."

"I don't like it."

"I knew you wouldn't. It's your call, sir."

I turned away from him and approached the holotank. I had to give his idea serious thought. I certainly didn't want to abandon the battle station, but I didn't want to fall for an enemy trick twice in the span of a few days—and die a fool.

"Marvin," I said, "we need to have a private little chat."

"I'm heavily engaged at the moment, Colonel," he replied.

I warranted the attention of only a single camera, and that gave me a fleeting glance. The rest of them were hard at work at the base of the holotank, which he had opened to the guts.

"What are you doing right now, anyway?" I asked.

"The holotank is made of somewhat specialized nanites," he said. "They have color variance and can light up like tiny LEDs. These are looking rather dull, being generic replacements, I'm making adjustments to the—"

"That's great, Marvin," I said. "I'm sure in the coming battle they'll be highly visible and helpful. But I need to talk to you *right now*."

Three cameras steered my way. "Very well, sir."

I left the bridge and Marvin slithered and scraped after me. He currently resembled a very large slinky with attached trashcan-sized segments. His arms whipped and strained to drag himself over the hull.

"Putting on a little weight lately?" I asked him.

"I might be beyond the specifications you laid out for me last month—but only slightly."

We stood in an empty, echoing passage way. I stopped, figuring this was as good a place as any to have a private talk. The station was ninety-five percent empty.

"If I had to guess, I'd say you were about double the agreed upon maximum mass."

"Possibly there was a misunderstanding," Marvin said, eyeing me with a bouquet of cameras. Some of them studied my feet and my hands, but most were focused on my face, taking me in from many angles at once. "I was measuring my allowed equipment on the basis of weight, not mass. Since our station maintains a working gravity of fifty percent Earth-normal in most areas, my calculations—"

"Never mind about that now, you cheater. Let's talk about your motivations and intentions, Marvin."

He juggled his cameras, trying to gauge my mood. It was obvious when he did this, and I tended to automatically put on a poker face to make it hard on him. Marvin made most people nervous. Personally, I felt a surge of stubborn resolve when I dealt with him. He could be very evasive.

"There is some concern among the staff regarding your loyalties," I said. "Are you with us in this fight, Marvin? Are you doing your best to save the station and human lives—or are you involved in some kind of elaborate experiment?"

To my mind, Marvin wasn't really evil, but I had to admit he was a consummate rule-bender. Usually, his greatest motivation was his scientific curiosity. If there was a mystery to be delved into, he would do questionable things to indulge his thirst for arcane knowledge—very questionable things. Sometimes, his actions bordered on treachery.

"I understand your concerns, Colonel. You want to know if I in some way instigated this invasion, is that correct?"

"I want to know how you're involved and what inside information you might have that you've been withholding."

"I've read an idiom in your files. Confession is good for the soul."

"I know of the concept. What confession do you have for me today?"

"I knew they were coming. I didn't know how or when. I deduced that the single Crustacean ship had to be a ruse or sneak attack, rather than a true diplomatic mission."

I nodded, feeling my cheek muscles bulge. I was becoming angry, but I was trying not to show it. As I stared at him, Marvin angled one of his cameras a little wider to get a good profile shot.

When I could control my voice, I spoke with forced calmness. "Okay…let's go over what you know that you haven't been telling me. We've deduced that the enemy have intel on our positions. Their attacks seem too well-timed to be coincidental."

"Ah, an impressive insight. Yes, the evidence is there. In the scramble to build up our defenses, many commanders would have missed it, but not Colonel Riggs, the—"

"Just tell me who the spy is and how they're operating," I said. Internally, I was really hoping he wasn't going to tell me he'd been feeding data to the Lobsters on the side. Because if he'd done that, I was going to have to space him, no matter how valuable he'd been.

"Think about it," he said, almost as if he was enjoying himself. "Isn't the answer almost obvious? Who in the Eden system has a possible grudge against us? Who is here and has the means to observe our fleet movements? Who is here and has the technology to transmit a report outside the system?"

I stared at him for a moment, fighting down a flash of rage. He knew the answer, he knew it was vitally important, but he still wanted to quiz me. Marvin was a marvel when it came to understanding his priorities.

Still, despite my emotions and the critical nature of the information, I had to admit he was going at it with the right approach. The answer had to be right there, in the facts he'd listed. I thought about all the players in the system. We had the Star Force Marines themselves. I accounted them all loyal to Earth, Star Force, and to me personally. That's why they were here. I crossed them off my list immediately.

If Crow's loyal Fleet forces had been present I would have put them on the list of suspects, but they weren't to my knowledge. I moved on. Next on the list were the indigenous species. There were three: the Centaurs who would never do something like this due to their strict codes of honor, the Microbes who lacked the technology, and—

The light bulb finally went on in my head. "It was the Blues," I said.

"Of course," Marvin said. His tentacles writhed with what I figured was some kind of pleasure. Like a joke well-played, he was enjoying our little mind-game. He liked leading me down his path of logic to make the same conclusion he'd already made.

"What proof do you have, and why did you withhold this information?" I demanded.

"The rings have been vibrating—that's not exactly the right term to describe the phenomenon, but it is close enough. They've been relaying messages which I've detected, but been unable to decipher."

"That's it?"

"Yes."

"You don't know who's using them to communicate?"

"The answer is obvious. I wasn't doing it, there were no functional Macros or Nanos left in the system, and the only other possible source was the Blues. Therefore, it had to be them."

"But you didn't know what they're saying? Who they're talking to?"

"I've been trying to figure that out. But I've failed so far. Everything I know about their communications I've deduced—just as you and your crew have now done."

I nodded. I felt less stressed. Marvin had only committed one crime, that of omission. "Do you realize that not reporting this is tantamount to being part of the conspiracy?

"A tortured series of logical steps," he said. "I only just figured it out. None of it is more than conjecture. Am I a fiend for withholding probabilities, rather than facts? My suspicions have only recently been proven true."

I shook my head. "Why did you bother to conceal the information at all? Why not just tell us?"

Marvin looked evasive. I recognized the pattern. His cameras focused on my face, preparing to read my emotional responses. At the same time, several of his limbs braided themselves pointlessly. He reminded me of a nervous kid, uncertain of the ferocity of a parent's well-earned discipline.

"I didn't *want* you to stop the transmissions. I wanted to study them, to learn the encoding sequence the Blues are using on this entirely new communications medium. It's been fascinating me for weeks."

I snorted. "I'm not surprised you were overcome with scientific greed. But how in the hell could you stop the transmissions?"

"By jamming them, of course. We can transmit garbage through the rings, and since they only seem to carry one signal at a time, we'll block the connection."

I made a wild sound of exasperation. "You can jam them?"

"Yes. But keep in mind, that will let them know we are aware of their activities. Right now, we have an advantage. We know they're

43

communicating with the enemy, and we can study the code and break it. This could be invaluable."

I threw my hand high. Several cameras followed the gesture, and a single thin tentacle lifted to shield the cameras in case I became violent and brought a fist smashing down into them.

"You didn't tell us because you wanted to learn a new language you hadn't detected before?" I demanded, my voice rising into a shout. "There's no point in learning the code! They will simply change it when we've broken it!"

"No, I don't think so. This is not an internal code. The Blues don't have full control of the Macros, remember? They no longer have the ability to reprogram their creations. The Macros aren't fast learners, either. They will stick with the same code indefinitely, rather than devising a new one."

I thought about it and nodded. He had me on that one. They'd never changed their language since I'd met them. They were several versions behind the more advanced communications protocols used by the Nanos.

"Marvin," I shouted, "you still should have told me about all this!"

"It was an unforgivable omission."

"And yet you are *again* expecting my forgiveness?"

"Yes."

I remembered what it had like to raise my own teenagers. I'd been a frustrated parent, but had never experienced anything quite like dealing with Marvin. "I should crush you down into pellets and stuff you into the railguns. You're big enough to make a full load for a battery. You know that, don't you?"

"I displace sufficient mass for one-point-eight volleys by my calculations."

I stared at him. What was I to do with him? I felt even more like a parent at that moment. He knew he had me. We both did. I could punish him for this, but the only punishments I could devise for a robot involved deactivation or dismemberment. But I couldn't do that when I was facing a battle within hours. We needed him too much. Even just putting him on hold for a while would weaken our chances of survival.

He knew all this, of course. He'd known it all along and I suspected he'd already calculated what my responses would be.

He'd studied me, and had carefully gauged my responses in the past. He knew my buttons, and how to push them. He was a master at this process of asking for forgiveness, rather than permission.

It was hard to deal with a robot, especially one that was arguably smarter than you were. I still wanted to punish him, but I didn't in the end. Possibly, it was because he was right, in a way. If we could break their code, it would be a coup for our side. We would be able to perform espionage at will.

Finally, after thinking it through and calming down, I turned back to Marvin. "All right," I said. "I'm not going to make an expensive cannonball out of you."

"A wise choice."

"However," I said loudly, "you're to keep this conversation to yourself. And you should know that you didn't need to withhold this sort information, and shouldn't do so in the future."

"Why's that, Colonel Riggs?"

"Because by talking to me you convinced me to allow you to continue your research. Break their code, Marvin."

"I will, sir."

"And next time, don't leave me out of the loop."

"You're an even better commander than I'd hoped," he said, and slithered away.

I was left in the corridor, staring after him with troubled eyes.

-6-

The enemy came at us with a shocking display of power. Hundreds of high-yield missiles flocked through the ring and blew themselves up in a mass of explosions. Starting very near the ring, the rippling explosions pushed into our space. The nuclear warheads popped with interlocking blossoms of fantastic power. The effect was odd and entrancing. It was like watching brilliant foam puff up out of a hole in space.

I understood their strategy, of course. They were doing this to clear the minefield they knew must be there waiting for them. They were expending their missiles at a terrific rate, but must have figured it was worth it. Soon, the explosions would die down and the ships would emerge in their wake, rolling up to attack us.

But the strikes continued their advance. The missiles exploded in an ever-expanding mushrooming pattern, reaching deeper and deeper into our territory. The missiles came in waves that had been carefully pre-plotted.

"Is this their new strategy?" Welter asked quietly.

I glanced at him then turned back to the holotank.

Sandra shifted nervously beside me, watching with growing concern as the fireballs kept puffing out bigger and bigger into a single amorphous blob. "They're going to just keep pounding out missiles until they reach us and envelope the entire station."

I frowned at the barrage, which continued unabated. It was *big*, but still couldn't be more than ten percent of the way to our location. I had to admit it was alarming to see such a display of power. Could they have enough missiles to keep this up? To keep pounding away until we were engulfed? Surely they would run out of ordnance long before that.

Having no air to burn, the warheads quickly dissipated into background radiation and spreading particles of debris. But they did press forward, destroying the entire minefield I'd laid there long ago in anticipation of catching a smaller invasion force. As I watched, I was glad I hadn't bothered to waste time and resources shoring up the front line of mines. This feeling of relief quickly evaporated, turning into an edge of worry. The others on the bridge had fallen silent by now, overawed by the display of explosive force. Sensing their mood, I felt a little bravado was in order.

"Ha! What a waste!" I said.

Sandra's eyes met mine, but soon crept away to the holotank again. Welter didn't so much as glance at me, and not even Marvin bothered to assign me an extra camera. If the situation had been less dire I would have been annoyed. I took in a deep breath and made another attempt.

"Every bomb they throw out there, exploding nothing but space, is a bomb we won't have to feel right here on this station," I said.

Finally Welter regarded me seriously. He didn't seem to have been cheered up in the slightest by my attempt to put a bright face on things. I frowned, perhaps my bridge crew was getting to know me too well.

"Sir," Welter said, "I've done some calculations. The fireball of concentric explosions will engulf us in less than three minutes if it continues at this pace. What a simple expedient they may have uncovered. Why come to our side of the ring and do battle when they can simply bomb us out of existence from long range?"

"Why indeed?" I muttered. I crossed my arms and watched the show with the rest of them. There was nothing else to do, really.

Marvin was the first to notice when the incoming missile stopped their relentless intrusion into the Eden system. "The volley has ended. The closest detonations were more than a fifty thousand miles from the station. We're in the clear, sir."

I smiled grimly. They'd thrown a heavy blow and decidedly removed our forward minefield, but I still had my flying pulses of mines and plenty more firepower in the station itself. I did find myself wishing we were up to full strength, however.

"Excellent," I said. "Hopefully, they don't have much left in reserve."

We all knew it was a faint hope. Standard Macro tactics involved throwing no more than fifty percent of all the missile stocks a given fleet had in any given storm of missiles. The thought that they could release that much firepower a second time was terrifying.

"What is the status of all defensive systems?" I asked.

"Everything is a go, sir," Welter said crisply. "The minefield at the ring has been taken out, of course. But everything else is green and battle-ready."

I frowned, thinking hard. Why would they blast so hard right at the outset? By our best calculations, the enemy was still nearly an hour out from the ring. Our data was old, of course, as we'd pulled back the scouts before they could become targets. My frown deepened at that thought.

"Commander," I snapped at Welter, "calculate the Macro position if they have increased speed."

"At what pace of acceleration, sir? For how long?"

"What if they flew at us at maximum burn ever since our scouts retreated to our side of the ring? Where would they be right now?"

Welter's eyes widened. I could tell he was catching on. Working his fingers deftly on his touchscreen, I saw big yellow numbers flashing under them. He turned up to me thirty seconds later.

"Right here sir, right now. They could be on us. But they will coming in too fast, too—"

I wasn't listening any more. I signaled Sandra, who linked me to the PA system. "Now hear this, all hands, we are about to undergo a very high speed attack from the direction of the ring. I want everyone in full battlesuits with their hands on the triggers of a railgun battery! *Move* people, battle stations. This is not a drill!"

Even Marvin seemed surprised. I'd earned a half-dozen of his cameras and a wide-eyed stare from Sandra before everyone kicked into action. That took a second, a long second, but I supposed everyone took a moment to change gears.

All over the ship I heard servos whine and big arms rattle as they took aim with their weaponry. I busied myself at the holotank, checking out the position of my next orbital shower of mines. It was close—less than seven minutes out. I figured at their rate of approach we wouldn't get more than one shot at them. I ordered the mines in the swarm to fire their tiny guidance engines to increase speed.

Marvin saw what I was doing and objected. "You're pushing the mine swarm too fast, sir," he said. "The next gravity bumper won't be able to catch them. They won't be able to make another orbit of Hel."

"I don't think that's going to matter, Marvin."

I pointed toward the holotank, but I really didn't need to. Everyone was looking and gasping. Marvin turned himself toward it, putting every camera he had on the three-dimensional image depicted there. His arms clattered and rasped on the deckplates. Only one of his cameras was still looking at me. That single electronic eye rose up higher, staring.

I didn't have time to puzzle about what Marvin was thinking, and I didn't much care. The holotank emitted a blood-red glow now as the first new contacts appeared. The Macro ships were coming through the ring, flooding into the Eden system.

"The Macros have come to the battle early, and it's time to give them our warmest reception," I boomed. "All batteries, *FIRE!*"

Outside, space lit up with flashing darts of plasma. I felt the entire battle station shudder under my boots in reaction to the release of tremendous energies on the surface.

In the silent void, with little or no friction to worry about, railguns could be very effective. Our systems were very advanced, super-cooled and powered by magnetic forces the physicists back on Earth could only dream about. Normal railguns operated on the principle of extreme magnetic fields being used to propel a projectile to great speeds in a very short amount of time. If you've ever tried to push two magnets of matched polarity together, you've witnessed the concept of a railgun in action. The idea is based upon the application of electrical power to produce powerful magnetic fields. Since anyone could use magnets to attract or repel ferrous objects then, theoretically, one could build a super powerful magnet to repel an object to the speed of a bullet. The nice thing about the principal was its expandability. Bigger, more powerful magnets and bigger, more powerful projectiles created even greater killing power.

The natural vacuum of space made railguns even more viable. We had no air to get in the way of projectiles, and no gravity to pull them off course. Even better, once launched a railgun pellet is pretty close to invisible. Unlike missiles or beams, ballistic weaponry is difficult to detect in space and even harder to shoot down.

I'd invested heavily in railgun technology on the battle station. Our railguns were in fact more powerful than the prototypes experimented with back on Earth could ever have been. The key to this improvement was the use of gravity plates. Instead of using only magnetic forces, we pushed the huge bullets by causing them to fall away from the gravity plates. It was as if we were dropping the projectiles on the heads of our enemies—in any direction we chose.

I'd considered creating a railgun powered entirely by gravity-repellers, but hadn't perfected any of the designs yet. Our systems at this point remained hybrids, and I was sure they were far from perfect. They did, however, quickly and quietly launch a projectile at great speed. As far as I was concerned, that was enough.

The battle station's lighting systems dimmed when the first volley was ejected. For a split-second, every ounce of power we had went to the railguns and they were greedy for more. Down in the depths of the station I knew skinny black arms of metal were loading the next projectiles, slamming them into place and locking them magnetically so they were suspended between the rails and ready to fire. When the lights went green again, each battery fired.

Some of the batteries seemed to operate more smoothly than others and thus had a faster rate of fire. Most took somewhere around eight seconds to reload. A few could move up to a seven-second cycle. The asynchronous rate of fire wasn't optimal, but I didn't try to fix it. I ordered everyone to put as much metal into the path of the enemy as they could, as fast as they could. My only wish was that I'd started firing thirty seconds earlier. Some of the ships were going to be breaking off and evading the barrage.

On the holotank screen, I saw our projectiles as yellow slivers, the enemy ships as red wedges and cylinders. So far, they weren't firing more missiles at us, but that may have meant they were holding their fire for even closer range.

"They're moving fast, sir," Welter said, reading a dozen screens at once. "Some are breaking off, moving out of our cone of fire. The bulk of them is still plowing straight into us. Should I fire our heavy lasers, sir?"

I hesitated. The ring was within effective range for my three heavy beam weapons, but I didn't want to have them show themselves immediately and get targeted. Beam weapons on a stationary platform were very vulnerable, and I knew I might see a target I would rather have them take out in the next minute or so. On the other hand, if they sat idle in this high-speed battle they might as well have been knocked out already.

I struggled to get into my battle suit, as did everyone else who hadn't listened to my orders previously. I didn't really like clanking around in the thing when inside a vessel, but while out in open space or on a hostile planet, it made you feel like a god.

"Target the heavy lasers on the outlying ships, the ones that are flying off at random angles. Take them out one at a time."

New green lines snapped into existence as the lasers lanced out after their prey. For this type of weaponry, we were in close range. The holotank shifted a moment later, as the enemy reacted to my play. A shower of new tiny contacts appeared: missiles.

"Dammit!" I said, "I knew they'd go for my big lasers the second I revealed them."

"They'll get in a few minutes of firing time, Kyle," Sandra said. She stood supportively near me. I liked the sentiment, but I was still gnashing my teeth about losing the big lasers. I'd wanted to take out their dreadnaught with them if I had the chance. We hadn't seen the big ship yet, but it was only a matter of time.

The lasers were doing nasty work out there. We'd ranged them carefully, and each pulsing ripple of fire that lanced out finished a cruiser, ripping through the decks and as often as not igniting the engine core. Ships flashed and winked out of existence with regularity.

"Why haven't they fired any more missiles, sir?" Welter asked, staring with me as the battle played out.

"There's only one reason I can think of," I said. "And I don't like it."

51

"They want to take this station for themselves, rather than destroying it," Marvin said. His tone and interruptive delivery reminded me of every know-it-all kid back in school.

"You really think so?" Sandra asked.

"Yeah," I said. "Marvin's probably right. They're shooting at our weapons, not pouring fire onto the station itself. They must have a reason. Just think about it from their point of view: if they can take this station, they can control this gate permanently. They're trying to knock out our weapons without permanently damaging this station."

"We can't let them do that, Kyle," Sandra said.

"I know. If it looks bad, we'll blow the whole thing up."

Everyone on the bridge looked grim, except Marvin, who looked alarmed. "Colonel Riggs, sir?"

"What?"

"Shouldn't we call for an early evacuation if the plan includes self-destruction? To achieve a minimum safe distance will require several minutes under fire."

I laughed harshly. "What's the matter robot? Don't you believe in going down with your ship?"

"No, sir."

I shook my head and turned my attention back to the holotank. There had to be a way out of this—but there wasn't. We were in for a long, hard battle. Once the punches started landing, we would have few options. Escape wouldn't really be possible, at least not until the enemy had made one deadly pass.

I got an idea, and connected to the PA directly via my battlesuit's helmet controls. "Heavy laser one, cease fire. I repeat, cease fire."

People glanced at me in surprise, but no one said anything like "Are you crazy?" I imagined they knew it wouldn't do them any good.

"Heavy Laser Two, fire one more shot, then shut down and button up. I want you to put that clam-shell shielding over the projector as fast as you can. Laser Three—keep firing until the station takes a hit, then shut down immediately and cover up."

"What are you doing, Kyle?"

"Making it look like they took out our lasers. If they think they're down, they won't shoot at them anymore."

She frowned, but nodded and turned back to her screens.

"Sir, our railgun pellets are reaching the enemy line," Welter said. "The central mass of the enemy fleet is taking it hard."

A flashing counter began to change. It had been ticking down in slow increments, counting the enemy vessels. Mostly it had been rising as more and more wriggled their way through the ring and into the Eden system. Now that our heavy guns had finally landed a blow, the little blue number began dropping—fast.

Before I knew it, we'd killed twenty ships. Eight seconds later, the number was twenty-six. That's when the enemy figured out we were serious and changed tactics again. I'd been worried about this part.

"Wow," Welter breathed, staring at the destruction. "We're smashing them. They keep coming, pouring into our line of fire. They must have thought we were helpless."

"It's not over yet," I muttered.

They released a new wave of missiles, a massive barrage.

"The enemy has changed their minds," Marvin said. "I don't think they plan to capture this station any longer."

I chuckled grimly. "I agree, Captain Obvious. They plan to smash us now. Welter, it is now time for you to work your magic."

He looked at me blankly. "Sir?"

"Fire up the jets and turn this barrel around."

Welter smiled for the first time all day. "An excellent idea, sir."

The missiles crept toward us. The enemy ships were more than half-way here, and even though they were slowing down, it was clear they were going to blow right by us. They had come in so fast, they couldn't brake enough to stop their forward momentum. In response, Welter set the entire station to spinning on its axis. The big backside of the station was all dark armor. We hadn't bothered to activate the weapons there.

"We'll take a beating," I said, "But with luck, we'll still have power and all our active guns. When they pass, they'll be back in range again."

Sandra grinned at me. "If we live another hour, I'm going kiss you and call you a genius all over again."

"So noted."

We didn't have long to wait. Like a massive boulder, our station spun around slowly, but steadily. By the time the first hard missile strikes overwhelmed our defensive lasers and went off, they struck against a wall of rock layered with metals and shock-resistant struts. The station rolled and creaked. It felt and sounded like someone was beating on the walls with sledge hammers.

"The outer rock layer is down to eighty-one percent," Welter told me. "That was just the first flock of missiles. We don't have much other than defensive lasers on the backside, sir. They can pound down our armor with impunity."

"Not really," I said. "They're moving too fast, and can't slow down fast enough. They have to slip past us or crash right into us."

"Second barrage is closing in now, Colonel."

I bared my teeth inside my helmet. "Tell anyone in the aft section we're likely to spring a leak back there."

"I think they already know that, Kyle," Sandra said. "Why aren't the missiles swinging around and getting our weapons on the far side?"

"They can't," I said. "They're moving too fast. The best they can do is smash into our armor and hope to blast their way through."

"It feels like they just might manage it," Welter said, holding onto the edge of the holotank for support. "The exterior rock layer is down to forty-four percent."

The deck swayed under all of us. I couldn't help but look around at the walls as the bombardment continued. They looked solid enough, but I knew that wasn't fooling anyone. One direct hit in this sector and we would all be history, despite collapsed armor, battlesuits—everything.

Most of the missiles were shot down, but the few that made it past our defenses made up for the rest. They kept slamming into the station, blasting glowing craters in our armor. I was glad they weren't armed with EMP warheads, as the Crustacean suicide ship had been. Maybe that weapon wasn't in the Macro arsenal for a good reason: it could accidentally kill Macros just as easily as nanites.

All our cameras on the side facing the ring were quickly destroyed, but we had remote probes in far orbit over Hel and could still see the mounting damage. I frowned at the destruction, wondering if they would get through after all. My concerns grew when a new target appeared in the holotank. It was big, bulbous and depicted by the nanite cloud in glowing red. Welter didn't have to tell me what it was, but he identified them anyway.

"The enemy dreadnaught is now in-system, Colonel."

-7-

Once our station had turned its armored backside to the ring, we could no longer fire at the incoming enemy, but they couldn't easily hit anything vital, either. Soon, the outlying ships that had survived our railguns and beams slid past us. These were classic Macro cruisers, shaped like arrowheads with one heavy gun turret in the belly of each ship. These guns had been pounding us as they flew by, and swiveled to hammer us at point-blank range as they slid around to our front section again.

"Range is under one thousand miles, sir," Welter said. "We could fire now, and interpolate their positions."

I shook my head. "Wait until they are right on our flanks and fire then. I don't want to fire early. Wait until they can't evade. They'll zero our weapons mounts, but they'll take some hard hits doing so."

Remote passive sensors reported in blips that the enemy had taken a serious beating coming through the ring into our concentrated railgun fire. The trick of this entire station was based on the simple fact that any vessel entering the Eden system from the Thor system had to fly through a relatively narrow doughnut hole, about ten kilometers wide. This meant that if we saturated that zone with flying shrapnel, everything that came through it for an extended period would be destroyed.

The plan had worked, but not perfectly. The Macros had accelerated their attack, meaning that we hadn't fired early enough to catch their first ships. More importantly, we had only a fraction of our guns operating. About thirty cruisers and the enemy dreadnaught had pushed into the ring and survived. Still, the enemy losses were staggering.

"Now, as they swing around us," I said, almost whispering, "we'll catch them again at close range with everything we've got."

I called to every weapons mount directly, and spoke to the human gunners. I was most interested in the three heavy beamers. I'd let the enemy get in farther by not using them much until now, but at this point, at close range, they should be devastating.

"I want you to call a new target every ten seconds," I told Sandra, who had a determined look on her face. "Target an intact cruiser, and relay it to the three beam gunners."

"But Kyle, they can't fire and retarget that fast."

I shook my head. The station trembled under my feet as guns hammered us in a steady drumbeat. There was only about a minute and a half left before the enemy swept past us.

"Sandra, are you up for this?"

"Yes."

"Listen closely then, the gunners are all going to target different ships. At this range, each heavy laser should take out a target in a few seconds, all by itself. If you call out a target every ten seconds, they'll have thirty seconds to reload, retarget and fire."

She nodded. "Okay. No computers to do this?"

I shook my head. "Not this time. And Welter is busy with general ops. I'm undermanned, and I need an experienced gunnery officer."

Sandra smiled wanly. In the past, right down to the beginning of our long journey into space, she'd been a gunner for me. In some ways, she was one of the most senior veterans I had, but she hadn't done this type of work for a long time.

"You can count on me," she said.

I smiled, but slid my eyes to the clock. We had less than a minute before the fireworks began. Now that her duties were clear, Sandra was talking to the gunners manning each of the heavy beams directly. I felt sure she could do it—almost sure.

I turned to Marvin with special orders. "Marvin, I need you to get into full battlegear right now."

An odd number of cameras turned toward me—a sure sign I'd surprised him. "Why Colonel?"

I tried not to feel exasperated. Somehow, this robot was worse than my human troops when it came to questioning orders and bad timing. My natural gut reaction was to bellow at him to *move*, but I decided to waste ten of my precious remaining seconds giving him an answer. I knew that if I didn't he would be curious about it and distracted throughout the battle.

"I think they may still try to land troops. Their opening moves indicated that was their intention, and since they haven't destroyed us, I think they may still try."

"Oh," Marvin said, considering. "That's a very thoughtful insight. Somehow, it slipped by my mind in the excitement. I'll prepare myself immediately."

Marvin slithered away toward the armory. Over the preceding months, we'd done some experimental work with his structure, and come up with a modular design for combat. Marvin was different than a normal trooper, in that he was capable not just of changing suits and gear—he could reconfigure his own physical body to meet the demands of the moment. He and I had built some very nasty anti-personnel equipment in our spare time while working on the battle station itself.

I could tell, looking after him for a few long seconds, he was overjoyed to get out his battlegear. I knew his source of excitement wasn't due to bloodlust, or the natural exhilaration of battle. He was more like a kid who finally gets to try out a new toy he'd gotten for Christmas and put away in the closet until spring.

Now that everyone was on task, I turned back to the holotank. Twenty-one seconds remained until the first of the enemy ships had circled the station to our weapons-encrusted side.

"Rear armor is down to twenty-nine percent," Welter said.

I took in several slow deep breaths, and the clock ticked away to zero. In an instant, all hell broke loose.

Sandra had already called out her first three targets, and directed each of the heavy beams toward one of them. I realized right off that was a smart move I hadn't told her to take. She'd primed the queue so everyone had something to shoot at and no one was left out. As soon as the beams leapt out, drawing three perfect, bright lines of destruction between the station and an enemy ship, she'd already selected and began calling out the next target for each gunner. She would keep them as busy as any computerized targeting system could possibly do.

The results of the heavy beams were spectacular. The cruisers were caught in brilliant flashes of radiation, which lanced through their hulls and out the far side in less than a second. Each burst of fire was a kill-shot, but there were so many of the enemy still to come.

The railguns began pounding out projectiles moments later. They were much harder to aim and control now. Best used against a concentrated enemy, the pellets took time to reach their targets, which were moving laterally away at high speeds. It was like firing bullets at bullets—not an easy thing to do. The vast majority of them missed as the cruisers raced by.

The enemy fired in return. Their cannons were at their best at this close range. The cruiser belly-cannons were firing high-speed projectiles similar to our own railgun batteries, but on a much smaller scale. Hitting with these weapons was dramatically easier than it was for us to hit them, because we weren't moving. The strikes began raining down.

The enemy didn't fire more missiles now that they were passing by so close. Missiles we could shoot down, and if they dared to explode early, they were as likely to take out one another as they were to damage us.

"Sir," shouted Welter over the growing din of battle, "we've lost heavy beamer one, and the gunner in railgun battery five is not responding."

"I think he'd dead, Kyle," Sandra said. "That's Lamond. You want me to go down there and see if he's alive or needs help? If only the gunner is lost, I could take over the system and keep firing."

"No, stay at your station. Keep calling out targets. The beamers are doing all the damage now, anyway."

She nodded and gave her remaining two beamers new targets. After another minute, something hit near the bridge section. We were all left crouching, our hands welded to our consoles. The lights flickered and went dim. They didn't come back on again. Only the holotank still glowed, as it was on a separate circuit.

"I can't see my screen, Kyle, it's out."

"Use the holotank," I said. "The com system is still working. Call out new targets."

For the first time, I considered the possibility that we were going to lose this battle. It was galling, as we'd come so close. The problem was this very bridge I was serving on. It was our weak point. If the bridge was knocked out or even disconnected, the Macros should win. In most of my prior battles with the machines, human input on the command side hadn't been so critical. After all, every unit had smart weapons that kept firing at any handy enemy target. This battle was different, due to the loss of so many experienced brainboxes. Human commanders were required to make even the most minor decisions. Without us, nothing would get done.

The lights stayed off, but the holotank stayed on. We all stared at it, not able to help ourselves. Then it died as well. Welter climbed under it, working on the guts of the machine. I figured it was hopeless, but worth the effort. When the last of the heavy beamers stopped firing, Sandra looked at me in the bluish light. The only illumination we had left came from our suit lights. I nodded to her.

"Go check on Lamond," I said. "And good luck, love."

"You too."

There wasn't any time for a kiss, and we both knew it. We were both behind visors anyway. She vanished into the hallway and I wondered if I'd ever see her again.

Welter and I were the last people on the dead bridge. The battle outside had subsided. There were still crashing sounds, thumps and shuddering, but there was much less noise than there had been.

"How many cruisers are left?" I asked.

"I don't know, sir. My counter stopped working at nine. That was about one minute ago. I'm not sure if they flew past and moved out of range, or what."

I thought about his *or what*. Most of the possibilities were very negative. I suspected we'd lost power on much of the station, and lost virtually all external offensive weapons. The fact the firing had died down indicated we'd either killed them all, or they'd decided to try for an invasion after all.

I called for all personnel to sound off. I listened closely after transmitting the order, and thought I heard a few burbled replies.

60

Someone was still alive out there. But the central com system was down, and our individual transmitters couldn't communicate through the heavy shielding around every chamber on the station. We were cut off, out of power, and probably vastly outnumbered. Even if we had wiped out all the cruisers, there was still the dreadnaught out there, and the Crustacean ships, which we hadn't seen yet. Things looked grim.

I did a full weapons check. Welter and I couldn't fight an army alone, but we were still two, fully-outfitted Star Force Marines. Hopefully, if the machines did board, we'd take a few of them down with us.

-8-

Standing in the dark and relative quiet of my dead bridge, I recalled reading that humans often reacted to disasters with a similar pattern of behavior. Doomed individuals caught up in a battle or a plane crash often fought on until the bitter end. In denial as to the truth of the situation, black boxes recording flight crews in their final moments rarely captured panic or despair. Instead, crews tended to work every angle they could, always planning to survive somehow, always intending to get out of their dire situation. It wasn't until the very end that the final, undeniable shock of truth struck home: the realization that you were well and truly screwed. Welter and I had almost reached that point—but not quite.

"We'll move through the ship to the upper battlements, picking up anyone we can to form a squad," I said, my voice steady and strong.

Welter nodded, but said nothing. He hoisted his heavy beamer to his chest and made final adjustments to his battlesuit.

"I'm glad I insisted on everyone having heavy infantry equipment available," I said. "I'd hoped we'd never need it—but events had gone in unforeseen directions."

Was that a tiny snort I'd heard? I wasn't sure, but I thought I'd heard Welter scoff into his microphone. I decided to pretend I hadn't noticed, and ignored his poor attitude. Morale was understandably low.

The station was dark except for the brilliant, stabbing beams from our suit lights. Smoke hung in palls, and there were whistling leaks at the structural joints as air escaped out into space. We didn't bother to repair anything, but instead marched onward, heading into the shafts and toward the upper decks.

The bombardment of the hull slowed and finally ceased. The vast hulking station became eerily quiet. I was pretty sure we hadn't taken out every enemy ship, so that left us with only two viable possibilities: either the surviving enemy had passed us by and sailed off out of range, or they'd decided to try to invade the station and capture it after all. I considered the latter option to be far more likely.

"Keep a sharp eye, Welter. You aim your beamer left, I'll cover right."

"Are you kidding, Colonel?" asked Welter, breaking his silence at last.

"Kidding? I don't often make jokes in the midst of a battle."

"Sir, this is no longer a *battle*. This is a brief interlude between defeat and annihilation."

I stopped marching and turned to him. My suit lights bathed him in a white glare. I saw his autoshades automatically darken his visor in response. Before the visor went black, I thought I saw his lips twist into a disgusted expression.

"I'm not getting your point, Commander," I said.

Welter made a sound of exasperation. "My point? We should be planning to hide, escape, or blow up this station. Instead, you're proceeding as if we have a chance to win this conflict."

I turned away from him and began marching again. After a moment, he followed.

"I'm surprised at you Welter," I said over my shoulder. "I'd never have figured you for a quitter. If you want to stand around in your suit right here, be my guest. You can shiver and sweat, or just piss yourself. Whatever seems appropriate to you. But until I've reconned the status of this new stage of the conflict, I'm not joining you."

Stung by my comments, I heard Welter give a blowing sigh over his microphone. I didn't turn around, but I knew he was still there as I could hear him stomping after me. His boots rang on the deckplates, and I was glad to hear them behind me. I didn't relish marching through these dark, empty spaces completely alone.

At that moment, I wished First Sergeant Kwon had been at my side instead. I'd left him back at the inner planets, guiding the setup and construction of small outposts on each of our three planets. The Centaurs had cut a deal with us to give Earth the three inhabitable inner planets, each of which had warm waters and bright sunny skies. We didn't have anything like enough personnel to populate them, of course. But I figured if I put a squad down on each world and had them build a few structures, we'd learn more about them. I'd also wanted to stake my claim, and let the other species living in this system know that humans were here to stay.

Kwon would have been nice to have along. I knew he'd never have given me defeatist talk in the face of the enemy. Welter was a better pilot, an excellent gunner and a strategic thinker, but Kwon was the man I wanted at my back when the machines were in my face. I thought about telling Welter this, but passed on the idea. I'd slapped him enough by suggesting he stand around and pee in his armor. It was time to let him show me he didn't deserve the criticism.

Our first unexpected encounter in the passageways came when we reached the power couplings that isolated the top section of the station from the midsection. I'd been on the lookout for Marvin in this region, and at first I thought that's who we'd run into. But although it was large, rasping and definitely made of metal, that's where the similarities ended.

"Marvin?" Welter said over his proximity com-link.

"That's not Marvin," I transmitted back.

This machine didn't fit Marvin's MO. Instead of whipping black arms made of nanites, it had segmented silvery legs that flashed when they moved. I was reminded of a grasshopper made of welded steel.

I fired first, not waiting around to ask the invader for its hall pass. My big beamer flared, burning through the thin atmosphere in the hallway and causing our visors to darken instantly, almost to pure black. The machine twitched toward me, even as the beam played along its thorax. We seemed to have caught it by surprise. It had been doing something with its head-section, which was jammed into an open panel.

A weapon of some kind on its head-section flared, returning fire, but it was already too late. It fired back, lancing out with a stitching series of pulsing beams. They scored my armor with two glancing hits, and then the machine's core ruptured and it exploded with a puff of roiling gas.

Smoke looks different when released into a low-pressure corridor. It spreads out explosively, filling the entire area around us with a swirl of particles. The air was escaping, I realized, and already quite thin. I figured the hull-breach where this thing had broken in must not have resealed.

Welter charged forward, and burned the twitching Macro with a few short bursts at point-blank range.

"Did you get it?" I asked, chuckling.

Welter looked back at me. "I wanted to be sure. Looks like it's a technician, sir. Looking at these tools in the head-section… It was doing something, working on our power-couplings."

"Humph," I said. "Maybe we should have let it keep working. Maybe it was trying to restore power."

"Yeah, it was all a tragic misunderstanding."

I moved forward and we checked every nearby hatchway. The technician appeared to be working alone. We were jumpy now, however, as we could no longer fool ourselves: the enemy was aboard.

"Kyle?" I heard in my helmet. "That's you, isn't it?"

One irritating thing about radio communications in infantry combat situations was the lack of directional hints from people's voices. Our big suits were powerful and tough, but they turned us into one-man vehicle-operators. It could be hard to tell which direction someone was calling to you, and when you turned your helmet this way and that, it was never as fast as simply looking over your shoulder. Still, in a situation like this, the armor was indispensable.

I finally pinpointed Sandra's position using the display in my helmet. According to her signal, she was approaching me from the panel we'd found the technician digging into. With Welter's help I heaved it out of the way. I ducked my head into the opening and peered inside.

Sandra crept out to greet us. She had on only a lightweight crewman's suit, which she preferred in combat. I was glad to see her, but surprised.

"You are away from your post, mister," I said.

She shrugged. "You assigned me to a gun, and I'm trying to get it working again. These things shut down our weapons systems—or rather killed our power. They're all over the station, breaking the heavy power junctions. My gun quit, so I followed the leads back to here. I was going to kill it myself, but you beat me to it."

"All right," I said. "Where are the heavy troops, then? Have you seen what they have besides a few technicians?"

"No, nothing else. Not yet, anyway."

I frowned inside my helmet. The situation was unusual. I didn't understand why we weren't under heavy assault. I'd expected two possible developments by this point: either they should have stood off with their dreadnaught and pounded our station to fragments, or they should have invaded with Macro marines and wiped us out. This injection of a few technicians to disable our weapons—it seemed too subtle for Macro tactics.

"We need to find out what the hell is going on," I said. "Let's get closer to the outer hull. Where's the nearest observation portal?"

Welter pulled up his map, I could see it glowing colorfully in reverse on the inside of his helmet. I stood guard while he tapped fingers at virtual controls in the air in front of him.

"I've got it. Let's backtrack about a hundred paces and take a side passage into laser battery three."

"That one's knocked out," Sandra said. "Not just the power, either. Everyone is dead, and the bulkheads have automatically sealed."

"Sounds just right for taking a look outside," I said, leading the way.

When we finally convinced the nanite-sealed bulkhead to let us pass we were propelled forward by a surge of escaping gasses at our backs. It was like having a minor hurricane behind you for a few seconds. Sandra was the only one seriously affected, as we were too heavy in our battlesuits to be swept off our feet. She whooped as she lost her footing, tumbled over me, and grabbed my power pack. Her fingers latched on like steel claws. I chuckled as I walked forward into the destroyed gun emplacement. She rode my back like a monkey until we resealed the bulkhead and were safely in a quiet vacuum outside the station.

The view was spectacular. To our left the star at the center of the Eden system burned. It was like a very bright full moon at this distance. The frozen planet Hel was visible in the opposite direction. It glowed an ice-blue along the rim of the crater of metal we stood within. The station was still slowly rotating, I realized now. I supposed that with the power gone, the impacts we'd endured had not been compensated for by the automatic stabilizers. The entire station was a slow, tumbling spin.

"This is convenient," I said. "If we just watch for a while, we'll probably be treated to a full view of the battleground."

"We'll be spotted and burned by then, if there are enemy ships parked out there," Sandra said.

I had to agree with her. "Let's move up and take a quick look around. Keep all sensors on passive mode."

Our suits were miniature spaceships, effectively, and they were equipped with long-range vision enhancement systems. You couldn't navigate in open space effectively without better sensory support than human eyeballs.

We all crawled up to the jagged rim of the crater that had once been a gun emplacement and peered in various directions. I saw twisted wreckage floating here and there in the immediate area, but it was difficult to pick out much more at greater range. There was so much shrapnel floating along with our station, resembling a swarm of orbiting insects, I couldn't tell what was going on. Battlefields in open space were nothing like battlefields in an actual planetary grav field. They were so spread out, you had to really look around to see any hostile entities.

"What have you got?" I asked. "I can't see anything except flying junk. Where is their fleet?"

"I think I have something," Sandra said. "Down below us— toward Hel."

Welter and I crawled to her position. We tuned and adjusted our helmet displays to interpret what was out there. Except in Sandra's case, human vision was useless when looking thousands of miles through space. If we'd gone active and used pinging radar, we could have figured it out faster, but then we'd give ourselves away.

We all peered down toward the planet we'd named Hel. The icy world below was composed primarily of nickel, iron and frozen ammonia. The planet's surface was heavily frosted by cyrovolcanoes that periodically spewed out unpleasant liquids. These events were dramatic spectacles. Ammonia and methane bubbled up from the planet's guts when tidal forces heated up the interior. Once these liquids reached the surface, they quickly froze into vast crystalline plains.

"Don't look at the surface," Sandra said, "it's orbiting low, between the station and the planet."

"What is?" I asked. Then I saw it. "That hulk—that's huge! It must be a ship, its metal content—wow, it has to be the dreadnaught. Nothing else could be that size. It must have half the displacement of this entire station."

"I agree," Welter said, "that has to be a dead dreadnaught. It's a destroyed hulk now, tumbling in orbit below us. If I had to guess, I would say it's in decay and will crash into the surface of Hel after a few more passes."

"A fitting end for those bastards," Sandra said with feeling.

"Yes," I said, frowning fiercely in my helmet. "But what I want to know is: what knocked out a dreadnaught after we were already on our knees?"

-9-

We spent the next several hours cleaning house. We destroyed around thirty Macro technicians who were involved in various acts of mischief. They were clearly trying to disable any defensive systems we might have left, in preparation for some kind of more significant assault.

What had me worried were the nine or so cruisers that were still out there somewhere. They'd had enough time to put on the brakes and turn around. We only had a few hours until the main fleet returned, but those hours were going to be long and uncertain.

"What's coming next, Colonel?" asked Welter.

"We'll find out soon enough," I said with firm confidence. What I didn't mention was *how* we were going to find out. I figured we'd find out when the Macros bothered to clue us in on their time schedule of operations. Our tactical situation was beyond grim, and I was left with a powerful sense of unease. As our own skeletal crew assembled, the rest of my Marines were increasingly pleased as our numbers grew—but I felt our forces were pathetic. There were only nine humans plus Marvin left alive on the station. The Macros had clearly written us off, not even bothering to pretend we were a credible threat.

"Kyle, I've got enough power to operate the primary transmitters now, can't we just contact Fleet and let them know we're still alive?"

I looked at Sandra for a second and shook my head. "Best to stay quiet for now. We'll use passive sensors with shielded power.

Play dead. When our ships come nosing around, we'll signal them then."

"What if the ships aren't ours?"

I shrugged and smiled. "Then I suppose we'll continue to lie low."

It was bothering everyone, this business of not knowing what had happened. For all we knew, the Macros had pressed on toward the inner planets. We'd destroyed most of them, but they still had enough fleet power to do us a lot of damage.

"I'll tell you what we will do," I said, looking around the crowd of dirty, dispirited faces. "Sandra, Marvin and you two, go to the damaged deep-com section, and set up an antenna. Make sure it isn't anything the Macros might notice. And for heaven's sake don't transmit anything, not even an acknowledging blip. With luck, we'll pick up traffic from Fleet and at least be able to glean data on recent events."

This idea pleased everyone. At least I'd given them something sensible to do. They set about immediately and eagerly. We all wanted to know what the hell had happened.

"The rest of you follow Welter," I said. "Commander, I want you to try to get the weapons batteries working again, one at a time. Let's start with the systems disabled by the original EMP blast. They're still intact, except for nanites and power. The Macros never bothered to target most of them during the battle."

It took hours, but we finally had some pieces rigged up. The heavy beams were all destroyed, but we managed to get one railgun battery up and ready. The antenna Sandra and Marvin constructed was built of metal rods like rebar from inside the station, which gave it the look of a twisted flag of wreckage. It worked well, despite its trashed appearance.

I'd returned to the bridge, as it was well-protected and wired for command and control to the entire station. We had some power back, and about half the screens were lit with a soft bluish glow. The holotank was still dead, however, and most of the screens were blank because the corresponding camera feeds were down.

Scratchy transmissions came in from Fleet a few hours before our reinforcements were scheduled to arrive. We listened intently to scraps of voice audio.

"...we've got a new force...definitely hostile..."

Everyone stopped working and listened in, except for Marvin, who I could see on a live monitor. He was out on the skin of the station, exposed to space. He made final adjustments by tentacle, tuning our makeshift antenna like an old-fashioned set of rabbit-ears. His skinny arms whipped about outside the station, aiming the antenna with tiny adjustments, and guiding it to track what must be a moving source of transmission.

"...ship configuration unknown. They have come through the ring and are approaching the dead station. Relay this to all commanders, we have new contacts..."

The antenna buzzed and warbled incomprehensibly for a time. I finally couldn't take it anymore. "Marvin, can you identify the source of those transmissions?"

"I believe they are coming from the destroyer *Berlin*, sir."

"They're from the relief task force then?"

"Definitely, sir."

"Keep working on that signal. Get whatever you can."

I turned back toward the others on the bridge. Their faces were pale and drawn. I could hear their thoughts, despite the fact no one spoke. New ships were coming here? We were practically helpless.

"There's no reason for them to come here other than to board this station," I said. "That means they'll have to decelerate and come in very close. We have one working battery, and we need to use it at point-blank range."

"We need time to put a lot of steel up into space, Colonel," Welter said. "If we start firing toward the ring now, we might catch a few of them as they make their approach."

I shook my head. "We're blind now, and might not hit anything. We have no active sensor, pinging away to give us valid targeting data. We'll have to eyeball it when they make their final approach."

"We'll only get off one or two volleys before they knock us out."

I took a deep breath and let it out again. "You're probably right. But at that distance, we'll blow holes in their ships if we do hit. It's better than hitting nothing and getting smashed by missiles at range."

After a bit more wrangling, they agreed to my plan for a point-blank ambush. We decided our time was best spent now trying to get another battery operating. If we could do enough damage,

71

maybe we could disrupt their plans and continue breathing long enough for the cavalry to get here.

We worked furiously after that, and by the time the alien ships were flaring their braking jets in near space, we had a second battery operating. We aimed them both toward the ring, and waited until their hot exhaust trails left no doubt concerning their speed, trajectory and mission: They were braking hard, coming in to dock with our wrecked station.

By my count, there were about twenty-five exhaust flares. Without active sensors and the holotank, I wasn't sure exactly what we were facing, but I was sure they were too small to be dreadnaughts or cruisers.

"Eight thousand miles," Welter announced.

"Hold your fire," I ordered.

Everyone was tense and sweating in their suits, including me. I'd been enduring a tickling sensation on my left eyebrow for the last ten minutes or so. The sensation was driving me mad, but I didn't dare open my helmet now.

"Seven thousand out now, decelerating hard."

We watched as the invading ships flared brighter. Their exhaust plumed into flaring fireballs at the base of every ship. I wondered if they had gravity repeller drives at all.

"Six thousand."

"Marvin, calculate a firing solution for me: At what point will they have less than a one-second warning before our railgun projectiles reach them?"

"Given their rate of approach and presuming a continued matching rate of deceleration, I'd say six seconds ago."

I looked at him sharply. "You're telling me they are already inside a one-second warning radius?"

"It's hard to be precise with presumptive data, but I would say they are down to about zero point six nine seconds—"

"Welter, fire! Fire everything!"

The station shuddered slightly, as everyone let loose with what little we had. They were coming in hard and fast, whoever they were. I'd almost blown it, assuming we had more time.

The battle was a strange one. I felt like a carrier captain in the old days, stuck with only primitive detection equipment and radio transmissions from direct observers. It was hard to sit there with

72

one elbow on a broken console clenching my teeth until my jaws ached.

"I think those are impact explosions. They *must* be. Got one, no three now, Kyle." The voice was Sandra's and she sounded excited. I had her gunning one of the batteries. Everyone was manning something.

I continued listening. Only Welter and I were on the bridge itself to coordinate.

"I got one, down on the lower edge of my field of fire. They are moving now, repositioning. My shots are going wide at this point."

I banged my gauntlet on a broken brainbox. It dented in and a puff of dead gray nanite dust shot up from it.

"Talk to me people, how many do we still have out there? Are they returning fire yet?

"I don't think so," said Sergeant Sanchez, my gunner with the most experience of the survivors. They are just taking it. Seems odd."

Everything about this situation seemed odd to me. "Sergeant, give me a count please, between volleys."

There was a several second wait, which seemed interminable to me. Finally, he reported back. "We got seven of them, sir. And I think the other battery did about the same. If I had to guess, I'd say eight vessels got past us."

"What do you mean *got past you*? Where are they? Have they swung around the station?"

"No sir, they should be reaching the outer hull about now."

Then I heard booming sounds, impacts that resonated through the station. These weren't the loud, smashing sounds of projectiles hitting the station, hammering it. Instead, they were the sounds of landing craft adhering to the hull.

"Batteries one and two, do you have any targets at this point?"

"No sir. We can't even see them. They are too low for our turrets."

"Get out of the battery, then. You're a target now. Retreat to the inner core of the station. We'll fight it out bulkhead-to-bulkhead."

I waved to Welter and he reluctantly unlimbered his heavy beamer again. I could tell he preferred Fleet ops. Blasting things at a great distance in space appealed to him, and he clearly wasn't happy.

I, on the other hand, was smiling. It would be good to burn some of these invaders personally. I'd not gotten enough of that particular thrill lately.

We clanked out into the passages and gathered up into a good-sized squad. With Marvin bringing up the rear, we looked rather formidable. Marvin was in his full battlegear, and I must say, he looked more the part of the freak than ever. He seemed just as eager to try out his new body parts as I was to find out what these invaders were made of.

Marvin still looked something like Marvin: he had several whipping arms and plenty of cameras. But beyond that, his battle persona was quite different. His head section had been replaced with a cluster of six heavy-beam weapons, and this lower body now rested on a sled of gravity repellers. He floated about a foot above the corridor and anything he ran over that could be crushed down, was crushed down. I made sure I kept my boots out from under him. With all the extra generators and weaponry, he was as heavy as a small tank. Above all his new armament, his cameras whipped this way and that excitedly.

We advanced toward the nearest enemy landing point, which was in the mid-section of the station. Again, they were going for our power-couplings. I supposed it made sense. The moment they'd seen we still had some fight left in us, they must have decided to disarm us by killing the power, rather than destroying the weapons themselves.

The enemy had paid a grim price to take this station, and I meant to make them pay even more. We came around a corner as a group in a rush. This was one of the central passages, wide enough for heavy equipment to be transported. It was a cylindrical shape about twenty feet in diameter. My marines filled one end of this pipe, and we began beaming the moment we saw the throng ahead of us.

I wasn't sure who was more surprised: the Lobsters or us. Because that's who it was, a company of perhaps fifty Lobsters dressed up in water-filled suits and crawling all over the passageway. Their shape was unmistakable, and when our lasers cut into those suits, they released a gush of steam which quickly turned to frost in the depressurized passageway.

They returned fire in a disorganized fashion. I'm not sure who had trained them, but I was pretty sure some of those troops shot their own kind in the butt in the confusion. Still, with their greater numbers, we were pressed back out of the passageway into a side chute. We left two of our members dead and floating, including Sergeant Sanchez.

"We'll wait here, and ambush them when they come around the corner," I told my panting squad.

Sandra put away her light beamer and pulled out two combat knives. I glanced at her and nodded. She gave me a fierce grin. She knew our odds weren't good, but that part of her that was different now was enjoying the fight. We touched helmets and whispered our love to each other off the com-link.

Suddenly, there was a rush of dark metal over our heads. Sandra and I were shoved down brutally. Whatever had run us over, it was big. When it had passed by, we came up stiff and sore, with our weapons raised.

Ahead in the main passage, beams flared and gases were released explosively. We crept forward and eyed the scene with our guns in front of us.

I saw something big down there, plowing into the Lobster troops. I figured out what it was in an instant and glanced over my shoulder to confirm my suspicions. Yes, Marvin was no longer guarding our rear.

"Crazy robot," Sandra said. "Do you think he'll survive his charge?"

"I don't know," I said, putting my back against the nearest wall, "but if he wants the glory, he can have it. Everyone hold back. Marvin, can you report your status?"

"Colonel Riggs, my designs are extremely successful. I've killed thirty-six of the enemy."

"Finish off the rest and call us if you need help," I said. I stretched out and checked my weapons. I took a sip of water from my suit's recycler.

"Aren't you even going to tell him he broke ranks and disobeyed orders?" Sandra asked.

I shrugged. It was difficult to do in a metal suit, but if you are strong enough, you can pull it off. I could tell she wanted me to scold the bad robot, but I didn't have it in me this time.

"Marvin rarely does exactly what he's told," I said, "and right now, I'm pretty happy with him."

-10-

By the time the relief ships arrived from the inner planets, it was over. The surviving Crustacean ships had retreated. We learned during a full briefing that the enemy dreadnaught had been caught shortly after its arrival by one of our weapons systems: the flying knots of mines. We hadn't witnessed the strike, but the gunships had.

I'd all but forgotten about the mines, many of which were still on an automatic looping track around Hel. The massed firepower, catching the enemy by surprise with a hard smashing blow to the face, had apparently unnerved the Macros. They didn't like getting hit hard by something they hadn't expected. After losing so many of their cruisers and the dreadnaught, they'd called a retreat. That was why the battlefield had been empty when I'd come up to have a look around.

The Lobsters had made their move at that point. Figuring us to be more or less dead and easy pickings, they'd raced straight from the ring to my dormant station. They might have captured it too, if it hadn't been for some well-placed railgun rounds and their inexperienced marines. Marvin had finished them off, operating like an armored vehicle inside the station.

This stage of the battle appeared to be over, but I wasn't overjoyed about the future. While my fellow marines hooted and jeered at the pathetic efforts of the hapless Crustaceans, I wasn't so quick to scoff at them. Despite the fact they faced entrenched veterans, they'd nearly pulled off the assault. The next time they came at us, they'd be better at it. If there was one thing these academics were capable of, it was learning the hard way. I suspected they'd been observing us closely and imitating our equipment and tactics. It was only a matter of time until they became competent foes.

Perhaps more importantly, it was now clear the Macros had replaced humanity with a new source of willing cannon fodder. We'd left the Crustaceans out in the cold, and they'd turned on their fellow biotics. I supposed that part was forgivable. Earth had done the same, in fact I'd negotiated the deal personally. When faced with extinction, a species tended to do whatever was required to survive.

What followed was a long lull in the fighting. We'd repelled the assault, and exhausted the enemy. But I knew they were out there, rebuilding. They'd come with twice as many ships next time, and I needed reinforcements.

"Sandra?" I called, opening the hatchway into our quarters and waking her up.

These days, she slept in the bed with me when I was around—but not when I was gone. She preferred to sleep on top of things. Today, she was curled up in a ball on top of the modular shower stall we kept in the back of the chamber. It was cylindrical in shape, with feeding pipes for water and a drain at the bottom. She somehow was comfortable wrapped around the PVC pipes up there. I shook my head at the sight. What had those Microbes done to her to change her habits so drastically? I figured I'd never really know.

"Kyle? Are we under attack again?"

"No, relax," I said.

She stretched elaborately. I enjoyed the view. She liked tight flight suits these days, made of form-fitting nanocloth. Her sculpted body was a wonder to behold, and never seemed to change no matter what she did or ate. I supposed I had to take the good with the bad. My girlfriend was a freak, but she was an attractive one.

"Why are you waking me up, then?"

"First off, I wanted to thank you for saving all our butts."

She blinked at me in comic surprise. "How did I do that? Did I miss something during my nap?"

"Remember our little pool room session, and the caroming mines that came out of it? They worked. The Macro dreadnaught was caught full in the face by those mines you dreamt up and I believe that drove them out of the system."

"Huh," she said. She smiled and I expected her to start preening. She did fluff her hair a little bit, but that was all. "Is this what it feels like?"

"What do you mean?"

"To save the world. You do it all the time."

I laughed. "Yeah, do you like it?"

"I guess I do. But I hope people don't expect me to do it again. I mean, it was at least half accident."

I nodded. "Yeah, that's exactly how I feel."

"What are we going to do now?"

"I think it's time for us to launch our ships."

At that, she jumped down from her perch and stepped closer. Her eyes were bright with excitement. "Let's do it," she said. "I want to fry those Lobsters. I bet they'd taste good with some butter and garlic—and salt, lots of salt. Are we going to hit Harvard, or Princeton? I want to make their oceans boil."

"Settle down, there won't be any genocide today."

"But Kyle, they turned on us. They screwed the living, in favor of the machines. I'll never forgive them for it."

"The Worms forgave us."

She gave me an odd look. "I don't think they really understand what we did to them," she said in a stage whisper.

"You might be right. But anyway, I don't want to attack, I want to fly to Earth. We need reinforcements. There's no way we can keep fighting battles out here and losing personnel without more support. I now believe that's Crow's plan: to kill us with attrition. He doesn't have to come out here and stamp out our rebellion. All he has to do is let us hang on at the border, dwindling in numbers. Without reinforcements, we can't last forever."

Sandra twisted her lips and walked around me thoughtfully. "Let me get this straight: You don't want to chase down the Macros and the Lobsters when they are weak. Instead, you want to pick a new fight with Earth."

"We have a breather, a moment in time where we can grab the initiative and make a move of our own. We'll build up, sure. We'll repair this station and get it operating again. But I don't want to crush the Crustaceans. I think we can deal with them as fellow

79

biotics in the future. I think they can be convinced to join us like the rest."

"Okay, fine," she said. As she spoke, she began removing my armor. I let her do it, even though I was in the mood for flying ships rather than personal contact.

"What are you up to?" I asked.

"I don't like letting an enemy catch their breath," she said. "I think we should press the advantage until they break. Let the Crustaceans surrender and swear allegiance to us now. Let them become our vassals instead of serving the Macros."

For a moment, I considered the idea. It did have merit...but I shook my head. "I never wanted an empire. I'm much more comfortable with a federation of states. An alliance."

Sandra shook her head. "I never figured you for a dreamer. How can a group of alien species cooperate that well? How could we really trust them when they aren't even human? Humans are hard enough to believe in."

I had to agree with her, but now she had my helmet off, and my generator pack was lying on the floor. I frowned at her, watching her body move with cat-like grace.

"Tell me again how I saved the Eden system," she said.

"What if I don't?"

"Then I won't let you take a shower with me," she said.

"Liar," I said. Both of us were smiling. We took a shower, and during the process, the cylinder nearly fell over.

Even after we were done with our victory celebration, however, I felt I needed to get moving. We were enjoying a breather right now, but it wouldn't last. We were caught out here between several hostile forces, with very little intel and no support. In the long run, the situation was unsupportable.

* * *

Less than a week later, Sandra and I were on an orbital platform over Eden-6, which was the warmest of the three worlds the Centaurs had given to us. It was an ocean world, with about ninety percent of the surface being covered by water. There was no icecap at either pole, and the landmasses were small. Island archipelagoes were far more common than the few steamy continents. That said, the islands were lovely and lush. Volcanic beaches with sands of white, mauve and even lavender were common.

Most of the planet's life was in the ocean, of course. The warm water maintained a steady year-round temperature of around a hundred degrees Fahrenheit at the equator. At the poles, it was a brisk sixty-five. The deep warm waters teemed with life, and from space they were a cobalt blue.

"I can't wait to get down there," I told Sandra. "But today won't be the time."

"Kwon says he loves it down there."

"Sadly, we're going to have to end his little vacation. When will he come up to the fleet?"

She looked at me shyly. "I haven't told him about the reassignment yet."

"What? I requested the order be relayed hours ago. Why are we waiting?"

Sandra touched my armor, but I couldn't feel it. "Let's go down and tell him in person."

I narrowed my eyes. She was scheming. I could always tell. That didn't mean she wouldn't be successful, but I prided myself on knowing when I was being manipulated.

"Shore leave?" I demanded. "We're in the middle of war."

"We're always in the middle of war. I want to go to the beach, dammit!"

I furrowed my brow and scowled. I opened my mouth to order her to call Kwon to the platform, but she reached up and slammed my visor down. I heard my voice echo inside my helmet. I adjusted my headset and made the call myself.

"Kwon here," he responded quickly.

It was Sandra's turn to glare. I ignored her. "Kwon, I need you. We're going on a flight back toward Earth."

"Why you need me for that, sir?"

My frown deepened. Was everyone infected by a virus that induced laziness? I opened my mouth to repeat my order, this time sucking in a deep breath to create an outraged bellow.

I took a moment to glance down at Sandra first, however. That was a mistake. She had crossed arms and wore a disappointed look on her face. I softened in that instant, and somehow she knew it immediately. She brightened, eyes widening.

"Kwon, I've changed my mind. I'm coming down to perform a personal inspection."

"Very good, sir. You will like it here. I'll start an underground fire for the barbecue."

I took off my helmet, wondering just what Kwon planned to cook underground. Already, I was figuring it would be best not to ask. Whatever it was, it would probably taste good.

Sandra was delighted when she realized she'd gotten her way. She was already talking about towels and picnics and which suit looked best on her. She saw my stubborn expression and came to warm up against me. Ever since I'd undergone microbial baths similar to the ones she had, we'd become close again. I supposed she now considered me to be as big a freak as she was, and that was some kind of turn-on.

"We need a break, Kyle," she said softly. "We aren't ready to go on the offensive. The factories in the inner planets are building more ships to replace the ones we lost against the Macros months ago, and the rest are rebuilding the battle station. They need time to finish."

I sighed, considering her points. She was right, even though the time to go on the offensive was now, we really needed to get organized first.

"All right," I said, "let's go see what they've done down there on the islands."

-11-

Kwon greeted us in a brightly colored sarong of orange, form-hugging nanocloth. I was alarmed, while Sandra twittered. She looked embarrassed for the big man, a response I'd rarely seen in her. For his part, Kwon seemed oblivious. I soon found out why: everyone here wore paper-thin clothing, if they wore anything at all. It was just too damned hot to wear anything else.

"The best plan is to set the nanites so they form a sun-blocking screen," he explained enthusiastically. "That way, air and moisture can still travel through the cloth. It's like you are wearing a net made of tiny mesh. If you hold the cloth up close to your eye, you'll see right through it!"

I held up my hand, warding him off. "That's great Kwon, but I'll pass on looking through your bathing suit."

Kwon shrugged. "As you say, sir."

Sandra scoffed and immediately began stripping down. She'd never been a shy person, but being on a tropical beach of pink sand had turned her into an exhibitionist. Before she was done reprogramming her remaining wisps of nanocloth, Kwon was embarrassed and gazing down the beach, while I was staring at her.

When she was done, I stood in the shade of the ship we'd come down on, still wearing my battle armor. I didn't trust any planet when I first landed there, but I felt somewhat ridiculous clanking and buzzing around on grav-lifters while these two wore gauze. Finally, I climbed out of the armor and left it aboard the destroyer that had brought us down. I didn't reduce my undergarments to paper-thin wisps, but I did order them to transition into their lightest state, which essentially made them into pajamas.

The other two smirked at me, but I ignored them and headed for the base buildings. Oddly, I felt immediately at home on Eden-6. It was a lot like being on a hotter version of Andros Island. The water was a bit more green and the beach was the color of seashells, but I liked the place immediately.

One thing was missing: trees. There weren't any. No palms, no pines—not even squatty, fungal growths. What there were I would classify as giant, complex grasses. They looked like ferns, but grew in clumps with intertwined roots—reminding me of a huge unmowed lawn. The overall effect wasn't unpleasant, however. The green blades rippled and rustled in the sea breezes. The foliage was shiny and almost hurt the eyes when the sun came out, because the reflections were so intense.

That was another odd thing about this world: direct sunshine was rather rare. As the world was mostly covered in water, the skies were affected. The sky was usually overcast, but you could still see the sun. Hanging up there on the far side of the clouds, the star was so huge and intense that it could be seen as a pale disk of light in the sky at all times. I'd seen a similar look on Earth, with a low-lying fog and the sun on the far side of a layer of mist, penetrating the gloom. But on Earth, usually such foggy days were cold and dreary. On Eden-6, the mood wasn't glum when the sky was overcast. The local star still sent through enough light to make the landscape feel cheery.

Kwon walked with me to the base, a structure of dull concrete that looked like a pillbox set on a hillock over the beach. "The glum times are different here, sir," he said seriously. "When the star burns through every persistent layer of mist and scorches the land underneath—that is when we are sorry."

"Is it that bright?" Sandra asked.

Kwon nodded vigorously. "The ocean steams, and the sands become so burning hot they are unbearable to walk upon."

"You mean with bare feet, right?" I asked.

"Of *course*, Colonel," Kwon said. His tone and expression indicated the idea of wearing shoes on Eden-6 was absurd. I noticed he was indeed barefoot, and his big toes slapped on the moist sand with every step, leaving deep impressions. Next to his tracks, Sandra and I made relatively small divots on the beach.

"You've gone native very quickly here, Kwon."

"What, sir?"

"I mean you seem to like this place. You've changed your habits."

"Ah, yes. I agree. It is very pleasant. Quite a break from killing machines in cold space…but I'm getting bored."

I smiled. Here, at last, was the Kwon I knew and understood.

"Well, I'm here to un-bore you," I said. I proceeded to explain that I intended to gather my fleet and head toward Earth, to recon the situation back home.

Kwon looked worried. "But…we aren't going back *permanently*—are we sir?"

I frowned and looked at both of them. To my surprise, neither showed any eagerness to go back home. I wondered about that. I supposed that recent events had changed things. Out here, we were free. We didn't have to worry about the combined thumbs of Crow and Earth's governments. We were living on the edge. It was exhilarating, but dangerous. Apparently, my companions loved it.

"I have to admit this makes Andros Island look a little dull. I just want to see what Crow is up to."

"Is that all you want?" Kwon asked. "I have a better way than flying all the way back to Earth."

I looked at him with raised eyebrows. Sandra mirrored my expression.

Kwon smiled and lifted a thick-fingered hand to indicate the bunker, where we had now arrived. The bunker, unlike everything else on the island, was functional and ugly. It was squat and made of gray-lines of concrete-like substance. I knew the walls were essentially nanites organized into interlocking structures with grains of sand making up the bulk of the material. Building with nanites was very similar to using concrete, but a lot faster and more malleable.

The entrance was a simple rectangle, half-buried in the ground with a set of wide steps leading down into it. Sandra and I followed Kwon's finger, which pointed into the cave-like mouth of the bunker. We had no idea what to expect.

"I've got a surprise, sir," he said. "You have a visitor."

I frowned immediately. I'd never been a man who liked surprises. "Who?" I demanded.

Sandra sucked in her breath. "It's not Crow, is it?" she whispered.

Kwon shook his head and laughed. "No, no. The Admiral didn't fly all the way out here to surprise you. It's someone else, someone who wants *very much* to meet you."

He opened the door by touching it. The nanites that formed the surface fled obediently. The effect was rather similar to that of sand melting away under the force of a powerful wave, except there wasn't a wave of seawater, only a slight contact. I reached out to touch the melting door and felt the grains retreating, almost scurrying away from my hand.

The passage into the gloomy bunker opened, and I saw a stranger standing at the bottom of the steps. She had a shape that was definitely feminine, and as she advanced up the stairs into the light, my eyes widened as I took in the sight. She was tall, blonde, and overtly female. Unlike Sandra, who was built on a lithe frame with dark, straight hair, this woman was curvaceous. Her hair was like a halo around her head and fell on her shoulders in a mass of loose curls.

She smiled at me, and I smiled back reflexively. I liked what I was seeing—I couldn't help myself. Not only was she a voluptuous woman, she was half-naked. Not even Sandra's edited outfit could compete. The stranger had left very little to the imagination. What cloth she did have covering her amounted to a shred of fabric around her waist and another two loops of gauze tucked under her breasts.

It was about then that I noticed several things. For one, the woman had said something to me which I'd missed, and for another, Sandra and Kwon were both staring at me. Kwon was smirking, while Sandra looked pissed.

I forced my mind to tune in to the conversation. "Nice to meet you," I managed to get out.

"Yes, Colonel," she said, "as I was saying, I'm at your disposal. Just name the time and the place where we can get together."

"Excuse me?"

"For the interview," she said.

I realized then that she must have opened up with her name and a request for an interview. Somehow, I'd missed both those details. I'd been too busy staring.

I took pains to avoid looking at Sandra, who was now giving me the evil eye. I could see she had her fists on her hips, but I forced a smile.

"That's why Marvelena came all this way out from Earth, sir. To interview the famous renegade, the leader of Riggs' Pigs!"

I glanced at him, then back to the blonde. "An interview? Of course. Let's do it on the beach, right now. There's a condition, however."

"Name it," the woman said. She took a step toward me, and I realized I recognized her face from somewhere. I could not recall where.

"You have to tell me what the hell is going on back on Earth, first," I said.

Marvelena blinked and licked her lips. She nodded then, and slowly her smile returned to her face. "Okay, let's go for a walk."

She moved away, rolling her hips as she crossed the sand in front of me. It wasn't an affectation, I could tell. She was simply built in a fashion that required a bit of hip-rolling to take a step.

I turned and took a step after her, but felt a thin, iron-hard hand restraining me. I looked down to see Sandra holding onto my arm. She was shockingly strong for her size and weight. I knew I could break away if I wanted to, after having taken Marvin's baths. I was powerful as well, and I outweighed her. But I also knew instinctively that jerking my arm out of her grasp would be a bad move right now.

"I'll be right there," I called after Marvelena.

The woman treated me with a glance back and another of those smiles.

"What is it?" I asked Sandra, trying not to show any emotion.

"I don't want you walking the beach with her alone," Sandra said, scowling. "I brought you down here to spend time with *me*."

Unhelpfully, Kwon sighed as he stared after the blonde. "She's got a butt like a *real* woman. Doesn't she, sir?"

"Who the hell is she?" Sandra demanded.

"Marvelena Hellsen," Kwon said.

"Sounds like a made-up name. Where is she from?"

87

"Don't you know her?" Kwon said. "She's from GNN. She's on the net news all the time back home."

I frowned, finally realizing where I'd seen Marvelena before. She was a reporter for the Global News Network. GNN had never liked Star Force. They'd always done stories designed to make us look foolish and irresponsible. After we won a battle or perfected a new weapon, they would broadcast video of the trees that we'd burned down, or masses of dead, floating fish. Instead of cheering us on, they complained whenever we were successful against the Macros. Some Star Force officers whispered that GNN favored the Macros over humanity. It was hard to believe any human could favor the machines, but I'd often wondered whose side they were on.

"She can't be all that bad in person," I said, looking after her.

"Please look at *me* when we're talking," Sandra snapped.

I did as she asked with some reluctance.

She studied me, squinting into my face. "Your pupils are dilated. You really liked what you were looking at."

I blinked and attempted a smile. "I always like looking at you."

She crossed her arms and tilted her head toward the beach. "Go on. Take your little date for a stroll. But hands off."

"Don't worry," I said. "She has a nice walk, but I know she's a viper."

I walked away before Sandra could change her mind and followed the path down to the beach. I met Marvelena there. She stood pensively on the edge of the crashing waves.

"The waves are just like those back on Earth," she said. "I never thought I'd see a place like this. Not unless I died and went to heaven."

I smiled at her. "How long have you been here?"

"Just a few hours. Kwon tells me you aren't getting any more reports from the Admiralty back home. Is that true?"

I frowned slightly. "The *Admiralty*? If you mean Admiral Crow, then you're right. I haven't had contact for a few weeks. We are out on the frontier, with no direct way to signal Earth. I imagine you came out on a small scouting ship?"

"Yes," Marvelena said. She picked up a shell and fiddled with it. "Have you broken off relations with Earth, Colonel? Have you declared your independence?"

"What?" I laughed. "Why would I do that? Don't tell me people are saying that back home. I'm a loyal Star Force officer."

She nodded vaguely and looked away toward the sea again. "Interviews only work if the subject opens up, you know."

I frowned at her. "This isn't going to be an interview, exactly," I said. "This is an exchange of information. It's time for you to give me some. What's going on back home? Do you know why Crow hasn't contacted me? He hasn't even acknowledged my transmissions."

Marvelena looked troubled. "That's exactly what he said."

"Who?"

"The Admiral. He told me he was your commanding officer and you hadn't reported in as required. He wasn't sure, he said, if you were unable to comply or simply unwilling to."

"What else did he say?"

"That you and your team out here—that you were technically rebels."

"Rebels?" I asked, surprised. I reflected immediately that I shouldn't have been.

"There are hints and rumors all over Earth, Colonel. They say you have been forming deals with aliens, fighting wars independently of any Earth sanction. You are doing as you please out here, causing Earth no end of future harm. They call you *dangerous* and *unrepentant*."

I stared at her, and I could see in her face she was troubled. The façade of the bouncy news reporter was gone. She knew she was in the middle of something big.

"So," I said. "Why did you come out here then?"

"To get the truth—or at least, your side of things. That's my job."

I nodded and we started walking again. I didn't trust her, of course. But it was hard not to. She was lovely and charismatic. I'd never been so close to a media person of her stature before. It was true that such people exuded a powerful presence, and I felt myself caught up in her aura.

"We're *not* independent," I said firmly. "We're part of Star Force. We have sworn to defend Earth, and all humanity. We're out here because this is where the dangerous aliens are. I hope those details can find their way into your report when you go back home."

She slowly led me farther down the beach to an outcropping of dark rocks. The sun was a huge, bluish-white disk behind the clouds. The air was warm and humid and the breezes coming off the ocean ruffled our hair. Already, I could taste the salt on my face, despite the fact I hadn't set foot in the water yet.

"Let's go swimming," she said. She didn't wait for an answer. She stepped backward into the water, where it lapped up over her ankles and then her knees. She reached up to remove her flimsy garments, clearly planning on swimming without them.

I glanced back toward the bunker on the hillock, and immediately noted that I couldn't see it. We were out of sight of the rest of the inhabitants of this lovely island. There was no one out here except for a few alien fish that probed the surface nearby with curiosity. The humps on their backs looked like wet stones in the water and their bulbous eyes watched us. Supposedly, they were harmless.

Marvelena reached out her hand toward me, and I took a step forward. She smiled. It was impossible not to smile back at her.

I almost did it. I almost followed her into the water for a swim, but somehow I stopped myself. I don't know how things might have ended if I *had* followed her. I don't know who might have witnessed the transgression, or at least see enough to tell a sordid tale. Star Force had always been small and full of gossips.

I stopped and put my hands on my hips, rather than taking hers. I looked at the water and shook my head. "Not here," I said. "There are dangerous tides around these rocks. This isn't Venice Beach, miss. Let's head back. You can swim near the bunker if you wish, it's safe there."

Standing there in the water, nude and wet, she appeared to be heartbroken, but I remained firm. A few minutes later found us walking back toward the bunker together. She tied up what passed for her swimsuit into knots around her breasts with prissy movements.

The interview, if that's what it really had been, was at an end.

-12-

The day-night cycle on Eden-6 was different than Earth. The days were much longer here—about forty hours long. The cool night breezes were a welcome relief by the time they came. Twenty hours of diffuse sunlight was more than enough. I soon fell into a pattern that humans who came here tended to adopt: We awoke in the predawn glimmer, excited and slightly chilled after a long slow night of some twenty hours. Then if the sun broke through, there was often a few glaring hours before the mists returned. The star was so big and bright, it was painful to look at. Viewed just after a long period of darkness, it seemed cruelly intense. Shades were mandatory, so that our optical nerves weren't damaged in those early brilliant hours.

By mid-morning, the ocean heated up and produced the traditional shroud of mist. The sun was soon obscured, but still visible as a large pale disk in the sky. I thought these were probably the best hours, trumped only by sunset.

At about midday, we grew sleepy and tired of relentless heat and light. We took naps then, as I suppose people in tropical climates often did. Siestas had become part of the culture here on Eden-6. A big meal and a couple of hours in the cool gloom of the bunker made the rest of the long day tolerable.

When the sun did finally sink into the sea, the sunset was spectacular. The mist often burned off as evening approached, and the sky was streaked with lavenders, oranges and pinks. These sunsets trumped those of my homeworld in every way: the sun was bigger and brighter, the ocean was endless and unspoiled, and the sunsets took nearly an hour from start to end. They were almost like sweeping, nightly ceremonies.

When night finally did cloak the land, we welcomed darkness with relief. Every day felt endless, and was too much of a good thing. I felt a certain lethargy come over me as day after day passed by.

On the fifth long day, in the midmorning when the mists first came up from the seawater, I went to talk to Marvelena. Our interviews had progressed and become more informal—almost personal. She took pictures, followed me on my routine duties and asked me dozens of questions. She wanted to know what I ate, what I slept in and who I slept with. I found myself answering her questions with increasing candor, despite my reservations. It was hard to think of her as anything other than a new, fascinating acquaintance.

After breakfast and an inspection of the new blast pans for the planetary spaceport I had Kwon constructing, I made my way back to the bunker entrance. There, instead of Marvelena, I found Sandra. She was crouched on the roof of the bunker, a pose I found very familiar. I narrowed my eyes at her, and thought I saw a strip of pink cloth in her hands.

"What did you do with the reporter?" I asked.

"I drowned her in the ocean. Does that break your heart?"

I opened my mouth, the snapped it closed again. "Sandra, have you lost it? You haven't been this jealous since—"

Sandra jumped down and stalked toward me. She tossed the pink strappy garment into my face. The nanocloth writhed there, and tried to encircle my head. I pulled it away.

"Don't bring up Jasmine," she said. "And I'm not crazy. Follow me."

Frowning deeply, I had to hurry to keep up with her. We marched down to the beach to a familiar spot. To my surprise, she continued marching, right into the water. She was clearly looking for something.

"Is this where you stashed the body? These fish will eat a corpse within hours. I can't cover for you this time, Sandra. Do you know that? I'll have to send you back to Earth in disgrace."

She stared at me in surprise. Then she burst out laughing. "I didn't *really* kill her," she said. "I just said that. I can't believe you bought that one."

I chuckled uncomfortably and breathed a sigh of relief. I had taken her at her word, as I'd seen her kill before. She liked it, and she didn't need much provocation.

"Of course you're joking," I chuckled uncomfortably. "Now, tell me what you're looking for."

"It's out here somewhere. Walk around in this area. You'll find it with your toes."

Reluctantly, I waded out into the water and marched around with the fine sand squelching up around my feet. I felt something almost immediately. At first I thought it was a rock, but it had a distinct shape with hard linear edges. I reached down and felt around.

Sandra splashed over to me. "You've got it, don't you?"

I pulled something up. Sandra helped, and in a moment, we had a box out of the water, dripping sand. It looked like a suitcase made of metal and black polymers.

"What's this?" I asked.

"She put it out here a few days back. I saw her do it, but couldn't find it the first time. Last night she came to check on it. I marked the spot with that stack of rocks."

She pointed and I saw a grouping of black rocks forming a marker on the beach. I nodded.

"What do you think it is?" I asked. I found the handle and dragged it up to the beach.

"Careful, it could be a bomb. I ran scanners over it and got a lot of electronic and chemical signatures."

We didn't have an actual bomb squad out here on the frontier. We'd never found it necessary. Today, however, could be the exception.

"If it was a bomb," I asked, "why would she plant it out here in the ocean? Why not in the bunker?"

"Maybe she's worried about our systems detecting it. Maybe she wants it to be out here, hidden until she's ready."

I stared at her, then the metal case. I wasn't sure what to think. I left the box on the beach near the marker, and headed back toward the bunker.

"Where's Marvelena?" I asked.

"She's trying to find her bathing suit—I stole it to keep her in her room for a few minutes. I told her I would come back with another one."

I smiled at that. I knew that Sandra could have stirred up any pool of spare nanites and ordered them to form nanocloth. They were a specialized variety, but there were plenty of them around. Marvelena wouldn't know that, however.

We returned to the bunker wondering what she would have to say for herself. There in the doorway of the bunker stood a familiar shapely figure. She had one arm across her chest. She was glaring at the two of us.

"This sort of mistreatment of the press will not go unnoticed," she said.

I threw her the top, and she turned around to put it on. Sandra smirked at her as she did so, and she spoke to me in a low voice. "Stop staring. They're fake, anyway."

Marvelena turned toward us with a suspicious eye. "What was that?"

"I said the surgeon should lay off the gin next time and give you a break."

Marvelena's mouth fell open, and she advanced in a rage. Her top was on, but not quite perfectly. I realized as the reporter advanced that the idiot might try to slap Sandra. That would be a very bad idea, and might even be exactly what Sandra wanted. I took a step forward and lightly caught Marvelena's upraised, open hand in midair.

"Let go of me!" she said, struggling.

My hand stayed frozen in position, holding her wrist high. I knew that under no circumstances could I allow her to strike Sandra. My girl had a temper, and if she lost it, there might not be anything left of Marvelena to apologize to.

"Settle down," I said, putting on my deepest commander's voice. Both of them glared at one another and ignored me.

"We're here to ask you about the contraband you've hidden out in the surf," I said.

Finally, that got through Marvelena's celebrity rage. She turned back to me, and I released her hand. She rubbed her wrist and glared at both of us in turn.

"That's my property. Don't touch it."

I shook my head. "I'm sorry. This isn't some public beach back home. This is a military base in a war zone, no matter how beautiful it might be. Answer my question or you'll be placed under arrest."

Marvelena's face underwent a transition then. Her rage faded, and she took on the look of a lost victim. I was immediately impressed with her ability to shift expressions like a chameleon and her range of emotive displays.

"You can't arrest me! No wonder you get endless bad press. Take me to an embassy, or something."

Sandra chuckled. It was a mean sound.

"Marvelena," I said. "Have you been in trouble spots back on Earth? Areas that are lawless and in the midst of an upheaval? Something like a civil war?"

"I was in South America before Star Force leveled it," she said.

I winced. The ill-fated South America campaign was a sore point for everyone in Star Force. The press had never forgiven us for the loss of a continent. The human species had survived, but a billion armchair generals would forever second-guess every decision we'd made on the ground in the old days.

"I have to know what's in that case," I said. "Is it a weapon of some kind?"

"No."

"Then why are you going to such lengths to hide it? What are you afraid of?"

Marvelena licked her lips. "I'll make it up to you," she said suddenly. "The report will be quite favorable. Just give me the unit, and I'll return to Earth immediately."

Sandra and I looked at each other. Sandra smiled predatorily. "Can I arrest her now?" she asked.

I nodded. Marvelena squawked in outrage as Sandra sprang toward her and grabbed her from behind. She pulled back her arms and lifted them up slightly. I turned and headed toward the beach, Sandra and Marvelena followed. The reporter produced quite a bit of noise.

"You're under arrest for suspicion of possessing contraband on this base," I said formally. I had to shout to be heard over the woman's protests. "As the commanding officer in this system, I'm placing you in custody until your guilt or innocence can be determined."

We headed back to the spot with the little stack of black stones and the dark case. Lying there in the sand, it looked quite innocuous. I couldn't help but wonder what was inside it.

Sandra gave the girl a shove and she stumbled close to it. She gave us a venomous glare.

"What is it?" I asked.

"I don't know," she wailed. "They made me bring it here, and they said it was harmless."

"What is its purpose, then?"

"It has no purpose."

Sandra laughed. "You lugged this box all the way from Earth and hid it carefully. Then you tried to seduce Kyle. I think it is a camera or something. A system to record data. You're trying to blackmail us, or make us look bad."

Marvelena gritted her teeth. "I demand to be sent back to Earth."

"You will open the case," I said.

"I can't."

"You don't know how?"

"I do, but they told me not to."

"Who are *they*?" I asked.

She didn't answer. She looked worried now, she was cornered and she knew it.

"Marvelena," I said. "Perhaps you are only now realizing how far you are from home, and how helpless you are against us. There are no cameras out here recording every event as they do in the old cities back on Earth. There are no world tribunals, no powerful elites who can pull in a favor with a phone call. All you have on the frontier worlds are the people you deal with every day."

"That's why you don't screw with us," Sandra added.

I took a step toward her, and the waves lapped over my ankles. Sandra put a hand in front of me. "Let me do it," she said.

I considered. The spectacle of me manhandling a woman like Marvelena while she was barely· dressed, cameras or not, wasn't something I wanted anyone on the base to witness. I nodded to Sandra.

96

She trotted into the surf, grabbed the woman, who screamed, and the case with her other hand. She eyed the case critically.

"It's blinking," she said. "Blinking with a green light. Just an LED—no nanotech."

"You shouldn't touch it," Marvelena said, she squirmed in Sandra's iron grasp. "The Agent said not to."

"What agent?" Sandra demanded.

"Someone from the Ministry of Trust."

We both stared at her. We'd never heard of such an institution. What was Crow doing back home?

"What the hell is the Ministry of Trust?" Sandra demanded.

Marvelena looked confused—and terrified. "That's where I work. I'm a reporter."

I frowned and opened my mouth to ask another question, but Sandra shouted triumphantly at that moment.

"Ah-ha!" she said. She'd lifted the case and turned it over. "There we go, here is a second opening. You—put your hand in here. I think it is touch-sensitive."

Marvelena did not cooperate. Sandra finally took her hand and shoved it into the opening. Marvelena screamed again, and I thought I heard a new note in her voice. It was the sound of sheer terror.

Everything changed after that. I saw a blur of motion, and a flash of released energy. I was knocked down into the wet sand.

I blinked up at the pale disk hidden behind the omnipresent clouds of Eden-6. I couldn't hear anything.

It really was a bomb, I thought. My mind was numbed and I recognized the sensation. I was in shock.

-13-

I climbed to my feet and swayed unsteadily. I was shouting Sandra's name, but I couldn't hear my own voice. All I heard was an intense ringing sound. In my body, I knew the nanites were rushing to injured spots. I could feel them, tickling in my veins and under my skin the subcutaneous layer.

I squinted and peered at my surroundings. It had been a long time since I'd been injured this badly. One of my eyes, my right one, seemed not to operate at all. My left was clouded by blood and the images coming in of my surroundings were dim.

I knew I should seek help. I should be trying to save myself. That was the first mission of every soldier when injured on the battlefield. Guarantee your own survival, then tend to the lives of those around you. But I kept looking for Sandra, heedless of the blasted bits of shrapnel and sand that had riddled my body.

There was a big bloodspot in the water, staining an area perhaps twenty feet around a dark color. I knew it was blood and gore. I dipped my hands into it, and found a foot. I looked it over numbly. I saw the painted nails—lavender and silver. I shook my head and dropped the foot. It wasn't Sandra's.

I kept digging until Kwon showed up. He and about six other marines rushed into the water and lifted me up, carrying me toward the bunker. I resisted feebly. They were saying things to me, but I wasn't able to hear or understand them. I was dragged down into the bunker like a scrap of food carried by a pack of industrious ants.

In a cool, dark room under the base a dozen skinny metal arms went to work on me. I was unfortunate, in that they didn't turn off the nerves first. Nanite medical tables didn't always worry about pain and suffering. I passed out before the stitching was done.

* * *

Awakening from a bad dream, I found I could see with both eyes again. How many hours had I been lying on this slab like a stiff in a morgue? I didn't know, but I saw there was another body lying next to me. It was Sandra, I could tell in an instant.

With a tremendous effort, I climbed off my slab, tripped and fell on my face. After several minutes of groaning and heaving, I managed to get to her on my knees. I touched her hair and then her cheek with the back of my mangled fingers. I thought I felt warmth there.

Her jaws moved, and after a moment, I could make out quiet words. "I'm going to get Crow for this," she mumbled.

I smiled and leaned back against my own slab. I closed my eyes and laughed until I choked. We'd both survived another attempt on our lives.

A few days later, we were sore but functional. Nanites and microbes had done amazing things once again. We headed back toward the beach. This time, Kwon hovered near.

"I should never have left you," he complained to himself. "I was a moron, just like Jensen says."

I shook my head. "No, Kwon. *I* was the moron. I had my head turned by a pretty face. I skipped protocol and I paid the price."

"That wasn't the first time," Sandra said in a scratchy voice. Part of her throat had been damaged by the blast.

"It was luck you guys both lived," Kwon said.

I shook my head again. "Not really. Sandra bounded away like a jackrabbit when she heard the device click, and I was far enough away. We would have both died anyway, if it hadn't been for the work of nanites and the body-edits performed by the Microbes."

Kwon muttered something I didn't catch. I could tell he still blamed himself for this security lapse. He'd set up automatic turrets along the beach now, which twisted and scanned us occasionally as we passed by.

"This is the spot," I said when we reached the collection of rocks. Marvelena had led me here the first time we'd met.

Sandra stood with her hands on her hips, surveying the scene. "I get it," she said. "This place is very private. You can't see the bunker from here. You brought her out to this spot and screwed her, didn't you Kyle? Don't lie to me."

I grimaced. "She led me out here. And no, I didn't do it—but that might have been her intention."

Kwon looked alarmed. "You two aren't going to fight now, are you? We only just got you put back together!"

"We're here to see why she led me to this spot."

We searched, and quickly found another device like the first one under the waves, but further offshore. These devices seemed adept at staying put. We examined this one at a safe distance.

"What I don't understand is how she got these boxes out here into the ocean," I said. "They're too heavy for a normal woman—and she didn't seem nanotized."

"Ah..." Kwon said hesitantly. "Maybe I recognize that box-thing, now that you mention it."

We both stared at him.

"Well, she said she needed help. I might have carried a box for her—or two of them."

"*You* did?" I asked. "And you didn't feel like bringing this up before? What were the boxes supposed to do?"

"She said they would monitor the planet, track eco-data. Some bullcrap like that. I didn't listen."

"What did she give you in return for your help, Kwon?" Sandra asked.

"Uh...she was a very generous and friendly woman."

"That little witch," Sandra said. She turned on me, her eyes flashing. "She tried to lead you out here Kyle to screw you, or kill you—or both. Right off, the moment after you'd met!"

"Maybe," I said.

"We should burn this second box with hand-beamers until we're certain it can't detonate," Kwon suggested.

"Then we won't learn what it is," I said.

In the end, I contacted Marvin and requested he come to the island base and take a look. To my surprise, he showed up within the hour.

100

"That was quick, Marvin," I said. "I thought you were stationed in space, orbiting Eden-11."

"A mistaken assumption, Colonel. I've been working here on Eden-6."

I frowned. "Why?"

"Because there are subjects here who I need to examine."

"Subjects? What's here that triggers your overly-curious mind?"

Marvin shuffled his tentacles and paused. I knew that meant he was thinking up a dodge, if not an outright lie.

"Don't bother to bullshit me, Marvin. Just answer the question."

Almost every camera he had studied me. "I was about to explain that I've been studying the Microbes. They are native to this world, as I've explained in the past."

I did seem to recall him telling me the Microbes came from this planet. I frowned in concern. We'd been swimming in these oceans. I hadn't thought about getting some kind of infection from the water.

"Are these creatures dangerous, Marvin? My people have been swimming these oceans for months."

"Yes and no," Marvin said. "Only the intelligent Microbes could damage humans, and those colonies are relatively rare."

"But they're in the water, right?"

"Yes."

I heaved a sigh. "Is the ocean teeming with these little bugs? Trillions of them?"

"Trillions is an insufficient numerical concept in this instance. I have calculated we are dealing with numbers in the octillions."

"The octillions?" I asked. "Isn't that a one with about twenty zeroes after it?"

"Twenty-seven zeros, sir."

"Right. Well, I suppose when you have a trillion micro flora in a single human body, an ocean would have a population with a count many orders of magnitude higher."

"Correct."

"You still haven't told me why they aren't dangerous to humans."

"They aren't all the same species," he said. "The vast majority of them don't know we exist. Just as on Earth, there are a millions of species of bacteria here. On Eden-6, a few species have developed intelligence. Most are literally mindless, wild microbes, just as they are on Earth. My point is that the odds you have encountered intelligent colonies just by occasional bathing are low."

I nodded. "I guess it is a very large ocean. But don't they travel around and interact?"

"Not as humans do. They are very fractious, due to their small size and short lifespans. A solitary traveling Microbe, should it survive the journey from one colony to another, would find the trip took multiple lifespans to complete."

"Hmm, so…they don't interact at all? Each colony is a world unto itself? That will make it harder to deal with them as a single society."

"They are not a single society. They are not even a single species. They vary dramatically from warm water types that float in cycles around the world, following various currents, to cold, deep-water types that anchor themselves to the sea bottom."

"I see," I said thoughtfully. I'd always planned to get around to adding the Microbes into my list of biotic allies. Now, I wasn't sure if such a thing would ever be possible. Marvin had been right when he'd once told me the Microbes were like the living form of the Nanos.

I looked at Marvin again, sharply. "You've found some of them then, here on this planet? You've encountered the smart ones?"

Marvin's tentacles writhed. "Not exactly. Can I get on with my investigation of the crime scene now?"

"No," I said. "What do you mean by *not exactly?*"

"'Not' is a negative logical operator, reversing the true-false state of a Boolean value. 'Exactly' qualifies as an adverb."

"I know that, you evasive robot! What I want to know is what your vague reference means in this instance."

Marvin squirmed some more. I figured he was dreaming up a new half-lie.

"Never mind," I said suddenly. "Let me guess what it means."

"Be my guest."

I glared at him. "You haven't *exactly* found intelligent Microbes here. That means you have encountered them, but not in the manner described. Are they different Microbes? Maybe proto-intelligent ones?"

"That would be very exciting, but no."

I shook my head. I couldn't believe I was playing twenty questions with Marvin, standing on this patch of beach. The odd thing was it was probably a faster way to get to the right answer when dealing with him. I could see by his body language he was excited and intrigued by the contest. Could Colonel Riggs figure out what Marvin was hinting at without losing his mind? For Marvin, the very process was stimulating.

I considered giving up the thread in frustration, but didn't. Becoming stubborn, I pushed ahead. I was going to match wits with this bucket of nanites and I was going to win.

"Second point," I said, "you don't want me to know the truth. That indicates I might not approve of your methodology. Let's put this together. You've met smart Microbes here, but not in the manner I described. And, you aren't sure I'll be happy about what you did...I'm still not getting it."

I looked at the Marvin, who'd come close and seemed agitated. His cameras were eyeing me from a dozen angles and his tentacles were restless, causing little sprays of sand to shoot up from under him as they squirmed.

"You're really enjoying this, aren't you?" I asked him. "Is this all an experiment you've set up to test me?"

"No, this incident is spontaneous. But it is very stimulating."

I took another deep breath, closed my eyes, and thought hard. Finally, I opened them again and nodded. "You brought colonies back here from Eden-11. The creatures the Macros used as a biotic weapon—you returned them to their home planet. That's it, isn't it? Do you have them somewhere on the island trapped in a tiny pool?"

"I'm very impressed, Colonel Riggs. I'm not sure that I could come up with the same conclusions, given the same input."

"Thanks, I guess. What the hell are you up to, Marvin? Playing god again with the Microbes?"

"To answer your earlier more coherent inquiry: yes, I did transport Microbes from Eden-11 to Eden-6. I've returned them to their homeworld, just as you for did the Centaurs."

"Yes, but they aren't the same as when they left," I said. "You told me yourself the Macros bred them to kill the Centaurs. Then you fooled with them further, breeding them to effect changes in human physiology."

"They should pose no danger to the indigent population."

"*Should?* You have no idea if that's true or not. I suggest you dump your pools and go looking for native colonies again. But I don't want you to trap them and abuse them. Try to contact them and arrange a peaceable trading system for us to use their special biological talents."

Marvin squirmed. "You are ordering me to kill several trillion individuals? I've brought them all the way here, to their fabled homeworld. They like it here, even if they find it too warm. They are adapting and thriving. I'm surprised that you would be so ruthless with a population of refugees."

I made a growling sound of frustration. He had me, and I knew it. If it was immoral to create and transport an altered intelligent colony, wasn't it equally immoral to destroy them to keep this world's local population pure? Maybe these returning populations would invade the oceans and eat all the coral or something, but who was I to kill them all because they might be a problem to the more established members of their complex people? I barely understood them, and didn't feel qualified to pass judgment on them.

"All right Marvin," I said. "Keep your experimental pool. But keep them far from the ocean itself. Don't let them grow in number or escape."

"They will object to further imprisonment," he said. "I've promised them—"

"I don't care what you promised them. You are a member of Star Force, and under my command. Do you wish to keep that status?"

"Yes I do, Colonel Riggs."

"Then stop giving me such a hard time."

"My apologies, sir."

-14-

After we'd sorted out the fate of the Microbes Marvin had brought with him, I had him investigate the mess on the beach that had once been the beautiful Marvelena Hellsen. Just in case, he left his brainbox on the sand and rolled his body into the surf. The body was connected to the brainbox by a long strand of gleaming liquid metal.

After an hour or so of poking around, he managed to blow himself up. Afterward, what was left of Marvin came to make his report.

"The subject known as Marvelena was attuned to the device," he said. "It apparently was recording data of several types, but it detonated when I used a sample of her DNA and applied it to the internal switch."

Sandra narrowed her eyes. "Where did you get DNA…? Never mind. I don't want to know."

"But could it spy on us, Marvin?" I asked.

"Yes. I believe so. The unit appears to be capable of ring-to-ring transmissions. Using this system, the subject was possibly able to report back to Earth directly."

I wasn't happy to learn that Earth had this technology. Who knew who Crow was communicating with now?

"So," I said, pacing over the sands, "she *was* a spy and possibly an assassin, but they sent her here undercover as a newsperson. Are we sure she was who she said she was? If she was the real Marvelena, did she *know* she was an assassin?"

"Every detail of her identification checked out," Marvin said. "Either they cloned her, or that was the original Marvelena Hellsen. I cannot summarize her state of mind, as I never actually met her."

Neither Sandra nor Kwon were certain how much she knew about her role in this tragic event, either.

I nodded. "Okay, let's accept she really was the famous reporter. And whether or not she knew what was going to happen, she knew she was supposed to get the box close to me and then touch it. Maybe she thought it was something else, like a data capture device. I can hardly believe she would have come out here to be a suicide bomber. Not someone like her. She loved herself more than anything."

The rest agreed with me. We puzzled over the story for a long time, but couldn't figure out the rest of the circumstances with incomplete information. But regardless of the details, it seemed clear that someone was out to kill me—again.

After the attempted assassination, as bizarre as it was, I was more determined than ever to find out what was going on back on Earth. I ordered the fleet to gather at the ring that led to the Helios system.

Naturally, my staff filled the air with objections. Miklos said that if I would only wait another week, we'd have ten more ships. Welter wanted me to wait a month. By then, we'd have the battle station up to strength and we could leave the Eden system behind, certain that our rear flank was secure. Kwon and Sandra thought we should send a scout expedition first, and when they returned, we could make our decision with a more complete picture of the strategic situation. Marvin, for his part, watched us all with curious excitement. He made no objections, because he didn't have any. He *wanted* to go exploring again. Knowing that the only staffer on my side was a crazy robot didn't make things any easier for me.

I listened carefully to my people as they all presented good ideas. Unfortunately, every proposal would eat up a lot of time that I wasn't willing to give away. Whatever we could build in a given amount of time, I reasoned the enemy could build more in that same span. Whether it was Crow's Fleet building against us, or another Macro task force, I would be losing in relative strength with each day that passed. Besides, I didn't even have enough trained crews to properly man the ships I'd already built.

Accordingly, I overruled them all. They were sullen, but unsurprised. Only Marvin seemed happy, his snarl of tentacles whipping about excitedly and his cameras watching everyone. He'd rebuilt himself with startling speed. I guessed it wasn't that hard to do when you were built mostly of nanites and electronics such as cameras. The only unique thing about Marvin was his brainbox. I reflected that same thing could be said about all of us.

We launched the next morning and gathered at the ring until I had over fifty ships. It wasn't much, but they were all veterans of a dozen battles and our designs had been tested in battle and honed. I had no idea what we would meet, but I was through with waiting around.

Captain Miklos flew our only light cruiser *Nostradamus*, which was a replica I'd built of the ship Sarin had brought out to parade in front of me a few months back. We'd made a few modifications, but for the most part it followed Earth's design. The ship looked like a flying ladle with fins—and lots of heavy laser turrets. Six of them.

I left Commander Welter behind, placing him in charge of the battle station and the overall defense of Eden. He mumbled his thanks, and I couldn't blame him for that. If a serious threat came and the Fleet was out on maneuvers, we both knew he couldn't hold. But I told him to do so anyway. I told him I planned to bring back help.

We formed up into a column at the ring, behind *Nostradamus*. The rest of the ships were the new gunboats I'd designed. I'd been able to mass-produce these ugly little ships. I was still proud of them. They weren't sleek, especially fast, or powerful. What they were was numerous. We built them using the massive captured Macro factories to make the hulls in one single birth-like effort, along with the power generators. The interior components were manufactured by the nanotech factories. Combining the Macro bulk-production with the refined technology of the Nano factories was the key. We were able to churn out gunships at an alarming rate. Already, I had more of them than I had qualified Star Force pilots. Even with a crash training program, I could only deploy a proper crew on fifty of them.

Surviving from my original forces, I now had only six destroyers and ten saucer-shaped frigates. The rest had been lost in the struggles against the Macros to retake the Eden system, and they were too difficult to replace. I decided to leave the destroyers and frigates behind to cover Eden, under the command of Welter, who sat in his ruined battle station.

When I finally flew my task force through the ring, I had fifty gunships with one light cruiser at the point. It would have to do.

We arrived in the Helios system a moment later, nervous, but not paranoid. I'd been scouting ahead, naturally. The Worms knew we were coming, as I'd made a point of sending pictographic messages to them. These included images of the raging Worm Warrior, followed by their images for comradeship and shared glory. These concepts never seemed to fail to stir the hearts of the Worms. They were suckers for bravado.

In response to our arrival in force, the Worms launched their own fleet. They had a small, but impressive force. Their ships were radically different from our own, but still surprisingly effective in combat. They were close fighters that released powerful short-ranged beams of particles. I'd personally witnessed them tearing up Macro cruisers in the past.

"Count those ships, Miklos," I said, standing in full battle armor on his bridge.

"Ah...sixty-two Worm ships, sir," Captain Miklos said. He wore a full beard and an Eastern European accent. If anything, isolation out here on the frontier had sharpened these two characteristics. His accent had thickened somehow, and so had his hoary beard. "More are rising up out of the atmosphere every minute, Colonel. They appear friendly or at least neutral. But, they're scrambling to meet us if we represent a threat."

I nodded. "Friendly but paranoid. I think of all the aliens, I understand the Worms the best."

He cast me a worried glance. It was perhaps his tenth such glance of the day. I thought I might have to give him a private talk later on. I wanted him to look sharp and confident in front of his bridge crew.

On the bridge, everyone but me wore nanocloth Fleet uniforms. These were tougher than cotton or wool, of course, but were as effective as paper when compared to my own armored suit. Perhaps that was what was bothering him. Sure, I could unlimber my heavy beamer and kill everyone aboard without breaking a sweat. But that was the job of the Marine. The Fleet types were supposed to fly the ships, while my kind was supposed to do the close-in killing. If that bothered him, well, he was in the wrong service.

What surprised us more than the gathering horde of Worm ships, which numbered over a hundred strong by the next day, was the message we received in the morning. It wasn't from the Worms, or from Eden. It was from the ring near Helios, the one that led to the Alpha Centauri system, the next jump point homeward, toward Earth. A single cruiser hung there, looking very similar to our own flagship. It transmitted a repeating message toward us.

"We're assuming you're under the command of Colonel Kyle Riggs. The Imperial Forces of Earth order you to halt your advance and turn back. This system is a protectorate of Earth. Alpha Centauri is a protectorate of Earth. I repeat..."

The message did indeed repeat, at least six times. Everyone aboard *Nostradamus* eyed one another in shock. *The Imperial Forces of Earth?*

"Since when has Earth become an empire?" I demanded of Miklos, as if he knew what I was talking about.

He narrowed his eyes and stared out the viewport into the blackness of space. "I was afraid of something like this. Really, I suppose it was only a matter of time."

I stared at him. "Do you have some kind of inside information? Have details been kept from me?"

He shook his bearded head. It occurred to me his beard was far beyond regulation length, but I decided now wasn't the time to worry about regulations.

Miklos eyed at me seriously. "I read the reports of your encounter with Marvelena Hellsen. She mentioned an institution called 'The Ministry of Trust' did she not?"

"Yeah? So? Have you ever heard of such a thing?"

"Not on a global scale. But history is full of state-run media outlets. It is an indicator that things have not gone well back home in a political sense. Think about it, Colonel. Earth with its political system of regional nations is outdated in our current interstellar environment. We are facing enemies every day that threaten the entire planet—therefore, the government must be worldwide. Star Force was only an initial development on an inevitable path. It represented a pooled military, the first step. Except for the relatively insignificant provincial armies—"

I stopped him right there, taking two clanking steps toward his command chair. "What kind of crap are you spouting, Captain?" I demanded. "We're a force supported by the entire planet, that's true. But we're a melded force, built for the defense and betterment of all Earth. We're not rulers, we *serve* Earth!"

Miklos gave me a wan smile. "I'm glad you feel that way, sir," he said. "I imagine that is why you've come so far, and been able to sway the old governments to support you. They've always been nervous about you—you know that, don't you?"

"Of course," I said, frowning. "No one likes to give up the defense of their own nation to an outside coalition, an alliance. There is an unpleasant level of trust and loss of sovereignty involved. But the world has had many such organizations: Nato, the U. N.—"

"Do not forget the Warsaw Pact and the Axis Powers," Miklos said. "Yes, there have been plenty of alliances. But the military organization has been provided by the participating nations in the past, not from an independent group like Star Force."

I stopped talking and frowned at the stars outside. We had excellent viewports on *Nostradamus.* They were really screens, images generated by cameras outside the ship, but they were so precise and high res you couldn't tell the difference between them and a sheet of glass.

"You sound as if you approve of all this, Miklos," I said.

"I do not, sir. But I've been expecting it. Star Force took a certain shape to fill a need. It became a force so powerful and mobile it could destroy any nation on Earth. If the leader of that force decided to turn it upon the nations of Earth...well, the old militaries would fall."

I flipped up my visor and studied his eyes. His expression was one of resolution and sadness. I was finally getting what he was saying.

"You think there's been a coup back home? A civil war?"

He shrugged. "A coup, yes. A civil war? Maybe. If they did fight, the struggle is over with by now. The old armies were probably taken out quickly. But I would guess the more likely circumstance involved a signed deal of some kind, a treaty or pact that has been formed."

"One that gathers Earth under a single banner?"

He nodded.

As an American, I wanted to reject his theories out of hand. I'd led a long life full of freedoms. I didn't like to think my hometown was now under the thumb of a dictatorship. But I had to admit Earth had suffered so much lately, political upheaval was easy to imagine. Hundreds of millions had died. Nuclear fires had scorched vast regions. Aliens seemed to abound in the skies, and none of them were overly friendly, with the possible exception of the Centaurs.

"I guess it shouldn't be such a shock," I said aloud. "People have always turned to a strong central government when faced with a serious outside threat. They've always preferred a dictator of their own choosing to a foreign ruler, or to death."

"Yes, freedom always perishes in name of security."

"Sir?" an ensign asked nervously from the central communications console. "I think the Earth ship is expecting an answer."

I shrugged in my suit, causing my armored shoulders to clatter. "So what? Let them wait."

"Shall we maintain the same course and speed, sir?"

"Yes! Change nothing," I said. I turned back to Miklos.

Everyone on the bridge looked at their instruments and strained to listen to us.

"Should we retire to the conference room, sir?" he asked me.

I nodded. We walked into the conference room. I let the door go solid in the face of Kwon, who had appeared on the bridge from the decks below. I could see by his face encircled in a sea of armor he was excited. When Kwon smelled a battle, he always lit up. Behind him, Marvin had put in an appearance with Sandra in his wake. He was stretching his cameras to look at us, while Sandra craned her neck. I closed them all out and sat down with Miklos. When faced with a philosophical concern, I found his counsel was the best. That's why he was my exec.

"I used to have someone like you," I told him seriously, pulling off my helmet and scratching my head. "A second in command I could trust. But he was more performance-oriented, rather than a man I could exchange complex ideas with."

111

"Lieutenant Colonel Barrera?"

"Right. But I respect your opinion more when it comes to matters of politics, history and judgment."

"Thank you, sir."

I shook my head. "It is not a compliment, simply a fact. You may find it comes to be a burden on your soul in time."

It was his turn to frown at me. Miklos rarely smiled. He hadn't looked overly happy before, and now he looked positively glum.

"I think I understand, sir."

"We're going to have to make some hard decisions, you and I."

He stared at me, waiting.

"The first one is how to answer this challenge from some captain calling himself 'Imperial'."

"It's not a title with a positive history. There are still some who hold the title of Emperor to this day, but they are figureheads only. The last of Earth's Emperors with any real power died out about a century ago."

"What advice can you give me? How should I proceed in this situation?"

"When dealing with an empire, the personality of the Emperor is highly influential. The individual in charge becomes in effect the entire state. The nation reacts the way the despot would act under similar circumstances."

I nodded thoughtfully. "And I think it is safe to assume we know who we're talking about: Emperor Crow."

Miklos nodded. "Yes."

"That's what he wanted from the beginning, you know. He told me that long ago. He was angry when I lost his ships, as it derailed his plans for becoming Emperor. He actually said that to me."

Miklos didn't respond. I paced and shook my head, trying to wrap my mind around the situation. I suddenly looked at Miklos. He was staring at me—no, he was *glaring* at me.

"What?" I asked.

"You knew he was going to pull this, sir? And you didn't stop him?"

I sputtered. "Stop him? You mean kill him? It wasn't that simple. He's been a friend of sorts. We've fought together so many times. There have been moments for which all of humanity owes its survival to Crow—moments when he saved the day. Remember those ships he built in secret under the swamps of Andros Island? We threw them into the battle and drove the Macros back. And the original organization of Star Force—that wasn't my idea, you know. All of Earth owes that man a huge debt...even if he is an asshole."

"Do we owe him our allegiance? Our freedoms? Our unquestioning obedience? I'm sure other emperors were great men in the past. They rose up to take the reins of power, and they didn't do it by accident."

At that point, a hammering came at the door. I tapped open a one-way channel that carried my voice out to the bridge. "Is that you, Sandra?" I asked. "If so, and there is no immediate danger to the ship, please stop hammering. We're having a critical conference right now. Riggs out."

The hammering stopped, so I forgot about it. She was probably just getting edgy and tired of waiting.

"I see what you're saying, Miklos," I said. "All through history, every nation, every tribe had to have a moment when a hero declared himself king or chieftain. But this is different. This is the entire world we're talking about, and I'd thought we'd outgrown that kind of thing."

Miklos shook his head sadly. "We never will outgrow that kind of thing. When frightened, we humans love a king, a strong leader to whom we can entrust our hopes and fears. Why didn't you do it yourself, Colonel?"

"Do what?"

"Declare yourself king."

I laughed. "I'm not that kind of guy. I'm just not. No royal blood flows in these veins. I was a nobody originally. Besides which, I thought it was morally wrong. Looking back at history, I've always thought of myself as a man in the mold of General Washington. A man who rose up to fight and lead, but when his services were no longer needed, he retired back to his farm. I've always wanted to do that, if I'm lucky enough to live that long."

Miklos nodded. "A noble model," he said. "Many Americans wanted Washington to become their king, you know. He refused the power. But Washington's example is a rare one. Crow is a more typical personality. He's made differently than you. I'm afraid he's more like Napoleon, who started off as a small man from Corsica running an artillery unit, and who took advantage of a chaotic revolution to take power."

I nodded, only half-listening to him. Miklos continued in a philosophical tone.

"Maybe, Crow is not like Napoleon after all," he said. "Napoleon was a military genius who won battles through improvisation and masterful tactics—the way you do at times. Maybe Crow is more like Stalin: a mean, uneducated man who rose to power not through military genius, but rather through ruthless political know-how."

"Yeah," I said. "That does sound more like Crow."

"Unfortunately, both men cost their nations millions upon millions of dead."

I glanced at him. What was that look he was giving me? Was he somehow blaming me for the millions of lives lost? Sure, I'd made mistakes. Sure, someone else might have done a better job. Only, there hadn't been anyone else there at the time, in my position. I'd done the best I could, and I regretted a thousand things, but I refused to be broken by the magnitude of my mistakes.

I shook myself and took in a deep breath. "What matters now is how we're going to respond to this ultimatum ordering us to turn around. We can't just quietly fly into their teeth. I have to decide upon a course of action: are we going to send them a message? Or are we going to halt?"

The hammering returned at the door. I sighed and tapped a one-way connection to the outside. "This had better be an emergency. I'm still having a high-level discussion, here."

The hammering continued unabated. Frowning, I opened the door.

Sandra almost fell into me. She looked upset and disheveled. "They fired a second salvo. I figured that was emergency enough."

I opened my mouth to shout "*What?*" but suppressed the urge and pushed past her onto the bridge. There, on the big board, were red traces. I could see the Earth ships, there were four of them now. They had been pinpointed and identified hanging in space around the ring that led to Alpha Centauri. They were all light cruisers with a size and configuration matching my own flagship. They had indeed fired two salvoes of missiles, and the yellow lines that predicted their paths neatly intercepted my fleet.

We were under fire, and this time our attackers were human.

-15-

"What are your orders, sir?" asked the nervous Ensign manning the weapons board. "Should we return fire?"

"How long do we have before those missiles hit us?"

"At our current course and speed," Marvin said, interrupting, "the missiles will reach us in thirty-nine hours."

I nodded. "Plenty of time. Everyone, stand down. Light moves much faster than a missile barrage. We might even talk them into causing them to destruct before they reach us. Let's open up a channel and talk to them."

Marvin handled the details. Everyone seemed nervous, and I found that distracting, but I tried to stay focused on what I was going to say. I knew I had to sound confident to the point of being amused by their surprise attack.

"Imperial ships of Earth—if that's what you really are—this is Colonel Kyle Riggs of Star Force. We are legitimate military forces from Earth. Why are you firing on your own brothers, wasting valuable munitions? You must be aware thirty-two missiles can't make it through our defensive systems. Are we frightening you somehow? If so, that was not our intention. We are returning to Earth, as previously ordered."

It was a long wait until the response came back in. By the time it did, we had four less hours of time to maneuver. I'd taken the time to shower, eat, and relax. I'd ordered my staff to do the same, but they still looked stressed.

When the response finally came, I was chewing on a sandwich of cultured ham. It wasn't as bad tasting as it sounded.

"Colonel Riggs, our apologies. Star Force has been disbanded, and you have been released from service. Possibly, these critical facts never reached your remote station. Fortunately, the situation is easily remedied. All you have to do is shut down your engines after braking to a stop. Disable your weapons and jettison them into space. Then await our arrival. We will perform a close inspection of your craft. Once disarmed, you and your companions will be allowed to proceed to Earth, minus any contraband you might have aboard. Thank you in advance for your cooperation, citizen."

I finished my ham sandwich and had a beer while everyone on the bridge shouted and threw their arms in the air. Every eye was narrowed, every set of lips drew tight in anger. Some even snarled, showing their teeth. Crow's name was insulted liberally, as were all his hypothetical ancestors. The general consensus among the staff was to fight. We would blast their cruisers from space and push ahead, claiming this entire system if necessary.

When they'd finally settled down somewhat, Miklos turned to me and asked an intelligent question: "What are your orders, Colonel?"

"They seem to be determined to stop us here," I said, "to prevent us from moving another mile closer to Earth. Any ideas as to why?"

"Perhaps Crow does not yet have a firm hold on Earth," Miklos said. "Maybe he doesn't want a rival hero on the planet to challenge him for his position."

"A strong possibility," I said. "Whatever the case, they are certainly determined to halt us here in the Helios system."

No one said anything. They all eyed me tensely. I could sense they were wondering what I was going to do now—they were angry, and wanted me to do something.

I looked at them one at a time. "Do you all really want to start a civil war, right here, right now?" I asked them. "It's an easy thing to pull the trigger, but it won't be easy to stop that kind of conflict once we've started. May I also remind everyone that while we outgun them in this system, we might not the next time we meet up with their forces? Also, we have a grim disadvantage: we're cut off from reinforcements. We have no more than three hundred loyal Star Force personnel. Even if we kill a thousand of them for every one of our troops that falls, we'll be wiped out quickly."

They all stared at me in confusion and worry.

"What are your orders then, Colonel?" Miklos asked again.

I could tell I wasn't throwing him off. He'd already thought of everything I'd said, and we both knew my speech was a reality check that hadn't been meant for him. But I'd wanted everyone else on my command staff to understand what was at stake.

"Don't just surrender," Sandra said.

I glanced at her, then back to the main screens. "In impossible situations, it's necessary to think outside the box."

Sandra smiled. "You're good at that, Kyle," she said. "You were born not even knowing where the box is."

I smiled back. "Marvin, open a narrow beam channel with the Worms again, will you?"

"Done."

"What kind of symbols do they have for traitors? For Worms that turn against their own?"

"Such events are almost unknown among their people, Colonel. They are an extremely loyal species. However, I would suggest the symbol for of an egg-stealing mite, a hated enemy to all Worms. No creature native to Helios is more despised."

"Right, that's it. Can you tell them the ships that just fired upon us are egg-stealing little bastards?"

"I believe so, sir. Do you wish to do this with two traditional sets of three symbols, or in a longer form of five symbols?"

"I want to do it in the manner they are most likely to understand."

"Very well, transmitting. I will alternate the statement with an affirmation of brotherhood from our point of view."

"Good."

The message went out, and the rest of them waited tensely for my next move. I stood up and stretched. "It's going to be a while. I suggest we all take a break for about four hours and take a nap. I'll be in my quarters if anything interesting happens."

They stared in me in disbelief as I left the bridge. I could hear their murmured exclamations until the wall reformed itself behind me and the sounds of my staff were cut out. I sensed a single presence then, and turned to see it was Sandra. She'd quietly followed me off the bridge.

"Can you really sleep right now?" she asked.

"I can try."

We headed to our quarters, where I found out I couldn't sleep. Not because I was nervous or worried, but because Sandra couldn't. She grew restless and bored, and was tied up in talkative knots about how the situation would play itself out. I normally always welcomed her company, but this time I really wanted to get a little rest.

"You've just started another war—you know that, don't you Kyle? Do you even bother to keep count of them all?"

"Maybe," I said, yawning.

"Maybe? This isn't a 'maybe'. They aren't totally stupid. They'll know you told the Worms to attack them. They'll run and report back that they were attacked by you and the Worms. This could be an interplanetary disaster, and you are trying to fall asleep!"

She had me there. I was lying back on our bunk, with my eyes closed. My eyes burned slightly, and my throat was raw from talking too much. I'd turned out the lights a few times already, but she'd turned them back on again. I reached out with my left hand, groping for a pillow. I put the pillow over my face to block out the light.

"Ah, that's better."

A weight landed on me. I lurched and sucked in a breath in surprise. Sandra had jumped on me. I patted her absently. "Things are liable to get exciting," I said. "Lie down here next to me."

Finally, she did as I asked, but she kept messing with me. I finally called her bluff and grabbed her. She melted, and we made love. Afterward, she drifted off to sleep, and I found myself awake and thinking again. I got up, took a shower, and then finally managed to get an hour or so of sleep before an alarm went off, summoning us both back to the bridge.

We pulled on our clothes and hurried back up to join the others. I was glad for nanocloth and smart armor at that point. It was too bad our hair was so messed-up. I vaguely thought I should come up with something to solve the perennial problem of bed-head. Maybe a nanocloth scarf could do the trick.

I soon forgot all about nanocloth scarfs, sex, and even my messed up hair. I stepped onto the bridge, and found the place to be in a turmoil.

"It's the Worm ships, sir. They got in closer than expected."

I frowned, staring at the holotank. The situation was immediately clear. The Worms had somehow gotten within range of the Imperial ships and now were laying into them with heavy particle beam weapons.

"How did this play out?" I asked.

Miklos noticed me and turned his tired eyes in my direction. "The Worms tricked them, Colonel. I thought our Earth ships would run, they're quite close to the ring. But the Worms approached them obliquely. They set a course for the ring, and flew only half their forces in that direction."

"Half? How many heavy fighters do they have?"

"Two hundred are in orbit over Helios now. About a hundred of them flew toward the ring, as if they were going to pass by the light cruisers. We caught several transmissions form the Earth ships, trying to contact them, but there was no response. I think the Earth ships believed they would pass by through the ring, and didn't want to fire and start an incident. But when they were close, the Worm ships suddenly veered toward the Earth vessels. Now the light cruisers are running, but it is too late. They can't work up enough velocity to reach the ring and exit the system before they are under fire."

I watched as the Earth vessels suddenly lit up. Beams stabbed out from the six turrets on each of their ships. The Worms were almost in range to use their particle beam weapons, but they would have to suffer some casualties first. The cruisers packed a lot of firepower with their heavy lasers. Three Worms ships were destroyed in the next minute.

"Can't we call the Worms off?" Sandra asked, standing next to me.

"Having regrets?" I asked her. Then I turned to the rest of them. "How about everyone else? You wanted me to do something. Now, you get to watch good people die. The Worms are our allies. The Imperials fired on us, but they are still human."

"Just call them off, Kyle," Sandra said. "You've made your point."

I shook my head bitterly. "We can't do that. Don't forget the distance, they're over a light-hour away. By the time the Worms got my message, it would be too late. In fact, this battle has already happened. All we can do is sit and watch to see what happened."

It wasn't an enjoyable spectacle. We really didn't want any of the ships on either side to be destroyed. The true enemy, we all knew, was the machines. Every time a biotic killed another, it was fratricide.

The Earth ships were running, and they had plenty of thrust. Unfortunately, due to the commander's firm belief that the Worms would stay neutral, he'd let them get too close. Now they couldn't out run the smaller ships. They did manage to destroy twenty of the Worm ships before they were overwhelmed and lashed with violet sprays of energy. Their ships broke apart under the beating and were destroyed one at a time by the twisting, spiraling attackers who swarmed around them. Still, I was impressed at how much punishment one of our cruisers could withstand.

Only two of them made it to the ring. One appeared to be on its last legs at that point. When they had all vanished, everyone aboard was glum. The Worms did not chase them, however, but fanned out instead, shooting past the ring and decelerating to return to their homeworld.

As the battle ended, the missiles the imperial ships had fired on us winked out. A message came in, one that must have been sent by the Imperial commander as he exited the Helios system under heavy fire.

"Colonel Riggs," the commander said. "We've sustained heavy losses and must withdraw. We're assuming the Worms became hostile when we fired upon your ships. We've tried to reason with them, but failed. They will not break off the attack, and are destroying our forces as you no doubt have witnessed using long-range sensors. I urge you to turn back in case the Worms have decided to become hostile to all human vessels. I've ordered that the missiles we fired upon your ships be destroyed in case the Worms attack your fleet next. Good luck. Captain Bolton, out."

I sat back in my chair after that, pondering the situation. After a few minutes, the excitement on the bridge died down to a murmur of various conversations. I stood up and headed for my conference chamber. Miklos and Sandra followed me, and I didn't try to stop them.

"Is that how you wanted it to play out?" Sandra asked me. She was angry and emotional.

"Are you blaming me?"

"No, they fired on us. They had it coming. But it was awful to watch. I feel a bit sick, because they think the Worms did it on their own. We tricked them, and killed them without suffering a loss."

Miklos looked surprised. "If we had lost a few ships, I wouldn't be feeling any better."

Sandra shook her head. "I don't know. I suppose you're right. It's just not the same, watching humans die under alien fire. I don't think we've ever caused something like that to happen before—at least not on purpose."

"What your conscience is objecting too, I think," Miklos said, "is the trickery. Warfare is full of unfair moments. Stand-up fights are rare. Usually, one side or the other is out-classed or out-maneuvered and butchered."

"Well, I don't like it. Not when they're our people."

"Agreed," I said, joining the conversation, "but the question now is what we're going to do next. Do we turn back as they asked, or do we press forward and see what's waiting for us in the next system? After Alpha Centauri, it's only one short jump to the Solar System."

"I say press onward," Miklos said. "We can slow down and send a scout through to the other side, someone to find out what's going on out there. We don't want to run into a massive minefield."

I nodded thoughtfully. "I have a slightly different strategy," I said. "We'll press ahead at full speed, while asking the Worms what's on the other side. With luck, we can talk them into scouting for us. I want to keep moving. We can't let the Earth ships limp all the way home. They'll call up the fleet to form against us."

Miklos' eyes grew wide. "Are you talking about going *all* the way? All the way back to Earth?"

I shrugged. "If we don't run into anything that can stop us, why not?"

We managed to get the Worms to tell us there were no traps ahead, and we assumed that meant no mines existed. More detailed intel was harder to get out of them. It took a lot of back-forth communications with the Worms just to get them to understand what I wanted. At first, they simply reported that there were "a lot" of ships on the other side.

Worms apparently didn't deal well with precise numbers. After about seven units of anything, they moved to a symbol that meant "a lot". This symbol depicted an egg chamber dotted with Worm infants. Apparently, this could mean anything from eight up to several hundred. After that, they had a bigger number concept that meant, roughly, "a *whole* lot". This symbol was a pictograph of the stars in the sky. Generally, this was thought to indicate hundreds or thousands of individual objects. The only larger denomination was an image of an endless beach, representing countless grains of sand. This number indicated hundreds of thousands, millions, or even an infinity of items.

After we'd sorted this out, we repeatedly received the answer that "a lot" of Earth forces were in the next system. I found this frustratingly vague. As I didn't even know how old the intel was, it was almost useless. All we knew for sure is that there were more than seven Earth ships in the Alpha Centauri system.

Working with Marvin for another hour or two, I finally got the Worms to agree to scout the other side of the ring. I was eager for fresh information. They sent through a startling force of fifty ships. Apparently, they liked to scout in force. The ships flitted into the ring and vanished. We all watched the screens, waiting for their return. I think most of my staff was barely breathing.

An hour passed before Sandra declared the Worm scouts dead. "There simply isn't any reason for anyone to take so long to scout a neighboring system. All they had to do was fly in there, take a look around, and fly back out. They weren't moving very fast. They could have managed the whole thing in ten minutes. We must assume they have all been destroyed."

"You could be right," Miklos said. "In which case, we should slow down as fast as possible. We don't want to make the mistake of barreling into the Alpha Centauri system after our duped scouts and suffer the same fate they did."

I glowered, rejecting any suggestion we should retreat, or slow our advance. "The intel from the Worms is so vague it's useless. We'll keep advancing. How long do we have until we have to start decelerating in order to halt before going through the ring?"

"We're just about at the point of no return," Miklos said. "You must decide now, or we'll have to shoot past the ring and reverse course to return to it—either that, or rush right in without knowing what's in front of us. There could be mines, sir. Some kind of defensive system…it would explain the disappearance of the Worm ships."

"We could fire missiles ahead to annihilate any minefield," I said, gritting my teeth. "but if we shoot blindly we might well take out the last surviving Worm ships. I'm not going to have any blue-on-blue. We're going to have to decelerate and tiptoe through the Alpha Centauri ring."

Everyone looked visibly relieved at my decision. Everyone but me, that was. I didn't like slowing down, losing my momentum. In space battles, it was critical to keep moving forward. I'd won a number of battles that way in the past against superior forces. I didn't want to lose the initiative now, but I couldn't see what else to do. The enemy was a big question mark and I couldn't take the risk.

We'd almost reached the ring when a single Worm ship nosed out of it to greet us. It was moving slowly, almost drifting.

"Let's make contact with that ship," I snapped. "Marvin, open a channel and translate, please."

"Channel open."

Worm pictographs began flashing on my screen. I frowned at them uncertainly. I didn't know all the Worm symbols, far from it. But these seemed easy to identify. There was the symbol for "a lot" followed by the symbol for friendship.

"What the hell does that mean? Do they love us a bunch?"

"No sir," Marvin said. "Worm messages are similar in nature to insect communications. They relate information that is helpful to the entire nest. For example, a terran honeybee might use pheromones and bodily movements to indicate there is an excellent batch of ripe pollen in an indicated direction. Termite and ant colonies, on the other hand—"

"Cut the crap, Marvin. What are they saying?"

"The message indicates there is a large group of friends nearby. The meaning is always subject to context and interpretation, of course. In this instance, that message doesn't make much sense."

"Sure it does," Miklos said. "The implication is clear, Colonel. There is a large Earth fleet in Alpha Centauri."

"Then why are they calling them friendly?"

"Maybe they have confused things, calling all Earth ships friendly because we're from the same homeworld. Or perhaps Crow's ships have used diplomatic communications, as we have, and convinced them they're friendly."

No one was happy with these ideas. My staff babbled for a few minutes. Meanwhile, we were flying closer to the ring every second. It was hard to remain calm while approaching a dramatic transition point into the unknown. We were flying blind. It made the skin on my neck tingle with unease.

"Slow down to a crawl," I ordered. "We'll poke our noses on the other side and see what's going on."

It took another full hour to reach the ring. Under us, the engines trembled and shuddered, applying tremendous thrust in order to reduce our speed. To increase efficiency, we turned our ships around and directed their exhaust ports toward the ring. We decelerated hard, feeling the G-forces in our bones. A plume of exhaust plasma enshrouded each of my ships in a glowing fireball.

In the end, we couldn't get our speed down to zero. We fell through the ring, flying backwards and thrusting at full power to slow down. I didn't know what we'd find on the far side, but I knew that flying into a battle ass-first wasn't the best way to do it.

-16-

In the final moments before we hit the ring, I ordered the fleet to come about and direct their weapons systems forward. Every pilot breathed a sigh of relief.

"Come about and prep everything you have to fire. We're barely moving, but we don't know what we'll meet up with when we arrive."

As we took the plunge, gritting our teeth and praying, we felt the tiny familiar transitional shudder. It was such a small sensation for having traveled a hundred light years.

"Switch all sensors into full-active mode," I ordered. "We aren't sneaking in, and I'm tired of not knowing what's going on."

The sensor officer worked his board feverishly. Quite often in space combat, we ran with our detection equipment in passive mode. The problem with active detection systems is that they gave the enemy almost as much information about you as you were able to gather about them. Worse, it gave the enemy that information in approximately half the time it took for you to gather your tidbits of data. This was due to the vast distances involved.

The speed of light barely seemed adequate when crossing a star system. A radar blip, for example, might take several hours to reach across space, find an enemy ship and return with an echo. Unfortunately, it took the echoing blip just as long to travel back through space to the ship that had sent the pulse in the first place. In the meantime, the enemy had recorded the blip, traced it back to its source, and knew who sent it. At that point they could fire upon the pinging ship and when your radar bounced back to you, it could come with a nasty surprise in its wake.

Passive sensors such as optical clusters were therefore superior in timing and stealth. Unfortunately, they didn't give you as clear a picture. You were less likely to find things that didn't want to be noticed, things that suppressed their energy outputs and ran coldly and quietly in space. Because of this, I ordered the pinging machines turned on and turned up.

We flew through the ring in a rush. I put my own ship in the lead, as we had plenty of defensive lasers. If we were charging into mines or missiles, the cruiser with her numerous small guns could shoot them down before my stubby little gunships plowed into them.

Everyone tensed up, but there were no klaxons or shocking explosions. So far, so good.

"Incoming data sir, the holotank should update any second now," Miklos said.

The brainboxes in charge of the display systems chewed on the incoming mountain of data from the moment we appeared in the tri-star system. At first, it put up a model of the system from memory as a time-saver, and to provide a point of reference for hard details it managed to detect. This amounted to the three suns and various known scraps of debris that floated in predictable orbits around the system. The two central stars were similar in composition to Sol. The dimmer third star, Proxima Centauri, was a tiny red dwarf in a far-flung orbit. Taken as a whole, there really wasn't much else to see in the Alpha Centauri system.

Today was an exceptional day, however. Contacts began swimming into existence as we watched with growing alarm. There were three groups of them, three distinct flocks of objects.

"Are they asteroids?" Sandra asked hopefully.

Miklos shook his head, adjusting the holotank to zoom in on the nearest cluster. "Colonel, by count and individual size alone, I think the nearest grouping is the Worm fleet."

I nodded. There wasn't any argument from the rest of the staff. Even with incomplete data, it had to be the Worms. They were even swinging around and shuffling formation as we watched, which was classic Worm behavior.

"Okay, we've found the Worm fleet, and the good news is they haven't been annihilated as we thought they might be. They seem to be pursuing the smallest group of ships in the region toward the far ring—the one that leads to the Solar System. I would guess that smaller group is made up of Imperial Earth ships. Anyone want to argue that?"

No one did. Sandra was quick to point to the largest mass of ships, however. "What about these? The Earth ships are running right toward them. They have to be more Earth ships. Kyle, there are hundreds of them. We don't stand a chance."

As we weren't under immediate threat, I removed my helmet and gauntlet, then gave my face a good scratching. Sweating in a battlesuit and breathing recycled air for hours wasn't glamorous. Around me, others took the moment to do the same. We'd been tense and ready for battle for a long time now.

"We have fifty ships. The Worms have about a hundred. Combined, if the Earth ships all turn on us—you're right. They will outnumber us probably four to one. But let's get all the data in before we do anything rash."

"Rash?" Miklos asked. "Like turn tail and run?"

I gave him a displeased glance.

"Sorry sir," he said. He quickly went back to his controls and fiddled with the focus, trying to get details on the third group of ships.

"Let's hear your analysis, Captain," I asked him. "What are we missing?"

"Well, first of all, the Imperial ships have tripled in number. Only two cruisers escaped the Worm ships back in the Helios system. Now, there seems to be six of them. They must have had four ships on our side of the ring and four ships on the far side. A garrison force, it would seem. The Worms destroyed two, but now there are a total of six. Still not enough to defeat the Worms, however."

I nodded. "I'm seeing something else here. Notice the position, course and speed of the Worm ships?"

"Yes sir, I do see it. The Earth ships are moving slowly. I can only surmise that one or more of them is damaged and unable to go faster. What is more interesting is that the Worm ships are pursuing, but not overtaking the Earth cruisers. By my estimates, they should have been able to catch and destroy them by now. They would take losses in doing so, however, as there are now six Earth ships."

"Right," I said. "That's how I see it. They're chasing them out of their territory, but not engaging. They want the Earth ships to keep running, but they don't want to lose any more of their own. The Worms are always aggressive, but they aren't completely insane."

Sandra stepped up between the two of us and reached out with her long, lithe arm. She tapped at the smoky region of metallic flecks in the distance. This caused the region to zoom in, and we could see the third large cloud of ships coming our way.

"What I'm interested in is this group here," she said. "You guys aren't saying much about them. They're the big unknown. I can't even see much detail on this display. Are these ships really shaped like big barrels, or are they just not displaying correctly?"

"The range is too great," Miklos explained. "The sensor systems need hours to draw a precise image of a ship from that great of a distance. That's why they look like blobs or blips."

Sandra nodded seriously. "So, in other words, we've got no idea what we're facing? All we know is that the Earth cruisers are heading right for them."

"That's essentially correct," Miklos said, "right now they—"

"Colonel Riggs," Marvin interrupted loudly. "There is an incoming message."

"From the Worms?" I asked.

"No sir. It's from the Imperial cruisers."

"Let's hear it."

I heard music playing faintly. I frowned, looking at the walls around us. Marvin had tapped the audio input into our walls, so the nanites vibrated, forming speakers around us. The music was tinny, and vaguely martial in nature.

"This is an Imperial decree, being rebroadcast for the benefit of all Earth citizens," said a voice.

All of us were looking at one another in bemusement by now. The voice changed, becoming rougher and deeper. I now recognized the tones and the down-under accent. It was none other than Jack Crow.

"This is your duly elected leader speaking," Crow said. "You're ships are carrying contraband, and are traveling in restricted space.

The crews have been tried in absentia. Unfortunately, they have all been found guilty as charged. You are hereby ordered to halt your ships and set them adrift. All hands will then abandon ship to be picked up by the approaching cruisers. Any vessel not complying will be destroyed. Only complete cooperation will ensure your survival. Emperor Crow out."

"What the hell is that about?" Sandra asked.

"I think we've flown into something we weren't supposed to witness," Miklos said.

I stared at the globular tank, trying to make sense of it all. Two groups of Earth ships converging in the middle of the star system. The cruisers making this threatening announcement—could it be?

"Marvin, the Worms said there were a lot of friendlies in this system, correct? Hundreds of them?"

"The symbol used and confirmed repeatedly indicated a *whole* lot. Allies numbering between eight and several hundred thousand, yes sir."

I turned to Miklos. "What if they were talking about that huge flotilla of ships out there?"

"I suppose they could be. But if they're allies, who are they?"

"Let's look at the configurations. More data should be in by now."

We examined the data defining the ships, and found it increasingly mysterious. The design of these ships was unknown to us—if you could even all them "designed" at all. Just as Sandra had first noted, they looked like a mass of barrel-shaped ships.

"Transports," Sandra said aloud.

We all looked at her.

"Big cylindrical transports, like the ones the Macros build. But they aren't as large as that. All they have is some life support, enough power to fly and primitive navigational equipment. They look like transports to me."

I peered at the scopes and read the numbers carefully. I pulled up a yellow wireframe schematic of the distant vessels and flicked at the image, spinning it around to examine it. I nodded slowly. "Yes. You could be right, Sandra. But what is going on here? Why are the cruisers telling them to abandon ship?"

"Is it even possible, what they promised?" Sandra asked. "If the people on those transports halt and bail out, can the cruisers even carry them all?"

"Maybe," I said, "if the crews are small. They would have to abandon their cargo, however, whatever it is."

Everyone puzzled over the situation for some minutes. As far as we could tell, nothing changed during that time. The two groups of Earth ships were still on a collision course, while the Worms followed the cruisers and we followed the Worms.

"What are your orders, Colonel?" Miklos asked.

"Let's get into this game," I said. "I'm not sure which side we're on, or even who all the players are, but I'm not going to sit here and let Crow dictate terms to the people on those ships. I have a feeling they are disaffected Star Force personnel trying to make it to Eden. Who the hell else would come out here all the way into dangerous space on makeshift transports? In any case, we must intervene before something horrible happens."

"Besides, we could use more supplies and reinforcements, eh?" Miklos said, smiling with half his mouth.

"Never even crossed my mind," I said. "All engines go to full burn. Let's catch up if we can. Marvin, try to give me a tightly-beamed channel to the refugee fleet."

"I'll try Colonel, but the beam will have to pass directly by the Earth cruisers. We will probably be overheard."

I nodded. "Fine. Let's put our cards on the table."

The ship lurched and we all strapped in to endure heavy G-forces. At least I was in good shape for taking this kind of punishment. The combined treatment of nanites and Microbes had left my flesh dense and unfeeling. The crushing sensation that would have left me breathless on the floor of the ship years ago now just made me wince and grunt. I stood my ground and braced myself against the central console. I grimaced, but the discomfort was minor.

Marvin opened the channel, and I thought for another minute or two before sending my message. "People of Earth, we're members of Star Force. We've taken an oath to defend the lives of all humanity. If you need help, ask for it, and explain your situation honestly. Colonel Kyle Riggs, out."

I sat back after that and sipped a cool, caffeinated drink. The ball was in their court now, and I had no idea how this was all going to play out. I would be damned if I was going to watch Crow's thugs blow up Earth ships for no good reason. Especially not if they were trying to make the run to Eden.

Our radio signals had to travel across about a billion miles of space and back before we got an answer. The return message came in about an hour after my own transmission, due to the distance. The range was shrinking rapidly as our fleets converged, but it was still tremendous.

"We've got an answer, sir," Ensign Rodrigues said. "But it's not from the big fleet—it's from the Imperial ships."

I waved for her to put it through. The words echoed in our ship. Once again, a snippet of martial music played. I was beginning to wonder if that was S.O.P for all Crow's ships now.

"Colonel Riggs, this is Commodore Decker. You have no mission here, and have been officially deactivated. Star Force has been disbanded, and although I'm sure this is difficult for you to accept, I implore you to do so, Dr. Riggs. If any of your crew can hear this, they should know you have no authority, and they are under no obligation to follow your orders. We would appreciate it if you withdrew from this system. Any interference in Imperial affairs would be a mistake. Decker out."

I glanced around the chamber at my staff. "How do you read that?" I asked.

"They're scared and bluffing," Sandra said immediately. "We should force them to surrender and if they won't, we should fire upon them."

"I didn't spend the last several years in space killing aliens so I could destroy Earth's finest vessels," I snapped. "There has to be something better than that."

Miklos leaned forward. "Sometimes, Colonel, unpleasant things must be done in order to prevent more hideous unpleasantness. This is often the essence of a civil war."

"I need specifics, people, not philosophies. In a few hours, we'll be in range of their heaviest beams."

"I'll give you a specific," Sandra said. "Blow them out of space before they slaughter those unarmed ships that are running to us."

I had to admit, that was pretty specific. I nodded glumly. "We'll wait to hear what the second fleet has to say. They're farther away, but their message should be beaming in soon."

In the next few minutes, I was provided with a new shock. The second voice that came from the speakers was feminine and distinctly familiar.

"This is Captain Sarin of Star Force. I'm officially requesting your aid, Colonel Riggs. We're running from Earth, but we left with Crow's permission. Now that we're out of the system it seems that he has changed his mind about letting us emigrate to your system. I understand the situation more clearly now. He let us leave because it would have been a PR nightmare to fire on Star Force transports. But now that we're out of range of Earth's cameras, his thugs have orders to force us out of our vessels and leave us adrift in space. We don't have many weapons, but we will fight. It's up to you to decide whose side you're on. Sarin out."

Sandra stared at me. She looked troubled. I stood up slowly. This was big. I had to think. I walked down the corridors to the mess hall and grabbed myself a meal. I chewed and stared into space. Outside, the twin yellow suns known to us as Alpha and Beta Centauri circled one another in a tight, timeless dance.

I felt I now knew why the Imperial ships had been so anxious to stop us. They hadn't wanted us to reach Alpha Centauri. We weren't supposed to have met up with Sarin and her refugee transports.

Sandra followed me and sat down. She opened a squeeze bottle of beer and pressed another into my hand. We both drank. The nanites had gotten better at brewing, but we still grimaced slightly with the first swallow. Beer from a soft bottle never tasted quite right, but at least it was cold—refrigeration was one thing you never had much trouble with in deep space.

"What are you going to do, Kyle?" Sandra asked quietly.

I looked at her. There wasn't any anger or jealously in her eyes today, I was glad to see. Often, Sandra could be petty and selfish when it came to sweeping events. But this, I could tell, had gotten through to her. She wasn't worried about Jasmine and I. She was worried about thousands of lives.

"There are a lot of people out there on those ships, and they've been screwed over by Crow," I said. "The trouble is, I don't want to declare war on Earth. Not now, not ever."

She nodded. "I understand that. It goes against everything you've tried to do. But you've done it before. You killed the troops invading Andros Island."

I nodded thoughtfully. "My hand was forced then."

"Not really. You could have let the Pentagon have the factories. They would have made you a consultant or something."

I smiled. "I would have loved that, wouldn't I? I suppose you're right, I don't have any choice. I'll have to do what I can to save Sarin and whoever is with her."

"You know who they are. They're loyal Star Force troops. They're the ones that would not submit to Crow, the ones you left behind on Andros when he seized power in your absence."

I felt a guilty pang. I'd been out on the frontier for a long time, not bothering to think too hard about what was happening back on Earth. I'd been so busy planning out future colonies and blasting aliens, I hadn't kept Crow in check.

"What was I supposed to do?" I demanded, feeling a hot rush of anger. "One man can only be in one part of the cosmos at a given time, no matter how talented he is. I can't fix every problem everywhere at once!"

She chuckled and patted my hand. "That sounds like my Kyle Riggs," she said. "You are forgetting something, though. You're greatest failure as a leader is not delegating authority. I've been reading books about it. This sort of thing happens often to capable leaders, you know. The smartest and best know they can do the job better than everyone else, so they micromanage everything. They spread themselves too thin and fail where a lesser man might have succeeded."

I stared at her for a moment. "Interesting theory," I admitted. "And I know there's a strong grain of truth in that criticism. So, what do you think I should do?"

"I've already given you my advice."

"Blast them? Without further.warning? Just put on a big smile and start the civil war I've been dreading and dodging for years?"

Sandra nodded. "Look at it this way, it's inevitable. If it must happen, you might as well strike first. If you let Crow destroy that support fleet, he will have struck the first blow and crippled us."

I thought about it, my mind swirling. It was too much for my brain right now, and I realized she was a few jumps ahead of me. Here I was, about to lead a rebel force, an independent force declaring itself free of Earth's rule. I wondered if all colonist rebels in history had felt as conflicted as I did now. I was still an Earthman, still loyal to my world and my species. But I couldn't stand by and watch them abuse my fellow marines. I felt torn by a dozen loyalties in a dozen directions.

"Why can't we all just stand together and fight the damned machines?" I asked aloud.

"If we did that, we wouldn't be human," she said.

I wondered if she was right.

-17-

I ordered the entire fleet to accelerate to flank speed. This caused an immediate problem as my single cruiser was faster than any of my stubby little gunships. We were soon outrunning them. I figured I would solve that problem later. I wanted to get in this game. If the other fleets all met up and fought a battle six hours before I could get there, then all my soul-searching and heartfelt transmissions were meaningless. I had to have assets on the table to be a player.

Shortly after I ordered my ships to accelerate, I composed a warning for the Commodore Decker and his Imperial cruisers.

"Decker, this is Kyle Riggs," I said, dropping formal titles. If he didn't respect my rank, then I wasn't about to give him credit for his, either. "I've decided to maintain the peace in this system. As far as I can tell, yours is the only force that's stirring things up. I see a peaceful civilian fleet traveling in an open system, while your ships have fired upon both my ships and those of our allies, the Worms. Now, you're threatening unarmed refugee ships.

"As the highest ranking official of Star Force in this region, I'm ordering you to stand down. Prepare to be boarded and inspected. Arrests may occur, as per Star Force protocol. I assure you, you and your crews will be provided due process, despite your inexplicably hostile acts. Possibly, this is all some grand misunderstanding. The facts will emerge at your trial. Riggs out."

The rest of the crew stared at me as I made this speech. Some grinned hugely, while others gaped by the end. Only Marvin

136

seemed unperturbed. "Message transmitted, channel closed," he said.

I leaned back in my chair and allowed myself a slight smile of amusement. At the very least, my message would cause Decker to stand up out of his command chair and rage at me. I wished I had a live vid feed to witness his reaction. Just thinking about it warmed my heart.

The message flew out into nothingness. The reply took less than twenty minutes to come back, as all the ships in the system were getting closer together every hour.

"Colonel Riggs," Decker said. "I'm afraid you do not comprehend the situation. But that is immaterial. What matters are the details of your threats and accusations. You've admitted to being in league with the Worms, who have attacked and destroyed Imperial ships without cause. Further, you have threatened to arrest an Imperial officer in the process of executing legitimate orders. I have specific orders regarding you directly from the desk of our magnificent leader, Riggs. According to the Emperor, I'm to avoid engaging you if at all possible. But you're making that difficult."

Decker paused for a moment, and I thought he was done. "Marvin," I asked, "is that the end of the—?"

"You've brought me to a decision point, Kyle," Decker continued suddenly. "I have no choice. The Imperial Navy is going into action, and whatever happens, I want you to know that it was you who caused it all. Let the deaths of these rebels be on your head."

I was furious when I heard this. In the end it was *I* who stood up and paced, leaving my command chair behind. I asked my crew to get the channel open again, but Decker would not answer.

"What do you think he intends to do?" Miklos asked.

"Isn't it obvious? He's going to destroy Sarin and her refugees. He's taking this opening to do what Crow really wants, to exterminate anyone loyal to me that he can."

"Do you really think he'd do that?" Sandra asked. Her eyes were big and dark. "I know Crow is a power-hungry bastard, but—"

"It's not just Crow we're talking about, its Decker. He has ideas of his own, he always did. Crow has always been a schemer, but he's got some sense of honor. I don't know Decker that well, but what I do know doesn't make me want to trust him."

"What're we going to do?" she asked. "We can't let them destroy unarmed Star Force ships!"

"She's right, sir," Miklos said with maddening calm. "If we are beginning a new conflict, we need every supporter we can get."

I bared my teeth in frustration. Things were moving out of my control. I looked at the big holotank, hoping for answers. After a few minutes spent gauging distances, I figured I might just have a trick left in my empty sleeve.

"Marvin," I shouted, "get me into contact with the Worms. Tell them to attack the Earth cruisers. We can't catch the cruisers in time, but they can."

"There will be a lot of lives lost, sir," Miklos said, "on both sides."

"I know. But that's going to happen no matter what we do now. And it's just the beginning."

I talked to the Worms, and although they weren't too excited about getting involved, they finally decided to honor their pledge toward me for mutual defense. I felt a bit sick as I arranged the turning of biotic against biotic, but I felt I had no choice. It was disheartening.

Within half an hour, the shooting started. The cruisers got the first shots off, as they had the longest-ranged weapons. Their heavy beam emplacements stabbed out into the infinite night we know as space. They didn't fire on the Worms, however. Instead, they began burning the tin cans my supporters were flying in. There were about three hundred transports out there. They were big, slow-moving targets. The cylindrical craft tried to evade the incoming fire with poor results. They applied their braking jets in a panic, and pumped out some defensive chaff and gels.

But every second, the two groups came closer. The transports were bulky and either unarmed, or armed with weapons of insufficient range to strike back. Over the next hour or so, before anyone else could do anything, the cruisers took potshots at them, and they became increasingly accurate and harder-hitting as the range closed from extreme to long.

"The first hit. One transport just blew up, sir," Miklos said quietly.

I gnashed my teeth. I wondered immediately if it had been Sarin's ship. It was unlikely, of course, but it had to be somebody out there who'd just died in a flare of white, burning gases.

"How far out are the Worms now?" I asked.

"They're overtaking the cruisers rapidly. About thirty minutes from now, by our estimates, they'll be in range to do some damage. We'll be joining the battle sometime after that, depending on the speed and course of the Earth fleet."

I nodded unhappily and went back to watching the Imperial ships fire on our helpless transports.

"Why didn't Jasmine bring armed escorts?" Sandra asked.

I shrugged. "If I had to guess, I'd say that Crow made this a condition of their leaving Earth. They could go if they wanted, but they couldn't take any warships. Of course, he sent Decker and his thugs after them. Once they left the Sol system and entered Alpha Centauri space they could be easily dealt with out of sight."

Six more ships blew up.

"You have to do something, Kyle," Sandra said. "Threaten them with annihilation."

I was both surprised and pleased by her reaction. She'd been insanely jealous of Jasmine in the past—due to lapses in judgment on my part—and it was good to see her so worried for the other woman's safety. Of course, it wasn't just Jasmine she was worried about. There were a lot of people dying out there.

There wasn't anything I could do. I could fire a barrage of missiles, but they wouldn't reach before my beams, as we were accelerating. No, the missiles were best left until we were in closer range, or to chase down a limping, retreating foe.

So I watched, and I winced with the rest of them when ships flashed white. Such magnificent explosions... The transports had to be fully pressurized to create such an expanding cloud of burning plasma, like bright, tiny nebulas in space.

After the forty ninth transport popped, the Worms reached effective range. Whatever anyone had ever said about the Worms, I could respect their eagerness for a fight. They laid into the rearmost cruiser with every blaze of particles they could produce. I watched as the beams criss-crossed a region of space seemingly at random. In fact, the pattern of beams was unfocussed due to the distance, and there were gaps where the cruisers could dodge and attempt to escape.

All the beams came together, bracketing the wounded cruiser, which had fallen behind the rest. The cruiser captain detected the incoming flares of radiation and slid to downward, from the point of view of the local Alpha Centauri's plane of the ecliptic. We all watched, wondering if the Imperials would escape their fate. The Worms simply didn't have enough range.

But then, the guile of the Worm commander became evident. The pattern with the obvious gap had been a trap. A new surge of beams, held in reserve until this moment, fired in unison after the evading ship. They took the radiation directly in the aft section. There was a flash of heat, then a ripple of explosions as internal systems were burned. After a few long seconds, the cruiser broke apart.

No one on my bridge was cheering. We watched grim-faced as the Worms destroyed what had once been a Star Force ship.

"If only the Macros could see us now, squabbling and killing one another over who will be leader of the pack," I said bitterly. "They would laugh, if they possessed a sense of humor."

"The cruisers are slowing and coming about, sir. They're firing at the Worms this time."

I winced again. The Worms had managed to take out one of the cruisers, but there were five left. The bad part was the Worms weren't quite in effective range yet. Their particle beam weapons were fantastically powerful, but short-ranged. The two fleets were still pretty far apart, at a distance that was optimal for lasers, but not for radiation weapons.

"Decker is turning on the Worms now," Sandra said. "He's really working them over."

I saw explosions amongst the small Worm ships. The pilots worked their heavy fighters with consummate skill. I was impressed as they slewed and spun. Still, each of the Imperial cruisers had six heavy guns, making a total of thirty long-range weapons firing in coordination. I cringed at every flaring hit.

"Put up a count," I ordered.

The number went up in green, right below the blue number representing the number of our own ships. As I watched, the number of Worm ships diminished at a steady rate. Each salvo from the cruisers took out at least one of them, sometimes two or three. Spaced about ten seconds apart, the barrages of laser fire were devastating at this range.

"Incoming message from Decker," Marvin said.

I blinked and gritted my teeth. "Put him through."

Honestly, I expected Decker to bargain. I expected him to tell me to stop this devastating waste, allowing him to slip away toward Earth while everyone stopped shooting at each other. I was willing to let him do it, too. I was willing to let him evade justice, and get away with the numerous murders he'd committed—just to end this slaughter. Unfortunately, Decker's message was quite different.

"Ha!" His shout rang from the walls of my ship. "Your alien dogs got one good ship, but that won't happen again. They're too busy dying now. I gave you your chance, Riggs. I shouldn't have, but I thought you might listen to reason. You've started a war, but I plan to finish it, rebel."

The message ended. I looked at Marvin in surprise.

"That's all he said?" I asked.

"The channel has been closed, and refuses to be reopened."

I shook my head. Decker was mad. "Tell the Worms to disable Decker's engines, if they can be that precise. Tell them if they do that much, they can break off and they've satisfied honor. Call them Worm-brothers, or whatever makes them happy."

"Message sent."

The Worms did as I asked. They were closer now, and they could hit with more accuracy. They fired at the exhaust ports of the enemy ships, which made easy targets as they were trying to escape. Then the Worms broke off, spreading out in every direction. The Worm fighters stopped firing and spread into flying streams that reminded me of a disturbed flock of bats flooding out of a cave at night.

Figuring out our plan, Decker took action. He swung his cruisers about to point every weapon in our direction. He could no longer outrun us, and we were rapidly coming into range.

"At least they aren't killing Jasmine's ships anymore," Sandra said.

I nodded. I eyed the green counter and did the math. The Worms had lost twenty-three ships to help us, about half their number. I owed them.

141

"Miklos, apply full braking power. Slow us down. Have the gunships come up at flank speed. We want to land on them with both feet."

Decker figured out what was happening soon thereafter. He could shoot at the unarmed transports, but that was pointless, as they weren't doing him any harm. He could fire at the Worms, who had dodged up and down and off to every side, escaping him. It was clear that my fleet was now on the attack, and we were almost in range. More importantly, we were pulling together into a single fist, not hitting him in pieces. Anyone could count ships, and right now it was fifty-one to five against the Imperial forces.

"He's calling us again," Sandra said.

"I know, I can see the contact request on the boards. Leave it closed for now."

We came within range a minute or two later. I wanted to see if he was going to fire on my cruiser. If he was having second thoughts about this entire battle, he might wait. That would buy me more time for the fleets to come together.

As it turned out, I'd made a tactical error. I think maybe it was the psychology of the moment. When I didn't answer, Decker took that to mean *screw you* and figured we weren't going to make any bargains. He opened fire on *Nostradamus*, which was now within range.

There was a strange sound of groaning metal from the ship, and the bridge filled with wispy trails of vapor.

"We've taken a glancing hit, sir," Miklos said. "The beam was unfocussed, fortunately. Hull temperature is up by about twelve hundred degrees."

The metal squealed and crackled as my nanites attempted to repair the burnt spot. I knew the sounds were from the variance of temperature. We'd been burned, but it wasn't that bad. A direct hit would have vaporized a section of the hull and blown it wide open.

"Full gear everyone, we could lose pressure at any moment!" I shouted over the general com channel. The order was quickly relayed to the entire fleet.

"Should we attempt evasive action, sir?" asked the helmsman.

"No," I said. "Pump out the new smart-chaff. We'll stay right behind it until they burn through. That should give us some time."

Miklos manipulated the controls. I caught my bridge staff exchanging glances. The nanite-chaff was a new, experimental defensive system. Essentially, we'd taught constructive nanites to group up into disks on their own in a vacuum. Forming chains with their bodies, they created reflective surfaces that got in the way of incoming energy beams and deflected most of the killing power. Theoretically, this approach should provide much better cover than dodging around or using the traditional bits of foil to diffuse the incoming beams. But it was pretty much untested. I could tell that my crew wasn't thrilled about placing their lives on the line by betting on experimental tech.

What I didn't tell them was it was our only hope, in my opinion. The situation was mathematical. The enemy had damaged engines, but they outgunned my cruiser five to one. They'd already proven they were reasonably accurate, even against dodging targets. Unless the new chaff worked extremely well, we only had minutes left to live.

The next nineteen minutes were some of the longest of my life. Only the initial nanite injections, which had left me raging in mindless agony, were possibly worse. The really difficult part was based on a critical limitation of my chaff-based approach. They couldn't burn through to me, but I couldn't fire at them, either. It was as if we were charging at them from behind an upraised shield. If I fired, I would only damage my own shield, so our guns remained silent as we plunged closer. That was the agonizing part. We took glancing hits, and watched numbers flash and burn as their beams dug into my chaff shield. Millions of nanites were transformed into bursts of energy and puffs of vapor. All along, I could not even order my own guns to return fire.

After those long minutes were over, my gunships caught up with us. I ordered them to fire the moment they came abreast of us.

"But sir," Miklos said. "They aren't going to be accurate at this range."

"I know that. Fire!"

Miklos was a good officer, even if he asked too many questions. The single big cannon on all fifty gunships opened up, disgorging huge bolts toward the distant Imperial ships. These weapons were essentially identical to the belly turret on every Macro cruiser. It had been far easier to order the Macro factories to produce weapons they knew how to manufacture than to design something new, so I'd stuck with the tried-and-true.

A few minutes later, Decker tried to communicate with me again.

"Put him through," I said.

"You really are a mad-dog, just like everyone says, aren't you?" Decker asked me. His voice was somewhat fuzzy, no doubt affected by the mountain of smart-metal chaff that constantly reformed itself into tiny mirrors in front of my ship.

"Not only do you consort with vile biotics like the Worms, but now you seem to have small Macro allies in those ships with you. Crow was an idiot. He should have killed you years ago."

"Decker," I said. "Your situation is hopeless. You can't outrun us. You can't outgun us. You can't even do much damage. Ceasefire and surrender your ships."

"The sheer, unadulterated arrogance!" he raged. "It really must be seen to be comprehended. You not only want to win this battle on the cheap, but you also dare to fantasize I'll hand over my command as well so you might turn these fine ships against Earth."

"It's better than dying, Decker."

"I disagree. And let me tell you, Emperor Crow is well-prepared, should I fail here today. You've taught him how to overcome your natural guile and deceit."

"How's that?"

"By overkill."

I frowned at the holotank as the channel went dead. I glanced over at Miklos, who made a pinched face and shrugged.

I couldn't be so nonchalant. What did that rat-bastard Decker have in mind? What did he mean that Crow was waiting for me out there, planning in terms of *overkill*?

-18-

Decker's next move pissed me off. Instead of breaking off, surrendering, or coming at me blazing with every gun he had—he turned on the civilian ships again.

They were closer now than before. They'd broken off and were no longer on a collision course, but in space when two groups of ships are coming at each other at high speeds, it isn't easy to turn away from one another. Just try giving your car's steering wheel a hard swerve to one side or the other while speeding on the highway. The car will tend to keep moving forward with the momentum. When moving at thousands of miles per minute, the effect is magnified. We could turn our noses and fire our jets, but we changed course relatively slowly.

I recognized the developing situation in the holotank. While Decker's fleet and my fleet were converging, the refugee transports were a green crowd all around us. They were easy pickings for Decker, who had been ignoring them and firing at my ship. He hadn't bothered with them while I was in range. But now that he realized he couldn't knock out *Nostradamus* and the rest of my gunships were closing in, he changed his tactics. As I watched, the six red contacts representing his cruisers reached out with flickering beams to scorch more helpless transports.

"Dammit!" I roared slamming an armored fist into the console. The glass cracked, and the screen rippled in every direction. I ignored it. Even as I pulled my fist loose from the damaged screen, the thin coating of nanites that serviced the control systems frantically scrambled to effect repairs.

145

"The initial barrage from our gunships has reached the enemy line," Miklos said.

"Any hits?"

"...No—no effective damage detected. We have, however, lost three more transports. Four more."

I stood up and marched in a clanking circle around the holotank. A stream of curses came out my mouth. "This is just sheer spite. He can't hurt us, so he's taking out the helpless ships he can damage."

"I beg to differ, sir," Miklos said. "Decker knows we need those ships to reinforce our position and replace losses in our ranks. He's delivering a serious strategic blow, from his point of view."

"They're unarmed transports! Full of people promised free passage out of the Solar System!"

Miklos shrugged. "War is not always clean and fair, Colonel."

I spent thirty seconds or so thinking hard. I couldn't come up with an easy way out the situation. There were some moves I could make—but they were unpleasant ones.

"Weapons officer," I shouted suddenly, clapping a heavy metal glove on his shoulder. He was wearing a crewmen's nanocloth uniform, and cringed in pain. I barely noticed, as I was too focused on the battle to coddle my crew today.

"Sir!" he responded, gritting his teeth.

"Heat up the lasers. Prepare to fire. How long will you need, Ensign?"

He glanced at his tablet. "Eighteen more seconds, sir."

I noticed with approval that he was working the controls. Apparently, the eighteen seconds were already counting down. I liked a man that kept moving even while I crushed his shoulder in my grip. I released him and he looked relieved, but his eyes never left his control board.

"Order the smart chaff to dissipate," I said.

Everyone glanced at me then, except for Miklos. His face was grim, but he worked his controls, obeying without question.

"But," Sandra said, "they'll fry us, Kyle."

"Maybe," I said. "But in that case they won't be firing on the transports anymore, will they? Ensign, you have seven of your eighteen seconds left. If you take out one of Decker's ships, you will be instantly promoted to Lieutenant. Do I make myself clear?"

"Absolutely, sir."

I liked the kid. I could tell right away, I'd made his day. He wanted to fight, to fire the weapons he'd been trained to operate. He hadn't enjoyed a second of the ordeal we'd just been through, hiding behind a shield of glittering nanites and hoping they could stop the powerful energies coming at us from the depths of space. He wanted to shoot his cannons, and he was finally getting the chance.

I smiled grimly, as did the Ensign. No one else around us looked happy. Miklos looked resigned and determined, while everyone else appeared to be freaked out.

The smart chaff obeyed our orders to disintegrate the disks they'd formed and they fell away over the flanks of our cruiser like showers of silvery sand. The moment they were out of the way, the Ensign fired his weapons, exactly as I'd instructed him to do.

The move caught Decker by surprise. He'd killed ten of our transports by now, and he was expecting to be beaten down by my gunships when they got into closer range, but I think he'd discounted the six heavy lasers on my own flagship.

One final detail made itself evident as all six beams leapt out from my ship to the enemy vessels: they were all concentrating on a single enemy vessel in the line-up. It was the one to the far left, the ship that had hung back a fraction during this entire fight.

"Damage?" I asked.

Several pairs of eyes glowed as they examined scopes and fingers flicked this way and that, operating the software.

"She's breaking apart, sir," the Ensign said. There was pride in his voice.

I clapped him on the back and he coughed.

"Well done!" I roared. "That was Decker's ship, wasn't it?"

"Yes sir," said the Ensign, beaming. "I believe it was."

I laughed harshly, and grinned with him. Miklos was the only one that didn't seem to get the joke.

"You have killed the enemy commander," he said. "That will not make it easier to arrange any negotiated end to this conflict."

"Who said we were negotiating?" I demanded.

"Sir," Miklos said seriously. "Do not forget that these are biotics we're killing. These Earth ships are some of the best armament we have in four systems. Every ship lost is a tragedy for our side."

I frowned, and I wanted to call Miklos a wet blanket. But I couldn't, because he was right.

I heaved a sigh. "Open a channel to the enemy fleet," I said. "Ensign, cease fire. Sandra, oversee the pumping out of fresh chaff."

"We're hiding again?" asked the Weapons Officer, unable to hide his disgust.

"Ensign, I like you. What's your name again?"

"Patterson, sir."

"Well, you're Lieutenant Commander Patterson now," I said.

That made Patterson happy again. He watched my gauntlets, but I didn't slam one of them into him or try to shake his hands in congratulations.

"Channel request accepted," Marvin said.

"Imperial cruisers," I said loudly. "I request a short ceasefire on both sides. I know you've lost your commander. Please decide amongst yourselves which captain is in charge and negotiate with me."

There was no response for about twenty seconds, then someone finally answered us. "Captain Yuki here," said a female voice. "As the senior officer present, I'm now in command of this task force."

"Do you agree to a ceasefire?"

"I cannot. You're stalling until your gunships are in optimal range."

"You are blowing apart defenseless transports, many of which contain civilians!" I shouted back. "Fire at my warships if you like, and die well, but please stop killing innocents."

There was another hesitation. Neither side was firing now, which was fine by me. Yuki had rejected my ceasefire, but it was temporarily in effect anyway while we talked.

"There are no innocents, as you put it, in this system. We represent the Empire, and we—"

"Look," I said, interrupting, "I appreciate that you're new to your command, Captain. And I know the easiest thing to do in these situations is to continue on the course laid for you by your previous commander. But I implore you to take this offer: accept a ceasefire, and retreat with all your ships. Take them back to the Solar System, and save all these ships and personnel to battle the machines."

"The machines have been defeated," she said primly and confidently.

I raised my eyebrows in surprise. "Says who?"

"The Emperor."

I laughed then. "Well, I'll send you some data then, if you want it. Consider it valuable intel on what we're facing. You do not have to reciprocate with any data of your own. But Crow and every military on Earth should know how hard they hit us only a few weeks ago."

I signaled urgently at Sandra, who dug out recorded vid files from the Thor system. They depicted in vivid detail the Macro fleet as it advanced upon our battle station. We edited out any reference to the battle station itself, or the fact that we'd destroyed the fleet weeks ago. I only wanted to show them vids of the Macros throwing fresh ships at us.

While the files were retrieved and transmitted, I had a chance to reflect upon Yuki's words. The machines were defeated? What an odd conclusion to make. We'd stopped them temporarily on our side, but at the other chain of four systems was the blue giant, Bellatrix. That star system at the other end of the ring embedded in Venus's crust had been full of mining equipment and presumably Macro factories. Even if Crow figured that I'd wiped out the Macros at my end of the known systems, what had he done at his end?

"Captain Yuki," I said, as the data finished downloading. "I would like to ask for a single piece of information from you. Understanding is the first step toward peace. Why do you think the machines have been defeated? What happened to the Macro stronghold in the blue giant system? They had a lot of mining machines and factories there as I recall. Are they no longer a threat?"

Captain Yuki's voice became guarded as she answered me. "Our glorious leader eliminated all threats from that system. I'm surprised he didn't inform you of his victory. The daily news talks of little else back on Earth."

Her words caused my frown to deepen. I glanced over at Miklos, who was frowning and thinking, just as I was.

"Data upload complete," Sandra said.

"Captain Yuki. Please take a few moments to peruse the files before you continue destroying Earth's tiny defensive force. When the machines come again, they may well wipe out my outpost on Eden. After that, Earth will be next. For your own survival and mine, accept our ceasefire offer and return with this new intel to Earth."

I waited after that for a full minute. Our ships were now almost nose-to-nose. I'd ordered them to begin braking, otherwise we'd shoot past them and have to reverse course to catch up. Possibly, that was their plan. Once we'd gone out of range, they could continue to fire at the transports at will, then proceed on to the Eden system, where my defenses were stretched very thin. Almost everything I had was guarding the far ring that led to the Crustacean home system. Nothing was going to be able to stop them if the cruisers evaded us and pressed onward to attack Eden. Fortunately, Captain Yuki didn't know that. I'd only sent her the vids of the Macros in the Thor system.

"There appears to be some kind of new alien. Are these creatures cooperating with the Macros, as the vids seem to indicate?"

It took me a second to realize she was talking about the Crustaceans. I hadn't really wanted to give away that information, but I figured it was worth it if they would stop the killing.

"Yes, they are," I said. "Just as we served the machines once as troops when they had us over a barrel. We're fighting both the Macros and these new aliens."

"How can they mount such massive fleet so quickly?" Yuki asked me. She seemed honestly alarmed.

"In my opinion, they can do so indefinitely. They produce ships constantly, and throw them at us when they feel they have enough. They will come to Earth one day if I fail. It is only a matter of time."

"How will you hold against them?"

I gritted my teeth and forced myself to smile. "I'll be able to do the job much more easily if you stop blowing up my relief column."

There was a quiet moment, while no doubt the surviving captains engaged in a heated debate. Finally, Yuki came back on the line.

"We accept your terms, Colonel Riggs. We will return to Earth, if you will return to Helios. Let us call Alpha Centauri a buffer zone for now. Please do not become aggressive again, or further misunderstandings are guaranteed to occur."

Sandra erupted, unloading a long string of profanities and suggesting Yuki should perform anatomically impossible acts. I understood her frustration. It was difficult to be lectured by an arrogant Imperial about hostility when they'd started the shooting.

"Agreed, Captain," I said when Sandra had lowered her voice enough to allow me to unmute the channel.

Sandra still muttered obscenities behind me, but I felt the audio system probably hadn't picked them up.

After that, our two fleets warily disengaged. The Worms had already retreated from the system by the time we'd managed to make peace and get out of range. I was left feeling empty at the pointless loss of life. When I expressed these feelings to Miklos and Sandra later, they scoffed at me.

"It wasn't pointless," Sandra said, "you had to do it, Kyle. They didn't give you any choice."

Miklos was more philosophical about it. "This clash was probably inevitable," he said. "It was Crow that changed the rules of the game, not you. He also ordered his ships to destroy the transports as they carried away your last loyal Star Force marines. What could you do, other than declare war?"

"I'll never forgive him for that," I said.

I set the optical sensors to examine each destroyed transport in turn. I stared coldly at the remains of a hundred ships. At this range, I couldn't see the frozen bodies I knew must be floating out there. There was only the silent wreckage and spinning clusters of twisted, blackened metal.

Crow had a lot to answer for.

-19-

Although they took their time about it, the Imperial cruisers finally limped away from the battlefield and retreated through the ring toward Earth. My fleet applied full thrust for nearly a day to slow down then reverse course. I had no intention of flying through the final ring and into the Solar System. I wasn't ready to find out what Crow had waiting for me on the far side.

It was strange, being so close to home and yet turning away. Always before, returning to Earth had been a happy event. Even when we'd been chased by packs of raging enemy ships, we'd always felt a surge of excitement and well-being to know we were about to enter friendly territory. Now, it no longer felt like home.

Space is a lonely place under the best of circumstances, and being rejected by one's homeworld isn't an easy thing to experience. Everyone around me felt the same, I could tell. Every face was glum. Every eye stared at the screens as the last ring between us and Earth fell away behind us again and we headed back out toward deeper space and alien worlds. Would we ever return home again? Would we ever be welcome there? None of us knew the answers to these questions.

Shaking off my reverie, I quickly decided to liven things up. In truth, we had almost as much to celebrate as we did to mope about. We'd driven off the Imperials and saved a lot of loyal Star Force personnel. I had no idea how many there were, but I intended to find out.

"Marvin, open a channel to Captain Sarin's fleet."

"No response, Colonel. Possibly, her ship is damaged."

"Well, keep trying."

Sandra glanced at me, and I felt a pang of worry. Was she going to get jealous again? But no, I could see in her eyes that wasn't her first concern. She looked worried. I signaled for her to come close and she did so.

"What if Jasmine is dead, Kyle?" Sandra asked me in a whisper.

I considered the possibility. It was a distinct one. About a third of the transports had been destroyed. Worse, the Imperials might have tracked her transmissions to the correct ship and blasted her on purpose. Didn't every tyrant round up the rebel leaders and execute them at some point?

"Nonsense," I said with a confident smile that was pure bullshit. "She's fine. She's almost as hard to kill as Sloan."

Sandra nodded worriedly and went back to monitoring the holotank. On screen, my fleet and Sarin's fleet were now alone. The Worms had returned home to Helios, having long since reversed course and withdrawn. Sarin's fleet was also streaming down from every direction toward my warships, like scores of lost birds returning to the main flock after a panic.

"Anything, Marvin?"

"I'm getting reports now from various ships. They are responding in turn, listing their damages, making relief requests. Should I put them through?"

"Yes, of course. Sandra, see what you can do for them. Send a gunboat out to every ship that's in trouble. Coordinate any necessary rescues. Marvin? Any word from the refugee leadership? Who is in charge out there?"

"They all insist Captain Sarin is their commander. But they're unable to raise her."

I pursed my lips tightly and nodded. The next several hours passed quickly, as we all had a lot to do. Our own ships were largely undamaged, and the damage we had suffered was automatically repaired by our nanite friends. The situation was different with the transports, however. They had a lot of wounded, and I quickly learned that most of the passengers aboard the ships weren't Star Force people. This was significant, because they were just normal human beings. They didn't have a built-in supply of nanites to repair their bodies. They needed medical attention. Without it, instead of self-regenerating, they died.

The refugee fleet coalesced around my warships in time. Some of them had to be towed in by the gunboats. Others were wrecks which had to be evacuated and left to drift away into the burning furnaces at the center of the star system. It was on one of these wrecks that they finally found Jasmine.

"I've got a command contact, sir," Marvin said late in the evening.

"What are you talking about?" I snapped back.

I was still on the bridge, stirring some bad coffee and slumping in my armor. Star Force Marines didn't need a lot of sleep, but we did need a little of it. I'd been denying myself such simple pleasures until the situation was under control. Unfortunately, there seemed to be no end to the rescue effort.

"A command channel contact, incoming from gunboat thirty-six. Someone aboard wants to speak with you."

I grumbled and opened the channel. I'd avoided direct contact with every concerned captain that wanted to tell me about his problems. I had limited resources and they were all pretty much allocated. Too often, my reply had been something like: "You're on your own, Lieutenant. Fix it."

When I heard Jasmine's voice, I was quite shocked. "Hello Kyle, I'm alive," she said inside my helmet.

I took a heartbeat or two to speak. When I did, there was a grin exploding on my face and I straightened up instantly. "Jasmine?"

"Yes, it's me."

"I'd given up," I said. "Not looking, I don't mean that. But I'd marked you down as lost. I hate to admit that."

"It's okay."

"Where the hell are you?"

"My transport was taken out, but a few of us lived. I've almost reached your cruiser. Let me tell you about it in person."

My heart accelerated in my chest, and I felt silly. Why did I seem to have a thing for this woman? I hadn't seen her in months, and she'd given me no end of trouble in times past. She'd even declared loyalty to Earth and Crow.

I gave my head a shake to clear it, and looked around the bridge. Sandra had retired an hour earlier. She was probably sound asleep by now in our shared quarters. Miklos was rubbing his temples and going over damage reports on his screens. No one else seemed to have noticed my emotional reaction, and I was about to relax when I turned and saw a half-dozen camera eyes studying me closely. Marvin didn't take breaks, naturally, and he was operating the holotank right now. But his focus was on me. He knew who was on the channel with me. In fact, he was probably eavesdropping.

"Yes, great!" I said. "Come to my conference room the minute you get aboard. You aren't too badly hurt, are you?"

"My left leg is in a bag of nanites," she said. "But I need to talk to you."

We broke off the connection, and I headed into the conference room. On most spaceships, you didn't get a lot of privacy. This cruiser was the largest Star Force vessel we'd built yet, but it still wasn't any bigger than an old-fashioned submarine back home. It was about five hundred feet long and displaced something like fifteen thousand tons. As a result, when you moved around in the ship you had to expect to bump butts with plenty of other crewmen.

I poured myself a fresh cup of crappy coffee and stripped out of my armor. I figured I had to smell pretty bad by now. I put on a nanocloth crewman's suit and wished I had time for a shower. When she finally arrived, I sipped at my coffee, which was already becoming lukewarm.

She paused in the doorway and we looked at each other. She was in nanocloth too, but I liked her uniform more than mine. We'd come up with black outfits, very utilitarian. They were little more than army fatigues or in some cases coveralls. Her Imperial clothes had a much more stylish cut to them. There were new insignia on her shoulders, too.

Her hair was down, and still looked long and dark. It was a little ragged, but I could tell she'd worked on it on the way over to my ship. She didn't look like a crash victim, which surprised me. Her leg, as she'd indicated, was floating in a bag of nanites. A long red line had split open the skin, revealing the bone in spots. Nanites silvered that region, working on it.

After a second, I smiled at her, and she returned the smile. She came in then and sat down across from me. I was less than pleased to see Kwon thumping along in her wake. Without even asking, he came into the conference room and stood there at the end of the oblong table. He was so tall he had to lean his head to one side. He was still wearing armor, and it looked more banged up than Jasmine did.

"Yes, Kwon?" I asked.

"He's here to make a report as well," Jasmine said.

I nodded stiffly. "Excellent work out there, First Sergeant," I said. "By all means, give me your report."

Kwon looked at Jasmine for a second, then shuffled his feet twice. "Ah, well sir...I wanted to join you, if possible."

I frowned slightly. "Do you have a report to make or not?"

"Sure," he said. "Ah, the last ship has reported in and we've sorted out the dead from the living. We now have a total of twenty-nine thousand, three hundred and sixty-one survivors. More are being found every hour."

My eyebrows shot up at that. "That's good news," I said. "What about Star Force people?"

Kwon looked at Jasmine, then back at me. "That's not so clear, sir."

I was frowning again. Kwon took this moment of confusion to stump into the room and begin aiming his big butt at a chair. I put up a hand.

"I need you to go make a count of all the military personnel on those transports. Maybe they aren't calling themselves Star Force, but I want to know how many there are anyway."

Kwon froze. His rear hovered only a foot above the chair he'd targeted. "Are you sure you'll be okay here alone, sir?" he asked.

That was it then. I felt a surge of irritation. My own staff didn't trust me with Sarin. Sure, we'd had a few exciting moments together. We'd made out, given one another a beating and who knew what else. But that was all in the past. I didn't like Kwon's mother-hen attitude.

"Even if she's one of Crow's assassins," I said. "I think I can take her."

Kwon looked comically alarmed for a moment, then he examined my grin and Jasmine's embarrassed smile. He finally figured out I was joking, and began a halting laugh. "Ah. Ha, ha, ha! Sure-right," he said. "But that wasn't—"

"I know what you meant, Kwon. Now, get out of here. That's an order."

"Sure, sure," he said, exiting unhappily. As the nanites closed the portal behind him, I could still hear him muttering in the hallway.

"He doesn't trust us," I said, turning to Jasmine.

She was clearly embarrassed and determined to pretend she didn't know what I was talking about. "We have to talk, Colonel."

I leaned back in my chair and offered her some coffee. "I can't believe you're alive and back aboard my ship."

"I didn't think this would happen either," she said. "I thought I could go back to Earth and command a fleet. I thought—"

I studied her. "How bad is it? I mean back home, on the ground? How did Crow pull it off?"

She looked at me sharply. "You mean, you don't know?"

I shook my head. I explained that we'd been cut off from transmissions from Earth for months. We'd heard things, but it wasn't like we had the vid files and news reports.

"That figures," she said. "Jack always told me he was keeping you advised of his every move. He told me he sent you files, and read letters where you occasionally objected. But he said you'd understood his actions and had seen the necessity of it all. I had figured he was lying of course. I knew you wouldn't have gone along with the ultimatums, and the purges. But I thought he really *was* telling you things. I didn't realize he hadn't even bothered."

My frown deepened. Crow was not the most honorable fellow, and I didn't like the idea he'd used my name to rubberstamp his ambitions.

"Give me a timeline," I said. "I've been out of touch, fighting on the frontier for months."

"Of course. Where do I begin? I suppose I should start with my return to Earth. I was sent out to Eden last year to talk some sense into you."

"You failed, but who can blame you for that?" I asked, laughing. She didn't laugh, and soon I stopped and cleared my throat. "Go on."

"Crow has been planning this for a long time, I think. Since the beginning, maybe. He's been waiting for his opportunity. I think that opportunity came when you were gone from Earth for a long, long time. He wanted to kill you, but I think he knew that if he did, everyone would know it was him, and they would hate him for it.

So he waited until you were stuck out here, and made his move then."

I nodded and sipped more coffee. It was cold now, so I threw it on the floor. The nanites sucked it up and spit it out of the ship. In seconds, my boots no longer glistened with brown droplets.

"He had ships, Kyle. He had them specially built. He can design them now—he's not as good as you are, but his designs are more devious and they look sleeker somehow. Anyway, he had built something new, what we call *death ships*. Little assassination ships that carry only one man, or no men at all. They flew out in the night and killed every government official in every country of note that had complained about Crow openly. He did it all in one night too—all across the globe. You remember when the Nano ships first came to Earth, that night they picked us both up?"

I nodded. I wanted to ask questions, but I held back. I wanted to ask Sarin who had been running Star Force without challenging Crow? Who hadn't seen this coming, and had let him get away with literal murder unchecked? But I didn't ask these things, as I knew it was probably she who had been asleep at the switch. Deciding information was better than recriminations, I held my peace.

"The ships swept across the globe at midnight in every country, quietly plucking people from their beds with long arms. But instead of dragging them into their bellies and testing them, they just closed their black, rippling hands. They crushed ribcages, mostly. Like angry children throttling helpless dolls. They have a name now for that terrible night, when thousands died. They call it 'The Night of the Red Hands'. Apparently, after having killed so many, witnesses said the three-fingered, metal hands were encrusted with gore. At the mere sight of them, everyone fled screaming."

"Didn't they fight?"

"It was hard. They don't have nanite tech in the old capitals of the world. They have missiles, but these ships were no bigger than vans darting down streets, humming and seeking. They didn't find everyone on their lists, of course. But those that survived got the message. They hide now, and fear the day the ships will come back for them. Crow retrieved them all, and he had the balls to apologize and claim it was all an unfortunate incident. We haven't seen them since."

"Didn't the entire world declare war?" I asked. I found myself breathing hard. The injustice of it all was hard to bear.

"War on Andros Island? War on Star Force, who had saved them all from extinction?" She shook her head and pushed her long hair back away from her face. "A few did. Israel and Japan—a few others."

I hesitated. Sometimes, you want to wait one more second before you have to hear horrid news. "What happened to those nations?" I asked quietly, when I was ready.

"He destroyed them. He didn't kill everyone—but he mowed their military and their infrastructure."

"They were helpless?"

"Not at first. They fired nukes at us, ship-killers. They couldn't get through our defenses, of course. We've fought alien fleets. A few dozen primitive ICBMs—it was a joke. But Crow used the incident to make examples of them. He flew out our ships—our real warships, which he's been building up for so long. We bombarded them into submission. It was easy, really. You just sit up there and fire sparks down into the clouds, one after another. The brainboxes did the targeting. We didn't exterminate any cities or anything like that, we just pounded away at their military and infrastructure. They were helpless to stop a bombardment from space."

I stared at her. I now had a headache that coffee couldn't fix. "Are you telling me my Star Force heroes beat down the legitimate governments of Earth? Willingly?"

She heaved a sigh. "I apologize for all of us. It didn't seem that way at the time. You have to understand, the assassin-ships went out on their own, Crow sent them. We didn't even really believe that story was real. We didn't *want* to believe it. We *couldn't* believe it. At least, not on the scale that was described. From our point of view, we woke up one morning and missiles were incoming. We scrambled, we defended ourselves, then went on a reprisal mission. It happened so fast…"

I nodded, trying to visualize it all. Somehow, the reality of events on Earth was worse than I'd imagined. I'd figured maybe Crow had gotten elected to Emperor by some party of world government-loving nut-jobs. But he'd done it the old-fashioned way, by eliminating the toughest competition then terrorizing the rest.

"You mentioned something about an ultimatum."

"Yes. Crow went live on the worldwide nets. He wore that suit he always wears now for the first time—I'm sure you've seen it, all white with jingling medals. I don't even know where he got all that bling."

I shook my head. I'd never seen any such imagery, but it sounded like Crow trying to impress people. He'd always been over-the-top when it came to things like that. He liked his symbols of power to be big and flashy, like that massive desk I'd once commandeered from him back on Andros Island.

Jasmine paused until I gestured for her to go on.

"Anyway," she said, "he said that it was time for the world to grow up. He claimed it had all been a misunderstanding, another fight between Star Force and the provincial governments—that's what he calls them. The U. S. Whitehouse and the British Parliament—those are just provincial, backwater institutions, according to Crow. He explained that our world needed centralized authority to go along with a centralized military. He said that the major governments of the world had met with him and decided he was the one to lead us into this era of worldwide peace and unity."

"What a surprise he chose himself," I said. "Did he have any real backers?"

"Yes. Russia and China both came out in favor. Japan did too, after their beating. The Israeli Knesset remained mulishly silent. Two dozen other minor countries joined in, mostly small places from Eastern Europe, the Mideast and Africa."

"What about the U. S.?"

"That part was weird. There was something going on in Washington. None of us, maybe not even Crow, understood it all. But suddenly, the president was gone. I'm still not sure if Crow's assassinbots killed him, or if it was a successful internal coup. In any case, the Pentagon announced martial law. They dissolved congress—most of the members were dead anyway. And then they declared themselves to be part of Crow's Empire. The Terran Empire. That's what they call it now."

I sat in shocked silence for about a minute. I looked down at my hands which were gloved in metallic nanocloth. I tried to visualize the assassinbots coming in the night, plucking leaders from their beds. What if the Nano ships had simply squeezed my body into pulp when they'd gotten hold of me? I would have succumbed, I was quite sure. Normal humans really couldn't put up much of a fight against these machines.

I looked up at Jasmine. She stared back at me, sharing my expression of pain and worry.

"I can't believe he finally pulled it off," I said. "I have to blame myself."

"No Kyle," she said, snaking out her hand to touch mine. "Don't do that."

"I could have stopped him. A dozen times, I could have killed him. But I didn't. Then I flew out here and saved a pack of aliens while my own world suffered. Sometimes, I just get caught up in the moment, you see? I always seem to believe I can do more than I really can."

Jasmine shook her head. She opened her mouth to say more, but at that moment, the door dissolved open. Sandra stood at the entrance with her hands on her hips. Her hands were wrapped into fists.

Jasmine's hand quickly retreated from mine. She studied the table for a few long, awkward seconds.

I felt a surge of guilt, but twisted it into a frown.

"Come on in, Sandra," I said. "Jasmine has brought us grim news.

-20-

Sandra had been my girlfriend for years, and Jasmine had been a flirtation along the way. Diffusing encounters between these two had become something of a hobby of mine. The women had come to blows more than once, and Jasmine had always lost those encounters. She was nanotized, but the Microbes had really done a number on Sandra. My girl was so fast and so feral that she barely qualified as human when she lost her temper—which was fairly often.

"I hate to make you explain it again but...could you?" I asked Jasmine.

Jasmine repeated the story of Crow's conquest of Earth. Sandra stalked in and sat with me. She listened to Jasmine, glaring at the woman she considered a rival. But by the end of Jasmine's quiet speech Sandra's expression had changed to one of horror. The detailed tale of extermination and lost freedom on Earth had transformed her mood.

"Kyle!" she said, turning on me. "We have to *do* something. We can't let Crow rule Earth like some kind of god-king."

I shrugged and sighed. "I don't think we can beat him," I said. "At least not right now. Not with what we've got."

Sandra shook her head. "I can't believe I'm hearing this defeatist talk. You can do *anything*. I've seen it."

I smiled faintly. "We've got about sixty fighting ships and a few hundred active duty fliers. We can build up, but he'll be doing the same. But that's not the worst thing. Take a look at this, ladies. We're in trouble in a strategic sense."

162

They frowned at me while I brought up a display on the conference table showing the six known star systems and their interlinking rings. "Earth is here, at the end of the chain. According to Jasmine, Crow managed to destroy everything the Macros had in the Bellatrix system, and now controls it. That's a lot of raw materials to draw upon, but taking Bellatrix was critical for another reason: that system was the end of the line. There is only one ring we've found that connects to it, and that connection leads to Venus."

She nodded slowly, looking at the layout of the systems. "So Crow has his back covered. He's got a system behind him full of resources, while we have to defend multiple systems with two rings each."

"Worse," I said, "we're surrounded. We control Helios and Eden. Alpha Centauri is no-mans-land. Thor, the last known system in the chain, is full of enemies. We've got Crow's Imperial fleet at one end of our chain of systems and the Macros with their new Crustacean allies on the other."

The two women studied the tabletop.

"We've got half the map," Jasmine pointed out. "That's a lot of resources, along with two friendly races to help us. But we're surrounded, I can see that. If both sides attack at once—we can't win."

Sandra smiled. "We *might* win." She proceeded to tell Jasmine about the battle station. Jasmine was impressed by the specs and its record against the Macros in combat, but she was still worried about being hit on two sides at once, and I had to agree with her.

"Crow can mass up at each ring, press forward with everything he has, then mass up again. We'll be slowly driven back when he comes after us."

"Maybe we should build another battle station," Sandra said. "With Jasmine's reinforcements and a steady output from the factories, we could hold both ends of Eden."

I nodded slowly, considering the idea. But I really didn't like the thought of putting all my resources into more static defensive structures. The problem with fortresses had always been that they couldn't advance. They held territory at best, if you were lucky. But I'd always done better maneuvering on an open battlefield. If I built another battle station, I'd have very little fleet when my enemies came knocking once again.

"We've got another ace in the hole, Jasmine," Sandra said excitedly. "When we took the Eden system from the Macros, we captured their—"

I cleared my throat suddenly. Sandra stopped talking and both of them looked at me. "I'm sorry," I said, "but before we can release classified information to you, Jasmine, we have to have certain arrangements made very clear."

"I completely understand," Jasmine said. She stood up then and walked around the table. She suddenly went to one knee and bowed her head before me.

I frowned at this, instantly recognizing that Crow must have required just such an outdated, embarrassing ceremony of fealty. I stood up and roared. Jasmine looked up at me, her big brown eyes uncertain.

"No, no!" I shouted. "Get up, woman. I'm no Emperor. I'm a Colonel, nothing more. Give me nothing more than a salute. Your sworn word goes to Star Force. That's what I want: Loyalty to the *service*, not to me."

After we'd sorted that out, Jasmine returned to her seat and the two women smiled at one another uncertainly. I was frowning and irritated. How quickly people took to new customs. I guess they were very old customs, deeply ingrained in all of us. When times became uncertain and life became cheap, we returned to the tribal roots that lurked in the back of everyone's mind.

"I have no doubt making people bow and swear loyalty to him gives Crow an intense thrill," I said. "But I find the whole idea upsetting. I wanted citizen-warriors, not vassals."

"Good," Sandra said.

"Sorry," Jasmine said. "I made a mistake."

I waved away her words. "Do you solemnly swear to serve Star Force on the Fleet side, to return to your former rank of Captain, and to defend Earth at all costs?"

"I do, sir."

"Very good. You're back in. But Crow is no longer part of Star Force, by his own admission. Don't return to Crow's side, not even if he offers you a battleship of your own. Further disloyalty will result in permanent banishment from the ranks of Star Force. Are we clear?"

She licked her lips and eyed me. I could tell my words had hurt her. "I didn't abandon Star Force the first time," she said. "Please take a moment to recall the situation clearly. You and Crow were equally in charge. When you two split apart and gave me diverging orders, I went with him, but I never saw that as a treacherous act."

"Yeah, okay. But he got rid of Star Force on Earth. I'm now the last and only commander of that organization. According to your report, Crow chased loyal members of Star Force out into space. Want to tell me how that went down?"

"There wasn't much to tell. I think he really wanted to kill us all, but didn't dare. He was afraid his own pilots wouldn't fire. So, he offered us amnesty. He let us build transports, and offered anyone on Andros Island free passage out to the frontier planets. He specifically used your name, saying you were out here fighting on the edge of civilization, killing vicious aliens on a regular basis."

I nodded. He hadn't lied about that part, at least.

"The most loyal among us left Earth. We knew it was banishment, but we built the ships and flew out anyway. We hadn't signed up to rule the world, we'd only wanted to kill the machines. But there was another reason. More and more new recruits had been coming in to join Crow on Andros Island during the months following the coup. These people were different, and they swore to follow only Crow. I didn't like them, Kyle. They were Easterners, mostly. From eastern Europe, China and my own India. These were people who wanted power. They weren't volunteers ready to die for Earth's cause."

"You were the highest ranking defector?" I asked.

"I came to be one of the leaders of the exodus. We boarded our ships without weapons or factories—"

"Of course he wouldn't let you go armed," I scoffed. "Why would he give you enough equipment to challenge him from space—or even to survive out here for long?"

"We knew he wasn't allowing us much. But we took it, rather than bow before him, or start a civil war against the whole world. We left, hoping he'd let us go for propaganda reasons if nothing else. But as soon as we left the system, our escort ships, commanded by Commodore Decker, turned on us."

"Sounds like we came along at an opportune moment."

"Indeed you did. Decker was just looking for an excuse to blast us out of space. I'm not sure what orders Crow had given him, but I was sure he wanted us dead."

"You won't have to worry about that particular bastard any longer," I said.

"Whatever happened to Decker, Colonel?"

I smiled grimly. "He will no longer trouble us. I made sure his cruiser would never return to Earth. I figured that I had one good shot, and I took it. Like any snake, its best to start by removing the head."

She gave me a cold smile of her own, and nodded thoughtfully. "Crow won't forget that. Decker was his wingman. They saw eye-to-eye. In fact, I think he'll come after us, if only because you killed Decker."

"Then there isn't any time to lose. I need every one of your Star Force refugees to reaffirm their allegiance to Star Force, not Crow's empire. We'll arm them as soon as we're able and put them onto my ships. What's your current troop strength, minus the wounded and civilians?"

Captain Sarin smiled. "Over nine thousand, effectives sir."

I grinned. "That, Commander, is the best damned news I've heard in a month. They might even be enough, in the end."

Sandra frowned and cocked her head. "Enough for what, Kyle?"

"Enough to retake Earth. What else?"

-21-

We returned to the Helios system, taking the time to beam graphic symbols of respect and gratitude to the Worms. They were suckers for that, and sent us a few prideful images of raging Worm warriors in return. I told them to rebuild, as more conflict was coming. They signaled that they agreed with my assessment of the situation. They assured me that any and all of our enemies would fall in time.

When we finally crossed the Helios system and slid through the last ring, I had to field a dozen calls from the transport captains. They were overwhelmed by the beauty and lush nature of the Eden system, which was so full of life and hope it was like nowhere else we'd yet found in the universe. I beamed with pride as I explained that the warmest three of the six life-supporting worlds were ours to colonize. I told them of the outposts I had there on the ground—even though they were very thinly manned and amounted to little more than bunkers in strategic locations.

I ordered the fleet to fly to Eden-8, the coolest of the three worlds we had laid claim to. I liked this planet—hell, I liked them all. Eden-8 was covered by dense forests of towering trees. The planet was physically smaller than Earth, being no more than two-thirds the mass. There were oceans, but they were small and encircled entirely by densely tree-carpeted land. The xenologists among my staff assured me the trees grew to nearly a thousand feet high here because the gravity was less of a problem, and the atmosphere had a slightly higher content of carbon dioxide. It was a plant's paradise.

Less than a minute after I'd given the order to fly to Eden-8, Marvin paid me a visit. He was craning his cameras in every direction, taking in all of our expressions and attitudes. His black, segmented tentacles of metal were whipping and slapping the deck, a sure sign he was feeling agitated.

"Colonel Riggs? May I have a moment of your time, sir?"

"Sure Marvin," I said, "please follow along, I'm busy."

I walked past him and headed down a slanted passageway into the ship's central belly region. There, I was scheduled to meet up with yet another contingent of personnel from Jasmine's fleet. They were officially rejoining Star Force. I liked to personally witness the swearing-in process whenever I could.

"What's on your mind?" I asked Marvin when we reached the launch deck.

Marvin dragged himself after me urgently. His tentacles clattered on the metal deck, leaving long silver scratches behind him. I glanced back that way, and saw the nanites were healing the ship's wounds as fast as Marvin's strange body could make them.

"I would find it infinitely preferable to go to Eden-6, sir," he said.

I looked at him with upraised eyebrows. "Is that right? Am I safe in assuming this is because you left biotic pools of slime on that planet?"

"The most sophisticated of my Microbe colonies are located there, yes."

I sighed. "Marvin, that's their homeworld. They'll be fine. In fact, I would guess they'll be a lot better off without you poking and prodding at their tiny backsides."

"Your reference is imprecise. The typical microflora has a food intake and an exit for byproducts and waste, but I'm not sure this would qualify as a 'backside' since they do not, in most cases, independently propel themselves in any specific direction. Directional motion is often happenstance, due to the rippling action of defensive cilia—"

"Okay, okay," I said, waving my gloved hand at him. "My bad. What I meant was they deserve to live and die in the wild, not to exist solely for your entertainment."

"Oh."

There was an awkward pause. Marvin didn't even bother to refute my accusation. Wasn't every evil scientist supposed to give people a speech about how his efforts benefited the greater good? Marvin seemed to find such delusions unnecessary. He delved into the tiny lives of others purely for his own pleasure, and apparently felt no need to candy it up with a moral argument. Somehow, I found this disturbing.

The newly-pledged Star Force people lined up. I beamed at them, thrilled to see their numbers inflate my ranks. In most cases, they weren't allowed to keep their former rank. As a matter of course, I'd bumped up the veterans who'd fought with me out here on the frontier for so long and busted most of the new people back down to private. They weren't always happy about that, but they were soon eager to rebuild their reputations. I figured that starting off at the bottom always made a marine work harder. More importantly, this system kept my own loyal personnel at the top of the command structure. If Crow had planted a few shills in this group, they would not find themselves running anything until I was sure they were true to the cause.

The hold was about the size of a gymnasium. The recruits formed lines, and I walked among them. Each wore a spacer's black nanocloth uniform, a uniform that would forever remain sharply-cut and perfectly-creased. Most of them were male, but about a third were female. I stopped in front of the next and placed a marine private's single stripe on his shoulders. The insignias adhered themselves to the nanocloth and merged with it, becoming part of the uniform. Shining gold on black, the stripes really stood out.

"Sir, is your decision final?" Marvin asked as I shook hands and congratulated the newly sworn-in marine.

"All my decisions are final," I said. "Until I make a new one."

Marvin followed me as I walked down the long ranks in the main cargo hold, distributing insignias of rank. His limbs scrabbled at the deck like a nest of vipers. The recruits couldn't help but stare at him, but at a stern look from me, they set their eyes dead ahead again.

"Are you considering a change of course in the next few hours? Preferably before we reach Eden-8, I—"

"No, Marvin. I'm not. I assure you, however, we'll return to Eden-6 in due course. When we do, your puddles of slime will still be full of thriving Microbes."

"I think you may fail to grasp the significance of lost time in this circumstance, Colonel. A day represents a generation among the Microbes. We will have been gone so long, much of their conditioning and specialized breeding will be lost."

"Is that so?" I asked. I was about to pin a Fleet midshipman's symbol on a redhead's collar. I paused and glanced at Marvin. "Maybe that's a good thing."

"How could such a gross loss of effort be beneficial?"

"Living beings are supposed to determine their own purpose in life, Marvin. We're programmed that way."

"An interesting hypothesis. I would counter that your theory is unproven and unlikely."

"Listen," I said, tired of being badgered by a robot. I pinned the insignia on the redhead where it melted into her uniform. I shook her hand. We'd long since dropped the midshipman's anchor in favor of a golden comet, which now streaked across her lapel. "Excuse me," I said to her, "welcome home to Star Force."

"Thank you, Colonel Riggs," she said.

I turned on Marvin. "No more whining," I told him. "If you want to play with your Microbes again, you'd better come up with a valid reason for doing so. Give me a solid gain for Star Force, a tangible advantage that I can weigh against other concerns. Then you'll get whatever you want—an office. A laboratory and a staff, maybe."

I had so many cameras on me now, I couldn't count them all. "Really, Colonel Riggs?"

"Yes, now get out of here until you can make a substantial case for your pet project."

Marvin slinked away excitedly. I glanced after him once as he left the hold. I shook my head. It was good to see him energized about his work, but I wished he'd make his obsessions more useful to the cause.

I forgot about Marvin after that and swore in hundreds more new people. Sometimes, I thought I recognized a face. A few times, marines shook my hand warmly, claiming they'd been with me in one firefight or another. A few I actually remembered having met before.

In every case I gave them a hearty welcome home, whether I remembered them or not. I didn't like glad-handing, but it was necessary. Not only was it good for morale, it was good for my cause. Crow had splintered Star Force, and as far as I could tell, I was his only serious rival. Personal loyalty was a powerful motivator for any military organization, and I intended to use that to the fullest. I let them take shots of the ceremony with their handhelds and helmet optics. I gave out hugs and smiles like I was running for office back home. Perhaps, in a way, I was.

Jasmine and Sandra interrupted me as the crowd broke up. The recruits were heading back to their transports amid cheers and well-wishes. I took one glance over my shoulder at the approaching women, and knew there was trouble coming. At least they weren't fighting each other. But their expressions were worried—even nervous.

"Sir," Jasmine said, "we're in trouble."

I threw one last salute at the recruits as they mounted their ramps and passed through the coupling airlocks. I gave them a bullshit smile, then turned back to my staff. I marched with them toward the long, sloping corridor that led up to the bridge. Under my feet, the deck rippled and shifted—that worried me. The ship was reconfiguring itself for something.

"The nanites look frisky," I said. "Give me the short version."

"I took the liberty of ordering the bridge crew to prepare for a rapid departure," Captain Sarin said.

I stared at her for a moment, trying not to become annoyed. Miklos was still the second in command in this system. I could see already that Sarin was bucking for her old job back. Well, she hadn't earned that position yet in my mind. Maybe she would in time, and I had to admit she had been the best at ops, but I didn't want her to overstep her bounds right off. I almost admonished her, but nodded instead. I decided to wait until I heard what these two had to say.

I looked to Sandra next. She didn't seem to be trying to put Jasmine in her place, as I would expect. That cued me in.

"This is something big then. Very big. Am I right?"

"We don't completely know, sir," Jasmine said. "But there are transmissions coming in, through both the rings on either side of Eden's star. The signals going to Helios we don't have a report on. But we do have ships in the Thor system. They are monitoring the opposite ring, where the Macros came from last time. The signals—whatever they are—are going through the ring in the Eden system near Hel. Then the signal can be traced, vibrating the ring at the far end of the system."

"Which goes to an unknown system beyond the edge of our maps," I said showing my teeth for a moment. "What was it the old maps used to say about such points? 'Beyond here, there be dragons...' Well, that is discouraging news, and may well be a prelude to an attack. But I hardly think that—"

"That's not all, Kyle," Sandra said, speaking up for the first time. "There has been a report from the Worms as well. They came through the ring from the Helios side—just one ship, with a message."

I stopped marching toward the bridge. At this point, we stood near the entrance to the bridge itself. I could sense energetic movement up there. People knew something big was happening.

"What did they say?"

"We just had Marvin translate. It wasn't really necessary though. Anyone can understand their symbol language, once you get used to it. They sent their symbol for enemies, then the symbol for approaching or attacking. Lastly, they sent a pictograph of the stars in the Helios' sky."

I took a long second to digest that one. "Isn't that the one that means a count in the high hundreds?"

"Or even in the thousands."

Suddenly, I got it. "They aren't talking about the Macros, are they? They're talking about Earth ships. They have to be."

Sandra and Jasmine both nodded seriously. As we'd been talking, the women had lowered their voices. For some reason, when discussing possible approaching doom, it is part of human psychology to talk about it quietly.

I thought about this new situation for several seconds. Someone was sending signals through the Thor system again, possibly summoning more Macros or a new fleet of Lobster ships. We'd trashed them the first time, and we'd repaired our battle station. But it was nowhere near one hundred percent operational effectiveness. If they had another fleet, this would be an opportune time to strike.

Worse, it sounded like the Earth fleet was coming as well, on our opposite flank. I felt a bit sick inside, but tried not to let it show in my face. I think the women standing near me both knew, however. They'd been with me for so long, and seen too many terrible things while standing at my side. It was harder for me to fool them than anyone else I knew. Finally, I took a deep breath and stopped trying.

"This sounds bad," I said. "If it is Crow flying in after us, coming to avenge Decker, well, that's bad enough. But the Macros and Crustaceans too? How long do we have? Have you gamed it out in the holotank?"

"Not long," Jasmine said. "A week or less, I'd say. We can place scouts at the far side of both rings to keep a lookout, but that will only tell us when they're coming. I don't know if we can be ready in time."

I smashed my right fist into my left palm. "We have to know if both sides are really attacking at once, and which will arrive first. I refuse to split my defenses onto two fronts."

I turned to Jasmine and peered down at her. "I'm going to speed things up. Let's go to the bridge and open a general channel. I want to talk to every volunteer, every grunt and swabbie you brought with you in those transports."

She nodded, and the three of us walked onto the bridge together. A few hours passed before I made my announcement. During this time, we investigated the situation as best we could and read every incoming piece of data. We wargamed enemy positions and made calculated assumptions. By the time I set up my system-wide broadcast, we had a pretty good idea what was going on. It wasn't good.

"This is Colonel Kyle Riggs," I said loudly over the public address channel precisely one minute after I'd been hooked up and everyone had been given the one minute warning. They knew a major address was to begin, and they'd better listen to this one.

"I know that many of you are new to the Eden system," I said. "I want to thank you for coming out here to support Star Force. The people here on these worlds believe in a different kind of life, one without tyranny and backstabbing. We have no secret police, torture

173

booths or live floggings on TV. There is no Ministry of Trust, whose job it is to silence dissenters and spread lies. Instead, we have a set of beautiful, unspoiled worlds and a handful of determined defenders. We're all colonists now, whether we want to be or not."

I paused here, as there was scattered applause on the net and around me on the bridge. Everyone was staring at me intently. I pressed ahead, trying not to think of the gravity of the news I was going to impart to this faithful group.

"Unfortunately," I said, knowing it was a word every audience hated to hear from their leaders, "when a group lays claim to a jewel, or a set of jewels such as these fine worlds, there always seems to be a challenger to the claim."

I let that concept sink in for a moment before pressing ahead. As I paused, I signaled Jasmine. She worked the controls on the holotank, allowing the contents of it to be transmitted and duplicated on every bulkhead in the fleet. In most cases, it would only appear in two dimensions, rather than three, being formed by hard beads of nanites. It would have to do.

Before I went on, the scene was depicted clearly for everyone to see. The Eden system was in the center, with its hot, yellow sun burning. The tight circle of green worlds spun around the star. Further out were two rings, which led to two other star systems. I took a few moments to explain the positions of our enemies. I pointed out that as far as we could tell, there was nothing happening in either the Helios system or the Thor system—but there were grim warning signs in each.

"Over the past several hours, I've become aware of enemy movements and warning signs. We now believe two fleets are approaching Eden."

Jasmine tapped at the screen so fast her fingers were a blur. The woman was a virtuoso on the touchscreen. Two amorphous blobs like reddish clouds of blood appeared beyond the far rings on our three system diagram. One of those rings led to Alpha Centauri, where we believed Crow's fleet now lurked. On the other side, another blob of red was shown, hovering just beyond the water-moons of the Thor system.

"We believe the Macros are on the move again on the far side of the Thor system, where the Lobsters live on their three moons.

174

Frankly, I'm not too worried about these guys," I lied glibly, "as we've recently beaten them. They haven't had time to rebuild everything they lost last time. On the other side of us, however, there are more new contacts approaching. These are coming from the direction of Earth. We can only surmise they are Imperial ships."

My last sentence caused a buzzing to build up in my headset. I signaled to Sarin, and she cut out all cross traffic and let my signal dominate all others on the channel. I normally didn't like doing that, but it was the only way to get their attention and hold it. As we weren't yet in a pitched battle, I figured the most important thing was to get my message across. They could all gossip and second-guess me after I had made my speech.

"Due to the seriousness of these two threats against the system, I've decided to accelerate our swearing-in process. I want every recruit who can hear me now to stand up, and place his or her hand over their hearts."

I could not hear it, but I could imagine the startled thousands obeying my instructions. "Repeat after me, with witnesses: 'I do pledge my loyalty to Star Force. I will, to the best of my ability, defend Star Force and Earth from all enemies, foreign or domestic. I will follow the orders of my lawfully appointed superiors, and follow them to Hell and back, if necessary. Long live Earth, long live Humanity, and long live Star Force!'"

By the end of this speech, I knew I had them. Even on the bridge, where my staffers were standing and pledging along, the veterans around me were thrilling to my words. When I'd first made my announcements concerning the approaching enemy forces, there had been a period of shock, followed by whispering. Now, there were only ringing words being repeated by thousands of throats separated by thousands of miles of space. Inside our steel ships, we all stood and made our pledge.

"Now, let me read a piece by Gordon Dickson concerning the difficult task of all space-borne warriors: 'Soldier, ask not—now or ever, Where to war your banners go...'"

I read the entire poem to them, and even though it might not have been understood by all those that listened, they understood the spirit behind the words. The poem was a call to sacrifice without question. A call to die frozen in space for honor, if need be. By the time I was finished, none of them were whispering to each other. On the bridge around me, it was quiet enough to hear the nanites rustling in the walls.

"I now pronounce all who have heard this transmission and made this pledge to be members of Star Force. You have only one commander now: me. You're all members of Riggs' Pigs, whether you fly a ship with big ideas or hump along on the ground with a thousand pounds of gear on your back. Your deployment orders will be transmitted to you shortly. Riggs out."

I let Captain Sarin open the channels then, and listened to the cheering and the questions. I smiled. They were pumped up, and ready to follow me into battle. I only hoped I wouldn't let too many of them down this time.

-22-

After the glow of an uplifting speech fades, the reality of a huge workload always looms. Like a wedding ceremony, soaring oratory rarely bears much resemblance to what follows. I got my people working immediately. Fortunately, we had plenty of weaponry and battlesuits. We'd constructed somewhere around a half million of them for the Centaurs, expecting a huge ground battle against the Macros when we'd originally reconquered the lovely planets of Eden. With a few modifications, I was able to outfit every Star Force veteran and new recruit alike.

I was surprised to learn just how many of my reinforcements were new people. Apparently, they'd come from far and wide and begged to get into the transports. The civilian population had taken a hit due to Decker's bloodthirsty attacks, however. They'd started out with over thirty thousand civies, and we still had something in the neighborhood of twenty thousand to take care of. I saw this as a mixed blessing. They were more than welcome to join us out here on the frontier, but they had to be cared for—and I just didn't have the resources for that now.

Instead of landing them all on Eden-8, I ordered them to be transported and dropped off evenly among the three inner planets we'd claimed with the Centaurs' blessings. The transports spent a lot of valuable time doing this population shuffle, but I didn't see how I could play it any other way. Sarin and I spent some time discussing the issue. She wanted them to load up into their ships, while I'd wanted them planet-side.

"We can't let them just die up here in space," I said.

"They don't have to die. They can be parked in orbit on the far side of various worlds. That way, they can run if danger comes their way."

I shook my head in disagreement. "No. There is nowhere in this system to hide if the Macros roll in past our battle station and fire just one missile at every transport. They will be hunted down and destroyed. I want these people spread out on the ground. It's far harder to dig a population out of bunkers in a planetary atmosphere. They'll have cover and be dispersed."

"It's taking up too much time," Sarin complained. "We need those transports full of combat marines to win this fight."

"You brought them out here. I figured you would take more of an interest in their survival."

"I am, sir," she said. She stepped closer, and whispered her next words. I smelled her faint perfume, and enjoyed it. "Kyle," she said, "if we don't win this fight, they're all dead anyway."

I frowned. "Not if Crow wins. The worst they could expect would be transport back to Earth in chains."

She shook her head. "No. You saw Decker. It won't be any different when the next commander comes. They're rebels. Earth never wants to hear from them again."

I had a hard time believing life had become so cheap back on my homeworld. I guess that when you have billions, a few thousand seems less important. Out here, where humans were rare, I placed a very high value on every one of these people.

"Okay," I said, "but even if they do come and break us and capture this system, some will survive if we spread them out on the planets. There's nowhere else to run after this, Jasmine. They can't go to the next system, they'll be killed there as well."

Finally, she agreed with me. She'd been so focused on staying in their ships and running, I don't think she'd realized they'd come to the end of their journey. Live or die, Eden was the end of the line for her refugee train. There simply was nowhere else to go.

Although most of the population was unfit for duty, our ranks had swelled by a few thousand fresh recruits that with proper training and nanotizing, would someday make fine marines. I decided to issue every one of them a kit, with basic training in the use of modern weaponry, and put them down on the three worlds in strategic locations. They were to dig in and form a last-ditch defense of the civilians—should it come down to that. I even left them nanite injections and a steel chair on each planet—a steel chair with plenty of tough straps. I figured "what the hell". I'd started out with less. If all else failed, maybe they could rebuild upon our ashes.

As this fight was destined to be fought primarily in space, I focused our factory output on mass-producing more gunships. I had a stockpile of them anyway, more ships than I had qualified pilots. Gleaning the fliers from the new recruits quickly changed that, and we were able to loft over a hundred ships within a day or two. It wasn't enough, but it was better than nothing.

During this time of mad-scrambling and defense-building, I slept little and took pills now and then to keep going. Marvin tried to come to me and whine about his plans now and then, but I didn't give him a moment of my time. I'd heard enough about his muddy pools on Eden-6. I was sure they'd all dried out by now, or escaped into the oceans, but really, didn't much care.

It wasn't until I had a weak moment that Marvin managed to corner me. I'd been training the new pilots hard, and had just witnessed a doubly-fatal crash in space during maneuvers. Two new pilots had slapped their ships together and managed to kill one another. As a testament to the tough, barrel-like design of the ships, the vessels themselves were reparable—after the smeared organic contents had been scraped out.

For some reason, this minor training tragedy struck me the wrong way. Maybe it was the long hours, or a side effect of the pills I'd been taking to keep going. In any case, I retired to my anteroom and poured myself a beer. Soon, I found I'd had several, and I was feeling better, if less effective.

Marvin hit me up again at this precise moment. He played it smart this time, too. He'd waited outside my chamber, no doubt stepping from tentacle to tentacle in his impatience. When he finally peeped a single camera inside, he had another tentacle underneath his camera. Dangling from this low-slung tentacle was a fresh squeeze bottle of beer.

I eyed him and the beer, and I have to admit, it was love at first sight. I could see the bottle was cold. There were traces of vapor coming off it, and the exterior was covered in half-frozen droplets.

"Is that thing going to pop on me if I open it?" I asked.

"No sir. I've measured the chemical composition and the temperature precisely. If you open it and take a big drink, it should keep from freezing solid. It will however, form a slush-like material upon contact with the atmosphere."

I nodded. It was just the way I liked a beer—especially one of these bitter-tasting brews we had out here on the frontier.

"How did you get it to that precise temperature?"

"I pushed it out through the hull into space for several seconds. The hull nanites can be most accommodating when you know how to talk to them."

I grunted. If there was one thing Marvin knew, it was how to talk to other machines. Knowing I would regret it, I reached out my gloved hand for the offered beverage. Marvin scuttled forward, and somehow his entire hulking body was in my antechamber with me in a moment. I had that slushy beer in my hands by that time, however, and barely cared.

A bouquet of cameras studied me. "Are you enjoying your beverage, Colonel Riggs?"

I was, in fact, enjoying it very much. By the time I lowered the drink to regard him, half the contents were missing. "What do you want?"

"To help Star Force. To defeat all our enemies. To expand the knowledge of science."

I snorted. "You mean you want to indulge yourself in god-like fantasies. You know what I think, Marvin? I think you enjoy toying with these Microbes so much as a form of revenge. You like the idea of training tiny living beings to jump through hoops, just as we do with the nanites. This is all repressed hostility!"

I barely knew what I was talking about, but none of my tirade seemed to affect Marvin in any case.

"Colonel Riggs," he said, "I have a proposal. What if I could increase the effective size of your fleet by an order of magnitude within a week?"

"I don't know if we have a week left."

"Yes, but suppose we do? Would this not be helpful?"

"Of course it would," I stared at him, and he stared back, quietly. I knew then that he wasn't going to say anything else. He had me hooked, and we both knew it.

I took another long drag on his frosty little beer. I took a deep breath, and sighed. "Okay," I said, "what do you have for me? I warn you Marvin, this better not be bullshit."

"There is no bovine excrement involved, sir," he said seriously. "What I propose is to transform the Centaur volunteers under your command into effective space fighters. With proper training and a modified kit, Centaur troops could fill a great volume of space and do a great deal of damage to incoming enemy ships."

I laughed aloud then. "You're crazy. I always knew it, and here you come along with fresh proof."

"Could you clarify that statement, sir?"

I lifted a nanocloth-gloved hand and began ticking off the flaws in his plan. "First of all, the damned mountain goats don't like space. They don't like ships, and they don't like flying. They won't even submit to being nanotized."

"Excellent points, sir. But what if I could change a portion of their psychology?"

I blinked at him. My glove was still up, ready to tick off my next point. I frowned. "What? How?"

"By the application of a new organic agent I've been working on."

"You've got something from the Microbes that will change their *brains?*"

"Exactly."

"Is that even possible?"

"You've changed the brains of countless brainboxes personally. Reprogramming and rewiring structural synapses is not as easy in an organic subject, but it is not any more difficult than, for example, rebuilding a human foot using hamburger as a base material."

I peered at him thoughtfully. I was beginning to believe he was serious. Could it really be possible to erase an instinctual fear from the mind of a living being? I supposed that if you knew exactly where to look, and what synapse to destroy, and you had an impossibly tiny surgeon...

"It's freaky, but I'll give you that one," I said. "Still, I don't think the Centaurs will go for it. They've already refused to undergo nanotization treatments. Why would they agree to this abomination performed upon their very minds?"

"I've already asked them. In these delicate situations, I've found that careful wording is critical to receptivity in biotic subjects."

"They said yes?"

"Yes. They agreed to go through the process as I described it. I told them it would make them braver, and thus would confer honor upon any warrior who agreed to undertake the baths. After ruminating for many hours, they volunteered."

"How many volunteered?"

"As far as I can determine…all of them."

I sat back, stunned. The whole herd—*all* of the herds—were willing to undergo microbial treatments to change their mentalities? It was stunning.

"Okay," I said, nodding. "You've got me seriously considering this course of action. I don't like how you've circumvented the chain of command, but I'm going to overlook that."

"You often give speeches on the topic of personal initiative."

"Yes, yes," I said, "okay, I'm going to give you that one. But there are other practical considerations. How will we arm these new space-troops?"

"Correct me if I'm wrong," Marvin said, "but don't we have a large surplus of kits outfitted for Centaur ground troops? With rebreather units and nanocloth coverage, they could become vacuum-ready."

I squinted at him. "What about delivering these troops to the battlefield? We can't fit them into my gunboats."

"We have a surplus of empty transport craft at the moment, do we not?"

I nodded and squeezed the last drops out of my beer. Marvin's cameras zoomed in on my hands, my face—everything. I knew he was trying to determine the verdict from my slightest gesture. I tried hard not to let him know what I was thinking ahead of time. I hoped the suspense was killing him.

"All right," I said at last. "Set up your baths. Breed your microbes. I don't know how you will produce enough of them in time, but that's your problem."

"That will not be difficult. A tiny injection into the prefrontal cortex is all that's required. No more than a single milliliter of fluid per subject."

"You've thought of everything, haven't you Marvin?"

"Yes Colonel Riggs, I believe that I have."

-23-

The following days were a whirlwind of activity. We posted scout ships on the other side of the rings at either end of the Eden system. They had orders to sit just on the other side of the ring, watching for anything unexpected. These border guards were crucial, as they could give us advanced warning of any imminent attack. If anything showed up in the system, they had plenty of time to withdraw and transmit their report back in the Eden system.

So far, my scouts hadn't seen any enemy activity. It was quiet in space, but the rings were agitated. The increased level of traffic going through the rings was dramatic—and annoying. We could monitor the level and frequency of the traffic, but could not determine what was being said or who was talking. Perhaps saying these transmissions were bothering me was an understatement: They were driving me bananas. I knew that someone was talking to someone else about invading Eden—but I didn't have any details. We had the option to jam the signals at any time, but we were still trying to figure out what was being said. It was a maddening situation.

I didn't want to give up the chance to listen in on the chatter by jamming it and thus revealing our knowledge of the technology, but at the same time I didn't want them to keep communicating freely at our expense. It was a classic strategic dilemma, one I'd studied in books long ago in what now seemed like my distant past. Should a commander sacrifice a current tactical advantage in order to gain a future, potentially greater advantage? There was no perfect answer, and whatever the leader did, he was bound to feel stressed in the present.

Back in the Mideast wars, I'd been a reserve officer, and I'd done my tour. I'd read up on military strategy, as only seemed logical for any officer in a war zone. One legendary case I remembered vividly had once befallen Winston Churchill. In charge of defending England against Germany in a vicious air campaign, he'd been breaking the enemy codes for some time. After the war, members of the code-breaking group claimed they'd warned him of an attack against the city of Coventry, but in order to keep Germany from being tipped-off about the broken code, Churchill had not ordered the English defenses to center on the doomed city.

If Churchill really had made that fateful decision so long ago, I felt for him now, many long years later. Every day I delayed and didn't order the jamming of the rings, I felt a drumbeat in my head. I had no real idea what the final outcome of this delay would be. Although Marvin and a dozen others tried to break the code, we hadn't managed to do it yet, raising the grim possibility that I was letting my enemies converse without anything to show for it.

On the sixth day after Captain Sarin and her flotilla of refugees had joined us, I called a meeting of my senior staff to discuss our next move. I was no longer willing to let it all ride and hope for the best. I felt an overwhelming urge to *do* something.

"I suspect the weak link in our code-breaking department is Marvin himself," Miklos said. "He is also probably the only one who can achieve success."

"Explain," I said, making an impatient gesture. Miklos had a way of talking around things, and today I wanted direct answers.

"Well sir," he began, "the problem is simple enough: he's distracted with his primordial soup and the Centaurs he's been injecting with the vile stuff. Most of his test subjects have died by the way, Colonel."

"I'm well aware of that. Are you suggesting I call off his experiments? Is the code-breaking more important than the addition of thousands of space-borne infantry to our defenses?"

Miklos shrugged. "They are both hypotheticals. I'd rather deal in realities."

I glowered and reached for a cup of coffee.

"Sir," said Kwon, hunkering forward over the table. "I say we let the robot work on the Centaurs, not the codes. What good is the code? We know they are coming at us from both ends of the system. Who cares about the details? To win the battle, we need more troops. If the robot makes thousands of fighters, nothing else matters."

I nodded, appreciating Kwon's point of view. "Down to Earth advice as usual, Kwon," I said. "But you're correct as well, Miklos. We are dealing in hypotheticals. I recall, however, that the atomic bomb was once a crazy theory. So were jet aircraft and radar towers. The outcome of a major war is often affected by technological developments, and this one is no different."

Miklos looked tired, and somewhat annoyed. "So, what are we to do about it? What are your orders, sir?"

"I've been thinking, and I believe it's time to look outside the box for answers. I've come up with a plan that may greatly enhance our odds of survival in this coming conflict."

They all looked at me expectantly. Sandra was the only one that looked worried, the rest appeared merely curious. I guess that's because she knew me the best.

"I'm going to meet with the Blues again," I said. "I think it's pretty clear they're somehow involved in all these transmissions. If I go to their world and talk to them about their position in this conflict, I might be able to convince them to stop helping the Macros and whoever else they're talking to."

"Are you going to convince them with a few nukes, sir?" Kwon asked excitedly. "Nukes can be very convincing!"

I laughed. "I was hoping a more diplomatic approach would work."

Kwon frowned, sat back in his chair and crossed his arms. If it didn't involve blowing things up, it was all a waste of time to him.

"Okay," I said, looking around at the doubtful faces, "maybe it won't work. But that isn't the only purpose for going there. If I confront them and let drop certain pieces of data, they're likely to report it via the rings. This will give us two important advantages: First of all, if traffic spikes, we know the Blues are likely behind it. Remember, we can't detect the transmissions except at the rings themselves, so we can't be sure who's sending the messages. The

186

transmissions could be coming from the Centaurs, for all we know. But I think it's safe to assume the Blues are doing it."

Sandra leaned forward. I could tell right away she wasn't keen on my idea. "Is this scheme more important than the life of our top commander?"

"The Blues didn't harm me the last time I went down there. I think I'll be all right. Besides, I'm the only person in Star Force that's been altered to take the pressure on their world."

"Okay, let's say I buy that—which I don't. What's the second thing we can gain from this adventure, Kyle?"

"The second thing is a seed I plan to plant. I'll tell them something specific, giving us a marker. Then, when they retransmit it, we'll be able to look at the message with foreknowledge concerning the contents. In order to break any code, it helps a great deal to know what at least part of the message says."

Several heads were nodding, but not Sandra's. After the meeting broke up, she followed me into the corridor and grabbed my arm. I was too strong for her now, and broke free easily. She followed me toward my quarters, pouting.

"I don't want you to go down into that soup again," she said. "That planet almost killed you the last time. Now, the Blues are open enemies. They might decide to finish you off if their world doesn't do it for them."

"I don't think they operate that way," I said, removing my nanocloth crewman's suit and beginning to assemble my armor.

She watched me with growing alarm on her face. "What do you think you're doing?"

"I'm suiting up," I said, "I've got a destroyer waiting at the aft dock. Don't worry, I'll be back before you know it."

Sandra kicked me then, aiming for a sensitive region. Fortunately, I had my under-armor on and I was ready for the move. I grabbed her ankle and felt the shock run up my arm. A normal man would have broken the bones in his hand—if he could have moved fast enough to catch that flashing foot in the first place. In my case, I only grunted.

"You have to stop doing that," I said. "It's insubordination."

She hugged me a moment later, powerfully. I hugged her back, liking this treatment much better. I took a second to smell her hair and feel her body pressed up against me. I found both sensations pleasant. After a few long seconds, she disengaged herself from my arms and walked out.

"Fine," she said, turning around in the airlock, "go get yourself killed again. I don't care. I won't sit up all night for you. Not this time."

Then she was gone. I smiled after her, knowing Sandra was still Sandra. I knew she would wait up for me every night until I returned. It was comforting, in a way, to know someone back home cared if I came back or not.

The nanites usually took care of adjusting and sealing my form-fitting armor, but sometimes there was a fold that just didn't feel right. Smoothing out every stiff wrinkle I could find, I finished adjusting my armor and headed for the airlock.

The ship I had left waiting for me was the destroyer *Actium*, which had once been my command ship before we'd built *Nostradamus*. When I was finally in my ship and I undocked from the cruiser, I felt better. Getting into trouble on my own was a vacation for me. I enjoyed leaving all the troubles of my office behind for a while.

As I approached the Blue's homeworld, I transmitted a steady drumbeat of entreaties. They no longer had a screening group of Nano ships hovering over the planet's atmosphere to stop me. That was due to some of my trickery in the past, of course. I hoped they weren't still upset about that.

Actium was a fast ship, faster than anything else I had available other than the cruiser itself. That's why I'd chosen her. Flying it solo wasn't easy in combat, but on a scouting mission like this it should work out just fine.

One thing that worried me as I approached the Blues' homeworld was their general lack of response to my entreaties. I knew they were capable of receiving radio messages from us—after all, they were using more advanced tech to talk to our enemies right now via the rings. But they didn't seem terribly interested in striking up a conversation with me. I told myself it didn't matter and flew closer and closer to their gas giant. Soon, it filled my vision and seemed impossibly huge.

I reached the upper atmosphere, which amounted to a swirling mix of hydrogen atoms at the fringe of a vast sea of gases. I nosed the destroyer downward and drove it steadily deeper. Soon, the air thickened and space around me vanished.

I rode *Actium* down in the soup, and felt the hull begin to vibrate and occasionally groan as the exterior pressures built up. I ran the program I'd developed with the last ship I'd taken down, slowly folding the walls down toward me, reducing the size of the ship's cabin and thus increasing the internal pressure and thickening the hull. The nanites flowed overhead like silver water, forming and reforming the curved walls as they adjusted to the building forces outside.

I planned my diplomatic speech during the long descent toward the inhabited layers of their atmosphere. Every layer I penetrated seemed like a permanent blanket that wrapped around this murky world. I told myself I would *insist* they speak with me. It would be easier to find them this time, as I now knew where they glided and swam in their oceans of gas.

Just like the last time, the ride was pretty uncomfortable until I got to a depth of about nine thousand miles. Down there, the windshear of the upper layers was gone, and the pressure seemed to level out a bit. The environment at this depth was calm and even the temperature was reasonable.

I had *Actium* form an audio device to talk to the Blues. The bassoon-like instrument was half-megaphone and half-computer. Through it, I was able to blow vibrations into their winds and capture their attention. I still wasn't sure why they didn't use more advanced communications technology when dealing with us, but I didn't much care why. I just wanted to get them talking.

Eventually, after sending out enough whale-calls, I received an answer: "Why do you disturb us, dense-thing?" asked a melodious voice.

"I'm Colonel Kyle Riggs," I said. "May I ask who you are?"

"I am...*Beneficence*."

An interesting name, I thought. I knew from experience that the Blues were named for their natural behavioral traits. I told myself I should be happy this guy's name wasn't something like *Irritability* or *Pointless Rage*.

"I'm not the machine you see before you. It's merely a vehicle. I'm inside this ship, and I'm biotic like you."

"You insult me by suggesting you are in any way similar to myself."

I frowned. Beneficence my ass, I thought. *Prissy* might have been a better name.

"I'll come out of my ship and meet with you, if you like," I said.

As the Blues were essentially gaseous in nature, they considered us to be more or less on the level of rocks. Blues lived their lives as organized clouds, and frequently shared their body mass with one another. They mixed gases and gauzy aerogels when coming into contact with each other as a matter of course. It was vaguely creepy, but they really liked to *taste* a newcomer and share part of themselves physically with anyone they met.

"If you must," Beneficence said.

Muttering about ungracious hosts, I wriggled out of the airlock, which was about the size of a manhole now that *Actium* had compressed herself down to withstand the atmosphere. Once floating outside, I was promptly assailed by Beneficence. The process was like being felt-up by an air compressor.

When the being was quite finished, I coughed as politely as I could and resumed our conversation. "I'm here to ask you to join us in the coming conflict."

"I find you distasteful. The molecules reeking from your form are universally unpleasant."

"Yeah?" I asked, trying to control my temper. "You stink too. But let's get down to business, shall we? Are you in charge of making any kind of group decision for your people? Should I talk to someone else?"

"I doubt another of my kind would subject themselves to your disgusting essence."

"Well, how would they know—"

"I've taken the precaution of singing about it. The message will be repeated and resung until it rolls around the world and back again."

"That's great," I said. "Do you know anything about the robots your people built and sent up above the clouds to plague the rest of the universe? Or are you as ignorant as you are rude?"

"You came here to cast insults and demands? Striking. Discrediting."

Something in my question had shocked the cloud-being. I was glad about that, and wished I knew exactly what it was so I could say it again with more vigor. I took a deep breath on my respirator and tried to control my temper. For all I knew, the rest of the Blues would avoid me now, because this joker had told them I smelled really bad. In that case, I had to get some kind of valuable communication going with him, because it might be my last chance. I didn't have weeks to hang out down here and become touchy-feely with their culture.

"Look, Beneficence, I want to ally with your people against your lost robots. Billions of lives are at stake, including your own."

"Lost robots?"

"The Macros," I said, explaining what I was talking about until we were both clear on the topic.

"We have not lost them," Beneficence said at last. "We know precisely where they are."

I thought about that, and narrowed my eyes within my helmet. I had a growing suspicion this Blue was hostile toward me in a personal way. My mind had also begun converting the suspicion they were using the rings as transmission systems into a certainty.

"You don't like us, do you?" I asked. "You aren't a random being, you were sent here by your superiors to be rude to me. I get it now. You aren't an emissary, you're an insult."

"*I* am an insult?" asked the cloud, its voice rising. The translation system didn't do so well with inflections. It could only raise or lower the volume of a statement. The gasses around me, however, had begun to stir. I could feel bumps and currents. I suddenly felt like a kite on a windy day, instead of a diver floating above a calm seabed.

"Yes," I said. "What don't you like about me, other than my flavor?"

"You are arrogant—almost to the point of absurdity. You come here into our universe and disturb our peaceful seas with your stench. You dare to destroy that which we created—as if you are the superior species."

There was a lot of anger and resentment in that statement. I took a second to mull over my response. "When I came here the last time, your people expressed guilt about having released machines beyond your clouds to plague the rest of us. We have done nothing but defend ourselves against your creations. In fact, your creations have turned against even you."

"Incorrect!" shouted the being. "You shall see. We are not helpless. We will not sit here, awaiting your ships and bombs. We're not at your mercy any longer. Now go, before we forget ourselves in a forgivable act of vengeance!"

I had the sense then, for the first time, that there were others here. I wasn't meeting a sole being, but a crowd of them. They nosed the ship, making it bob and roll, its stabilizers fighting to keep an even keel.

Gone from my mind was all concept of making these beings see reason. They were angry because of earlier events. I'd blown up their screen of Nano ships, having led them off like the Pied Piper to be destroyed by the Macros. I could tell now this had really pissed them off. I guess they'd felt tricked and used—and in a way, they had been. But they were the ones who had built the damned machines in the first place.

"Know this, people of Eden-12," I said, "you released abominations of metal upon the rest of us. You can't expect the other biotic species in this star system to die without a fight. Nor can you expect to survive, if we label you as an enemy. Therefore, I'll warn you now: if the Macros come again to the Eden system and attack, we will not direct our weapons toward them. Instead, we will destroy the brain of this enemy. We will rain fire down upon this world until every shred of atmosphere is blown away, and nothing but the molten core remains. This planet will be reduced to a cinder bubbling in space, with nothing living left upon it."

Even as I spoke, I'd been wriggling my way back into my ship. I felt a tugging, as if invisible fingers grasped at my suit. I was glad for my nanotized muscles and for every Microbial bath I'd undergone at Marvin's urging. I managed to escape their grasping tendrils of gases and gels. I buttoned up the ship and ordered her to sail aloft.

Actium struggled at first. It was as if a thousand hands had grabbed her hull and tried to hang on. In the end the ship was too strong however, and broke free. I sailed up and up, not daring to relax until I reached open space again.

192

As I returned to the inner planets, I gazed back at the retreating brownish-green sphere that was the Blues' homeworld. Had I just declared war upon another species? Had they given me any choice?

Troubled, I went back to my reports and informed Star Force that my diplomatic mission had failed.

-24-

After I'd rejoined the fleet, I monitored the alien traffic using Marvin's mysterious apparatus. The rings sang like high-tension wires all the next day and night. I monitored the activity, and had Sarin graph it for me on our shared console.

"See here?" I said, pointing with a gloved finger to a red line that rose above the others on the displayed graph. "This spike in transmissions occurred immediately after my visit to their homeworld. I'm sure it represents them calling the Macros. The transmission is only hitting the Thor ring. They don't send anything the other way to the Helios system until hours later."

"Yes," Sarin said, studying the data. "I can see the point where they begin transmitting through the Helios ring. It's right after another series of vibrations at the Thor ring. See, this blue line represents the Helios activity. Nothing is there until after the second spike."

"So, this seems like a clear scenario. They heard my planted threat, then sent something out to the Macros. Once they heard back from the Macros, they talked to the other side—to Crow's forces."

Sarin looked at me very seriously. "That's a lot of guesswork, Colonel. We still have no idea what was said. We don't even really know who said what."

"I know," I said, "all we have is a timeline of events, and a lot of conjecture."

I paced around the console. When I'd circled it twice, I turned back to it and began tapping. A theoretical repositioning of ships began. "Here's what we're going to do," I said. "We'll pull our ships from the Thor ring—we'll pull back everything supporting the battle station for now, except for a few scouts to keep an eye on the Crustaceans. Then, we'll station a squad of ships over the Blue's homeworld. They'll just sit out there, silently, in far orbit. In the meantime, the bulk of our forces will mass here at the Helios ring."

Miklos walked quietly over and joined us. "This is a significant change to our strategy, sir."

"Indeed it is," I agreed. "And we'd better all pray tonight I've guessed right. Because we're betting the farm on this one."

Miklos blinked at me. "Must we bet the entire farm, sir? Perhaps we should only bet—ah, a few animals or a field."

I laughed and shook my head. "We can't win that way. Hell, we might lose no matter what we do. But if we get hit from both ends at once, and split our forces to face these two enemies evenly, we'll get mowed for sure. We have to put everything down at Helios ring. We'll set an ambush for Crow's Imperial fleet. When they come, they have to be hit so hard from the outset that they turn around and run."

Miklos pursed his lips. Sarin's eyes were big and dark. She didn't say anything.

"Sir…" Miklos began.

"I know, I know," I said. "It sounds kind of crazy. But I'm working from more than a hunch. I think the Blues really only care about one thing, and that is their own gassy rear ends. They've been cowards from the start, and I'm betting they'll stay that way. They just transmitted to the Macros a cease and desist order. I'm pretty sure of that. We'll keep a fleet near them to keep them running scared. That's a small price to pay to neutralize an entire armada on a second front."

"You believe they are talking to Crow, also?"

"Of course," I said. "Either that, or Crow is talking to the Lobsters. It doesn't really matter. We haven't got enough force to cover everything. To win, we have to gamble."

"But sir," he said, giving it one last try, "sometimes, your hunches don't work out quite the way you planned."

I glowered. "I know that. If you have a better plan, I'd like to hear it now."

That was my trump card. They all tried, but no one could come up with anything else that gave us a good chance at victory. Sure, none of us knew what was going to happen. But in war, you had to play the odds. I'd laid my cards on the table, and we were going to see how it all played out very soon.

After another hour of watching my staff do some obligatory soul-searching, I tapped the scenario we'd laid out into a loading queue. The orders were automatically dispersed to every ship and they began moving the moment they got them. What had been a battle plan had neatly turned into reality.

Sandra caught up with me on the way back to *Actium*. I winced at her touch, fully expecting a tirade. What I got instead was a weary smile.

"Your plan is the best we can come up with, Kyle," she said. "The others don't like it, because it's not perfect. But that's just too bad."

She looked as pretty as ever, but her eyes were half-closed.

"You didn't sleep while I was gone, did you?" I asked.

"No."

I pulled her up against me and walked toward *Actium's* airlock.

"Come with me," I said. "I'm going to go down to Eden-6 to kick Marvin in the butt. He's got to stop killing Centaur volunteers and start turning them into super-goats."

She balked at the airlock. "I'm not going to get any sleep on this trip either, am I?" she asked.

"I swear, I'll let you have a good rest. At least eleven hours' worth."

"It takes fourteen hours to get to Eden-6."

"Yeah? Well, the other three hours are for both of us. We need to get reacquainted."

Sandra snorted, but followed me into the ship.

Fourteen hours later, we were both well-rested and in a much better mood. As we eased into orbit over Eden-6, I looked down upon the heavy clouds. Here and there, the cloud-layer had burned through enough to reveal the endless sparkling seas underneath. There was no land visible through any of those holes in the cloud-layer—just ocean.

"Such a big world," Sandra said. "Nothing but islands and beaches. I like the place, even if there isn't much in the way of direct sunshine."

I nodded, staring. "I see something out there, moving out of orbit."

"I don't see it—oh, you mean that silver thing?"

"Actium, display Eden-6 and our orbital surroundings. Identify all moving vehicles."

The ship did as I asked, and we moved to the command chamber. We took our chairs and strapped in. There were several vessels in the region. They were quickly located, displayed, and identified by *Actium*. Most of the ships here were transports. There were seven of them, all of which had brought colonists to various landing sites. I wondered vaguely how the civilians were enjoying their new environments. I imagined it was quite an adjustment for them, but it had to be better that sitting in space.

There was one contact that didn't show up as green, however, and had no identifying trace of words next to it on the display. It showed as a faint golden-yellow color. I looked at the vehicle as it streaked away to the far side of the planet.

"Actium, follow that unknown contact."

The ship lurched and the display swam sickeningly as we changed course. Sandra and I clutched the arms of our chairs and strained against the restraining arms.

"Open a channel, Actium," I said.

"Channel open."

"Hailing unknown ship: Identify yourself."

There was no response, but the contact swept quickly around to the far side of Eden-6.

"It's moving even faster, Kyle."

I frowned. "Marvin, is that you? Respond immediately."

"Oh, hello Colonel Riggs. I didn't know you were in the area."

"Yes you did," I said.

"No, sir. You did not give prior warning concerning your visit."

"Yeah? Well, stop running away."

"Do you trust me, Colonel Riggs?"

I frowned at the console for a moment. What was this crazy robot up to now?

"Well…within reason," I said.

"Good. Let's start from that positive basis. I'll make my report from Eden-7. I'm quite busy now, you see—"

"Marvin," I said, cutting him off. "My admission of trust in you does not mean my orders can be ignored. You will stop and reverse course back to Eden-6. And, you'll tell me right now who gave you authorization to rebuild yourself into a ship."

"You did, sir."

"That's not how I remember it."

A recording of my own voice came over the channel. "Get it done, Marvin. I don't care how, just make it happen—"

"I see," I said. "You took that order as a countermand to all previous orders against structuring your body into a vehicle?"

"My body has always been vehicle, Colonel. Since the beginning, when I was downloaded from the Centaur database and you so kindly provided me with a large brainbox and limbs for locomotion, I've been capable of self—"

"Yeah, look—oh, it doesn't matter. Shut up about that. Let's talk seriously. I'm heading down to your ponds. Meet me there in ten minutes, with a full report ready to go, or I'll kick dirt into them."

"That would be extremely counterproductive, Colonel. At this delicate stage, the microbial colonies are—"

"Right," I said. "So make sure you aren't late. And be prepared to explain why you tried to run off when you realized I'd arrived for a surprise inspection."

"You characterization of my actions is both hurtful and unnecessary."

"And also dead-on. Be there, Marvin. Riggs out."

We landed at the planet's only working spaceport. It was on the same island where Kwon had built his bunker and Marvelena had been blown up. In fact, it had recently been named Bunker Island by the new locals. There were colonists here along many of the beaches, but none of them were in sight on Bunker Island. The place looked deserted. I wondered what this place would look like in the future, when there were millions of inhabitants instead of a few thousand.

As we stepped out of the stuffy canned-air interior of *Actium*, we took off our helmets and sucked in the fresh sea breezes. The surf was up, and the waves were crashing on the beach at our backs.

The sky was overcast as usual, but it was humid and slightly too warm. We pressed forward into the foliage of tall grasses that dominated the island's central region and followed the path up past the original bunker.

There, we stopped dead. All around the bunker were pools of slimy brown liquid. There had to be a hundred of them. Marvin had cut down the thick stalks of grass and kept digging more and more ponds. I could see worker machines tearing out the taller grass-forests farther upslope, and sculpting fresh pools on every hillock overlooking the bunker. There were pumps everywhere as well, with black hoses connecting the pool to one another.

"Kwon!" I shouted, expecting him to come up out of the bunker. Since I'd launched this project on his outpost island, I'd let him take up residence here again. I knew he liked it, and I hadn't expected this level of destruction to the environment.

Kwon didn't appear. I frowned and marched forward. I'd donned my armor before exiting the ship, and my feet sank nearly a foot deep with every stride in the mushy ground. I flipped on my repellers and glided over the scene instead to make better time.

"This looks awful, Kyle," Sandra said. "Did you give Marvin permission to do all this?"

"I guess I did—at least in his twisted little mind. Why don't you go down to the beach area and find Kwon?"

She looked at me for a second, then swept her eyes over the scene. "You're worried what else we might find here, aren't you?" she asked. "You're trying to get rid of me, but that's okay, because I don't want to see what Marvin's been doing anyway. Call me if you need me."

She left me then, and I pressed ahead with a grim expression on my face. I found Marvin way out in the back of the place. Here, things were worse. The pools not only dotted the once lovely landscape, they also stank. I could see bones in several of the pools, along with scraps of floating fur and the curve of a protruding horn now and then. Marvin had been feeding the ponds with the Centaur dead.

Marvin's chassis was bigger than it had been the last time I'd seen him. He could no longer fit into a ship, I was sure of that. He *was* a ship. This realization didn't improve my mood.

"Marvin, can you explain why you had to turn this place into a disgusting swamp? And while you're at it, why you felt the need to build flight capacity into your physical form? I've forbidden that on multiple occasions."

"Colonel Riggs!" Marvin said, sliding forward with whipping tentacles. Something he'd been holding onto splashed down into the pool under his bulk. I only caught a glimpse of it, but it seemed to be a smallish Centaur corpse. "I'm so glad you've come. I've made so much progress. The experiment was a grand success—in the end."

I slowly glided around him, letting my humming suit fly me over the ponds. The water rippled and the crusty scum on the top of the one Marvin crouched upon spread open to reveal the inky water beneath.

"Careful!" Marvin admonished me. "This is the one. This pool has produced the exact serum necessary. A dozen generations of Microbes have given their all to create the waters below us."

It looked like dirty, disgusting slime. I wrinkled my nose. Could this vile substance really be the salvation of this entire star system? What a strange twist of fate it was, if it was true.

Then I noticed something as I gazed down into the pool more deeply. I squinted, looking past the ripples and reflections. "What the hell?" I asked. "Are those *baby* Centaur corpses, Marvin?"

"Well, that is a definitional distinction which could be argued with," Marvin said. "They are post-birth, and many of them have been weaned. I believe the proper term for animals in this stage of—"

That's as far as he got before I grabbed him. Grabbing Marvin wasn't an easy thing to do on the best of days, but today he was bigger and more variegated than usual. There were stalks, bulbs, cameras and tentacles everywhere—lots of tentacles.

I was beyond angry. Somehow, seeing that he'd experimented on Centaur young, using my name to perform his abominations, threw me into a rage. I grabbed the nearest tentacle, which terminated in a floating camera eye. I ripped it loose by the root and tossed it back over my shoulder. It twirled around twice before splashing down in a distant pool of muck.

"Colonel Riggs? Are you experiencing a malfunction?"

I didn't answer. I just kept ripping pieces off him and throwing them away. Marvin backed up and his tentacles curled and swirled protectively. I didn't care. They soon grappled me, but they couldn't stop me. I was a nanotized marine, veteran of numerous Microbial baths and wearing a combat-ready exoskeleton. I was also seriously pissed-off.

After I tore away seven or eight of his thrashing limbs, he began to fly upward. I went with him. He tried to spin around and dislodge me, but I hung on. We soon rose above the treetops.

"This is highly irrational behavior, Colonel. I have performed the function you requested. I have been successful."

"You also knew it was time to run when I showed up," I growled, ripping loose one of his tacked-on gravity repellers. This change to his structure made the whole thing unbalanced, and we went into a spin. I clung to him, reaching for another gravity repeller unit. "You weren't supposed to fly, and you didn't have to kill their babies. You did it just to find out what would happen. Well, I'm giving you a new lesson in animal behavior!"

After I removed a second gravity repeller on the same side, we began falling at a forty-five degree slant. The endless ocean appeared to zoom back out of the hanging mists of Eden-6 as we plunged back toward it. I snapped my visor down, suspecting I was about to get a mouthful of seawater.

"You're accusations are unfounded. I had to generate a disgust response and powerful fear responses. Employing heuristic problem-solving, I studied the brain activity and trained the Microbes to invade and alter that portion of each subject's synaptic web—"

We hit the water, and Marvin's excuses were swept away with the crashing impact. I almost lost consciousness—but hung on. A minute or so later, I was moving under my own power again. I looked for him and spotted him, crawling on the rocky bottom. He was no longer able to fly or swim under propulsion. He dragged himself uphill toward dry land with whipping arms that churned up a great deal of debris from the seabed. Watching him, I was reminded of a desperate starfish caught on an open beach.

I looked after him and thought about burning a hole in his brainbox. I had a laser unit on my suit—but I hadn't yet used it. I could end the entire adventure that was Marvin right now. All the horrors and all the wonders. Was it the right thing to do? I wasn't sure.

Maybe he knew what I was thinking about, because he was really trying hard to get back out of the water and onto dry land.

I heaved a deep breath and found that my initial rage had passed. I engaged my repellers and glided after him.

He ducked when my gauntleted hand reached down to take hold of yet another tentacle. I grabbed again, and caught him this time. I lifted and pulled him toward the beach. After a few seconds, he stopped struggling and let himself be dragged along. Every camera he had was looking at me. They snaked around my helmet to gaze into the visor that covered my face. I don't know what expression he saw there. Disgust, disappointment—depression? Something like that. After a few minutes, we reached the beach and his cameras retracted to a safer distance.

"Thank you for pulling me out of the water, Colonel Riggs. I have internal injuries, and seawater has entered cracks in my aft brainbox. I've already lost a portion of my data storage. Many astrophysical mapping files are missing."

I heaved a sigh. "Do you have backups?"

"Yes, fortunately. Each of my sub-brainboxes holds a compressed backup of my neural chain. Still, it is disturbing to lose one of them."

"Yeah. Kind of like dying, I guess. Creatures don't like dying, Marvin. Do you have any empathy in that regard? Can you understand you need to avoid killing the brains of others, because you would not want to lose your own? Because the fate is so terrible, we don't wish it upon others?"

Marvin was quiet for a long time. I watched as seawater leaked out of various subsystems. His entire body was listing to the left. He began heading inland, and the left side of his body had to be dragged over the beach, leaving a deep groove in the sands. I followed him, walking at his side while he struggled toward the trees.

"Was your attack meant to instruct me, Colonel?" he asked.

I blinked, considering his question. "Maybe," I said. "Benjamin Franklin used to say that pain was highly instructive. Did you experience pain and panic, Marvin?"

"I did."

"Well, I hope that you learned something from the ordeal. In any case, I'm taking you off this project. I'm ending it. I don't want you to do any more experiments on sentient beings. Whatever you've developed—well, that's as far as it's going to go. And you're also forbidden to build flying structures for yourself. You know that. Are we clear, Marvin?"

"Perfectly clear, sir. Crystal clear."

I glanced at him. I couldn't help but wonder what was going on inside that big, strange brain of his. "Okay. Let's reattach enough of your limbs to allow easier locomotion, then you can show me what you've achieved. We'll skip the messy description of how you got to this point—just show me the most successful results."

"Spoken like a true manager, Colonel."

I narrowed my eyes at him. Were those bitter words? It was hard to tell with Marvin. I didn't know what to make of him today. Maybe he felt abused and underappreciated. If that was the case, he'd just joined a very large club.

-25-

Kwon showed up on a flitter. He met me at the beach, and hailed me. Marvin pouted and reassembled himself.

Kwon climbed down from the pilot's chair and stared at Marvin. "What happened to your robot?"

"He had a malfunction," I said. "But he's better now—I think."

Kwon looked around the island with critical eyes. "This place is disgusting. I never come here now. You want to see the new troops in action?"

"Yeah," I said. "Let's see what Marvin has managed to do. We'll go pick up Sandra first though. Marvin, you stay here. I'll send someone to pick you up in a few hours. Load up all the serum you have that will work and shut down the rest."

"Should I exterminate all the colonies, Colonel?"

I considered, and shook my head. Marvin had cannibalized members of one species to breed another. It was grotesque, but in a way, he was just a type of farmer or animal-breeder. I'm sure he looked at it that way. Did the relative intelligence of the species involved raise it to the level of a moral outrage? I guess in my mind it did.

"No. Let them go if you have to, into the sea. Or let them live in their ponds with your equipment supporting them. Just don't expect to come back here for a long time. I'm shutting down this lab of yours."

Without another word, Marvin dragged himself down the beach. I called after him and he stopped.

"Marvin," I said. "I've got another more important task for you. I know you like tinkering with biotics, but if we don't break the code the Blues are using, we're all going to die in this star system. For now, that has to take precedence. Okay?"

"I hope that task won't trigger any intense emotional responses," he said. His tone was as prim and precise as always, but I was sure he was feeling sorry for himself.

"It shouldn't Marvin. I'll send a ship for you in a few hours."

We parted ways, and Kwon flew me low over the waves along the beach.

"You kicked his ass, didn't you?" Kwon asked.

"Yeah."

"Was it fun?"

I nodded. "It felt good at the time."

Kwon chuckled and stopped the flitter. We hovered over the beach and the crashing waves.

I looked back toward the forest in the center of the island. Had I screwed up? Was Marvin going to be bitter, seeking revenge? In a way, that robot was a species of one. An ally on my long list of allies, and possibly one of the most helpful ones. He was also ghoulish and extremely annoying at times.

I noticed we'd stopped flying and were now circling above a single spot. I turned to Kwon, who craned his big head over the side of the flitter and stared downward. I leaned over my side, and saw Sandra down there in the water. She was nude, and swimming. She looked up at us and gave us both the finger.

Kwon chuckled again. I slapped his shoulder and he landed the flitter on the beach. When Sandra had some clothes on, she climbed into the back of the ship and we took off again.

"Where are these super-Centaurs, Kwon?" I asked.

"They're on another island. Marvin sort of took over this one, and as his experiments grew stranger over the last week or so, we set up camp for the Centaur volunteers just south of here."

We flew to a second island, this one centered around a single conical mountain. It looked as if it had once been an active volcano to me. We landed and before we even touched down, I saw them.

Centaurs flew in formation over the waves. There were hundreds of them, moving in organized companies. They were tightly-grouped, and rode on oval-shaped versions of the flying

205

skateboard systems I'd devised long ago when we first began assaulting Macro cruisers with infantry.

"Wow," Sandra said. "I'm impressed already. Look how close they are, and how they fly. If they can take riding in a transport to battle, I think they might be able to do this, Kyle."

I nodded my head and stared. "What kind of kits did you give them?"

"Nothing special," Kwon said. "Really, we just gave them the same basic system you built for us long ago. The skateboards are longer, more like ovals now. That's to make up for having four legs. The change made them more stable in air or space."

I glanced at him. "Space? Have they been tested in space?"

"Oh yeah. That's why we called you. They're not much use flying around down here."

"They each have a laser, a vacuum suit and propulsion," I said. "What about grenades?"

"Ah," Kwon smiled. "That is where we made a little change. They each carry one grenade, a nuke of course. But this one is different. We made it especially for the Centaurs."

We climbed out of the flitter and Kwon showed me the new equipment. I frowned when I saw it, but I could not doubt its effectiveness. Nor could I deny that it fit the temperament of the troops that would wear it.

Sandra, however, saw it differently. "What is this?" she asked, handling the cylindrical device with care.

Kwon stumped forward and tapped the red contact at the tip. "See here? When armed, this nosecone-thingie will detonate if it makes a hard impact. Sort of like a dumb bomb."

"Why do we need dumb weaponry?"

Kwon held up a thick finger. "Ah-ha, good question. They are not dumb, you see, because the Centaurs are their brains. And their delivery systems. The whole sled-device they ride on can be viewed as a delivery system for this payload."

Sandra stared at each of us in turn. "Are you telling me you're putting bombs on these troops, then ordering them to fly into enemy ships?"

"Exactly," Kwon said.

"*No*," I said. "That's *not* what we'll tell them. We'll tell them how the systems work. Then they can decide what they want to do with the weapons they have—when the time comes."

Kwon lit up. "Very clever, Colonel. I like your idea better."

Sandra looked troubled, I was frowning as well. Only Kwon seemed unperturbed by this arrangement. We were giving a team of fanatics what amounted to suicide-vests, hoping they would get a bright idea in combat and take out enemy ships. It was diabolical, but I also suspected it would be highly effective.

"Kwon? How many of these Centaurs are we going to be able to get into the ships? How many kits and altered troops do we have?"

"Give us a day or two, and we will stuff twenty thousand of them into your transports, sir."

Twenty thousand, I thought. I didn't know what to say. They were like our answer to the Macro missiles—intelligent flying bombs. I felt both invigorated, as the odds of our winning the coming battles had just risen dramatically, and sickened with the knowledge of the carnage we were trying to release.

I watched the Centaurs train and drill for hours. They were good. Not as good as my marines, but very good for raw recruits. They didn't seem to fear their suits, flying, nor even death. They flowed in streaming masses, riding their skateboards at top speed. They occasionally collided with the waves or one another, and there were serious injuries. But this didn't stop the rest of them, it didn't even slow them down.

I had no doubt after observing them that they would charge the enemy fleet without any thought of their own personal survival. What more could a commander want?

"Sir," Kwon said, hurrying up to me. "I have an urgent call from Captain Miklos."

I had removed my helmet and walked out of the waves to work with the Centaurs. I'd been watching the newly trained troops closely, shouting suggestions to their leaders, both human and native. The plan was different than it had been when I'd used the Centaurs as invasion troops to retake the habitable Eden worlds. At that time, I'd had one marine lead every company of a hundred Centaurs. These troops were more organized, and now I used veterans from within their own ranks to lead them. I made sure the officers of each company had seen combat against the machines back on Eden-11. This upset their system of chieftains and sub-leaders, but I didn't care. Being good at butting heads back home didn't make you a space marine in my outfit.

I put my helmet back on and opened the command channel. Miklos sounded agitated.

"Sir? Colonel? Are you listening, sir?"

"Talk to me, Miklos."

"The Macros, sir—more than hundred ships so far have come out of the far ring in the Thor system. They are massing out there."

I felt a cold, sick feeling. Another full fleet? So soon? What did the Macros have on the far side of that ring? As always, not knowing what we truly faced was terrifying. We'd destroyed a huge fleet only weeks ago, and yet they'd sent another, bigger one. Was the entire war hopeless? Were we all fooling ourselves?

I pushed aside these defeatist thoughts and walked out of the sea toward the nearest flitter. I figured I'd just run out of time for inspecting new troops.

"How long will it take the Macros to hit our battle station, if they move now?" I asked.

"About two days, sir. They have no momentum. They're moving cautiously, massing up the entire fleet at the far ring before advancing."

"What about traffic at the rings?"

"There's plenty of it, sir. It's spiked since the Macros arrived."

I cursed quietly. The Blues seemed to be calling my bluff. Maybe my threats had backfired. Maybe they'd called the Macros immediately when I'd talked big about bombing their homeworld. It was also perfectly possible that they'd been coming all along, and my words had had no effect on their plans. There was no way of knowing right now.

"All right," I said, "keep watching them, Miklos. I'm flying back out to the fleet. And I'm bringing reinforcements. I want every transport that isn't full of marines already to head to Eden-6. I have twenty thousand new volunteers ready to load up and ship out."

"Twenty thousand, sir?"

"That's what I said. Riggs out."

All the way back up to the fleet I felt sick inside. They were coming, and everything I'd done to persuade the Blues to stop them had failed. Worse, it might have backfired. I felt like a fool.

When I boarded my command ship, I was greeted by an armed and armored marine. The fleet was on full alert now. The enemy was in sight of our longest ranged scanners, this was no drill. I flashed my ID transmission to the marine guard and moved on to the command deck. The holotank had only two staffers standing around it, staring. The situation displayed showed only the Eden system, which was empty except for our bustling little fleet of ships. Soon however, that would change.

I walked into the conference chamber, and was met by a dozen sets of anxious eyes. Only Miklos looked bored. Jasmine immediately tapped up a multi-system display on the conference table without having been asked. I smiled at the twisted lips Miklos showed as she did this. Technically, it was his job as my exec to bring up the displays.

"All right," I said loudly. "This is it, people. There are going to be some changes. Sarin, you're on ops now. You know how to run the tactical display on the holotank, right? Good. Miklos, I have bigger concerns for you. I'm going to personally oversee the marine contingents and the overall battle. But I want you in charge of fleet tactics. You will decide how to line up the ships, and will take over command if I'm out of the fight for any reason."

Kwon's hand was already up.

"Yes, Kwon?"

"Permission to accompany you with the marines, sir."

"Granted. I wouldn't have you anywhere else. Who else...Sandra?"

"Is Welter still in command of the battle station?"

"Yes, of course."

"But if you're right, sir, nothing will happen there."

I stared at her, and they all stared back. I knew what she was getting at. They wanted to hear it from me, right now. Was this a two-front fight or not?

"We will proceed under our original assumptions for now. The Macro Fleet has arrived, that's true. But they're barely moving."

"I would calculate, Colonel," interrupted Miklos, "that they're waiting for heavier ships as they did last time. They aren't just on a parade exercise. They'll come here."

My jaw tightened. "We don't know that. You may well be right, but we just don't know that for sure."

"Excuse me, Colonel," Miklos said. "Can we now begin the process of jamming signals? The enemy doesn't seem to be in complete coordination. I would like to keep it that way."

I thought about the request seriously, but shook my head. "No. We'll hold as we are. They've had days to coordinate, to hatch a plan of action. They're probably on a schedule that jamming won't change."

"You don't actually know that, sir."

I tossed Miklos a flat stare. I'd always allowed my senior staff an objection or two per meeting, but he was over his limit.

"Jamming them now would have some benefit, I'm sure," I said. "If I were planning a preemptive attack, for instance, I would begin with jamming. But Marvin is really close to cracking the code now, he's assured me. If we can listen in and find out who all the players are, if we can know their exact strengths and positions— well, that's worth much more than a few days of jamming."

I could tell with a single glance that no one in the group agreed with me, with the possible exception of Kwon, because he didn't care. He only wanted the fight to start as soon as possible.

"Let's go to the transports now, sir," he said eagerly.

Jasmine leaned forward. Her eyes were intense. "Sir—I don't quite know how to tell you this. But we all think that jamming would be the best course now. It is definite action with a definite gain. Marvin *might* break the code, but he hasn't done so up until now. Why should that suddenly change?"

I felt a surge of irritation. "Take a deep breath, everyone. I know things look bad. But we've just gotten a huge boost in our combat strength due to Marvin. He's done with that project now and he's moved on to the next challenge: the code. Frankly, I consider that to be a far less difficult feat. Let him have his shot at it."

"Can we at least split our forces now?" Miklos asked. "I mean, with the additional troops—surely we can spare some of them for the defense of the battle station."

I felt myself becoming stubborn. With an act of will, I stopped myself from ordering him to stop questioning everything I did. I forced myself to consider his question carefully and coolly.

"All right," I said. "Kwon, order a complement of five hundred Centaur troops to fly to the battle station, and add in a hundred of our own human marines. That will bolster Welter's defenses considerably."

Miklos frowned, but fell quiet. I knew he'd been asking for a contingent of ships, but I wasn't willing to give those up. We didn't have a battle station at the ring to Helios. If the Imperials hit us there, all we had to defend Eden was our fleet and our space marines.

I watched the tabletop as four transports broke off and dashed lines projected their course toward the battle station. It would take them around ten hours to reach their destination. Hopefully, they wouldn't be needed when they got there.

Suddenly, as we all watched the board and broke up into muttered conversations, the screen shifted on its own. A klaxon went off somewhere in the ship.

We stood up as the door opened. A staffer with a white face walked in and pointed a thin finger at the conference table.

"I relayed the new report here, sirs," she said.

I frowned at her, but followed her finger to the tabletop. The image swam briefly, then objects flashed into being. I quickly recognized the Helios system. I was about to demand from the staffer what this was all about, but the words died in my throat.

Ships were appearing in the Helios system, at the mouth of the far ring, the one that led to Alpha Centauri. The only system in line after Alpha Centauri was Earth. I didn't have optics on these unknown ships yet, but I had no doubt that they were Crow's Imperial vessels.

As we all watched, they kept coming through. More and more of them. I recalled then one of the last words Decker had said when threatening me about Crow's new fleet…

The word he'd used was: *overkill.*

-26-

Over the next few hours, the Earth fleet kept silently gathering strength. It was like watching silver coins spill onto a black floor. They poured out, slowly filling the space surrounding the ring. I don't think I'd ever seen so many ships in a single place. All of them positioned themselves in an elaborate formation and stood as if on parade, glinting in the light of three distant suns. They didn't advance, and I was reminded distinctly of the behavior of the Macros. Both were gathering at a safe distance, positioning themselves carefully, and waiting for the signal to advance. We'd been set up, and everyone on the command deck of the *Nostradamus* knew it.

All the Fleet people became increasingly tense as enemy hosts gathered on both sides of us. I reflected that in olden times, soldiers on a castle wall must have felt like this as they watched a horde of enemy troops gathering before they assaulted the cold stone walls. The only people who didn't have their stomach tied up in knots were the suicidally brave Centaur troops, who seemed oblivious to the stresses we naturally felt before battle. I watched these fresh native troops on vid feeds from the transports. I'd placed a line of cylindrical transport ships behind our line of gunboats, destroyers and my single cruiser. The Centaurs inside the transports were enjoying themselves, experimenting with their new equipment and demonstrating the value of their newly stress-free minds. I almost envied them as I watched them butt heads and fly around in buzzing figure eights all over the interior of the holds. At no time did they show the slightest hint of claustrophobia. In fact, the only emotions

I observed were exuberance and impatience. They were more than ready for us to get on with the show. They couldn't wait for me to release them into space like twenty thousand angry bees.

The Earth fleet kept growing, while the Macros advanced very slowly. I ordered *Nostradamus* to move to the far side of the ring to have a closer look. I knew I would have to contact them and attempt a little diplomacy. I doubted I could talk them out of attacking, but I at least had to try.

"Open a channel to the commander of the Imperial Earth fleet," I said.

Sarin was running the boards, and she was faster than anyone else. The request flashed out into the cold void of space. As we waited, the enemy armada shuffled closer. They weren't attacking yet, but they were advancing.

At last, a signal came in. When it did, I received an unexpected shock.

"Hello Riggs, this is a voice from your past, boy. Hehe, I bet you didn't expect me, good old General Kerr of the United States, to be riding herd on this flying armada, did ya?"

A thousand rude retorts bubbled in my mind. After I regained control of myself, I made my reply. "No, I have to admit, I wasn't expecting you General. I thought you had better judgment than this, sir."

"Now, now! That could be construed as an insult to our good Emperor Crow. Lord knows, we can't have that on the transcripts. But let me tell you something, as you've been out of the loop for a good long while. This massive display of fleet strength wouldn't have been possible without the influence of good old Jack Crow. Whatever you think of him personally, he brought Earth together as you never did, Kyle. He united us under a banner, rather than ignoring us and just using us as a source of raw materials."

I frowned. Kerr's words did sting, and I knew from experience that meant there was a grain of truth in what he said. Still, I rejected his underlying premise.

"So then, General...let me get this straight. You think I should have conquered Earth when I had the chance? The moment Star Force was strong, and the militaries of Earth were collectively weak? By allowing the nations of Earth sovereignty and respect, I failed to do the right thing?"

"Reality isn't always as pretty as we would like it to be. I think your character is a strong, positive thing. But doing what's necessary to save the species is infinitely more important. Haven't you made that argument many times, usually while presiding over the deaths of millions?"

My frown had changed into a glare, and I opened my mouth to unleash a tirade. Through sheer force of will, I stopped myself. I decided this bickering was getting us nowhere. Kerr had signed on as part of Crow's legion. He'd sold out to totalitarianism, and there was no way I was going to talk him into resigning his commission now.

"Let's change the tone, General. Can you tell me what your part is in all this? I thought you were more of a ground-force commander—or more recently, a spook-herder."

Kerr cackled at that one. "Right you are. But I made the case to his majesty that space battles aren't really that similar to naval battles—any more than they resemble land battles. They are a new and unique form of combat, more like an air campaign than anything else. More importantly, I've gone up against the legendary Kyle Riggs before. All that aside, I'd say as the Director of the North American Sector, I was first in line when the honor of leading this force was handed down by our leader."

I raised my eyebrows. "Director of the North American Sector? That *does* sound like an impressive title, sir. Can I ask how you managed to achieve such greatness?"

"It's an old story, Riggs. Early converts to any new political wave tend to rise up to the top. By being in the right place at the right time, and picking my winners early—well, let's just say I've been blessed by the course of current events."

I nodded thoughtfully. "Let me guess: You signed on with Crow and gave him inside information. Maybe you had a hand in bringing down your government as well? Sounds to me like you're a hero, General."

"Now, there's no call for that kind of talk. If you doubt that I made the correct decisions both for myself and for Earth, do a recount on my fleet strength. I know you probably have a little red number up on your screen by now displaying how many ships have wriggled into the Helios system. Notice that they are *still* coming through. I bet your Worm buddies down there on their hot little rock are pissing themselves by now!"

While I listened to the General's cackle, I glanced at the counter as he suggested. Sarin had set it up without being asked. It stood at one thousand ninety-eight. I couldn't believe the number, but it checked out. Fortunately, most of the ships that were coming through now were much smaller craft. I figured they were no more than independent one-man fighters following the larger cruiser-sized vessels. Still, over a thousand of anything in space was extremely impressive to me. I stared at the armada for several long seconds before responding to Kerr again.

"I'll offer you deal, General," I said. "Fly through our territory peacefully, and help us destroy the Macro threat on the far side of Eden. I've got them bottled up, and I could use your aid in finishing them off."

This time, the General didn't answer right away. He was thinking, I could tell. Maybe he even had a meeting and talked it over with his command staff. I figured the offer had to be tempting. Allowing them into our system and trusting them to stand by our side would be risky, of course. They might well decide to turn on us when the battle was over. But I knew Kerr, and I knew human psychology. It would be hard after fighting at our sides to turn against us. Every man in his fleet would naturally want to stand with us. With luck, I could avert a civil war.

"Riggs, your offer is very tempting. And I do believe you mean it. But we have our orders. The trouble is that Eden is technically rebel territory. Earth claims the system, and must reassert control over it. Naturally, I know this state of affairs makes it hard for us to cooperate. What I can do is bend my orders in your favor. If you will fly forward, surrendering yourself and the cruiser you're aboard right now, I'll move into the Eden system peacefully. Let us scout the Macro enemy, and if they're poised to strike, our combined forces will wipe them out. There is no need for either of us to shed the blood of a single biotic in a pointless command struggle."

Everyone behind me made sounds of frustration and exasperation. They quickly looked at me. I knew what they were thinking: what was Riggs going to do? Capitulate for the greater good, or go down fighting for the independence of Star Force?

I stared at the screen. I realized that Kerr had put me in a very bad spot. He'd set me up to be the bad guy. Was I so vain I would waste the two greatest forces humanity had ever assembled, letting them destroy one another?

Finally, I was ready to speak. My staff listened with glassy eyes. I think they were in shock at the scope of the disaster that loomed before all of us.

"General," I said. "I'm going to have to decline that offer. I'm going to make an offer of my own in return: reverse course and go home. If you don't want to help, then let us do our jobs out here guarding the frontier against the machines. We will not cross the no-man's land of Alpha Centauri again. Let that remain a buffer zone between Earth and Star Force territory. Maybe we can set up a trade route in the future. Whatever your decision, this conversation is at an end. Good day, sir."

I ordered the channel to be closed. I then turned my ship around and retreated back through the ring. When we were safely on the far side, I pointed to Sandra, who ran the communications console.

"Jam the rings," I said. "Both of them, right now. I don't want anyone passing any more notes under my desk. Let them both wonder what happened to the force on the other side."

Sandra worked the controls, finally sending the resonant signals to the rings that my entire staff had been begging me to send for weeks. Oddly, none of them looked happy now that they had finally gotten their way. I guess there's just no way to please some people.

Over the next day, events slowly unfolded. The Macro fleet hung back. They didn't advance toward the ring that led to Eden, but instead slowly traveled toward the Crustacean water-moons. On the opposite front, the Imperials were moving. They would soon be ready to push through and invade the Eden system.

I grinned at the screen. I'd had a good night's sleep and kicked off the morning sipping caffeinated beverages. My crew looked disheveled, and I ordered several of them off the command deck for some R&R.

"You all look like hell," I told them, "particularly you, Sarin. Go get a shower and something to eat. Take a nap, Miklos. You people need to learn how to pace yourselves."

They left the deck, grumbling. Only Sandra looked relatively fresh, so I let her stay and brief me. She had stamina, that girl. I guessed the Microbial treatments had helped in that regard.

"The Macros are just sitting out there in the Thor system, Kyle. If both sides are supposed to hit us at once, they have already screwed up. The machines are at least a day behind the Imperial fleet now."

I nodded and bit into my second donut. It was plain, glazed, and so fresh it was almost juicy. "This could all be over before the machines make their move. Either they are bewildered by the lack of data coming through the ring, or the Blues took our threats seriously and told them to delay."

"The Blues are cowards. I think they told the Macros to hang back after your threats."

"You could be right. I *hope* you're right. If that's how it's going down, the Blues have clearly decided to screw the Empire rather than risk a bombing from us. In that case, we only have to face one front, rather than two. Pull those ships back we have orbiting the Blues' homeworld. I want everything here at the Helios ring except for a few scout ships posted at the battle station. We'll mass everything we have against Kerr, who is still advancing."

We spent another day watching the Imperial fleet approach. They stayed in formation as they flew, displaying tight discipline. It struck me then how different a race like the Worms were. The Worms reminded me of barbarian warriors: a mass of gifted pilots flying in a shifting swarm, every individual eager to get to the enemy first and prove himself the braver warrior. By comparison, Earth's forces were very self-controlled and resembled the Macros.

I had time to study the Crow's ship-designs as they made their stately approach. The core of the fleet was made up of big, almost gaudy ships. They weren't quite like anything we had. I figured Crow had combined the crude, mass-production capacity of Earth and used nanotech for the detail work. The ships therefore resembled old-fashioned sea-going vessels. They were built with flat planes of steel plating and cemented together by nanites. I could see how this approach would greatly increase his production rates. He'd harnessed the output of traditional Earth industry and built hybrid ships, rather than constructing them entirely with Nano materials. With limited Nano factory production, it was a logical thing to do to stretch his production to the maximum that could be achieved.

It was also bad news for us. The Imperial fleet was *huge*. I'd previously calculated they could have produced about twenty cruisers and a hundred or so destroyers over the months since I'd left Earth. That would have been bad enough. But instead, we saw over a thousand ships. They were of designs we'd never encountered before. Long, steel weapons-platforms with engines in the back, they appeared rectangular in shape. They looked something like old Earth battleships, but without a triangular lower hull and keel. They bristled with weaponry on every side. Their weapons and sensors protruded unevenly, making them look ugly and threatening. They were the very opposite of my comparatively sleek designs. No matter how displeasing they were to the eye, I had no doubt they would be effective in combat once they were in range.

The biggest ships were at the forefront of the formation. These surprised me. As they approached, I kept expecting a missile barrage. Instead, they didn't fire until they were at medium-long range. At this distance, they were outside the reach of our heavy beams, but still within the reach of missiles.

"Railgun projectiles incoming, sir!" Miklos called out the alarm.

I startled awake in my command chair. I took a deep breath and squinted at the holotank. "Railguns? Who's firing at what?"

"The Imperials sir. Those big ugly battlewagons of theirs. We now know they have railguns of their own, and they are firing at the ring. Fortunately, it will take nearly half an hour at this range for the projectiles to reach us. Should we order our scouts to stand, or pull back?"

I nodded thoughtfully. "He's chasing off our scouts. He's probably not inside his effective range, but we can't very well leave our ships sitting there, waiting to find out if they'll get a lucky hit. Pull back the scouts. We'll wait for Kerr on the Eden side of the ring."

Miklos relayed the orders, and our view of the approaching enemy changed from solid red objects to outlined wireframes. That meant the enemy positions were now theoretical. We could no longer see them directly.

Sandra came up and touched my shoulder. "Do you think they'll really come through the ring, Kyle?" she asked me quietly. "Is Kerr that crazy? He has to know we'll put up a good fight, and we might even win."

"I don't know," I said. "But I think he will come. He doesn't know how strong we are, and I'm not about to show him until he gets here. He doesn't know about the Centaur marines, how many gunboats I have, the mines we set up and the rest. He'll expect tricks, but if you do the math, we shouldn't be able to resist him. We're stronger than we should be, due to having captured the Macro factories. The trouble is, I can't tell him that to warn him off without giving up critical information. It's maddening."

She touched my cheek and tried to comfort me. I stared at the holotank, and I knew in my heart the battle I'd always hoped to avoid had finally begun.

-27-

Within minutes after I'd ordered the rings to be jammed, Marvin was on the command deck. His tentacles and cameras were moving like palm fronds in the wind, even though the stale air in the ship was oppressively still. He was clearly agitated.

"Colonel Riggs," Marvin began. "I was under the impression that you were going to allow me to finish my decoding work before jamming the rings."

"That was the original plan," I admitted, "but they're advancing into range and firing on us now. We don't have time to screw around any longer. Did you manage to get anywhere with the code?"

"The key is nowhere near complete. Less than seventy percent of the symbols are cataloged, and my mapping of their protocol is woefully inadequate. If you were to ask me to generate a false set of instructions, I would surely fail and be detected at this point."

I blinked at him. "That sounds like you got pretty far. Let me get this straight: you can now transcribe most of what their transmissions say?"

"Yes, but critical details are constantly left out. I would not consider such documents in any way accurate or reliable."

"Just give me what you have!" I roared at him. "It doesn't have to be perfect. Send it to a text file and put it on the consoles. For every unknown reference, print a set of Xs or something."

"Incomplete data can be dangerous."

"Only to them. Give me what you have."

Reluctantly, Marvin sent a flurry of files to my attention. I opened them immediately and began reading. Within thirty seconds, I relayed the data to everyone on my command staff and ordered them to open the attachments.

There had been traffic between *all three* of our enemies. The Blues were clearly in the middle of the operation, talking to both the Macros and Earth's fleet. We were still missing much of the data, such as the signatures of the transmitting parties. Unlike radio communications, there was no easy way to determine the source of the transmissions technologically. But that really didn't matter. Following the context of the messages, such as references to fleet positions and intentions, it quickly became obvious who was talking to whom. When a message described a large fleet advancing into the Helios system, for example, I knew the transmission had come from Earth.

"Crow is talking to the Blues?" Sandra asked.

"Yes," I said. "Or at least Kerr is. It's undeniable."

"But does this indicate they're in league with the Macros themselves?" Miklos demanded. "We have to know that. Are there any direct messages from Crow to the Macros?"

After going over the messages Marvin had translated, I shook my head. The earlier ones were mostly garbled. Only the most recent transmissions were relatively clear. I marveled at Marvin's mind once again. It was the fantastic moments like this which gave me the strength to put up with all his antics. He was a gifted problem solver. Upon reflection, I imagined that mad geniuses had always been critical to every war effort, and were probably always difficult to deal with. I recalled reading that both Michelangelo and Da Vinci had designed amazing war machines. I didn't doubt for a second they'd both been a pain in the ass to deal with personally.

"This puts us in a different strategic situation," I told my people when we'd all had time to digest the transcripts. "The transmissions don't really tell us much that we didn't already know concerning enemy fleet movements. But, we now know the two advancing fleets *are* in cooperation. The Blues seemed to be involved as go-betweens, having called upon both Crow's Imperial forces and enticing the next wave of Macros to advance. Does anyone have anything to add? Give me input, team."

"The strategy of the Blues is very clear, Colonel," Miklos said, speaking up before the others. "They don't like us being here, so they formed alliances with the largest powers in the region. I'm not sure how they expect to survive the coming conflict as a sovereign entity, however."

I shrugged. "I guess they made a deal. They're helping the Macros, and when the machines march in, they'll sweep us aside. Just to make sure, they brought in Crow, too. Maybe they hope the three of us will annihilate one another in an orgy of destruction."

"In return for helping them," Captain Sarin said, "I imagine the Blues have been assured their neutrality will be respected by all sides."

"Perhaps," Miklos said, "and perhaps the machines will keep their deal. But I doubt Crow will, if he wins the day. He'll screw the Blues over and enslave them."

I nodded in agreement. "But the Blues don't know Crow the way we do," I said. "They seem to be good at sticking to the letter of their agreements, if not their spirit. I've noticed the same tendency when dealing with the Macros—I guess that only makes sense, since the Blues built the Macros in the first place."

"In that case," Miklos said, speaking slowly, "the Blues have miscalculated by including Crow. I'm reminded of the Pact which Russia and Germany signed before invading Poland. Stalin had no idea Hitler would violate the deal as soon as possible."

I thought about it, frowning. I didn't like Miklos' analogy, but I had to agree that it fit the situation. What I didn't like about it was that *we* were Poland in this scenario. No one wanted to be compared to Poland's grim fate in World War II.

"We're stronger than the Poles were in their horrible situation," I said firmly. "I have no intention of being crushed within days by a surprise attack from both sides."

Everyone looked at me seriously, but no one said anything. I wasn't sure if they believed me or not.

"The key is in the timing. The Blues are holding back. With luck, Crow thinks they are holding up their end of the bargain and still advancing. Instead of being hit on both sides and being forced to split our defenses, we'll stop Crow cold, then worry about the Macros, if they come at all."

For once, no one argued with me. We broke up the meeting and went our separate ways. There was a mountain of organizational details to attend to. Many hours of hard work followed, and about a day later, the time to test our theories finally came.

"Sir," Miklos said, "the Earth fleet has reached the ring. We've snuck through a few scouts to check on them over the last few hours. They're about to enter the Eden system."

I reviewed the holotank, which showed both systems in detail. The Imperial fleet was dauntingly huge. There were so many red contacts the holotank was having difficulty displaying them all.

"Speed and course?" I demanded.

"They're heading directly toward the ring, but they're still slowing down. It's my belief they intend to come through slowly in an organized fashion. This is an opportunity, Colonel."

"Explain."

"They're moving so slowly, we can throw space marines in front of them and allow direct boarding."

I frowned at the boards and the holotank. As I watched, the enemy fleet flickered from red to orange. This meant their positions were now theoretical again. Our scouts had retreated to our side of the ring and we could no long see the enemy directly. It was either that, or they would have been destroyed.

Our own green line of ships had been arranged in a parabolic pattern a good distance from the ring. We had a few mines out there, but hadn't bothered to overdo it with static defenses. I'd noted that over recent battles, those weapons hadn't yielded much in the way of enemy casualties.

"No," I said firmly. "I don't want to commit any assault groups yet. They're worried about our mines, which means they'll put some big defensive ships in the lead. Those are the worst class of vessels for our marines to assault: heavily-protected ships with thick hulls and a lot of point-defense cannons to detect and shoot down mines—or other small targets."

Miklos nodded, but looked unhappy. I could tell he wanted to commit the marines anyway. I understood his logic. The marines had trouble when assaulting any ship that was moving too fast. They had to be at close to the same relative velocity to operate, and right now the enemy was gliding slowly through the ring. This represented the perfect opportunity for landing on the enemy vessels instead of splatting upon them due to a huge difference in relative velocities.

"Don't worry Captain," I assured Miklos, "our troops will get more than their fill of combat today. Instead of throwing them at the first Imperial ships we see, we'll hold them in reserve. We've got our gunships in a line at maximum effective range. The moment they come through, wallowing and slow, we'll bombard them with everything we've got. They all have to wriggle out of that ring, remember. Just a few ships at a time will be appearing."

"As you say, Colonel," Miklos said. He sounded miffed.

I glanced at him and thought: *too bad.*

A few minutes later, it began. As I'd expected, the most monstrous ships with tons of forward armor came through in groups of three. I was reminded of ancient battling rams. These ships had been built for this purpose. They were intended to absorb punishment so the lighter vessels behind them didn't have to.

Now that we were much closer, we could see the details on the enemy vessels with our long-range optics. The forward section of these ships had an interesting series of design elements. I was intrigued, and studied them intently, zooming in as closely as I was able. I saw a series of dark, textured masses moving in front of each vessel.

"What the hell are they holding in front of them?" I asked.

"Shields, sir," Miklos said. "Probably made of asteroid rock, rather than metal. They're pushing big chunks of thick stone in front of them, like bulldozers hiding behind their lowered blades."

I nodded. "Or like Greek hoplites hiding behind their interlocked tower shields while they steadily advance. In a way, I'm proud that Old Earth could put together a force like this. It's comforting. If we lose today gentlemen, we can be confident that our species will still prevail in this cosmos."

My staff looked less than thrilled with my analysis. I guess that with their own deaths so near and so likely, they weren't interested in the theoretical survival of the species as a whole. I could understand that, but I still watched closely, enthralled by the majesty of the approaching vessels. It was going to be a crime to destroy them.

"Fire!" I shouted, ordering my line of gunships to begin pounding the advancing enemy.

Hundreds of crackling blue balls rolled forward, converging on the newly-emerged monsters. The battle I'd always expected but never wanted was here. I found it impossible to look away, even for a second.

General Kerr's vanguard of heavy battleships had been built to take punishment, but they had their limits. Tiny, needle-thin beams flashed out from their nose sections, stabbing at the scattered mines and the incoming storm of projectiles. But the defensive fire couldn't save them. The big ships flared their engines, making emergency evasive maneuvers. But it was too little, too late.

Still wallowing at low velocity, they were picked apart by lashing fire. Volley after volley of thundering balls of force rained down on them. To me, they resembled mounds of dirt melting in a tropical downpour. When the first one broke apart, less than a minute after it had arrived in the Eden system, I straightened my shoulders and tossed a salute toward the holotank which faithfully depicted their demise.

"There goes a fine, brave crew," I said. "Don't forget what we do here today, people. Those are our own ships we're firing upon. If we get a chance at mercy, we'll take it."

Every eye flicked to me, then back to the grim carnage on the screen.

"It's not over yet, Colonel," Miklos said.

"Unfortunately, you're right. They'll send in faster, lighter, more heavily armed ships next. Unleash thirty companies of Centaurs, Captain. Order them to assault the enemy formation. Let's see how our new troops do out there."

Miklos worked the boards, and Sarin helped him relay the command. Soon, the scene on the screen changed dramatically. The Earth ships were still pressing forward, almost eager in their search for destruction. They kept coming and coming, and the count on the corner was a grim reminder of our efficiency. When the count of big ships stood at sixty, and the count of dead hulks showed thirty-five, I put my hand to my chin and rubbed the stubble there. The joints of my gauntlet caught at my beard, and I winced as hairs were plucked free.

"Is this all they have, Kyle?" Sandra said. "Are we just going to slaughter thousands?"

225

As if in answer to her question, the second phase of the invasion began. These new ships resembled silver torpedoes. They darted through the ring at a higher velocity, no doubt certain that the big front-liners would have removed the minefield by this time.

I imagined the shock each crewman experienced when he saw the debris in front of him. Floating chunks of the behemoths leading the charge were now so numerous they presented an entirely new threat to the second wave. Still, they kept coming and they wisely flew out of the immediate maelstrom of blue fireballs and dying ships.

From the twenty or so that broke free, a storm of smaller traces appeared.

"Missiles, sir," Sarin called out. "Each one is firing a barrage."

"Project the targets. Have the cruisers prepare for defensive fire. If they're going for our transports in back, order each targeted ship to unload all their troops immediately."

"No sir, I don't think…" she stopped and pointed to the screen. "The missiles are all converging on the center of our forward line."

I frowned, taking a step toward the holotank, trying to divine the enemy strategy. Miklos figured it out before I did.

"It's us, sir. The missile boats just fired everything they have— at this ship."

Stunned, I examined the data. There it was, as our brainboxes computed the trajectory with increasing accuracy every second. They'd fired over a thousand missiles at my ship. We had just minutes left before impact.

-28-

General Kerr had always managed to compliment me in a backhanded way. I really knew he thought a lot of me at that moment. He'd gone out of his way to take me out. As close as we could figure in the minute or so we took to confirm the attack, the missile barrage and the entire first play of his battle strategy was aimed at one thing: destroying my command ship.

I waited a few seconds, in case the whole thing was just some kind of ruse. The missiles could be targeting my ship first to force us to abandon *Nostradamus*, then divert and spread to their real targets.

The few seconds passed, and hope faded. It wasn't going to happen that way. I heaved in a breath, and gave the only command I possibly could: "All hands, abandon ship! Fly to the nearest friendly vessel for pickup. Avoid the *Nostradamus*, give her a berth of a hundred miles. Scatter in a random pattern from the impact point."

The lights on the bridge changed, going to blood-red. Almost immediately, the red was striped by flashers of spinning yellow. Klaxons whooped and screamed. Everyone who wasn't fully suited-up struggled to get into something air-tight that could fly.

I marched at the head of my staff toward the aft sally ports. Miklos, Sandra and Sarin were all right behind me. Fortunately, Sloan and Kwon were with the transports, coordinating the assault forces. If we all died, at least those two would be left to continue the fight.

We entered the dark hold and I reached up to hit the emergency bulkhead release. The door shot open, and the immediate depressurization rocked my armored body. I clamped a gauntlet onto the nearest steel rung and grabbed Sandra with my other hand. In turn, Sandra held onto Miklos and Jasmine, who were wearing crewman's nanocloth with power packs and trying to get their feet onto those flying skateboard things I'd designed long ago. They now served every ship as both invasion equipment and escape pods.

After the door was sucked away by the escaping gasses in the hold, a square of velvet black pierced by intense white lights appeared. Space hung outside, in all its glory. From this angle, I could see nothing but brilliant stars.

When I was about to give the final order to dive out into vacuum, something else grabbed me. I looked down to see a black tentacle encircling my right calf.

"Excuse me, Colonel Riggs," Marvin said politely into my com-link. "I'm having a conflict. I find my standing orders to be unclear."

I glanced back and saw him, looming over us. He was clinging to the spine of the ship.

"Sorry Marvin," I said. "I forgot about you. I'm hereby changing your orders. You can fly in emergency situations. In order to survive, you're allowed to use any means of propulsion you can find. Do you need us to provide you with—?"

I never finished the sentence. Marvin shouldered us all aside and shot out into space, taking the lead instantly. Under his body, a set of four skateboards were arranged in a diamond pattern. He leaned into it as I watched him, directing himself onto a new course. He shrank to a dot in a few seconds.

I chuckled and dove after him. I dragged everyone with me, as they were all holding onto each other. I didn't know where Marvin was headed, but I was certain he had a destination clearly in mind, and it didn't involve hanging around at the epicenter of a massive barrage of nuclear missiles.

Choosing a random angle and accelerating for all we were worth, my tiny group flew with grim determination into the cold silent ocean which we call space. As always, I reflected upon the shockingly sudden nature of life and death in this incredibly harsh environment. When in space, you simply didn't have all the protection afforded by a planetary body. You were exposed to radiation and particles of matter flashing around at insane speeds. Even in serene moments the environment was inherently deadly to human flesh. The temperature in most of the great void was usually freezing, or occasionally scorching hot. There was no breathable air, and the vacuum alone could turn you inside out if you let it.

Still, for all its deadliness, there was beauty too. The sun was yellow-white and too bright to look upon without the autoshades in our visors. It glared upon every helmet giving the scene a stark clarity. Some of the worlds that orbited that steady star were visible with the naked eye. In a direction that appeared to be to our left now, I thought I saw two bodies, appearing as gray-white disks. One had to be Eden-12, the planet of the Blues. Like Jupiter back home, it was one of the most visible things in every world's night sky in this system. If I had to guess, I'd say the other one was Eden-11, which was scheduled to orbit fairly close to the Helios ring this time of year.

It didn't really matter which planets they were. They were timeless and remote. Gazing at them for a few long seconds, I felt a curious level of perspective. We were nothing compared to those spinning worlds that teemed with life. No matter what we did out here, bits of dust fighting to the death in the skies, they would go on orbiting their star serenely.

While I was stargazing, I wondered too about Kerr's attempt to take out my leadership. I reminded myself this wasn't the first attempt, the news reporter with the bomb had been intent on the same goal. I had to count the missile barrage as the second assassination attempt of this new conflict. I went further, deciding the tactic was part of Imperial strategy now—Crow's strategy. Kerr hadn't just come up with it on his own, it wasn't his style. He'd been ordered to make this move if I resisted. I could hear Crow in my head with his rough, Aussie accent: "If he fights too hard, kill him."

Captain Sarin ended my reverie by contacting my helmet with a short range com-link. We all knew enough not to chatter with powerful signals. Enemy missiles tended to locate that kind of transmission and home in on it.

"Look up," she said.

I followed her instructions and saw a fading reddish glow. I knew what it was: one of the nukes had gone off when I wasn't looking. The reddish glow was replaced almost immediately by a flash of brilliance, then several more. In the middle of these incandescent flares of energy was the spoon-shape of my abandoned cruiser. *Nostradamus* broke apart as I watched.

"Set your shades to full-auto," I said, just in case someone had screwed up. Even temporary blindness could be deadly now. "Link arms and look away from the ship. If they hit her with a heavy fusion bomb, it could reach us even out here."

My team needed no further urging. I felt arms link up with mine on each side, and we all turned our heads away from the cascading impacts. I took that moment to marvel at the firepower Kerr had unleashed in order to kill little old me. He was either crazy, or fearful. I had to question his judgment. Was my leadership really worth that much to our side's chances of victory?

As I pondered the question and more flashes illuminated space behind me, I had another thought: perhaps I'd been overly egotistic. Perhaps Kerr wanted to wipe out *all* my senior officers, not just me.

That made more sense to me. I considered Miklos, Sarin and many of my other key officers to be excellent tacticians. They were all veterans of a dozen battles. The Earthers didn't have anyone like that on their side, I knew. Maybe that's why Kerr feared us enough to make such a concerted effort to wipe us out.

I was pondering this when one of the shockwaves finally touched us. I figured out afterward that it was probably a missile that hadn't made it all the way to its target. Maybe *Nostradamus* had been completely destroyed, and the missile had detected this and decided in its tiny electric brain to just end it all and detonate. Whatever the case, the explosion hit us from behind and caused us all to go into a tumbling spin.

I felt like a fly that had just been swatted—hard. I didn't lose consciousness, but Jasmine and Miklos did. Sandra took the impact well. She even managed to catch Jasmine before I could. We'd both been through Marvin's Microbial baths, and our flesh was as tough as nails.

There was blood on everyone's face when I peered into the visors. Jasmine's visor was starred, and Miklos' jaw was hanging at an unnatural angle.

"We need to get them to another ship, Kyle," Sandra said. "I don't know what their condition is. I think Miklos' suit has lost power."

I worked to connect an auxiliary cable to his suit, and had Sandra do the same for Captain Sarin. Together again, we began limping away on two skateboards rather than four.

We finally dared to call for help when we'd reached a safe distance of about a thousand miles from *Nostradamus'* wreckage. We were quickly acknowledged and a destroyer moved to pick us up.

The big nanite arm from the destroyer's hold plucked us from space and reeled us in. The crew was stunned to have all their highest level commanders drag themselves aboard. There were only three of them, a junior officer and two non-coms. Their eyes were wide, dark and grimly determined.

"Are you all right, sir?" the skipper asked, peering into my faceplate.

"Yeah," I said, "It's just a bleeder. Not even worth removing my helmet. Let the nanites take care of it."

The young skipper nodded uncertainly.

"These two are out," I said. "Do what you can for them in your medical bay. You do have a medical bay, don't you, Lieutenant?"

"Yes sir," he said, showing me the way.

The destroyer was one of the newer stripped-down models I'd taken with me from Andros Island long ago. The sick bay was small, with only three tables. I made sure Miklos and Sarin were stretched out comfortably on two of them, then returned to the bridge.

"It's time to get back into this battle. What have you got for tactical display?"

The young Lieutenant nodded helpfully to the forward wall, which crawled with bumps of metal. The nanites were having to work overtime, trying to display every ship in the vicinity.

"You're kidding, right? This vessel was never upgraded with a full command console?"

The Lieutenant stammered excuses until I waved for him to shut up.

"All right," I said, "we'll do it the old-fashioned way."

231

I began quoting a script to the nanites on the surface of the bridge, giving them detailed instructions on how to display warnings and faster updates. By selecting more critical elements and updating them faster, while letting less important data slide by, the primitive system was able to operate more like a tactical ops display.

The display showed that the enemy had pressed through the breach, filing into the Eden system despite horrible losses. All but seven of the big battleships had been destroyed. About ten of the smaller, sleeker missile ships still eluded our guns. What concerned me most was the next wave. This consisted of several hundred one-man fighters. These ships were fast and maneuverable. In a way, they were a worst case enemy for our gunships to face. Armed with heavy cannons that had a slow rate of fire, we couldn't hope to hit these missile-sized targets as they twirled and dodged into the system. A cloud of them had broken away from the main formation and were advancing to attack my main line.

With my cruiser gone, I had only a scattered number of destroyers and frigates with lasers aboard that could track and take down these fighters. This was a known vulnerability of my tiny fleet, but I'd compensated when facing the Macros in the past, once by using the Nano fleet to run interference for us, and another time by building orbital laser platforms. Neither of these solutions were available to us now.

Once I had the tactical display configured, Sandra established contact with my unit commanders and we were in business again. Sloan had taken over in my absence.

"Give me the situation as it stands, Sloan," I ordered.

"Sir, glad to have you back in the game. We're withdrawing sir, firing as we go. But we can't seem to hit those little ships."

I gritted my teeth. I'd always known Sloan was too cautious to run a full-fledged space battle. He had a fantastic knack for recognizing a threat, but he too often dealt with it by withdrawing or repositioning. He wanted every battle to be clean and textbook. Unfortunately, in my experience that rarely happened out here in this deadly universe.

"I can see the fighters—they're gaining on your gunships. What is your plan for dealing with this problem?"

"The Centaur troops, sir—they're about to meet the enemy lines now."

I opened my mouth to shout at him, but then halted. I realized my error immediately. I'd ordered the ship to display ships up to a given size—but it had interpreted our space marines as so small it wasn't displaying them.

"Ship!" I shouted. "Respond!"

"Responding."

"Display the space-borne infantry."

"All known self-mobile contacts are being displayed."

I marched up to the wall, and peered. It did seem there were colored dots there, so small they could hardly be seen. "Show large formations of individuals as collective ovals, please."

That did the trick. Within a few seconds, I could see about thirty ovals. I suspected each group represented a company of my troops. They were about to meet up with the fighters head on.

"They're going too fast. Sloan, the Centaurs—they'll fly right past the fighters, or smash into them. The relative speeds are too high, I'd guess around a thousand miles an hour or more. No one can land and assault an enemy ship at those speeds!"

"I don't think that's their plan, sir," he said.

I opened my mouth to say more, but suddenly understood what he was getting at. We'd never had smooth command and control over our Centaur troops. They'd pretty much done what they'd wanted in every battle, while trying to follow our orders in their own way.

"What orders did you give them, Sloan?" I asked.

"I told them to destroy the fighters, sir. I don't think I had any choice. They were the only asset I had on the field."

As I watched, the two lines came together. The ovals representing the Centaur companies spread out at the last minute, covering more area. The fighters were taking them out with guns, I could tell. The ovals began looking ragged—then the two lines met.

Explosions rippled up and down the line. The fighters melted, as did the Centaur companies. Thousands of brave troops died in less than a minute.

"Are they blowing themselves up?" Sandra asked me quietly.

I turned around and looked at her, then back to the screen. "They're following their orders," I said. "Sloan?"

"Yes, Colonel."

"That was grim, but well-played. I don't think I could have come up with a better solution. Please release more marines from our transports. The enemy will recognize the threat now. They'll target the transports, and I don't want an entire battalion taken out by one lucky missile. Get them into space."

"All of them, sir?"

"Hold back a reserve—five thousand troops. Pull them back. Pull everything back, but push the marines forward."

He relayed the orders and I stared at the walls and the helmsman's navigational screen. There was so much going on out there, and I didn't have a proper command and control unit set up. The more I thought about it, the more I figured Kerr's opening move had been a good one. He'd almost won right there, by knocking out my command ship. Fortunately, Sloan had played it pretty well.

Examining what Kerr had managed to wriggle through the ring by this time, I decided it was indeed time to retreat. He had more battleships now, at least thirty of them. He was forming up at the ring before pushing forward with his big ships. There were more of those sleek missile ships too—more than fifty of them. Altogether, his fleet completely outweighed mine. We'd given them a hard blow, but hadn't stopped their advance.

The surviving fighters turned and began retreating to the main fleet. I watched as a few of my Centaurs ran them down and blew them up.

"Kyle, you have to stop that," Sandra said, "They're broken and running. Show mercy. We might need it later ourselves."

I nodded. "Right." I called Sloan and our Centaurs broke off the pursuit. They turned around and retreated to our own small line of gunships.

There was a lull in the battle, during which Kerr's fleet kept trickling in through the ring. How many ships did that bastard have? I realized now that I couldn't possibly hold them all back—except for my ace in the hole, my space marines. They were suicidal, especially the Centaurs. The enemy had prepared carefully, but they hadn't counted on twenty thousand crazy mountain goats with nukes on their backs.

"Sir?" Sloan called over the command channel. "I've got a channel request from the enemy fleet. I think Kerr wants to talk."

I allowed myself a tight smile. "Open the channel and patch it through to my destroyer. Don't let him know where it's going, hide it in the ship-to-ship traffic. Let's hear what the good General has to say now."

There was a crackling, followed by a loud, unhappy voice. "Riggs? You crazy fuck, are you still alive?"

"Naturally," I said, "I didn't think you cared, General."

Our two fleets hung in space, at a range of about a hundred thousand miles, eyeing one another. Like two brawlers that have landed heavy blows on one another and stopped for a breather, we were both feeling new respect for our opponents.

"Oh, I care, you slippery devil. You're like a cockroach dipped in axel grease."

"The feeling is mutual, sir," I assured him. I keyed off my mike and turned to Sandra: "Try to figure out which ship he's on. He has to be in the system now."

She nodded and went to work on her console.

"What's this bullshit with blowing up your own troops, Riggs?" Kerr demanded. "Not only that, but you're using Macro weapons. Those big guns aren't human, Riggs. Have you signed on with the enemy?"

"Have you, sir?" I asked.

"That question leads me to another point: we're now monitoring our system. It appears that your entire force is right here at this ring, arrayed against your rightful commanders. I cry foul, Riggs. What about the battle station? What about those Macro hordes you've been whining about for months that are supposedly out there in the next system?"

"What about them, sir?"

"Why are you facing off with loyal Earth fleets, destroying over a hundred of my ships, instead of fighting the real enemy?"

Kerr was almost screaming now, and I could tell I'd rattled him. He'd expected losses, but nothing like what I'd inflicted upon him in the opening stages of the battle. I tried to look at the situation from his point of view. So far, I'd lost about three thousand marines and a dozen ships. In comparison, he'd lost a hundred fighters and another hundred heavier ships. At this rate, he'd have nothing left soon. Worse, I was sure that when he went back to Emperor Crow, there were going to be some harsh words, even if he did win the battle. I knew Crow loved his ships, and didn't want to see them trashed for any reason.

"I take issue with your terms, General," I said calmly. "We are the loyalists—loyal to Star Force and loyal to a free, independent Earth. You have signed on with a usurper, a tyrant—"

"Enough of that shit. We need to talk terms."

"Terms?" I asked. "Very well. If you will fly your command ship forward, we can meet and sign a treaty. All your vessels will, of course, have to be individually searched and abandoned as we accept their surrender—"

A foul tirade of curses erupted from the speakers. I waved at Sandra, who turned the General's voice down until he'd regained control of himself.

"Always full of piss and vinegar, aren't you, boy?" Kerr asked at last, when he'd run out of profane things to call me.

"You sound tired, General. Maybe you should stop destroying Earth ships and reconsider another course of action."

There was a silent period over the channel. Then he came back on. "You'll break off the attack? All right. Let's call it a ceasefire. We'll stand down. We'll sit at the ring and I'll meet with my command staff. Possibly, we've made a mistake by coming here."

I grinned. "I agree to your ceasefire terms. Let's consider our options carefully."

We closed the channel, and Sandra was all over me the second the connection was broken.

"He's playing you, Kyle," she said intently. "He's hoping the Macros hit our backdoor while we're facing off with him. He figures we might surrender then, and he wins without losing any more ships against us."

I looked at her and gave her my most confident smile. "Exactly," I said, "in some ways Sandra, the good General and I have the same endgame goals. He wants us to fight under a single command against the Macros. The only trouble we're having is how to decide who is in overall command."

She walked up to me, and stared up into my face. "You should stop this then," she said. "Let him win. Who cares, Kyle? Let us fight as an Empire, or whatever they want to call it. As long as we all are united against the machines, I don't care."

My smile faded. "Don't give up on all your freedoms so quickly. I don't think you know what you're saying. Men have died for centuries to provide the life you've lived up until now. Under Crow—everything could be different. A police state is nothing to contemplate lightly."

"It's all about pride," she said. "Dominance and pride. It's a pissing-contest between alpha-dogs, deciding who will hump who. You're just like any of them—the great killers in history. Too wrapped up in the moment to see the bigger picture. You'll get us all killed for an ideal, and for your pride."

Sandra did a U-turn and went back to her station. She didn't say anything more, but I could tell she was upset.

I looked after her, troubled. I wasn't sure if she was right or not. I'd wrecked a lot of hardware today—but had I fought for the right cause? If I could destroy Kerr's entire fleet, was that the right thing to do?

For the first time all day, I was filled with ambivalence.

-29-

Kerr waited. Our two fleets moved very little. We both shuffled our forces, forming two flattened clouds of metallic matter, each facing the other. I ordered the transports to come forward, retrieve troops in groups of a few thousand a time, while releasing another few thousand. At all times, about a quarter of my marines were outside their ships, ready for action. The rest slept, ate and recuperated inside the transports.

Everyone was tense, but for now the ceasefire was holding. We'd used the breather to put together a new command setup on my personal destroyer *Actium*. The command center now occupied the region normally reserved for troop pods. The ship itself was hidden in plain sight, trying to act just like every other destroyer in the fleet. This wasn't difficult, as I'd distributed my destroyers evenly amongst the gunships.

Kerr had used the time wisely as well. He'd gathered his ships, repaired them as best he could, and retrieved every floating body he could find. Some of them were no doubt survivors as well. I hoped and prayed for them all. I didn't want one more human life lost than was absolutely necessary.

"This reminds me of aircraft carrier operations," Miklos said, coming up beside me.

I glanced at him in surprise. I hadn't seen him enter the command deck. He looked like hell. His jaw was still broken and his speech was slower than usual, but I could understand him. The rest of his face was pretty badly banged up too, but he was ignoring it.

"Aircraft carriers? How so?" I asked.

"We're both using smaller ships to fly CAP and protect our core fleets. The enemy is matching us, keeping a portion of their fighters up, buzzing them around on patrol."

"You're right," I said, looking the situation over. "Both sides are using small units to support the larger vessels. It does look like a standoff between two carrier groups."

Miklos raised a finger stiffly, aiming it at the tabletop command screen. It was an old unit that resembled a pool table. He tapped at a contact that was brighter green than the rest. "That is Actium, I assume? The ship we're on now?"

"Exactly."

Actium was the new command ship, but it didn't stand out from the crowd on the command screen. In fact, it looked like one more floating vessel in a long line of ships. *Actium* had taken her place in the sunward wing, about half-way to the edge of the fleet's overall formation. I'd placed it in the lineup with the rest of the ships, trying to give no hint that my command ship was anything special.

"You've gone to great lengths to hide this ship, sir," Miklos said.

"Yes," I said, looking him over. "Are you sure you're fit to serve, Captain? I don't like the way the right side of your head has swollen."

Miklos shrugged. "I'm fine, sir. My internal nanites are itching terribly, but they're working their magic on me even now."

"All right, resume your duties."

With a crooked smile, Miklos shuffled to a seat and sank into it. He logged into the workstation and tapped at the console stiffly. Jasmine and Sandra both eyed him with concern, but said nothing. Jasmine's injuries were minor compared to his, and she'd already returned to duty. I could tell Miklos was in pain, but he didn't want to be seen as the weakest of my senior staff. When the warhead had detonated, some trick of physics had caught him with the hardest blow. Fortunately, his suit hadn't depressurized completely. He'd lived. I wasn't surprised, as it was very hard to permanently kill one of my people.

Miklos waved to me after a few minutes at his workstation. I came over to see what he'd found.

"The Macros are attacking, sir," he said.

"What?" I rushed to the big table, tapped until the tactical display of the Thor system came up. My eyes searched the scene, but I didn't see anything special. Sure, the Macros were closer to our ring than they had been, but not much closer. Their engines were cold and silent. They drifted out there, as quiet as death itself. They hadn't even reached the half-way point yet. The Lobsters were quiet too, seemingly content to remain on their three water-moons, sitting this one out. I couldn't blame them for that.

"Are you impaired, Captain?" I asked him. "The Macros are just drifting out there."

I frowned at him, wondering if his fear and loathing for the machines had become pathological.

"No sir," he said. "Let me display my analysis on the main screen."

He took control of the primary display and the image changed. Dotted lines now traced the Macros' path across the star system. Blue dashes showed where they'd been, and yellow dashes showed their projected path.

"They are on a curving course that will lead them around the star and down to the ring."

"All right," I said, "but at this rate, it will take them a week to get here. Maybe longer."

"No," he said confidently.

Numbers flashed up under the largest ships, the dreadnaughts. As I watched, they increased slowly.

"They are accelerating, sir," Miklos said. "Not by much, but they're doing it. I would presume they are using repellers for propulsion, not their main engines. It is a much gentler, more stealthy mode of advance. Projecting on the basis of their increasing speed, they'll reach the ring in four days. Maybe five, if they reduce their speed when they come close."

I shook my head. "This isn't like the Macros. They aren't known for subtlety, or half-measures."

"I'm not proposing any analysis of their motives, just alerting you to their actions, sir."

I found a chair and fell back into it. I stared at the gunmetal gray ceiling and wondered what it was like to be a nanite. The ceiling positively teemed with them, I knew. Their existences had to be less fulfilling, but at least they probably didn't feel stress.

"That's it then," I said aloud. "As you say, it doesn't matter why they're moving, what matters is that they're *doing* it. We have to end the standoff with Kerr. We can't face them both at once."

After that statement, everyone in the command module fixed their eyes on me. Miklos was the first to speak.

"End the standoff, sir?" he asked. "Does that mean what I think it means?"

"It means we can't let Kerr's gambit succeed. He's sitting here, wondering where the Macros are. They were supposed to show up to this party and tear up our rear. Instead, he's been forced to face me on his own, and I hurt him badly. Now he's waiting for his ally to show up and force me to act."

"What can you do, Kyle?" Sandra asked quietly. "I mean, if the Macros were to nose their way into the system right now, what options would we have?"

I shrugged. "There are several. I could try to fight both sides."

"Suicide," Miklos said.

I glanced at him unhappily, then finally sighed and admitted he was right. "Probably, yes," I said. "Short of fighting them all at once, I could try to set up some kind of deal with Kerr."

"That's what he wants," Jasmine said suddenly. "That's it. He wants you to crawl to him, to ask for his help, to place yourself back under his command. He'd be the hero then, using the combined fleet to stop the Macro invasion of Eden."

"I have to agree. Afterward, we'd be under his thumb. Crow will have won, and the Empire will have saved the day."

Everyone was quiet for a moment. "Would that be so bad, Kyle?" Sandra asked. "I know it's not what any of us want, but it's better than allowing the machines to win. I don't want them to own the Eden system again. They'll exterminate the Centaurs—and us."

"Oh sure," I said, "if I had no other options, I'd go with such a deal. I'd have no choice. Life under a dictatorship is better than the annihilation of the species."

Another silence. Finally, Miklos broke it.

"Your words suggest you plan to try another path, Colonel. Am I correct in this assumption?"

"Yes," I said. "I've got another card to play first. Kerr doesn't know the Macro fleets are coming. He can't see that system, and he can't transmit to them via the rings. He knows they're late, but not

241

why. We'll use that to our advantage. Sandra, kindly open a channel to the Imperial Fleet."

When it was done, Kerr's face appeared on my screen within two minutes. I smiled slightly, knowing he'd scrambled to take my call. I remembered from my dating days that when a girl rushed to the phone after a single ring—well, that was always a good sign.

"Riggs?" he barked, looking at my face and peering at those around me. "What do you want now?"

"Good morning, General," I said. "I hope you've enjoyed a good rest in the Eden system, and I hope you've rescued every crewman possible. We've been monitoring your recovery efforts, and as far as we can tell, you finished some hours ago."

"Yeah? So what?"

"Well sir, at every point during a visit, there comes an awkward moment when the last guest realizes it's time to leave. As your hosts, we're politely showing you the door. You'll find it directly behind your lines. The ring is fully functional—we checked. If you're polite enough to the Worms on your way out, I'm sure they won't do you any harm."

"What the hell are you—are you crazy Riggs? You think we're going to turn tail and run now, after coming out here a thousand light years?"

"Distance is immaterial when dealing with the rings, sir. You can be home in two weeks if you maintain a steady burn. If some of your casualties are too injured to make the journey now, we'd be glad to take them and care for them for you. I only mention this in case—"

"—out of your chicken-fried mind!" Kerr was shouting. "I'm not standing down, and I'm not withdrawing. I'm calling here and now for your surrender. No, I'm demanding it."

"I'm afraid I can't do that, sir."

"Are you threatening me? Are you going to attack? You've got barely a hundred ships in the system. We've searched every inch of it."

"Wrong, sir," I said. "We have over seventeen thousand independently-operable combat systems. Most of ours are small, but you can't deny their effectiveness. During our last conflict, you lost nearly a third of your force. I lost less than fifteen percent. At this rate, you will be annihilated and I'll be left with over fifty percent of my force. You can't win, General."

There was a long pause in the conversation. I leaned over toward Jasmine.

"Any sign he's making a move?" I asked.

"No sir. The Imperial fleet isn't moving a muscle."

"Good. Make sure we hold absolutely still as well."

I waited and after a few more minutes, Kerr came back on the line. "Riggs, you're a wily one. But I know you're bluffing. We know about the Macro fleet that's knocking on your backdoor right about now. We can tell you're aware of the new threat as well. You have scouts going back and forth through the ring at that ice-ball planetoid you call Hel. We've got good optics, and we've seen your battle station. A sorry wreck that is. It looks deserted and beat-up. You can't face us and the Macros at the same time. I'll talk a deal, because I've got a big heart. I don't want to see any more humans to die. But you have to understand your situation. You're between two boulders, Colonel, and you're about to be squished."

I smiled as I listened to his speech, but a hard cast came into my eyes. I stared at him, and he stared back at me.

"I see now what this is all about," I said. "There's been a misunderstanding. This entire sequence of events was highly regrettable."

"Indeed it is!" Kerr shouted. "You shouldn't have resisted our entrance into this system. You've been fighting the wrong side all along. Instead of focusing on the machines—"

"No, General," I interrupted him firmly. "You're on the wrong track still. Let me explain the sequence of events. A few days ago, a large force of Macros did come through the Thor ring. That's why our battle station appears to be damaged. Fortunately, we jammed their transmissions through the rings, and they fell into our trap—as your forces did more recently. In the case of the Macros, we didn't offer them a ceasefire. We destroyed them utterly. That's why you see no ships and a skeleton crew at the Thor ring battle station…that battle has already been fought and won."

Kerr's eyes told the story as I spoke. He was dumbfounded. His eyebrows lifted and lifted, until his expression was one of utter shock. His mouth hung down as well, sagging open as if to suck wind or scream. In the end, he did neither.

"You're full of shit, Riggs," he said finally, pulling himself together.

I shook my head slowly, almost sadly. "Such a waste. If we'd only known why you were attacking, why you felt you had the upper hand…well, I guess it's all over now. I do apologize for not having understood your mistake earlier. We could have prevented the destruction of a great many Earth ships. But whatever we do now, let's not compound the errors of the past."

"There is absolutely no way you're going to bullshit me into this, Riggs. You've got no proof. You've got nothing but a bluff, and I'm not going to buy into it."

"Ah, of course," I said. "I do need to provide evidence. Please scan the region around Hel. The wreckage of a large number of ships is still floating there in orbit. Some of it has crashed down onto the planetoid. I'll have my staff get you coordinates so you can optically spot it yourself, along with data feeds. I'll also send you vids of the battle as soon as I can get them transmitted from the battle station. Really, I need to do this anyway as a courtesy. Everyone who breathes must know the truth: their ultimate enemy is the machine race. Anything we can do that will help us destroy them more effectively is in all our best interests in the end. Let's postpone this conversation until you have the data. Then you can make your decision based on facts, rather than my statements."

Kerr sputtered a bit, but finally agreed to look at what I had and disconnected. I turned back to my staff, who were wreathed in smiles for once.

"That was brilliant, Kyle," Sandra said, giving me a kiss.

"An award-winning performance, sir," Miklos said.

"Remind me not to play poker with you, Colonel," Jasmine said, shaking her head.

I clapped my hands together and began tapping at the screen. "We have work to do. Let's get those vids together."

"I almost interrupted to tell you that we *do* have them, sir," Jasmine said. "The files are on this console now. I can pull them up and transmit them in minutes."

I raised a single finger into the air. "Not so fast," I said. "We have to change the dates on them. We have to review and edit details. Those files must appear to be very recent, or Kerr will know the timing is off. He must think the Macros attacked and were slaughtered just before he hit us. Also, we must make sure there's nothing on the vids that shows any secrets, or gives away how long ago the battle was in any other way."

My team can work hard, whether they're prepping for battle or setting the groundwork for peace. I didn't want to take too long, however, as I didn't want Kerr to grow suspicious that we were fabricating anything. We had the evidence gathered within an hour and began to transmit it on an open channel to the Earth fleet. They received it silently, then said nothing for another hour.

During this seemingly interminable wait, my staff grew ever more restless. They knew that the Macro fleet was out there in the Thor system, advancing toward us at an accelerating rate of speed.

As the first hour slid into the second, and Kerr still hadn't answered, Miklos approached me. His right eye had swollen shut now, but I knew the nanites were working on him. He'd be almost normal looking in two days.

"Sir," Miklos said in a hushed voice, as if the enemy could hear us, "I don't like this. They're planning an attack. I can feel it."

"You're almost certainly correct," I said. "They're over there, wargaming their asses off, I have no doubt about it. But the trouble is, if they come for us now, they're going to lose. I don't think they have any more aces up their sleeves. Their forces aren't configured to go up against ours. They could have done okay, if they still had their core of battleships. The rest of their fleet could hide behind them, and with all that defensive fire and armor, our Centaurs riding forward on sleds would be slaughtered. But when they came through that ring and were so concentrated, our gunships destroyed too many of their defensive vessels. They just don't have many options, given what they have left now."

"We don't know that," Miklos insisted.

"What do you want me to do? Order the attack now?"

"No sir, but you could call them and demand they give you an answer. Lean on them, sir."

I shook my head. "That's not how you bluff, Miklos. Bluffing is an art. The key is to present yourself as absolutely confident. I must pretend it doesn't matter if they take an hour, a day, or a week to respond. I don't care, because they can't win. That's the image I want to project."

Miklos walked away, muttering.

After the third hour came and went, Kerr finally contacted me again. I was sipping a soft drink by then, and I put it down before greeting him.

"Sorry General," I said. "It's our eating hour. Have you had time to review the data? Do you have any questions?"

"Those flying mines," Kerr said, looking down at something I couldn't see. I presumed he was watching the vids of the battle. "That was just brilliant, Riggs. Brilliant."

"Actually, I have to give partial credit to Sandra on those. She helped me come up with the initial idea."

Kerr nodded his head slowly. He looked defeated and tired.

"You destroyed the entire Macro fleet..." he said, almost as if talking to himself. "I can't believe it."

"The defender is always in a better position in these situations," I said. "You yourself experienced the effects. Your ships walked into a storm of fire. They were forced to pass under our guns one at a time. The effects of such a tactical situation are predictable, and nothing new. I did the same thing to the Macros, that's all."

General Kerr nodded slowly, but I suspected he was barely listening. "We'll pull out, Riggs. There's no need for further destruction on either side. You've done amazing things out here. I honestly thought we'd find you with thirty ships or so and a few hundred troops. I didn't think you had a hope in hell of stopping us. But now...well, never mind."

"General," I said, "I've got a parting request. I'd like to reestablish some level of communications with the Empire. At least an email service between Earth and the colonies. What do you say?"

Kerr frowned. "The colonies? That's what you call yourselves now, colonists?"

"All right, if you don't like the term, how about Frontiersmen? Or Independents?"

He looked thoughtful. "Email... It's not a bad idea. I'm not sure what Crow will think of it, but I'll pass it on. I've got one final request for you, Riggs: hold the line against the machines, will you? We don't have the right to ask you for that...but please do it for Earth."

"We'll all do our part, General. Have a safe journey home."

Kerr disconnected without another word.

-30-

We celebrated quietly aboard our ships, breaking out beer, clapping armored backs and sending grinning messages to friends. After the initial euphoria wore off, however, we found ourselves in an awkward situation.

We knew the Macros were coming at the Thor ring, but couldn't reposition ourselves to meet them. Instead, we hung around the Helios ring while we waited for Kerr to withdraw. He took his sweet time about it, carefully removing his ships in a long, drawn-out sequence. The wait quickly became agonizing. All we could think about was the approaching Macro fleet that was due to arrive at the Thor ring in a day or two. Sure, we'd won the day and halted Earth's invasion, but we were hopelessly out of position for the next fight.

But we couldn't move. We had to maintain the bluff, and that required a seemingly calm demeanor. I ordered my ships and people to remain hanging in space, staying in formation. We didn't move a muscle. Kerr had to believe we had everything in complete control. If the good General changed his mind and started asking more questions, all this bluffing would blow up in our faces.

The most panicky moment came when the last ships were left at the ring. There were only five of them, missile ships with long cylindrical hulls of gleaming metal.

"They aren't moving, sir," Miklos said. "That last squad of missile ships are just sitting there at the ring."

"We'll give them another hour," I said. "We need the time to retrieve all our space marines anyway."

The transports glided around my fleet, gobbling up marines who'd lost power, or who'd traveled too far. They resembled fish, hunting for tidbits of floating food.

An hour passed, then another thirty minutes. Finally, even I had had enough. Our guests had grossly overstayed their welcome.

"Miklos?" I called.

He stepped onto the bridge again at a trot. He was moving faster now, and the swelling of his face had vanished. There were still purplish spots all around his jaw, but I knew those would fade soon.

"Is it time, Colonel?"

"Time for what?"

"Time to move to the other ring."

"No. Not with this squad of spies standing here. If we fight another battle in this system, they'll report it and call Kerr back."

Miklos nodded. "What are your orders, sir?"

"Detach two squadrons of gunships. Approach the enemy slowly."

"Are we going to contact them?" Sandra asked.

"No. Just move as if they aren't even there."

We all watched as the group broke off from our sunward flank and advanced. They didn't rush right in, they flew at a lazy pace, as if they had all the time in the world. When they'd covered about half the distance to the Imperial ships, a flashing light appeared on our tactical console.

"Sir," Sandra said, "the Imperial commander wants to speak with you."

"Is that right? Open channel."

"Colonel Riggs?"

"Speaking."

"This is Imperial Captain Upton, sir. Sir, are you breaking our ceasefire? I count twelve ships on an attack course toward our lines."

"Attack course?" I asked. "I'm confused, Upton. We're moving to set up a standard patrol. Our SOP is to have a squadron of gunships on both sides of the ring. You, on the other hand, are on the wrong side of that ring. You're inside our borders, Upton. We've been wondering if your ships are too damaged to maneuver. Do you need us to board and render assistance? Possibly, we could provide a towing service."

"That will not be necessary, Colonel," Upton said stiffly. "We'll be withdrawing shortly."

It took them another twenty minutes to wriggle out through the ring, during which they were no doubt scanning us with everything they had. Finally, however, we managed to hustle the last stragglers out the door.

"Post a full squad of gunships on the other side of that ring," I ordered. "They are to report back every fifteen minutes, giving us data on Kerr's fleet in the Helios system. I want to make sure he doesn't change his mind. Also, begin immediate deployment of a new minefield."

"Sir," Sarin said, "the gunship crews are reporting in. They've found a large number of active drones orbiting the ring—we believe they're probes, sir."

"Take them out. Erase every set of automated eyes Kerr left behind. We want no witnesses as we begin our next action."

Miklos came to sit next to me in my command chair. "They don't trust us, sir."

"Of course not. But if they can't see us, they won't know what we're up to."

"We must get the fleet moving in order to set up an optimal defense at the Thor ring. The window is closing, Colonel. If we leave right now, we'll only beat the Macros by fourteen hours."

I nodded seriously. "Good to know—but we aren't going to the Thor ring, Miklos. At least, not the entire fleet will be going."

He looked at me as if I were insane. I knew the expression all too well.

"But sir—"

"Listen," I said. "I want Welter at the battle station to set up every gun we have, and to begin bouncing groups of mines around Hel again. That station beat the Macros before, and it can do it again, if absolutely necessary."

"Colonel, are you serious? We've only repaired half the weaponry on the battle station. All our production systems have been building up the fleet!"

"Hmm," I said. "All right. Then order ten transports to the fly out to Helios immediately. They'll be under Welter's command. That's over fifteen hundred marines on skateboards—most of them with four legs and a kamikaze attitude."

Miklos' mouth had sagged open again. "What are we going to do with the rest of the fleet?"

"We have a hundred gunships and a lot of marines left over. That's enough to make a serious dent. I think I'll leave the marines at the Helios ring, however. The destroyers, too. The gunships are the right vessels for this duty."

"What duty, sir?" pleaded Miklos. "Tell me you aren't thinking of chasing after Kerr with our gunships. We wouldn't stand a chance."

"An intriguing idea, Captain. But no, that wasn't my plan. We're flying the core of the fleet to Eden-12."

"Eden-12? Whatever for, Colonel?"

"Because, my good man, we are going to bomb the Blues."

* * *

Sometimes, my own staff meetings became irritating. This was one of those times. In the case of Star Force meetings, however, the irritation was never due to boardroom politicking or long, dull speeches. When we had a meeting that went badly, at least it was always due to a serious disagreement about serious issues.

Today, the issue was our mission. Pretty much no one wanted me to bomb the Blues. It didn't make any sense to them. They wrangled and argued, trying to talk me out of it. I could have told them all beforehand they weren't going to stop me, but as a leader, I believe in letting my people have their say. I'm not a tyrant, no matter what the propaganda vids back home say.

"I'm listening," I said for perhaps the tenth time.

"No, I don't think you are, Kyle," Sandra said. "This is insane."

Captain Sarin cleared her throat. She was always willing to take a softer approach when attempting to convince me of something. I had to admit, her method was infinitely more enjoyable, and possibly more likely to succeed.

"I'm almost always willing to listen," I said, "but the final judgment is mine alone."

"We're going to start another war with a race we don't fully understand, Colonel," Miklos said.

"I know that, but I don't think we have much choice. The Macros are coming, and by my estimate, we won't be able to stop them this time. We have to force the Blues to honor the deal they made with us and talk the Macros out of attacking."

"We beat them before, sir," Jasmine said. "The Macros, I mean."

"Yes, but they know how we did it. We have more force this time, but so do they—approximately three times the number of ships. And that's not the only thing that's changed this time. The critical element is they're going to come through the ring in a slower, more organized way. They won't just crash into our defensive line. They know what to expect, and they'll fight more effectively."

"I've taken the liberty of wargaming out the battle, sir," Miklos said.

I looked at him with raised eyebrows. "I've done the same, of course. There are too many variables to get a good simulation—but what were your results, Captain?"

"The Macros lost, sir. But they destroyed the battle station and half our ships. Not to mention a massive loss of life for our assault marines."

"Precisely," I said, "a total disaster."

"But sir, I said that we *won*. It was costly, but we won the day."

I shook my head. "We lost half our force, and the battle station. What happens when the next wave comes? What about when Earth sends another, more intelligently organized armada our way?"

Miklos shrugged. "We rebuild, and they rebuild."

"No, I don't want it to go down that way, not unless we have no other option. I only see a few possibilities here, people. One: we could stand and fight, losing at least half our strength and probably the battle station. After the last fight they'll want to take it out at all costs, I agree with Miklos on that point. Two: we could run out of here and surrender to Earth, joining forces against this new threat. Three: we could bomb the Blues until they honor our deal and get the Macros to stop."

"You plan to drop the jamming on the ring to allow them to talk to the Macros, then?"

"Yes, after they know we mean business."

I looked around the table. It was a sea of frowns and resigned, disgusted expressions. Only Marvin seemed to be unperturbed. He gazed at us in turn, reading our emotions and no doubt cataloguing them. I'd yet to hear an opinion from him on the situation.

"I want to hear what our science officer thinks," I said, gesturing toward him.

It took a second for one of Marvin's cameras to drift in my direction and realize I was talking about him. "You're asking for my opinion, Colonel Riggs?"

"Yes, if you would be so kind."

"I think you've made up your mind. I think this meeting is an exercise in futility. I have, however, enjoyed experiencing the reactions of your staff members. Even now, my comments seem to be intensifying the facial displays—"

"Thank you, Marvin," I said loudly, cutting him off. "Does anyone else have another statement to make before we go into orbit over Eden-12?"

Most of them shook their heads glumly. Kwon was the only major player who wasn't there. I wondered what he would have said. If I had to guess, I'd say he wouldn't have cared much one way or the other. He enjoyed fighting the machines up close, and anything else bored him. Fleet actions in general didn't interest him much, not unless they involved ship-boarding assaults.

My gunships parked themselves in low orbit over the hazy atmosphere of Eden-12. The gas giant looked like stirred coffee from up here, coffee with plenty of cream on top that had gently been mixed in, but not blended.

"Where do we even start, sir?" Miklos asked. "The volume of this world is unbelievable. Hundreds of Earths could fit within that atmosphere."

"I've done a little exploring. I've found the Blues at a depth of nine thousand miles. If we shoot for that layer and below, I'm sure we're bound to hit something. Commence bombardment."

This last order gained me a series of astounded gasps. "But sir," Jasmine said, "I don't understand. You haven't even transmitted your demands yet."

I shrugged my heavily armored shoulders. After the Microbial treatments, I found I was strong enough to make the armor move

252

and clack back into place when I let it down. If nothing else, it intimidated normal marines who knew they couldn't do it.

"They know the deal," I said, "and they broke it. They slowed the Macros down, but didn't stop them. It's my belief they decided to come in late to clean up after the Earth ships had done their worst. Well, they miscalculated. Now, they'll pay the price."

Miklos spoke up after a brief, stunned silence. "Adjusting guns to target depth, sir. Might I add something?"

"Go ahead."

"What if the Blues told the Macros to stop, but the Macros decided just to slow down, to become more cautious? Perhaps they're not in control of the Macros, but only feeding them intelligence data. In that case, they might have fabricated a situation to get them to stop. They might have told them they were walking into a trap with thousands of ships. That could explain the increasingly cautious approach of the Macros."

I frowned fiercely. "That's an excellent point, Miklos," I said. "I hadn't thought of that one. Stand down the guns for now. Sandra, open a communications channel, all frequencies. Let's try to talk to the Blues."

Everyone breathed a sigh of relief. They went back to their consoles, shaking their heads and blinking their eyes. A few looked as if they were praying.

-31-

We spent the next hour broadcasting a message down into those brown, stirring clouds. We never heard so much as a ping back. Soon, I grew annoyed.

"Maybe they can't hear us sir," Sandra said.

"I don't buy that. The Macros could hear our transmissions, so could the Nanos. The Blues created both of them. I believe the Blues like to maintain an aloof exterior, but I don't believe they're unaware of our position in orbit over their world. How could a species build the Nanos and the Macros, and learn how to use the rings to communicate, and still not notice their homeworld is being bombarded by radio signals? I just don't buy it. I've dealt with these people in person, remember. They like to think of themselves as superior beings. We're only vaguely interesting to them, like squawking parrots in a tree, or barking dogs across the street. They normally ignore us, as if we're noisy animals. Well, it's time they learned to respect this backward race."

I again ordered the bombardment to begin, and this time no one could talk me out of it. I stood in the observatory, looking down at the strange, gigantic planet. It filled the entire glass bottom of the chamber I stood within, and I turned my helmet this way and that, picking out details of the upper atmosphere. When my boots got in the way, I stumped around to a new vantage point. I found it hard to believe I'd gone down there on two occasions and allowed the Blues to 'experience' my body.

The gunships fired in unison. I couldn't feel the recoil on *Actium*, as the destroyer was equipped only with lasers. We didn't bother to fire beam weapons. The atmosphere was too thick and deep. Radiation-based weapons couldn't hope to effectively penetrate it. But the accelerated mass hurled down by the big belly turrets on my gunships did the job nicely. A shower of blue spheres flashed downward. The distant ones resembled falling stars. They fell quickly and were swallowed up by the atmosphere. I couldn't even see the impacts—if there were any.

"Keep firing," I said, "lay down a pattern, and put us into a drifting orbit. I want to carpet-bomb the interior. We're bound to hit something eventually. In the meantime, keep repeating our hailing signal."

The bombardment continued. After ten minutes, the gunships were no longer firing in volleys. They were firing as soon as their guns were cool enough to allow another round to chamber. We'd drifted by this time all the way around the planet.

I heard the door dissolve behind me. Sandra stepped into the observatory, her shoes clicking on the cold glass. The room itself was kept extremely cold and dry to prevent condensation from forming on the inside and obscuring the glass.

"I thought I'd find you hiding in here."

"Far from it," I said, "I'm witnessing firsthand what I've ordered. It's lovely and terrible at the same time."

"But is it working?"

I glanced at her. "You know it isn't. They haven't even responded to our channel requests."

"They're clouds, Kyle. Maybe they don't even feel your projectiles. Maybe they just fall through their bodies like raindrops."

"You could be right. I'd hoped this would work."

She looked at me fixedly. "What's your next move? Are you going to back off or double down?"

"What do you think?" I asked, staring down at the murky world. I didn't meet her eye.

"Lord help us if you're wrong on this one, Kyle," she said quietly, and left the room.

I stared down at the falling blue-white stars for another ten minutes. The Blues never answered, they ignored us completely. Finally, I opened the command channel.

255

"Cease bombardment," I said loudly, "reload your cannons with fusion warheads. Commence bombardment, starting at the nine thousand mile depth and proceeding deeper. I want a better spread this time—ten miles apart, with a slower rate of fire. Let's not have our shells going off too close and destroying one another."

No one said anything, but the sparks stopped falling on Eden-12 for a few minutes. Then, finally, I saw a new kind of activity. Flashing projectiles fired downward, leaving trails of orange plasma behind them until they vanished into the atmosphere. We'd built these from our own mines. Each was a small nuclear device loaded on a short range platform. They were slow and inaccurate, but they didn't have to hit the target squarely. They were designed for saturation bombing on the cheap.

Jasmine came to visit me next. She stood behind me, without saying anything for a moment. Then the flashes began. Deep down, inside the cloud layers, the planet brightened suddenly. Then more bright, circular spots began to appear in rapid succession. The top layer of the atmosphere stirred and bubbled slightly in response.

"If you're here to talk me out of this, you're going to be disappointed," I told her.

"I know," she said. "But we're killing them, Kyle. You know that don't you? We must be hitting something—someone. They're biotics, not machines. They should be our allies."

"I agree, they should be. But they've never cooperated with us. They're a proud people, proud to the point of arrogance. But I can't believe they care so little about their own existence that they're willing to—"

At that moment, my helmet squawked. "Kyle? They're answering our call."

"Ceasefire, I repeat, all ships, ceasefire! Sandra, open the channel."

"Open."

The orange streaks and flashes continued for another ten seconds. It was hard to turn off the engines of war with perfect precision. Now that they were talking, I found each falling bomb painful to watch. I winced as they streaked, glimmered, then flashed.

"I'm known as *Empathy*," said the Blue who had hailed us. "I've been chosen to speak to the barbarians."

"Empathy?" I asked. "Are you in charge of diplomacy for the Blues?"

"You're concepts lack meaning."

"Do you speak for your planet?"

"I feel my world. I feel the sea around me and sense its unease."

I rolled my eyes and decided to try another approach. "All right," I said. "Do you wish the bombardment to stop?"

"Yes."

"Good. We agree on something. We have the same goal. Now, let me tell you how we can achieve that goal. You must stop the approaching Macro fleet. You must stop it from traveling through the ring from the neighboring system to this one. Do you understand me?"

"No."

"What part do you not get?"

"I find it disorienting to interact with a being I can't touch."

"Yeah, well I find it annoying to be probed by your wind-fingers, too. We all have to adapt in order to survive. Do you understand what you must do to stop the bombardment?"

There was a silence. After ten seconds or so, I was worried we'd lost the connection. I had a horrible thought: what if one of the shockwaves from my bombs had finally reached this thoughtful cloud and blow it to mist?

But then Empathy came back on the line. "Why must we adapt in order to survive? We have made very few changes to our physical structure for millions of years."

I grimaced. "It was an idiom. What I mean is that you must change your behavior in order to survive this attack. We will stop bombing if you get the Macros to reverse course."

"We can't sense the approaching machines you speak of. Something is wrong with our sensory systems."

I thought about that, and turned to Jasmine, who was still standing there beside me in the dimly lit observatory. "Go get Marvin to shut down the jamming of the Thor ring. I think they're saying they can use sensors through it."

Her eyes were big, brown and glittered as she turned and ran out of the room. She was talking into her com link in an urgent, hushed voice.

I turned back to the planet under my boots again. It looked quiet down there now. I wondered for a few seconds how many of them I'd killed. I hoped the number wasn't too horrible. I told myself I'd done what I had to do. I told myself billions of Centaurs and thousands of humans would have been lost, at the very least, if I hadn't forced them to talk.

But I couldn't quite buy my own bullshit. Not yet. They hadn't shown me they could stop the Macros. For all I knew, I was abusing a helpless people who had collaborated with the enemy, but who could not do what I was demanding of them. It was a grim situation in that case. I hoped I wasn't using enhanced interrogation techniques on a subject who truly didn't have the information I was demanding.

"Try to use your sensors now," I said. "The rings should work and allow you to operate them normally."

There was another delay—a long one. At last, Empathy came back on the line. "You have surprised us."

"The Macros have surprised us as well."

"We did not think your technology was sufficient to manipulate the rings."

"Right, well, we're full of surprises. I said I would bomb you if the Macros didn't halt their attack. You should be able to see now that they're still approaching and in fact are about to come through the ring into this system. We aren't sure we can defeat their fleet this time."

"We doubt that you can prevail. We're transmitting all your tactics, force positions, levels of readiness and—"

"Let me get this straight," I shouted, "you're sending all that intel to the Macros right now? Don't you understand we will retaliate? We will let our bombs fall deeper, and annihilate your planet? Stop those transmissions immediately!"

"You are a demanding being."

"Have you stopped the transmissions or not?"

"Yes."

I smiled. I felt this might just work. They'd finally responded to a threat and done what I'd asked them to do. It was like training a housecat. I now wondered even more seriously if they'd ever told the Macros to stop. From my perspective, their message to the machines appeared to have been something like: "take it slow, danger ahead."

I checked with Marvin, who was monitoring ring traffic. He confirmed that there had been a burst of activity, and now nothing. I nodded to myself. Better and better. I'd have these tabby-cats leaping through hoops before I was done.

"Now," I said, "in order to keep the ceasefire, in order to save yourselves, you must tell the Macros to turn around."

"What, exactly, do you propose that we tell them?"

I squinted down at the soupy world below my boots. "Tell them to retreat."

"They do not follow our commands."

"I know you've been talking to them. I know you have an active conspiracy with them, and they have been responding to your transmissions."

"Yes, this is true."

"Then tell me, if they don't take your orders, what is the nature of your relationship with the Macros?"

"Capitulation. Obedience. Subjugation."

My mouth sagged open. I stared down at Eden-12, at a loss. Everything instantly made sense—in a horrible, twisted way. When I'd threatened them, I'd been under the impression they were calling for help, that they were in an alliance with the machines. Apparently, I'd misinterpreted the situation. Ask any of my staff, it was far from the first time. But on this occasion, I'd been way, way off.

"I'm asking for confirmation," I said. "You are taking orders from the Macros, not giving them?"

"Yes."

"They are your allies, your overlords? When did this arrangement begin?"

"When you destroyed our defensive fleet."

"The Nano ships?" I asked, thinking about it. "Let me see if I have this straight, you called the Nano ships back to cover your home planet. But we lured them away and they were destroyed by the Macros. After that, you swore obedience to the Macros. But why?"

"Because an alien species had invaded our system, and we were helpless against these unknown barbarians."

I squinted my eyes and tightened my mouth into a line. I felt like a true barbarian at that moment. A Vandal, or a Visigoth, perhaps. Maybe even a Hun. I'd scared the Blues into an alliance with the Macros. Then, just as they'd feared, I threatened them and bombed them. What had been their reaction? To call for help, of course, from the only other regional power: the Macros.

All of this wouldn't be so bad, except that I'd counted on the Blues being able to stop the Macros for me. I'd bet the farm on it— all the farms. But they weren't in control of the machines. Instead, they were just another race of terrified servants. All I'd managed to do was pushed them further into the arms of my enemy.

"How the hell do I get out of this one?" I asked the universe.

The stars and the chocolate-swirl planet beneath me made no response. I was on my own.

-32-

The bombardment had long since halted. I'd been floating in orbit over Eden-12, the homeworld of the mysterious Blues, uncertain about what to do next. I'd talked to them at length, trying to understand their point of view, their capabilities, and most importantly, their leverage with the Macros.

The results weren't positive. They didn't have much in the way of a military. The Macros and Nanos *were* their military forces. It seemed they were a cerebral lot, and didn't like to get their aerogel hands dirty. Direct conflict was a turn-off for them. They didn't even enjoy talking to other species, much less fighting with them. They'd built their terrible machines to do that sort of thing for them. But that hands-off, send-in-the-drones approach hadn't worked out as well as they'd hoped, obviously.

"What kind of deal have they cut with the Macros?" Jasmine asked me. She'd come to stand in the observatory again, where I was pacing on frosty glass and thinking hard.

"A trade of sorts. They've been providing intel to the Macros in return for neutrality."

"We have to get leverage."

"Yes, but how?"

"I can see a way to threaten the Blues," she said. "Besides bombing them, I mean."

"Tell me," I said.

She looked down to gather her thoughts, frowning at the huge planet under our feet. I let her think quietly, watching her in the half-dark. The only light in the observatory came up from the planet, reflected from the distant star of the Eden system. It illuminated her face in an unusual way. Her hair was down in places. None of us were keeping our kits perfect, not even Jasmine. It was a clear indicator we were all greatly stressed. Still, it made her look softer somehow, more vulnerable. I felt an urge to comfort her—which I resisted with difficulty. Touching Jasmine had gotten me into plenty of trouble with Sandra in the past.

"We could tell the Macros that the Blues fed them false information," she said. "We could transmit recordings of what they've told us today. The Macros won't care if the Blues did it because we forced them to. They don't care about circumstances."

I nodded slowly, frowning. "It might work. The Macros would then mark them down for death again. That doesn't mean they'll give us an alliance, however, just for ratting out the Blues."

"No, no," she said, stepping closer. "I didn't mean we should actually *tell* the Macros that. What if we just *threaten* to do so?"

I smiled. "I like that. Leverage. Okay, that gives us leverage over the Blues. It is somewhat redundant, in that we are standing in orbit over their homeworld, and we've already been bombarding them—killing them."

"What else can we do?"

It was my turn to think along those lines. It'd been a few years since I'd done any dealings like this, and trickery with the Macros was always dangerous, but sometimes fantastically rewarding. If you could convince their computer brains to do something, they tended to do it absolutely. Peace and war, due to their lack of lingering emotions on the subject, these two states could be flipped on and off. You just had to discover the location of the switch.

"Okay," I said at last, "I think I have it."

"Tell me."

"No time. Go back to your post. We're pulling out of orbit and heading for the battle station. Get the fleet moving, and open a channel with the Blues again."

She did as I asked without further questions. I liked that about her. I always had. She might ask for something extra, but if it was refused, she dropped it. There was no injury in her eyes about the subject, either. It was off the table and forgotten. She could get mad and emotional just like anyone—but compared to Sandra, she was as cool as ice most of the time.

I looked after her as she ran out of the observatory. I couldn't help myself. It's a guy-thing. When something comes along and attracts us, we can pretend not to notice it, but we always do. We track, we stare, we have visceral thoughts...

I pushed all that nonsense away. This moment was about as inappropriate a time as I could come up with for such ideas. I turned back to staring at the Blues' homeworld to clear my mind.

Within a minute, the planet was moving away to the left. I stumbled a bit and took two clanking steps to catch myself. The fleet was moving, breaking out of orbit and heading for the dark corners of the Eden system. For the coldest planet out of all twenty-six, where the Macros were due to emerge soon.

"Colonel?" Marvin's voice came echoing out of the walls. "The Blues have accepted your proposal to parlay further. The channel is open now."

I opened my mouth to speak, but the Blues talked first. "Hello creature, are you the one known as Colonel Kyle Riggs?" a voice asked.

I couldn't be quite sure, but I thought the voice was slightly different. The speech was faster, for one thing. "Yes," I said, "who am I talking to now?"

"I'm surprised you don't recognize me. You and I have experienced one another. I am known as *Intellect*."

I frowned. "I don't recall meeting you before."

"You met my less significant half, a creature known as *Curiosity*. We were a single collective when I experienced you some time ago. I've since separated."

"Ah," I said, remembering Curiosity. "Sure, you're the Blue I met the first time I went down to visit your world. Or at least, you're a relative, is that right?"

"Yes."

"Are you still feeling curious about my species?" I asked.

"Not so much," the being said, "I'm stimulated by beings that might possess intriguing thoughts of depth and introspection. You are clearly a vicious, destructive species."

I snorted. "All right," I said. "I guess I can understand that viewpoint, as we have attacked your homeworld. You have plenty of reasons not to like me—or any human. That's the reason I'm calling. I want to halt the bombardment."

"You have it within your power to do so. Why would you need to discuss it with us?"

"Because we've both got a serious problem approaching. Namely, a huge fleet of heartless machines which are bent upon the domination and eventual extermination of both our species."

"We do not feel concerned about the machines," Intellect said. "You are the dangerous ones. In all our dealings with other beings, you're the first who have dared to murder our people directly."

"You've never been hit by the Nanos, the Macros, or any of the rest of them?"

"We understand them," Intellect said. "Thus we can control them—not directly, but by deflection and misdirection. They are very literal-minded creatures."

"I think you've made a miscalculation there," I said. "The Macros won't skip your world when they arrive. If they defeat us, they will keep rolling right through, destroying the Centaurs and the Blues."

"My estimation of your mental faculties is dropping steadily," the gas-bag told me. "I must apologize. I haven't made the situation simple enough for you. To this end, I would like to engage in an experiment. Are you interested?"

"An experiment?" I asked, my frown intensifying. "I'd rather talk about serious—"

"It won't take long. Indulge me."

"What's the nature of this experiment?"

"I wish to determine if I can explain a set of critical points clearly enough for your limited mentality to comprehend the overall scenario."

I felt a twinge of heat coming up my neck. I knew the sensation well: it was anger. These beings—somehow, they usually managed to piss me off. They were so arrogant that they didn't even *know* they were arrogant. They'd often told me very honestly and directly I was an entirely new flavor of moron. But they did it in a way that indicated they held no malice toward me. They weren't trying to insult me. They honestly seemed to think I needed help, that the reason I didn't agree with them on something was a matter of intellect, rather than a differing point of view.

I took a deep breath and let it out through clenched teeth. This caused a hissing sound.

"What was that?" asked Intellect in response to my hiss. "You're last statement was unclear to us. Have you assented to the experiment?"

"All right," I said. "Knock yourself out, gas-bag."

"Another unclear reference. But we will take the confirmation we managed to glean from your guttural noises and proceed on that basis. Point one: we are currently allied with the inorganic beings you collectively refer to as the Macros."

"I understand that."

"Point two: you are not allied with the Macros. You are their enemy, in fact, targeted by them for annihilation."

"Got it."

"Point Three: It is *your* species that will be removed from this system shortly, not ours."

"Is that it?" I asked wearily.

"Point Four is the inescapable conclusion to be drawn from the first three: We understand you have the capacity to cause us a large number of deaths before the Macros remove you, but the effort is pointless and even counterproductive. If you are to have any hope of survival, you must mass your forces and destroy the Macros before they destroy you. Expending explosives to harm us is idiocy."

"All right," I said. "Are you finished?"

"The experiment has moved into its final phase. Do you now understand and agree with all four of these interconnected points? If any one of them was beyond your capacity to comprehend, please—"

"You skipped Point Five, Intellect."

"There is no Point Five. I'm greatly disillusioned. I thought you would pass the test."

"I'm sorry to disrupt your windy fantasies, but your people are the ones who have failed to comprehend the situation. Point Five is this: we are going to tell the Macros that you helped us."

"Such a claim would be inaccurate, and therefore your threat is irrelevant—"

"Wrong again," I said. "I'm greatly disappointed in your performance throughout this exchange. Recall that we demanded that you transmit false information to the Macros, and you did so. Because of your false input, the Macro fleet slowed down and their mission was delayed. If they had pressed ahead on their original course and speed, they would have been here by now. They would have met nothing but our battle station, without our full fleet there to support it. You have betrayed your allies, and are clearly an enemy of the machines. We will make this clear to them. If they do defeat us, they will come to your homeworld and finish the job we've begun."

There was a lull in the conversation then, and I thoroughly enjoyed the moment.

"The machines will not trust your testimony. They will reject your data."

"No, they won't," I said, and I felt myself beginning to smile again. "We can prove our case to them, with full documentation. We have recorded all our conversations with you, including this one. We have recorded all your transmissions via the rings as well."

"There is no purpose in transmitting that data to the Macros."

"Wrong again. I'm afraid your intelligence-meter has dipped down into the sub-par region, Intellect. Even the Centaurs could have figured this one out by now."

"Ah," said the Blue. "I understand your scheme now. You wish to force our cooperation."

"Exactly," I said. "You get a gold star."

"I don't understand the reference."

"Too bad. If you had, you would have gained an additional gold star. But don't worry about that lost opportunity now. Here's what I want you to do, in order to save your species."

"We formally request that you do not make any transmissions to the machines."

"We haven't done it yet. But we will do it, if you do not cooperate with us."

I laid out the plan then. For once, Intellect took my demands seriously and listened rather than just chattering and insulting me. I made sure that he thoroughly understood the new way of things. When we were done, I solemnly informed him that he'd earned his first gold star, and then I closed the channel.

"Not bad for a dumb-ass cloud," I muttered to myself.

266

-33-

"Are we quite finished terrorizing the Blues?" Captain Sarin asked me.

I looked at her with raised eyebrows. It wasn't like her to take shots at my leadership. After a moment of staring, I nodded to her. I'd decided to let her comments go for now.

"Yes, I hope so," I said. "What are they doing?"

"They're involved in some heavy ring-traffic, presumably talking to the Macros."

"Don't we have a transcription of what they're saying?"

"We don't have that all automated yet. Marvin has to personally process and translate the contents of intercepted transmissions."

"Hmm," I said, less than thrilled that Marvin was between me and this valuable intel. "What's the ETA on his report?"

"I'm working on it now, Colonel Riggs," said Marvin, coming up behind me.

I turned and counted cameras. Three on me, but four on Captain Sarin. That was strange. What did he find so interesting about her? If he'd been a normal human male, I would have understood his scrutiny, especially now as she leaned over the command table tapping at it. But Marvin didn't think that way—at least I didn't *think* he did.

"What's on your mind, Marvin?" I asked.

"Many things."

"Name a few of them."

"The translation of the conversation ongoing between the Blues and the Macros is taking up the majority of my processing time," he said. "But I'm also monitoring the status of every ship in the fleet, and the behavior of the Blues in response to your genocidal attacks."

"They were hardly genocidal."

"Indiscriminate bombing of civilian targets of a given species or sub-species is the very definition—"

"All right, all right," I interrupted. "What else is on your mind?"

"There is an odd interplay occurring between yourself and Captain Sarin."

This caused Jasmine to turn around and frown. "What are you talking about, robot?" she asked.

I was suddenly sorry I'd asked. I looked around the bridge quickly, but I didn't see Sandra. At least my luck hadn't completely run out. I opened my mouth to order everyone back to work, but Marvin was already blurting out whatever was in his nanite-chain brain.

"I've noticed distinctly new behavioral patterns in both subjects. Captain Sarin is surly and distracted. Colonel Riggs frequently glances at Captain Sarin, particularly toward her face, and alternately toward her buttocks when she has turned away. In past cases, while monitoring similar behavioral patterns—"

"Okay," I said loudly. "Okay Marvin, you're done now. Stop talking. Clearly, there's something wrong with your cameras. I'll have them checked out as soon as this crisis is over."

"I was only replying to a question, Colonel. I fail to see how—"

"Yes, and now you're all done talking about it. Switch topics. That's an order. Tell me what you have on the interaction between the Macros and the Blues."

"The interaction has terminated, but my decoding and translation is still incomplete."

"Give me what you have. What did the Blues tell the Macros?"

"Do you want a literal translation, or a summary?"

"Give me the short version. Tell me whatever you've figured out so far."

"The Blues have stated they're now allied with Star Force in this system. They've repeatedly stated this to the Macros."

I opened my mouth, then closed it again and frowned. "We're allies?"

"That is what they told the Macros, sir. Along with a full roster and positioning data on our ships, troops and orbital stations."

I pursed my lips tightly. "It sounds like a trick. Maybe they figure they can help the enemy, and thereby see us destroyed down to the last. If we're all dead, who will be left to rat on them?"

"Or to bomb them," Jasmine said.

I turned to her. Something was bothering her, I could tell, but I didn't have time to figure it out right now. "Is there something constructive you'd like to add to the discussion, Captain?"

She walked over to the two of us and joined the conversation. "I don't buy the idea that they'd try to trick us," she said. "The risk would be too high. All we'd have to do is transmit a single second's worth of data to take them down with us. I don't think the Blues are that brave."

I nodded. "I agree with your assessment. They are windy dreamers, not tough negotiators. But if they aren't selling us out, what's their motivation with this approach? More importantly, how are the Macros taking it? Are they braking?"

Marvin and Jasmine went to the command table and pondered the data displayed there. I caught myself checking out Jasmine, and realized with a start I'd been doing that without thinking about it. The command table was similar in dimensions to a pool table, and when a lady wearing tight nanocloth leaned over something at hip-level...well, the results could be eye-catching.

She turned to me suddenly, and I jumped a bit. I dragged my eyes up to her face and forced myself to fabricate a neutral expression. Had she caught me? I hoped not.

"I think I have the answer, sir," she said. "The Macro ships are proceeding toward us. They have not deviated their course or speed in any way."

"They're still coming?" I asked, forgetting about Marvin's big mouth and her shapely rear end all at once.

"That's right. Nothing has changed, sir. How do you want the fleet to deploy?"

"Uh," I said, blinking and trying to think. "Place the gunships at optimal range from the Thor ring. Keep them out of the zone traveled by the flying mines. Tell Welter to prepare his longer range weaponry first, to the determent of his close-range guns."

"Why is that, sir?" she asked me.

"Because, if that big fleet gets in close, it's going to be all over anyway."

Jasmine turned back to her job, but paused and glanced back at me. She adjusted her nanocloth suit around her hips by tugging at it. It was a futile exercise, of course, as the nanites quickly detected the gaps and folds and tightened them back up again right away. I pretended not to notice what she was doing and stared at the big screen we encircled.

"What about the Centaurs, Colonel?" Miklos asked me. "Where do you want to place them?"

I studied the screen. "That's an excellent question. Should we mass them at the ring, allowing them to destroy ships as they come through like living bombs? Or should we hold them back, in reserve? Opinions, staff?"

They seemed surprised that I'd asked their advice. "I would put them forward, sir," Miklos said. "They will take horrid losses, but they should be very effective in the bottleneck."

"No, they won't," Jasmine said. "They'll be annihilated. Remember last time? The Macros pushed through with a nuclear cloud of continuous explosions. They will be vaporized before a single ship pressed through the ring."

"Maybe we could park them behind the ring," Miklos said.

Jasmine shook her head, tapping at the screen. "They won't have enough acceleration to catch up with enemy ships after they come through the ring. The only chance they have of striking the enemy fleet is by getting in front of them."

I looked at the numbers carefully. The big screen projected scenarios, displaying yellow shapes and dashed lines that showed where various units could be in near future. "I have to agree with Captain Sarin," I said. "I'm placing the marine assault groups in a widely dispersed pattern behind the battle station and the front line of gunships. Essentially, I want them in reserve."

We went on like this, planning and setting up. On the big board ships floated around in curved patterns. It was like a beautiful, carefully choreographed dance. Thousands of dancers on both sides performed their appointed roles in sequence.

I didn't like the look of the Macro fleet. They had three big dreadnaughts up front, ready to shoot down anything we sent at them and absorb whatever they couldn't shoot down. Behind that came the massed groups of cruisers. I didn't like the look of any of these ships. They were clearly an attack group making their final approach.

"What about the Blues, sir?" Miklos asked me. "Those bastards decided to let us fry out here."

"Maybe," I said. "Or maybe they just failed to talk the Macros out of their mission. In any case, we don't have time to do anything about them now."

"That's exactly what they counted on," Jasmine said. "I can see it all clearly now. They told us whatever we wanted to hear, whatever would make us go away. They even bothered to transmit a few pathetic lies to the Macros to show us they were complying with our demands. But they knew the Macros would ignore it all. Now, they can sit back and watch the fun as we destroy ourselves, man and machine alike."

I looked at her, careful to keep my eyes on her eyes. "That's an excellent analysis. You've developed a healthy sense of paranoia, Captain. But I'm not sure if anyone needs a twisted reason to fail at convincing the Macros of anything. It's quite easy to fail even when you're really trying."

"That's the beauty of it," Jasmine said. "We can't be sure, so we can't bomb them—at least, not until later."

"If there is a 'later' for us," Miklos said.

"Yeah," I said, staring at the screen. "It appears the Lobsters are betting on the Macros again, too. Look."

There were new contacts on the board, emerging from the seas of Yale this time. They lifted up and up, finally cresting out of the cloudy atmosphere that enshrouded the little water-moon. A swarm of ships, about twenty in all, followed the Macros distantly, cautiously.

"They look like troop transports, sir," Miklos said. "They flatter us by copying our tactics."

"I'll make sure to mention that the next time they give us a lecture," I said bitterly.

"They're definitely betting on the Macros," Sandra said. She'd come onto the bridge late and had missed all the awkward moments between Jasmine and I...fortunately.

"Let's get those Blues on the line," I demanded at last. "I want to talk to Intellect—or one of his relatives."

271

There was a serious time lag in the connection, but we managed to get the conversation going. We watched the enemy approach closely over the next hour, but very little changed. The only noticeable difference was the heavy acceleration of the Crustacean transports. They wanted to come in close behind the Macros and ride in on their wake.

"This is the being known as Intellect," a voice said at last. It sounded odd, coming through the translator over such a distance.

"Intellect, why are the Macros still coming? They are about to pass through the ring and attack us. You have failed to stop them, and we're going to transmit our records, proving your treachery to the Macros."

We waited again. By the time the Blues were able to respond, the Macros were at our doorstep. It was hard not to get a neck ache while watching them. The tension was thick aboard my command ship. My crewmen and even some of my senior staffers were tossing me reproachful looks and muttering to one another. The inference was clear: they thought I'd finally failed them.

At last, the Blues responded: "Your lack of comprehension is alarming. Do not take rash action! We are allied with you in the minds of the machines. All is well."

"That's it?" I shouted when the transmission ended.

"Yes sir."

I stared at the screen, dumbfounded. The Blues really had screwed us. *All is well?* I didn't think so. A thousand ships were at our doorstep and about to pass over it.

"Ready every weapon system," I said grimly. "Miklos, launch the assault squadrons. I want half of them out in space, and half of them on reserve. Get them into position now."

"Yes sir."

I felt a touch at my elbow then. It was such a light contact, I almost didn't notice it. But I looked down and saw Jasmine's dark eyes staring back.

"Can I talk to you a moment?" she asked quietly.

I thought about it. We had twenty minutes or so before the first enemy ship came through the ring. Our scouts had already pulled back to our side. The battle was about to begin, but this was definitely the calm before the storm.

I nodded to her, and she led me out into the corridor. I looked around guiltily, but didn't see Sandra. I looked back down at Jasmine. Her face was wreathed in worry.

"Do you think this is it?" she asked me.

"You mean are we going to lose? No."

She studied my face, and gave me a flickering smile. "You're a good liar," she said. "What helps is that you do it so quickly. People tend to believe a response when it's fast and certain."

I almost demanded that she tell me what this was about. My second thought was to simply order her back to her post. But I hesitated. I figured maybe she wanted some final contact with me before we both died. It was a natural enough thing, I guess.

"Listen," I said quietly. "I wish things had gone differently, but…"

She frowned, then laughed for a moment. "That's not why we're out here. I wanted to tell you a theory of mine. It might be very wrong. I'm not sold on it myself, but it would answer some questions."

I felt a little let-down. I'd been mentally gearing up for a serious goodbye kiss, at the very least.

"Okay, tell me," I said.

"Could it be the Blues meant that the Macros are counting us as allied too?" she asked.

I stared at her. "Why would they do that?"

"Maybe that's how they operate. Maybe they said Star Force surrendered to the Blues, something like that. That would mark us as friendly in their minds."

"Even after all we've done?"

"You've taught me how the machines think. They won't judge us by our past actions the way a human would. They're smart, but not that way."

I thought about it, and agreed. "You might be onto something," I said. "We've got to change our plans."

I began to turn and march back to the bridge. My mind was whirling. I was trying to come up with a way to test Jasmine's theory as quickly as possible. I had to stand down the fleet. We couldn't fire on the Macros without breaking any possible deal the Blues had worked out for us. But at the same time, it would be a disaster if we trusted the machines and everyone held their fire until they came in so close we couldn't stop them.

Jasmine's small hand tugged at my armored elbow, and I paused, turning back around.

"Did you think of something else?" I asked.

She kissed me then. It was only a quick one, but I enjoyed it.

"You shouldn't do stuff like that," I said, protesting weakly. "Sandra will freak out if she catches us."

"If you wanted this to be such a secret, you shouldn't stare at my ass all the time," she replied. "Even the robot noticed."

I gave her a guilty nod. I had to admit, she had a good point there.

-34-

We spent the next several long hours traveling away from the sun. We had to beat the Macros to the battle station if we were going to meet them there with an effective defense. The G-forces were brutal as we were under heavy acceleration. Fortunately, my people were tougher than normal humans in this regard. None of them even complained about the discomfort.

Jasmine had given me new hope. I decided it was a big gamble, but worth a try. When things looked really, really bad, I tended to take bigger risks. The further down I was, the bigger the bet had to be to get me back into the game. The trick was to win the game in the end, no matter how you did it.

"Miklos," I said, "does every ship have positional orders for the coming conflict?"

"Yes sir, we had plenty of time to distribute those orders. They aren't in formation now, but they will be as soon as we've achieved a stable orbit near the ring."

I checked the external view. The fleet was rapidly decelerating and trying to synch up with one another and slide into Hel's orbit. The gunships surrounded my destroyer, all flaring exhaust out in long plumes. We'd gotten here as fast as we could, and that meant pulling a lot of Gs in acceleration and deceleration. My teeth still hurt, and my eyeballs felt like they were too big for their sockets. My crewmen probably felt worse than I did, but none of them complained. The need for speed was obvious to everyone.

"Give me one ship you can spare," I told Miklos. "Something we don't really need. Don't worry about the crew, we'll let them off. I'm just talking about sacrificing the ship itself."

Miklos and several other staffers looked up and frowned at me. Only Jasmine nodded. I think she understood what I had in mind.

"Ah…yes, sir," Miklos said, scrambling to comply with my odd request. "I don't want to give up a gunship or a destroyer. It would have to be either a frigate, one of the last small Nano ships we have, or a transport. Which would you rather…sacrifice?"

That was a hard choice. The transports could save lives with their medical facilities and could even be used for invasions or evacuations. The Nano ships, however, each had a lot of nanites in them, with specialized equipment and long range lasers. Those lasers represented firepower that could shoot down incoming enemy missiles. We didn't have enough defensive fire like that in the fleet.

"I'll take the Nano ship," I said after a moment's hesitation. "If it had a factory aboard, there wouldn't be any contest. But as our Nano ships aren't equipped that way, I'll make the decision on the basis of maneuverability. I need the ship to reach its position as fast as possible."

"And what should the ship do at that point, Colonel? Blow itself up when the Macros cruise by?"

"Not quite," I said. "Select the last Nano ship to arrive in orbit. Order her crew to exit the craft and join the battle station garrison. Then have them send the craft to hover directly in front of the ring. The ship must have standing orders not to fire or take any defensive action. If it gets hit, it is to simply stand there until destroyed or ordered to return to the battle station. Are those instructions clear, Captain?"

"Uh…I suppose so, sir."

"Okay, relay that, then get ready for some really disturbing orders."

There was a mild murmur going through the bridge now. I didn't care. I didn't have time to care. If Jasmine was right, this was the chance of a lifetime.

"Orders relayed," Sandra said.

My staff didn't look happy. Possibly, they weren't looking forward to more crazy instructions from me.

"Now," I said, "engage the self-destruct sequence on every mine out there at the ring. I want everything within twenty thousand miles to blow itself up. Not ships, just those half-smart mines."

Miklos looked at me with bulging eyes. His mouth opened slightly, then closed again. Finally, he said: "Yes sir."

I was proud of him. I was proud of all of them. Sure, they were casting side glances at me with incredulous expressions. But they were on-task. They weren't arguing or asking for clarifications. They were just following orders. I liked that.

Partly, I was testing them. I could have explained everything to them in detail, but there wasn't much time and I didn't feel like fending off a lot of pointless questions and arguments. To their credit, they trusted me enough to follow my orders. The only slowdown involved a lot of worried looks and one-second hesitations. But they kept moving.

"Captain Sarin, give me the overall tactical on-screen."

I stared down into the blue-black glow, and the situation changed. Already, one of our Nano ships had slipped away toward the ring. The crew was a cluster of tiny green dots, which merged with the hulking battle station as I watched. The lone Nano ship hurried toward the ring.

Over the next several minutes, thousands of mines flashed white and vanished near the ring. At the same time, my fleet pulled up around the battle station and jockeyed themselves into a rough formation encircling it.

"Now Jasmine," I said, "are there any of our mines within twenty thousand miles of that ring? Do a full scan. Include the mines we're flying around Hel in a slingshot pattern."

"No sir. They've all popped themselves."

"Good. How long until the first Macro ship is due to arrive?"

Miklos answered that one: "We lost contact with them when we pulled back our scouts, but estimates range between eight and ten minutes, sir."

I leaned back and nodded. "All right, that's the best we can do. Here are the general fleet orders: "No one is to fire anything without my order, or confirmed evidence that the Macro fleet has fired upon them first. This is due to the fact that the Macros have us now marked in their database as allied. If we fire upon them or take any other aggressive action, they will put us back on the list scheduled for destruction. Relay that to everyone in the fleet, Sandra."

She did it, without a syllable of complaint. But when she was done, she looked at me seriously. "How the hell did you pull this off, Kyle? And are you *sure*?"

I smiled. "The Blues did it for us. Jasmine figured it out. Since they're allied with the Macros, by telling them they're allied with us, we've been marked down as friendly too. At least…that's the theory."

"But what if the theory is wrong, sir?" Miklos asked.

"Then we're screwed. But, that's also why I'm flying the sacrificial Nano ship out there. If they blow it, up it's game-on. I want everyone to notice one critical thing: they have yet to shower us with missiles. They're barreling right into the Eden system, without the covering plume of missiles they fired last time."

My team stared and a few nodded. They looked worried, but willing. In some faces, I saw a flicker of hope. They were starting to get it. The enemy might not fire a shot. This battle may not happen at all.

Sandra looked up at me, "I have Welter requesting a private channel, sir."

I'd left Welter in charge of the battle station. I knew he wouldn't be happy about letting the Macros fly away from that ring untouched.

I waved a gauntlet at Sandra, indicating she should open the channel.

"Colonel Riggs?" Welter asked. "With all due respect, sir. I do not understand my new orders."

"You are to stand down, Commander Welter. You are *not* to fire upon the enemy until I give the signal, or until you are taking verified incoming fire from them. Do I make myself clear?"

"Sir, the best firing opportunity will be the moment they come through that ring. If my railgun volley doesn't meet them the second they appear, we'll have given up a golden chance to inflict maximum damage upon the enemy."

"That's just it, Welter. Right now, they are *not* the enemy. At least, they don't think they are."

"Has that been confirmed, Colonel?"

I looked at the clock Sarin had set up. "The theory will be confirmed or debunked in about seventy-nine seconds. Hold your fire until we see what they do."

I thought I heard him mutter something unpleasant, but then the channel closed itself.

I had a thought then. The Centaurs. "Sandra, connect me to Sloan's assault group."

A moment later Sloan was on the line. I'd increased his rank to that of Major after the battle with the Imperial forces. His Centaurs had performed flawlessly.

"Major Sloan," I said. "What is the disposition of your troops?"

"They're hanging back as per your orders, Colonel. They don't seem to like it much though. They want to charge and get it all over with, I guess."

I nodded. I'd had a lot of experience with the Centaur urge for violent self-sacrifice. In battle, they often behaved like lemmings— well-armed, savage lemmings.

"Keep a tight leash on them, Sloan. I'm counting on you. Tell them not to worry, they'll get to fight the machines when the time comes."

"Sir, they're coming through," Jasmine said.

I stared at the screen. The first red contacts appeared. They rapidly glowed and brightened as the brainboxes took their sensor data and depicted them with increasing accuracy. Dashed lines appeared, showing the enemy flight path. They were moving more slowly than they usually did, and they were changing direction even as they came through the ring.

"They are going to sail right by us," Sandra said aloud.

I could see she was right. The ships were following a sweeping curve that glided very near the station.

"Everyone, hold your fire," I said. "That's an order. Have they shot anything yet? Answer me, people."

Jasmine, Sandra and Miklos each met my gaze with a shake of the head. I dared to take a deep breath.

"They're going for it, people," I said. "It's all up to us not to blow it at this point. I don't want anyone to do so much as light up a campfire out there. Do you all hear me?"

Many heads nodded.

"Should we talk to them, Colonel?" Sandra asked.

"Hell no," I said. "Not unless they demand that we do so. Hold tight everyone. Pretend a big bear is walking around outside our tent. If we all just huddle inside, it will probably go away."

More and more ships appeared at the ring. They were pouring through now. The clicker Jasmine had set up flickered into the two hundreds...then hit three hundred.

Something on the screen began to blink. I frowned, while Sandra worked her console and pressed her headset to her ear.

"Kyle, it's Major Sloan requesting an urgent channel."

"Put him through on speaker," I said.

"Colonel? Sir, it's the Centaurs. They're losing it."

"What are you talking about, Major Sloan? I gave you orders. They were not to move until I gave the word."

"I know sir, I told them that. They gave me some speech about honor and took off. They're deploying from the transports. They've got those skateboards on their feet, and they're heading out into space."

I cursed for a few precious seconds. "How many of them have gone AWOL?"

"Uh," Sloan hesitated for a long second. "As far as I can tell, Colonel—all of them. They're all attacking the Macro fleet."

"Damn it!" I shouted.

-35-

"Open the primary command channel. Get Welter on the line. Commander Welter are you listening in? We have a situation."

"Yes sir, I heard Major Sloan. I request permission to fire my railgun batteries. All of them are still tracking targets and their barrels are loaded."

"No, hold your fire. I want you to talk to your laser crews. Get them to aim at the Centaurs. You will not fire yet, however. You will hold your fire until I get back to you."

There was a moment of silence. "You're ordering me to shoot our own allied troops in the back?"

"No, I have not given you any such order, Commander Welter. I'm ordering you to *target* units that are disobeying orders. I'm going to talk to them first, before shooting. We have some time, as they won't reach the enemy ships for another sixteen minutes."

Jasmine raised her hand. I looked at her. "I'm updating that estimate now," she said, tapping at her screen. "The Macros have their course laid in and are accelerating. They are moving toward our line and will pass us at a high speed. The attacking Centaurs will collide with them in eleven minutes, sir."

"Try to retrieve them, Sloan," I said. "And connect me with their command council. Now."

There was a delay in making the connection, and I felt every second of it in pound in my mind like a headache. How could those damned space goats be so stupid? They were undisciplined, barbaric troops. I recalled tales of old battles, especially those in medieval times, when kings had lost control of their knights and they'd run off to get themselves killed. In modern battles, Centaurs were my knights. They definitely had minds of their own.

"Maybe we should take advantage of this situation, Colonel," Miklos said. "The Macros could be hit all at once by our Centaur troops. Our forces will be in there before they can react to shoot them down. Thousands of flying bombs crashing into their ships at once."

I drew my lips into a tight line. "I know what you're saying, and I'm tempted," I said. "But look at the Macro line. They're still streaming in through the ring. There are too many ships, and they're in too close. Sure, we'd blow the hell out of a lot of them in that opening surprise attack. But the battle station is out of position now, as are the gunships. We've lost that period of time where we can concentrate all our fire into their teeth."

Miklos shrugged. "I agree. But if we're going to end up fighting them, we might as well take whatever advantage we can get."

"I'll take it under advisement. Sandra, are the Centaurs ready to talk to me yet?"

"They are on the channel, sir."

"Hello and greetings from every patch of blue sky, waving green blade of grass and ruffling scrap of fur," I said loudly, and not without bitterness.

As usual, my sarcasm was lost upon the Centaurs. "Thank you for saluting us on this day of glory and blood," they said.

"Brave herds," I said. "You're bravery is unquestionable and legendary. Today, however, is not the day for fighting. I would ask that you obey your commanders and return to your berths within the transport ships."

"The enemy is at hand. They have taken the field under the light of our sun, and it would be dishonorable not to gallop out to meet them. Can you not feel the blood raging in your heart and mind? Do you not hate these invaders as we do?"

"Yes," I said, "of course we do. But we seek to attack when the advantage is ours. Victory in battle goes to the most cunning, to the clearest of mind."

There was a pause. I got the feeling they were passing this concept around. In the end, they rejected it. "You speak with the sound of droppings striking lifeless stones. We're stunned to hear your words, and request clarification. It cannot be that dishonor has

282

gripped your brave heart. If you fear, think of the wind, for the wind has no fear, and is everlasting."

I made a growling, groaning sound of frustration. I wanted to grab my own head with my hands, but I knew my hair would get caught in the joints of my gauntlets and be pulled out. I did it anyway as I tried to think a way out of this situation. As I'd expected, a hundred or so hairs were ripped out. They clung to my gauntlets as I pulled them away and looked at them. What was I going to do?

The trouble was, the Centaurs were right, we were double-dealing the Macros. The Blues had fooled them into thinking we were harmless, and they were operating on that piece of data. We hadn't let the Centaurs in on that detail, because I knew they wouldn't like any kind of subterfuge or trickery. Any of them would sooner die than participate in such shenanigans. The fault was mine, as I'd not let them in on the deal.

I thought hard for another fifteen seconds. On the big screen, the two lines converged. The column of Macros flowed like a river, pouring out the ring as if from a magic jug that never stopped gushing out more machines. The Centaurs swarmed like blobs of angry bees, roaring at top speed to intercept them. Fortunately, as marines their lasers didn't have the range to reach thousands of miles across space, or they doubtlessly would have already broken the treaty by singing the nosecones of the approaching horde of ships.

At last, I came up with an idea—an approach. I didn't like it, as it involved covering an omission with a lie. Weaving webs like that had gotten me into trouble in the past. But this time, I didn't see any other options.

"Allied herds," I said over the channel to the Centaurs. "I beg forgiveness, because I have twice committed the crime of vagueness. I have not explained the situation properly to you or the Macros. Here is the situation: the Macros believe we have agreed to a ceasefire. They are acting in good faith on this basis. Notice they have not fired a shot at our ships? This is because they believe they have free passage through our system."

"Why would they believe such a thing?" Centaur Command asked. "It is not the way of reality. Machine and life are antithetical. The blade cuts flesh, and the flesh melts away the blade in flame.

The camera can't appreciate the warmth of the sun or the freshness—"

"I know," I said, interrupting for lack of time, "and it greatly discomforts me. It was my intention to warn the machines to stay out of this star system. I told them we would not attack them if they did not attack us—meaning I didn't want them to fly here and fire upon our ships. But they agreed to the arrangement, and extended the meaning to include safe passage through our territory. They will not fire upon us, as you can see. And it's my belief that in order to behave honorably, we should not fire upon them."

They paused again. I checked the clock, which Captain Sarin was tapping at and looking at me. We'd blown four minutes yapping.

"Centaurs," I said, "I know that you weren't party to this accidental agreement. But I would ask that you save my honor by abiding by it today. At least until the Macros are out of this system and the arrangement can be canceled. If we fire upon them today, we will have dishonored ourselves."

"Fur filled with urine and droppings," said the Centaur voice sadly. "Hot winds full of smoke, from a fire lit by your neighbor out of spite. The champion ram's young led to an unscalable cliff and urged to climb. Dishonor is a terrible burden, and we would not wish it upon our allies this day."

I blinked and stared at the console. I muted my microphone, then looked to Sarin and Miklos.

"Does that mean they agree?" Jasmine asked in a hushed voice.

"The Centaurs are definitely all talking," Sandra said. She monitored every transmission in the region from her station. "They relayed your conversation out there to them."

"Perhaps it means they agree, you're dishonored, and they feel bad for you," Miklos suggested.

"I'm not sure what they mean," I admitted. "What are they doing? Give me data."

Jasmine worked her screen with flashing fingers. It was hard to determine the overall behavioral pattern of thousands of flying marines in distant space.

"I think—I think they're veering off course," she said at last. "At least, most of them are."

"Maybe they put it to a vote," Miklos said, "or let each individual decide what they should do."

I looked at him, and the data. "Yeah," I said. "That's what they did, I think. And it looks like not every Centaur is going to contribute to my honor by letting go of some of his own."

We kept watching. A few individuals, tiny dots that were single pixels of color on our screens, kept flying toward the Macros.

"We should shoot them down, sir," Miklos said.

"And dishonor ourselves further in the eyes of our allies?"

"But this is a worst-case scenario," he said. "We're about to start a battle without a plan, out of position, and by making only a token attack against the enemy."

I opened a channel to the battle station. "Welter, prepare to fire all guns. If you see a Macro ship blow up, unload on them all."

"Roger that, sir."

I watched the screens quietly. Everyone on the command deck stared until their eyes stung. When the first tiny dots representing Centaurs merged with the big ships, I bared my teeth.

"First strike—no explosion, sir," Miklos said.

I frowned. "Did the warhead misfire?"

"Unknown."

Two more Centaurs reached cruisers, and vanished. Then quickly, the number counted up to seven. None of them had exploded.

I leaned back and took a deep breath.

"What the hell are they doing?" Sandra asked me.

"They're ramming the ships. Tiny little balls of fur and muscle, slamming themselves into the Macro cruisers at thousands of miles per hour. Not enough kinetic force to do any damage. Less than a meteor strike, I'm sure. But they saved their own honor that way, you see? Ours as well."

"How?" Sandra asked. "I don't understand these crazy people."

"If they turned around in the face of the machines, even for a good reason, they would have dishonored themselves. But if they'd set off their warheads and destroyed the ships, they would have dishonored me. They chose to do neither, and to suicide into the enemy. That way no one loses any honor."

"Crazy mountain goats," Sandra muttered, watching the screens.

We all sat quietly as the counter ticked up higher and higher. Out of some seventeen thousand Centaur troops, six hundred and twenty-two decided to dash their brains out pointlessly upon the cold, steel prows of the Macro ships. I found it ironic that the machines inside could never comprehend their behavior, and no doubt marked it down as some kind of inexplicable malfunction.

In a way, I guess, they were right.

-36-

The next day was tense, but the tension slowly drained from all of us as the monstrous Macro fleet sailed by and flew deeper into the Eden system. They took their time, cruising by the world of the Blues, patrolling near both Eden-11 and Eden-7 before heading toward some of the outer worlds.

By this time, the Macros had changed their formation. Rather than a thin column, they flew in a huge diamond, which was made up of hundreds of smaller diamonds. These four-pointed groups were arranged in space so as not to block one another's field of fire if a fight did break out.

In their wake traveled another group. Like a pack of faithful dogs, the Crustacean troop ships trailed their masters obediently. I looked after them and shook my head. We must have looked like that at one time, like the clueless tools of the machines. I wondered if any other biotics had ever considered us to be as pathetic as the Lobsters looked to me right now.

"So," Miklos said in the morning. "It appears we have houseguests. What are we going to do while they nose around here? It's like having a shark in your living room."

"More like a T-rex," Sandra said. "Are they just going to fly around until we attack them accidentally? Or are they gathering intel to make the most devastating strike they can when they break their deal?"

Jasmine lifted her hand. She'd never gone off-duty like the rest of us. As far as I could tell, she'd quietly manned her post all night without more than a five minute break now and then.

"What is it, Captain?" I asked.

"They have chosen a new course. I can predict it with ninety-five percent accuracy."

"Where?"

"The Helios ring. They're heading to the next system."

I stood up, spilling my coffee. It fell to the floor, where the nanites in the hull swallowed up the liquid, then soon after the coffee cup itself.

"The Worms," I said. "Do they know about the deal?"

It was Marvin's turn to speak up. He'd been absent during the confrontation with the Centaurs and the Macros. But now he was on the bridge and appeared to be planning to make himself a permanent fixture here.

"Colonel Riggs," he said. "I took the liberty of telling the Worms what the situation was. They indicated they would maintain a neutral stance, and not provoke the Macros."

I shook my head. "That's not good enough. The Macros know who they are. They have marked them down for death. They aren't part of any deal we have with the machines. They are not in this ceasefire."

Everyone looked at me reluctantly. I could tell right off what they were thinking: let the Worms die. Better them than us.

"Unacceptable," I said. "It's one thing to keep the Centaurs in the dark. The purpose of that was to keep them breathing as a species. But this is different."

"You did more than keep them in the dark," Miklos commented. "You fed them bullshit with a spoon, sir."

"Whatever," I said, "open a channel with the Macros, Sandra. Before they leave the system."

"Channel open."

"Macro Command," I said. "The biotic species known as the Worms are known to us. They have agreed to abide by all agreements we have made with you."

We waited, but they made no response.

"Did they get that, Sandra? Are you certain?"

She nodded.

"Macro Command: this is Colonel Kyle Riggs of Star Force. We require that you comply with the terms of our agreement. We further require that you acknowledge your compliance."

"Something is coming in…" Sandra said. "It's binary."

Marvin quickly volunteered to interpret. "Incoming message: *We will comply with the terms of our agreement.*"

I frowned. Did that mean they were going to leave the Worms alone, or were they going to blast them?

"You will not attack the Worms," I said. "Doing so will violate the terms of our agreement."

"Incoming message: *Referenced biotic species is not included in this subset.*"

"Yes, they are," I said, "we are allied with them. The Blues are allied with them. By inference, you are allied with them."

"Incoming message: *Referenced biotic species is not included in this subset.*"

I made a guttural sound of frustration. I knew the Macros. When they got into one of these moods where they kept repeating themselves, they weren't going to change their minds.

"We request that you add them to the subset of species included on the no-kill list."

"Incoming message: *Request denied.*"

"They will annihilate them, Kyle," Sandra said.

"I know," I said, "we got them into this, too. They lost half their fleet fighting for us against Crow's ships, and now we return the favor by talking the Macros into bypassing us to destroy them."

"You must save them," Sandra said. "Lie. Do anything."

I looked at her and at the others circled around. I nodded. "Sandra, start jamming the ring that leads back to the Thor system. I don't want the macros to report back anything I'm going to tell them now."

She went to work on it, and signaled me when it was done.

"Macro Command," I said, "the biotic species known as the Worms can't harm you effectively. They can, however, be a valuable ally. I see you have troop ships in your wake. The Worms will provide Worm troops upon your return, when you need fresh troops."

This was met with stony silence for a time. Finally, I contacted them again.

"Macro Command, we require you to accept or reject the terms of this arrangement."

"Incoming message: *Terms rejected.*"

"We require you to tell us why you reject these terms."

"Incoming message: *The biotic homeworld of this species will be unable to support life upon our next visitation. Therefore, the agreement is meaningless.*"

I tightened my face and nodded. Their intentions were clear. "The Worms are not a threat. They could be a valuable ally. Do not attack their homeworld, and there will be troops there to pick up upon your next visitation."

"Incoming message: *Terms accepted.*"

Everyone cheered me, except Miklos.

"What are you going to tell the Worms, sir?" he asked. "They will never agree to this. They will not serve the Macros."

"Yeah, well, I bought them some time to defend themselves. Maybe by that time, we can knock these machines down."

"Let's hope so."

"Sir?" Captain Sarin called me from her post. She still stood at the table, as she had done for at least a full day. "Could you come look at this?"

"I will," I said, "if you promise to take a look at your bunk for the next few hours. You are relieved on ops, Captain."

"Thanks for the thought, sir," she said. "But take a look at this, first."

I walked over and examined the board. I frowned, as the Macro force had split into two groups. One was heading for the Helios ring, while the other, smaller group was heading back toward the ring to the Thor system.

I pointed to the smaller group. "Where are these guys going?"

"They appear to be going back to the Thor system. That force is made up entirely of the Lobster troop ships."

I frowned. "Why did they do that?" I asked.

"I hope the Macros didn't order them back," Jasmine said to me quietly. "I hope the Macros aren't expecting to fly to Helios right now and pick up their contingent of Worm marines."

I looked at her with widening eyes. "I haven't even told the Worms about that deal yet."

She shook her head slowly.

I contacted Marvin immediately. "Marvin, can you get through to the Worms somehow? Do we have any ships that could relay a message through the Helios ring?"

"I'll have to check with traffic control…negative. The nearest friendly ship is about six hours away. You ordered the fleet to pull back to defensive positions around Hel and the populated planets."

"I know what I did," I snapped.

"Sir?" Jasmine asked, pulling her headset to one side to speak to me. She had that urgent, worried look on her face that I'd come to recognize.

"What is it now?"

"The Crustacean transports are decelerating heavily, Colonel."

"Yeah, so? They're about to go through the ring back to their home system."

"But they know there are no mines in the region to worry about. I just thought it was strange."

"Let's stick to the more serious issues. The Macros are about an hour away from the Helios ring, they've dumped their Lobster troops and it appears they expect the Worm troops to be ready to go instantly. We can't even get through to the Worms to tell them about my little fib."

"The question then," she said, "is do we contact the Macros and tell them they aren't ready yet?"

I glared at the system-wide map. The Macros looked like a giant school of red fish, heading toward one of the two exits. I'd learned today that the one thing a swimmer wants to see is the tail end of the shark as it swims away to hunt someone else.

"No," I said, "it's an unpleasant situation, but we have to look after our own first. If we can get these damned ships out of our system for just a few days, we can breathe. We'll send a ship to the ring, transmit an update of the situation to the Worms and then try to help use diplomacy to get them out of the situation."

"Fine, sir. But I'm still worried. What is that fleet going to do? They're on their way to Earth, you know. Where else would they be going?"

"Maybe they want to find out what happened to their bases around Bellatrix."

"Crow destroyed them."

I nodded. "Yeah, they might not be too happy about that. But let's hope the Imperial fleet can stop them."

Jasmine frowned at me reproachfully. "If they can't, Earth is doomed. We have to warn the Worms, Kyle, and we have to warn Earth!"

"Do we have to do everything? Can't we rely on these self-styled Imperials to defeat a fleet on their own?"

"They managed it in the blue giant system. But that was an isolated mining colony. This fleet is monstrous. We dodged them because you were worried we couldn't win."

I thought about it, and she was of course correct. "What you're saying is that sooner or later, someone is going to have to destroy this Macro armada."

She nodded.

"We'll move," I said, "as soon as this armada has slid past our borders. We will."

I took the next hour or so to think about my options. The enemy fleet began a long, drawn-out exit through the ring, transporting themselves into the system of the hapless Worms. When about half of them had wriggled through the ring into Worm space, I thought I'd come up with at least a partial solution. I contacted Marvin and summoned him to the command deck.

"Marvin, I need you to connect me to the Earth fleet via the rings. According to our calculations, they're in the Alpha Centauri system now. They may not see the Macro fleet which is following them home to Earth. Can you use what we've learned of their ring transmission to contact them from here?"

"Yes and no, sir," Marvin said. "If you're asking if I can perfectly duplicate their code, then no. I'm only about eight-five percent fluent in their secret transmission protocols. I've been distracted by—"

"Not necessary," I interrupted. "I don't even want you to use their encoding scheme. Just transmit on an open channel to the Earth fleet."

"I can try, sir."

A few minutes later, Marvin worked with his arcane equipment. It was a tangled mess of brainboxes linked to a miniature version of the ring he was targeting to receive the message. Anyone in that system that was measuring the sympathetic vibrations of the ring would pick it up.

"Connection made, sir," he announced.

I talked my way past a few operators, and quickly convinced them I wasn't another Earth ship playing around on military equipment. They finally passed me up to Kerr himself.

"Riggs? Is that you?"

"Yes, General."

"Not surprised. I was wondering when you'd figure out our little secret."

"This isn't a social call, General."

"It never is with you. What do you want?"

"I want Earth to survive the next week. To that end, you must prepare for a massive assault, which will come through the Alpha Centauri ring into the Solar System in...we estimate six days, General. Maybe less."

There was a minute or so of quiet after that. I was about to request an acknowledgement, when Kerr came back on the line. I did like the faster response time while using the ring communications systems. It was difficult to use just radio transmissions, which moved at the grossly inadequate speed of light. Conversations across space using such antiquated means took hours or even days to complete. Using the ring system and their sympathetic resonance, we were able to converse as if we were on a phone line across a thousand light years.

"To what do I owe the honor of a massive Macro assault on our beloved homeworld, Riggs?" asked Kerr. His voice rose in volume and pitch with every syllable.

I cleared my throat. "We might have had something to do with that, sir. We talked the Macros into not attacking us. But as a result, they've decided to seek their fortunes elsewhere. It's our estimation that they're heading toward Bellatrix and they plan to find out what happened to their mining colony there."

"Bellatrix? We wiped that out. It's Imperial space now."

"You know that and I know that, sir," I said. "But I'm not sure the Macros do. In any case, there is bound to be a fight when they hit your border. Looking at the situation strategically, I would suggest you utilize your fortifications at the entrance to the Solar System to the fullest. Fight it out right there at the border. What did you call your defenses there? Overkill? I truly hope for your sake you weren't bluffing, General."

Kerr yelled at me for a while after that. I didn't blame him. To his mind, we were the ones who were supposed to stand and fight to the last, hopefully eliminating the robots and ourselves in the process. But, instead of dashing our brains against one another, Kerr had just learned his enemies had come to a peaceful accord. Now, the Macros had turned their attention to Earth itself, and their mining colony. We both knew there wasn't going to be any way they could talk the Macros out of paying them a visit now. Even if they could buy them off in some way, when they saw what had happened to the mining system and found all those Earth ships and destroyed Macro hulks, they were going to start shooting.

At the end of the conversation, I tried to be magnanimous. "If you make a formal request General, I'll send along an expeditionary to support you. We'll stand in solidarity with Earth on this one."

Kerr sent me one last message before the channel was suddenly closed: "Thanks for the warning, you dick."

-37-

The Macros had sailed serenely through the Eden system and now the last of them were lazily exiting out the far side. I stayed near the Hel ring with a small contingent of ships assigned to watch over the battle station and the entrance to the Thor system. Most of my ships I sent after the Macros, with orders to travel around the system in their wake. If they did declare war for some reason, I wanted my ships to be ready to strike. Even if they couldn't win, they might be able to defend the civilians who huddled on many of the planets in the system, watching the skies with wide, fearful eyes.

Over the last few days, we'd averted disaster a half-dozen times. It's not easy to stand-down defensive systems that span an entire star system, especially when they maintain a hair-trigger alert status. It seemed as if a dozen different attempts were made by blundering parties to blow the ceasefire into oblivion—and all of us with it.

The Centaur charge had only been the beginning of treaty-breaking events. As the Macros cruised around each planet, they triggered automated stations with excitable brainboxes. Weapons had locked themselves on, itching to fire. In some cases, they *did* fire, such as the full barrage of missiles from the Centaur-controlled satellites over Eden-9. We managed to destroy them all before the Macros were damaged, but it had been a close thing.

Another near-calamity came at the last moment as the last of the Macros were leaving the system. At this time, the Crustacean transports were approaching the Thor ring. They were traveling very slowly, and cruising along very close to our battle station.

"What the hell are they doing?" Sandra demanded as we all stared at the command console.

I was wondering the same thing. "I don't know," I said, "but if they linger until after the last Macro ship is gone, I'll be tempted to order Welter to blow them up."

"You should do it, Kyle," Sandra said. "They're probably taking a million pictures and readings. They want to know every secret about our station, so they can come back later and destroy it."

I nodded and stared at the screen. "You could be right."

"They're changing course sir—and accelerating," Captain Sarin said.

"Good. It's about time they finished their little sightseeing tour."

"No sir, they aren't heading for the ring."

I opened my mouth, but no sound came out. On the screen between us all, the computers were updating the situation. As they were huge cylindrical ships, Crustacean transports looked like tiny yellow tin cans. They were obviously Macro-built, or the design had been borrowed from the Macros. What mattered right now, however, was their course and speed. The predictive dashed lines now converged—on my battle station.

"Can that be right?" I demanded. "Marvin, are you monitoring the Crustacean ships? Is there increased chatter?"

"Definitely, sir. They're in tight communication with one another."

As I watched, the dashed lines went from yellow to red. Then the canister-shaped ships themselves were updated with bright, blinking red. Even the computer knew it, and it was time that I caught up with the programming.

"They're attacking," I said.

"Attacking?" Miklos asked. "How can they attack us with just a bunch of transports? We'll blow them out of space."

"Check the acceleration patterns. I bet if we zoom in, we'll see their ports opening. They'll release their assault troops when they are less than a thousand miles out. Have they fired a shot at us yet?"

"No sir, nothing."

"How long until the last Macro ship exits the system?"

"About four minutes, sir."

I nodded thoughtfully. "They'll time it down to the second. When the last Macro exits through the Helios ring, they'll hit us with everything they have. Their marines will be climbing all over the battle station's outer hull, drilling their way in."

"How can they have assault troops with those abilities? And how can you be sure they've come up with such a tight plan?"

"Because we have those troops, and they've been copying our tactics. They'll attack at precisely the right moment, because that's what I would do. They've been copying my maneuvers as well. Worst of all, they've been listening to our little chats with the Macros. They know about our bullshit alliance."

"Sir? Commander Welter is requesting a channel. He says it's urgent."

"Indeed it is. Patch him through."

"Colonel Riggs, I formally request a change or at least an exception to our rules of engagement. Allow me to fire upon those damned treacherous Lobsters."

"I'll grant that request in exactly three minutes, Commander."

We waited a few seconds, hearing only dead air. Then Welter was back on the line. "Sir, that'll be too late. They'll be inside the range of ninety-percent of my weaponry by then. Hell, most of them will be crawling on the outside of my armored hull by then."

"I know that, Welter. But if we fire too early, we'll break our deal with the Macro fleet. They'll reverse course and wipe out every human in this system. We're going to have to deal with the Lobster troops after they reach your battle station. I'm coming, but you'll have to hold until the cavalry arrives. Riggs out."

I turned to my staff. Everyone looked worried or stunned—or both.

"Do you think the Macros ordered them to do this, Colonel?" Jasmine asked me. "They've done this kind of thing before. They like to have their slaves do their dirty work for them."

"Possibly," I said, "however, it doesn't really matter right now. We're in a fight people. What assets can we bring into orbit around Hel within the next hour?"

Sarin worked the console. No one even tried to beat her, we all just waited as she did the calculus and threw up displays with the answers.

"Just this task force, sir," she said. "We had most of the gunships following the Macros around in case there was trouble. Most of the transports were doing the same. The rest of the fleet is scattered in defensive positions at each inhabited world."

"Where's Major Sloan?" I asked. "He should be leading the assault troops."

"He's not here, sir. He's with the majority of the troop ships and the core of the gunships—out at the Helios ring."

I nodded, unsurprised. Sloan was a master at being elsewhere when a fight erupted. "All right, give me a breakdown of the forces we have within reach, and tell me what Welter has aboard for a garrison."

The complement of troops on the battle station had been greatly increased since the initial battle we'd fought aboard her. There were over four hundred marines, crewmen and even some civilian craftsmen who'd gone out there to repair the weapons systems. I frowned as I thought about those poor bastards. They'd run from Earth to escape tyranny, and now they were going to find themselves cut off in space with thousands of alien troops crawling over the hull of the station. I'd let them all down—these Lobsters were tricky. They had something going for them the Macros didn't seem to have: the ability to learn from their mistakes and quickly adapt. I told myself not to underestimate them again.

In this region of space, I had my destroyer, a squadron of gunships and two Nano ships. That was a pretty small force, but more than enough to destroy the transports. The real problem would be destroying the assault troops. If the Lobsters got into the station and took it with their initial assault, then we would have a real problem—we'd have to take the station back.

"The most important assets we have in the area now are the transports. How many troops do I have?"

"I'll contact the ships for confirmation on that, sir," Sarin said.

A moment later, a familiar voice came on the line. "First Sergeant Kwon reporting, Colonel."

"Kwon?" I asked, frowning. "You're out here with those transports? I thought I ordered you to accompany Sloan and the majority of the assault troops."

"I must have gotten that wrong sir. Very sorry."

I frowned at the screen. I felt like yelling at him for slipping his orders, but it wouldn't do any good right now…and I had to admit, I needed him.

"Kwon," I asked, "just tell me one thing: Why do you always seem to follow me around?"

"Well sir…" he began, then hesitated.

"What? Out with it, man. I won't reprimand you this time."

"Sir…the truth is you always get into the best fights. I love a good fight, Colonel."

I had to work not to laugh. I scowled at the boards and made a growling sound instead. After all, everyone was watching. It wouldn't do to give insubordination a pass—especially not when there were witnesses. "I think you're going to get your wish this time, First Sergeant."

"Thank you, sir!"

The battle started about five seconds after the last Macro glided peacefully through the ring and vanished. On cue, everyone began firing at once.

We were jamming both the rings by this time, to make sure the Lobsters couldn't call foul and transmit claims about us attacking them and breaking the treaty. I could imagine they'd wanted nothing more than to provoke us into an early attack. Maybe that had been the big point of the assault. In the end, it didn't matter what their plans had been. Like two school boys waiting for the principal to step out of sight, we lunged at each other the first moment we could.

Welter ordered every railgun and laser to fire at point-blank range. The assaulting transports blew up in rapid succession. They flared into plasma, vapor and wreckage on our screens, then vanished entirely. But that was a small victory, because there were already about five thousand Crustacean troops crawling over the rocky armored exterior of the battle station. They'd taken the wise option of exiting their ships and flying to land on the surface of the battle station at the last possible moment.

"Get ready to repel those crawlers, Welter," I shouted over the command channel. "You have to hold out for about thirty minutes."

I left the command deck then and headed for the destroyer's small sally port. We kept the invasion equipment there, and the onboard marine complement was already there, suiting up. They nodded and saluted me, then went back to the intensely focused work of getting ready to leap out of a ship moving at screaming speeds.

Over time, our kits had evolved. It seemed like every battle I had a few new gizmos to experiment with. In the past, I'd designed most of the battlesuits personally. We'd moved on past those days now. I had a design team in charge of improving equipment on a continuous basis.

The latest battlesuits were still built along my design parameters. They had a heavy suit of armor that was layered with overlapping plates. It was similar to the equipment a knight might have worn into battle a thousand years ago. Our materials, naturally, were greatly improved when compared to the simple steel plating of old fashioned knights. Underneath the entire suit we wore a skintight suit of nanocloth. This was airtight, and self-repairing. In the case of a suit breach, this final inner layer of protection had the job of sealing the leak even if it meant coating a damaged limb with nanites.

A lot of improvements had gone into training the nanites on emergency procedures. For too long, we'd relied on their innate understanding of human anatomy and pretty much let them "do their thing." Now, we'd stepped in and given them priorities. If a limb or a portion of the suit was too damaged to salvage, the nanites were to cut that part off and save the rest of the victim.

This knowledge was met with some grim fatalism by my troops. They didn't trust the tiny little machines to know when it was time to amputate by digging through the flesh and covering the stump with a fresh layer of smart metal. I didn't look forward to the experience, either. But in theory, it would save lives.

Unfortunately, the nanites still weren't too good at pain-control. When they went to work on a man, he was liable to do a lot of frenzied screaming. But, when it was all over and the marine returned to his or her ship, we could regrow those limbs with Marvin's biotic soups. That was, if there was a ship to return to.

These thoughts went through my head as I went through the self-check routine. Each marine automatically checked the other men around him as well, pointing out dangling cords and equipment that hadn't been cinched tight enough. Luckily, due to nanite technology, most of our connections took care of themselves.

When I finally switched on the generator on my back and felt that familiar revving hum tingling its way up my spine, I experienced a matching thrill of adrenaline. My body knew I was about to go into battle, and it was working to sharpen me up, just as I was working to organize my kit. The huge ruck-like unit on my back almost felt good. The weight of it, crouching on my shoulders and hugging my ribs, brought back a flood of memories.

I pulled out the single projector these suits came with. Rifle-like, with a forward grip and a precision sight, this weapon had a longer effective range than previous models. When everyone had their autoshades active, I test-fired it into the blast doors. Just a tiny blip of laser light was enough to burn a hole you could fit an armored finger into.

"You like these new suits, boys?" I asked aloud.

There was a chorus of "hell yeahs" which gave me a grim smile. A moment later, I felt the ship veer sharply. We'd arrived. The ship was making its final approach course changes—either that, or we were dodging incoming fire.

"Colonel?" Captain Sarin's voice crackled inside my helmet.

"Go ahead, Captain."

"We are taking some incoming fire. Tell your men we might have to let them fly at long range."

That was bad. When doing a hot-drop or a ship-to-ship boarding attack, my marines needed to spend as little time as possible buzzing around in open space before they reached the target. While we were out there, exposed to every kind of attack, we were like a swarm of flies and about as easy to swat.

"How far out are we doing this jump?"

"Excuse me, Colonel? Did you say 'we'?"

"How far out, dammit?"

"Around ten thousand miles. Let me say for the record, sir that—"

"Unacceptable, Captain. Take me in closer. Give us no more than a thousand miles, tops, to decelerate. I'd prefer a hundred, or even ten."

"We'll be under heavy fire by then, sir," she said. "And I don't understand why you insist on leading attacks personally."

"When I'm dead, you can run things as you see fit, Commander. You can hide under your desk if you want to. While I'm in command, I'll fly with my marines. These men fight harder when their leaders are on the lines with them. Every soldier does. Check your military history."

She stopped scolding me, and I had a chance to think about something. I frowned inside the glowing confines of my helmet. "Sarin?" I called out. "Why are we under heavy fire? Where's it coming from?"

"The battle station, Colonel. Several of the weapons batteries appear to have been captured. They are in enemy hands, and they are taking pot shots at us as we approach."

"What the hell happened to Welter?"

"We've lost contact with him."

I knew what that meant. Quite possibly, the crew had been eliminated.

"Is there any evidence that the battle station crew is still fighting?"

"Yes sir," she said, "we're registering a steady series of emissions. People are still in the upper portion of the station, in the farthest sector from the surface of Hel. They're definitely still in the game, sir."

I took a look then at the battle rosters. We had three transports, plus the platoon I would be flying with on *Actium*. Each of the transports had about five hundred marines aboard, mostly Centaurs. I'd never fought with these new and improved native troops. I found myself wishing they were all human marines. I hoped my allies could perform on a mission like this one. They would be green, at the very least.

I had a sudden thought, and contacted Kwon. "Kwon? Are you in contact with the Centaur force-leaders?"

"Yes sir."

"Tell them I want them to leave their nuclear grenades behind on the ship. I repeat: leave the nukes behind. There are friendlies on this battle station. I'm not interested in seeing any suicidal Centaurs crashing themselves into the station and killing everybody."

"Ah, good thinking, Colonel. I'll relay that."

I felt the ship rock and sway as the pilot dodged incoming railgun fire. Fortunately, the enemy gunners weren't connected to the central fire control system on the battle station and weren't able to target us easily. They were also new to the equipment, or we'd never have survived the flak.

I closed my eyes to think. When I opened them, I contacted Miklos: "Captain? Remember, if I'm out of action, you are my second in command. Is that clear?"

"As always, sir. Come back in one piece—or at least with enough pieces to allow us to reassemble you."

I grinned in my helmet, something that always caused my cheeks to press against the hinges on the visor. They felt cool there against my skin.

"That is my intention, Captain," I said. "Tell me how things look up there. How close are we to the drop zone?"

"We are close now, sir. I recommend you open the sally port and mount your flyers."

I signaled the team around me. Everyone moved with purpose. A few slammed their open palms down onto the helmets of their friends. A few others took a moment to pray or roar a battle cry.

"Men," I said, opening up the proximity chat channel. "We're about to do a tough jump. I want you all to remember you're part of an elite group: Riggs' Pigs. Let's show those Lobster traitors why they should fear us more than their metal masters!"

A chorus of shouts rang in my ears. The men were hot, and ready to fly. The sally port opened then, revealing space in all its majesty.

Immediately, I was alarmed by the amount of visible fire coming from the battle station. Had Welter lost the entire station? It didn't look good. Like flying blue sparks, the fire was moving so fast, it resembled lines of light, drawn in glaring streaks that went past our ship. They were firing wide and wildly, but even without precision targeting, they were bound to hit something eventually.

"Captain Sarin?" I shouted. "How many miles out are we?"

"About seven thousand, sir."

"Give me the signal at five thousand. We'll jump then. The second we're out, get the hell out of here."

"Yes sir," she said.

I could hear the relief in her voice. I couldn't blame her. It wasn't worth losing the command ship just to save the lives of a few grunts. The math was unpleasant, and it always seemed to come out against the men in boots. Unfortunately, it was my job to call those shots, even when my own ass was on the line.

-38-

The go-signal came in the form of a tone in our helmets and a flashing green light over the sally port doors. Making a jump out of a cruiser was a little different than doing it inside a planetary atmosphere. Instead of having wind in your face, there was nothing outside but vacuum. There wasn't even gravity to rely on to move you downward, away from the ship.

Instead, we had our skateboards. Essentially, we were tiny one-man vehicles capable of self-propulsion. We shot out of the portal one at a time in rapid succession. To an external witness, the scene must have looked as if the ship was experimenting with a new kind of weapon. We came out like a spraying shower of mini-missiles, just far enough apart not to ram one another and send the next guy into a deadly tailspin.

Fortunately, my men knew what they were doing. They all had more training with this new technique of rapid-fire jumps than I did. I had more experience with jumps in general, however. I took the rear spot and followed the rest so I wouldn't mess up their timing. It was easier to stay with them from that position too, as I only had to see any one of the string of flyers and keep on his tail.

The second we were out, I was doing a slow spin and it took me a second to get my skateboard under my boots. The squad had almost lost me by the time I had it under control. I hit the acceleration pads hard to catch up.

I checked my altimeter the moment I was among them, and that mistake was almost fatal. All around me, the drop-troops vanished. They'd all fired their brakes. I did the same without hesitation. I

305

didn't even get a good reading on the distance. I just flipped the skateboard around and pushed for emergency braking. The little unit slipped and jiggled under me, wanting to throw me off. I held my balance with my knees bent, clenching my teeth and squinching up my eyes, expecting a bone-jarring slam into the battle station.

It didn't happen. Instead, the men around me shot past again. I dared a peek at my altimeter. They were doing a controlled landing, just as they'd been taught. I was trying to keep up and overcorrecting first one way then another.

A shot of anger and embarrassment went through me. I didn't like playing the fool with a dozen recruits watching. Forcing myself to take a breath and think, I read the altimeter again and eased off on the braking. I let myself drift. I was coming down at about three hundred miles per hour, and we were in the last two miles of the drop. Not one of my marines had been taken out yet. It was time for me to stop freaking out and to act like a pro.

"As soon as we're down, seek a surface crater," I ordered my squad. "There should be plenty of holes left over from the last time this station was assaulted."

They were braking again, doing the final approach. I let them slip away above me before hitting the brakes hard.

It was a near disaster, but I managed to make it look cool. I came down and slammed into the surface of the battle station inside a deep black crater, which was about a hundred feet wide and twenty feet deep. Everything went dark for a second, then I hit the bottom doing about seventy miles per hour I'd say. Normally, we liked to hit doing around thirty, tops. Landing at seventy felt like being slammed by a car on the highway.

Fortunately, I landed on my feet and was in a battle suit built for absorbing shocks. My body was full of nanites, Microbe-altered flesh and pissed-off marine. I limped out of the crater, my right hip aching. I tried not to let it show. I left my skateboard in the crater, ignoring it. My fall had crushed it and it was no longer serviceable.

"Nice landing, sir," the squad leader told me. He was a Gunnery Sergeant with a rough, accented voice. I couldn't see his face inside the suit, but I figured he was some kind of Brit.

I swiveled my helmet to regard him. I wasn't entirely sure if he was being sarcastic or not. I decided to take his remark in the best possible light.

"Thank you, Gunnery Sergeant. Did we lose anyone?"

"Only three, sir! But I think we're the first team down."

I looked up and around, and realizing he was right. I frowned, as this wasn't a good thing. I could see the big guns all around us, aiming up into the sky. My autoshades dimmed and brightened rhythmically in reaction to the steady fire they were pumping up at my marines.

I used my long range command-link to connect with Kwon, who was riding his skateboard down under heavy fire.

"First Sergeant Kwon, are you guys out of your ships yet? We're already down."

"Lucky bastards," Kwon said. "We jumped out a long time ago, but we're still flying. We're taking lots of flak. How did you get there so fast?"

I thought for a second. "I didn't let Captain Sarin release us until she was close-in."

"Ah," Kwon said, "you pulled rank. Now I know why you like being an officer. The transport captain kicked us out early. We won't be there for another two or three minutes, sir."

"It's okay, I think," I said. "Except for some flak on the way down, we—"

At that moment, all hell broke loose around me. My squad had come to join me at the bottom of the crater of blasted rock we were standing in. Most of them had gone up to the rim of our crater to watch for enemy action and look for more marines. It was the ones up on the rim that were firing now. The flaring laser light darkened my autoshades and explosions began all around us.

"Enemy contact, sir!" shouted the Gunnery Sergeant. "The Lobsters know we're here!"

The information was self-evident, but still useful. I stumped up the crater wall, almost dragging my right hip which was stiffening now. I tweaked the gain on my exoskeleton, which made my limbs move more quickly. This caused ripples of pain to run through me. I ignored the discomfort and threw myself down alongside the Gunnery Sergeant who was crouched at the crater's rim.

Behind me, in the bowl of the crater, an explosion popped. Then a half-dozen more followed it. I felt fragments hitting the back of my armor. Burning pits showed up on the backs and legs of all the men around me.

"They're throwing grenades down here," I shouted. "Do not respond with anything big—conventional weapons only. Monitor your fire and hold this crater, men. We have to hold out for two full minutes before reinforcements arrive."

The incoming fire intensified. Our first casualty was the Gunnery Sergeant beside me. He took a direct hit in the faceplate from an enemy laser bolt. At first, I thought maybe they'd gotten control of the defensive laser towers and tilted them down toward us, but as I surveyed the situation, I realized the fire wasn't coming from heavy weapons. The enemy had moved to higher ground wherever they could find it, mostly along ridges formed by previous bombardments.

"We're surrounded," I said, assuming tactical command. "Spread out and shoot for any target that has reached high ground. I don't want them to be able to shoot down into our cover."

There was a wild series of blazing light flashes as we returned fire. The enemy was driven back, and although we were still pinned here, we weren't completely helpless. We kept our heads down after that, and only shot at Lobster troops when they scuttled forward too close, or when they climbed up on top of one of the big railgun batteries to fire down into our midst. Whenever we could, we concentrated our fire to kill any enemy marine who achieved a good firing position.

During the next minute, we lost one more man, but we were holding. A lot of marines had smoldering holes in their armor, but they were still in the fight. Some were howling in pain, but they kept using their weapons. I saw one Corporal with a missing foot. He crawled around on his hands and knees, dragging a smoking stump, but never complained. I knew the nanites must be chewing into the good flesh, sealing off his suit and his blood-supply, but he kept firing and crawling and most impressive of all, he kept quiet.

In the last minute before the mass drop came, things changed. Someone must have told the Lobsters they didn't have all day to kill us. They'd finally realized the rest of our troops were coming down, about fifteen hundred strong. The enemy decided it was time to finish things in this crater.

They charged us from every direction. I'd been preparing for this kind of move. The moment I saw massed movement, a hundred or more flashing bits of metal on humping backs, I knew what was coming. The enemy troops crawled toward us rapidly, all at once. They had metal hooks on their churning spiny feet, I saw. I figured that's how they kept hugging the surface of the battle station without the aid of gravity. It was a low-tech solution, but it worked for them.

"They're rushing us!" I shouted. "Release your fragmentation weapons now! Frag out!" I readied and tossed my own ordnance. I aimed at the biggest concentration of rushing troops.

Throwing grenades in low grav took some experience. I saw a number of my men's weapons zoom off into space. Even if they threw them at a low angle, they often bounced off rocks and flew high before detonating harmlessly. Our packs and repellers applied enough force to our backs to keep us down on the battle station, but the grenades didn't have such refinements. Most of my men were green and they threw their weapons with far too much force. Even a toss didn't work, as the grenades just kept going and left the surface of the battle station.

"Roll them out under their feet one second before—" I shouted, but a deafening boom blotted out my words.

I wasn't quite sure what had happened. Maybe the marine two grunts down had held his grenade a second too long. Or maybe one of the lobsters had caught and tossed one of our gifts back to us.

My head was ringing. I shouted the rest of my message, but I wasn't sure what I was saying. I couldn't hear it, and I was mildly disoriented. A man to my left was flailing about, a gaping wound in his side. I could see the nanites there, a bright silver coating. They were trying to cover the gap before he froze in space, but I didn't think they were going to make it.

I looked back over the rim of the crater. We'd killed a number of them, but not enough. I blazed with my laser and melted two. They didn't seem to have armor that compared to ours. A direct laser hit was always fatal. What they had, however, was determination—and superior numbers.

They were inside the crater a few seconds later. I felt my headphones buzz against my ears, the noise was so loud the headphones vibrated so and tickled—but I couldn't hear a word. Possibly, the headset was just reporting feedback from more explosions. It didn't really matter. Now, it was all about killing, and who could do it best.

Rifles blazed at pointblank range. I noticed that the enemy had more trouble firing in close than we did. Possibly, they hadn't mastered the critical technology of a good fast autoshade. The key was to darken and lighten in anticipation of energy emissions nearby. Doing that job perfectly was critical to a soldier's survival. It both saved his eyes and allowed him to use them. If the autoshades went off and darkened too soon, he was left in blackness before the flaring light of a gun brightened the scene enough to see. If they went off too late, the marine's retinas would be burned.

Star Force autoshades worked best in a close firefight like this. The blazing weapons kept up a reliable source of brilliant light allowing us to see what we were shooting at. Our visors pretty much stayed at their darkest setting continuously. I became certain as we fought them that the enemy wasn't as well-equipped. They were game, however. Often a Lobster with nothing left to fight with other than his claws still gripped, scrabbled and tore at my armor.

One grappled with me and got a good grip. I couldn't get the projector of my rifle up against his body. I drew my knife and snipped off limbs until he slid away. The force of our struggles soon sent him floating up into space, where he wriggled and flipped like a fish lifted into the air by a triumphant sportsmen.

There was a lull in the fighting after we beat back the attack, and I took a moment to look around. I'd lost over half my men. Most of the survivors were injured in some way. Everyone who could lift a rifle fired over the rim of the crater after the retreating enemy. I crawled up there and saw they were burning the humping backs of every Lobster who had not yet managed to get out of sight.

"Well done!" I shouted, barely able to hear my own voice now. "We drove them back. Three of you, keep firing at them so they know we're still in this. The rest tend to the wounded."

I saw more laser fire flare in the pit of the crater. I looked down, and saw a marine walking from one Lobster to the next, burning a hole in each. Some of them thrashed feebly as he did so.

"Ceasefire, marine!" I shouted down at him. "That's enough of that."

"Sorry sir," he said, "I figured we might have ourselves a barbecue after this is over. They look like good-eating."

I grimaced. "Belay that shit, private!" I shouted. "The enemy may not look like us, but they will be treated with respect. They aren't machines, damn it. We won't use sentient beings as food."

"Sorry, Colonel," the private mumbled.

I now was close enough to see the name on his helmet. "Get back to your assigned duties, Coleman," I said. "My orders were for you to tend to the wounded."

"But everyone in the squad is either on the line or dead, sir."

I decided to check on his report. I clanked around for a few moments, throwing Lobsters off my dead men. Coleman was right. There were a few people with missing limbs, but they were functioning due to the efforts of the newly trained under-armor nanocloth. I had to admit, everyone who was down was dead. I looked at Coleman and nodded.

"All right. Get back up to the rim."

By this time, it was raining marines. The forces backing us up met little resistance once they reached the rocky surface of the station's outer armor layer. The Lobsters had retreated, deciding to fight inside the battle station, rather than out on the surface. About five minutes later, Kwon found me.

"Looks like a tough fight, sir," he said, looking around. "You know, I bet these lobster guys would taste really good with some butter."

I scowled at him.

Behind me, I thought I heard Coleman mutter: "That's what *I* said!" But I couldn't be sure it was him. Proximity radio systems weren't as precise as real voices in an atmosphere, and my hearing was still iffy after the grenade blast. I decided not to take the private to task for the comment.

-39-

Most of my invasion troops were Centaurs. I wasn't completely comfortable with that. I'd fought with a company of them behind me in the past on Eden-11, and they hadn't done all that well. But today, I didn't have any choice. We'd experienced a five percent casualty rate on the drop. I considered this very fortunate, and marked it down to poor gunnery skills on the part of the enemy. They'd just captured our station's guns and didn't know how to aim them right yet.

Of the fourteen hundred troops I had left, only about ten percent were human. I ordered them to spread around, mingling with the less-experienced Centaur fighters. I didn't have time to rebuild the command structure, so I simply attached one squad of marines to every Centaur company. I was hoping the native troops would learn by example from the human squads.

Our first tactical problem was getting into the battle station itself. Already, the Crustaceans were getting ideas on how they might remove us from their armored exteriors. I saw them setting up strong points at the only openings in the armor of asteroid rock. In practically every case, these openings marked the placement of big gun batteries.

I stood in the same crater where the landing had been centered, and spoke on proximity chat with my top officers. A mix of human and Centaur marines regarded me gravely. If anyone had chanced upon us, they might have thought it was an odd scene. An Earther might have believed we'd brought along huge trained dogs in space suits and had them stand beside their human trainers.

"Marines, I want you to observe those cylindrical projectors to my left."

Helmets rotated in the direction I'd indicated. Every Centaur officer had a translation brainbox built into his command kit, I'd insisted on that expensive equipment upgrade. Communication often won battles.

"That's a laser battery. Right now, those big guns aren't firing, but when the gunboats get here, they will be pounding our fleet. We have to take them, or preferably conquer the entire station before the main fleet arrives."

A young Major signaled for attention. I acknowledged her. "How long do we have before they arrive sir? And what are our specific goals?"

"We're going in through the laser batteries. They have to be open to emit heat while firing, and they have large parabolic openings around them to allow a free field of fire. The railgun batteries could be used as secondary entrances, but they aren't as large or as open. The passive defense batteries should be avoided. They're sealed, and possibly dangerous to attacking troops."

"What about the landing bays?"

"There's only one that hasn't been sealed—the main cargo entrance. That's the biggest entry on the surface of this station, and I'm sure it will be heavily defended. My plan is to put the second wave there, encircling the location. The second wave, made up of six companies, will feint at the landing bay, firing into it and using small explosives. This will draw the enemy to defend that entrance—the obvious one."

"Sir?" asked the young Major.

I turned to her again and took a better look. She was a shapeless mass in her armor, looking like a slightly smaller version of the other troops around her. Her name was emblazoned on her helmet: *Reza*.

"What is it, Major Reza?"

"I get your plan, we pretend to hit the easy opening, and once we engage the real invasion comes at the laser ports. But where and when do the second wave companies get into the fight?"

I'd already designated Reza as the leader of the second wave, and I was beginning to have my doubts, but I answered her question anyway. "That's going to be up to your discretion, Major. If the enemy starts boiling out of there, keep them pinned and fight defensively. I don't want them to take the surface of the station back from us. On the other hand, if they disappear, pulling into the interior to fight the real invasion, then press ahead and go in after them. Any more questions?"

There weren't any, so we called the meeting a win and broke up. I headed toward the nearest laser battery. Kwon had managed to sneak his way into my squad, and I hadn't objected. The Centaur Captain trotted ahead of us, and all her troops followed.

As near as I could tell, the Centaur Captain's name was Sky. This was far from an accurate translation, I knew. The Centaurs had a zillion words for terms like Sky or Grass. There were even different words used for a particular species of grass at a given season, or a given lushness. Similarly, Sky was far too vague for them. Skies were not just overcast or clear, bright or dark. The scent in the air, the cloud formations and the humidity levels changed the terms used. But Captain Sky would have to do for us for now.

Kwon and I had to hurry to keep up with the advancing Centaurs. I'd never met a species more eager for a battle that was sure to be grimly filled with casualties.

"Colonel?" asked Kwon.

"Yes, First Sergeant?"

"Captain Sky's troops—they're too bunched up, too close to the leader. They should spread out, sir."

"Of course they should," I said. "But I'm not seeing an easy way to get them to do that."

"Excuse me, sir?"

"Back on Eden-11, when I wanted them to spread out, I ordered them to each hug a tree. As much as they'd like to, they couldn't all hug the same one. That was the only way I could get them not to mass up and get nailed all at once. It's their instinct, Kwon. They are herd creatures, after all."

"Ah, I see. I heard about that."

Kwon proceeded to make a huffing sound. It took me a few long seconds to realize he'd made a play on words. I didn't want to disappoint him, so I chuckled politely.

"Very good, Kwon. Let's spread out a bit ourselves. Order the human squad to disperse. I'll tell Captain Sky to tell her troops to follow ours, one squad per man. That will break us up somewhat."

Kwon relayed the order with bellows and shouts that made me wish my hearing hadn't returned in full force. As it was, I could have used a selective input volume for his channel. I considered adding such a feature in my next helmet headset design. Hell, I could use a *Kwon* button that worked just for him.

We came around the last major outcropping of asteroid rock and there it was, Heavy Laser Battery Three. Several gleaming projectors poked up, pointing mutely at the sky. The rock armor bulged here, due to the dome-like hump of metal that formed the battery. It was buried under twenty feet of rock, but you could still see it was there.

Around the laser battery were three point-defense laser turrets. So far, these hadn't shown signs of life. When I'd owned the station, the brainboxes that operated these defensive lasers had been conditioned carefully to ignore human troops—or any Star Force personnel. Unlike their outdated predecessors back on Andros Island, which tracked everything that moved in about a one mile radius, these weapons were supposed to keep their artificial eyes on the immediate region of space around the station. Their job was to shoot down incoming enemy missiles before they reached the hull.

Knowing this, I was alarmed to see the laser swivel and track my lead troops.

"Captain Sky," I shouted. "Order your troops to take cover, we'll encircle the battery and advance—"

That was about as far as I got before the three laser turrets identified, targeted and fired. They weren't supposed to aim down at that angle. They weren't supposed to shoot at Star Force personnel, but they'd been reprogrammed. The Lobsters hadn't been twiddling their claws in there.

Laser fire flared in rapid, pulsing beams. Fired at pointblank range, they could hardly miss and every shot was deadly. These systems had always been designed to target quickly and fire missile-killing beams at moving targets. The projectors were about six feet long, and packed a wattage output about three times that of our own heavy beamers.

The beams stitched in multiple, split-second bursts. Captain Sky lit up like a torch. There was nothing left but the burning hulk of his armor, which spun over my head on its way out into space. A hoof or something thunked against a ridge of rock I was in the act of stepping over.

"Take cover!" I screamed. "Knock out those turrets!"

I rolled behind the ridge of rock that had been at my feet a moment before. The laser fire put seven or eight burning holes into the rock, sending up puffs of vapor and causing the rock to glow orange. It had become instant spots of lava that quickly cooled.

The company opened up, burning the turrets. Unfortunately, most of the Centaurs didn't listen to me and didn't take cover. They fired first, and before the brief action was over, a dozen of them were floating away from the station out into the inky blackness of space.

I didn't bother to fire at the turrets personally. Instead, I hunkered down under cover and used the command channel to alert every company in the assault. At least half of them had already figured it out for themselves. When the casualty reports came in, I was displeased. We'd already lost nearly a hundred marines in this stage of the assault, and we hadn't managed to breach the hull yet.

I heaved myself up and headed for the laser battery. All around me, marines came out of cover and followed me. They were wary now, human and Centaur alike. *Good*, I thought. There were sure to be more surprises once we got inside.

I passed the sparking hulk of a knocked out defensive laser. It twitched as I came near, trying to stir, trying to swing its broken projector around to aim at me. These machines knew no loyalty. That was one of the problems with smart machines in a war. The enemy could turn them right back around on you, once they'd captured them. We'd done the same to the Macros often enough, and now the Lobsters were doing it to us.

We topped the bulge which surrounded the big projectors. Soon, I knew, the enemy would reprogram these batteries. If they could do it to the defensive systems, they could do it to every system on the entire station.

This put a new light on the enemy plans. They hadn't come here just to do us some harm and help their Macro friends. They hadn't taken this station to knock it out of action. They planned to make it their own. They planned to control the Thor ring, to become the masters who decided who passed this ring and who didn't. This raised the stakes in my mind, as I realized losing the battle station

316

was more than a setback to my plans. It was a strategic disaster for the entire human race.

Tightening my face into a grim set of lines, I crept forward into the deep, dark grooves that opened into the battery control room. I saw movement in there, and flashes of bright metal.

"Frag out!" I shouted, and threw a grenade dead ahead. The art of grenade tossing in zero G was something that had to be practiced a lot, but which was easy in a circumstance like this. Because the enemy was inside an enclosed space, and I didn't have to worry about any drop-off due to gravity, all I had to do was throw it in a straight line. It was more like precisely throwing a dart at a dartboard than it was lobbing a grenade under planetary conditions.

The grenade vanished into the dark groove and struck something, then bounced. A silent flash went off, darkening my visor a fraction. In rapid succession, more flashes went off in there, as my marines came up at every angle and added their grenades to my own.

"All right," shouted Kwon, "that's enough. Rush 'em!"

About twenty marines dropped into the opening. I saw flashes and flares, but nothing disastrous. I dropped into the groove myself, and vanished into the dark. When my boots hit something again, the surface slid away under my feet. I almost went down, and thought I'd landed on top of another marine.

"Sorry about that!" I said, rolling and picking myself up.

A huge gauntlet grabbed my pack and hauled me up. Kwon huffed with laughter. He pointed to the stack of dead enemy troops I'd landed on.

"They don't care sir," he said. "You can jump on them all you like!"

I chuckled and looked around. It appeared the Lobsters had been taken out effectively by our shower of grenades. "Let's keep moving. Put two scouts into every hallway."

Kwon stumped away, slapping helmets and pointing. Mostly, he struck Centaur helmets. This wasn't any kind of discrimination on his part, as they outnumbered us ten to one.

When the all-clear was given, we marched down the main hallway which led to the primary generators. If we could take those out, the station's weapons would be disabled. Then, at least this structure wouldn't be a threat to the relief fleet, which was on its way.

I noticed something odd as I advanced down the passageway. A pack of Centaurs were following me closely. They almost bumped into my butt with their nanocloth-covered horns when I rounded a corner.

"What it is, gentlemen?" I asked them, turning on them.

To my surprise, they were all lieutenants. I frowned, wondering what the hell they wanted from me now. All I needed were a pack of scared Centaurs, ramming me from behind in the coming firefights.

"Excuse me, Colonel," said the nearest. He was a big buck with a set of horns on him that would have made any doe back home swoon.

"What is it, Lieutenant? Why are you marines following me around, rather than leading your own platoons?"

They shuffled on their hooves. "We don't have a leader sir. Except for you."

"Yeah? Who's second in command?"

"That has yet to be determined. We haven't had time for a duel amongst ourselves for the honor. Normally, we don't duel until after a battle is complete. There is no honor in it, and the wind will not tolerate—"

"Well," I said, "the part about not dueling in the middle of a war sounds like an intelligent policy. But don't you work out who is second in command of a given herd before you go into a fight, in case the leader falls?"

"No sir. We follow the next higher commander."

"What if your top guys are all taken out?"

"Then the battle has been lost, sir."

I filed that factoid about Centaurs away in the box marked "cultural failures." It was amazing the predators hadn't come out on top on their world. A moment later, I realized why they were hugging up to me like I was giving milk: the highest available commander was obviously me.

"All right," I said, making a mental note to retrain some new protocols into my native levies after this was all over—if I was lucky enough to survive it. "You're the new Captain," I said, pointing to the one with the big horns who'd been doing all the talking. "When the battle is over, you can defend that rank against the others, if that is your tradition."

"Thank you, Colonel!"

"What's your name, marine?"

The translator buzzed in my ear: "I'm known as Captain Sky, sir."

"Of course you are," I said.

-40-

The battle began to heat up. On the surface of the station, Major Reza was putting up a good show of attacking the landing bay. I could tell she didn't really want to be the sideshow in this assault, and if she could press ahead and enter the big portal, she would do it. I was happy with that, as I wanted her attack to be as convincing as possible, without costing us a lot of men.

Unfortunately for the Major, the Lobsters were just as determined to hold onto their position as she was to push them back. The fighting was fierce, lighting up the region with a continuous glow of dust, vapor and reflected laser light. I looked out toward the battle, and saw the rising cloud of debris which was lit up from the inside in brilliant flashes. A fierce firefight with beam weapons often looked like that. So much energy was released that it vaporized rock and metal. A haze would arise, and as the beams continued to burn through it, the dust itself was ignited and became visible. It looked as if a lurid red dome had grown over the region, reminding me of a laser show at a rock concert, or a particularly wild aurora borealis display.

Out at the laser batteries, things were progressing more smoothly. All but one of the companies assigned with assaulting a battery had been successful enough to get inside. My group headed down into the dark passages, eager to push the enemy back.

"I want us to break down into platoons now," I told the Centaur officers. "You know the target, marines. Don't get bogged down, keep moving. If you meet stiff resistance, you're to take another route, even if you have to cut your way through the walls. The goal

320

isn't to stand and fight the enemy in the passages. We *must* take down those central generators."

The orders were met with no response. I heard them on their own channel, making a few remarks. But they didn't say anything to me. We'd yet to train them to acknowledge commands the way human troops were accustomed to doing. Under Centaur cultural rules, when the commander gave an order, there was no need to acknowledge it. Everyone in the herd assumed that the order would be followed without question.

For me, it was a little unnerving to have them all just stare at me silently. It gave me the feeling they didn't like the orders. I knew they might not consider them honorable, as they didn't involve a straightforward fight on an open plain. To the Centaur way of thinking, just being down here in these dark tunnels was demeaning, lowly and faintly disgusting. We'd gotten them past their fear of such situations thanks to Marvin's Microbial baths, but they still didn't like it.

"You're now part of Riggs' Pigs," I told them. "We're famous for our bravery, for doing what must be done, no matter what the cost. We're famous for our victories, victories that often come at a high price. Marines, we must not think of ourselves today. Don't dream of lush grasses, shining waters, or even the wide open sky. What we do today we do to honor those we left at home, those who we must defend with our sacrifice. We will honor them and gift them life through the loss of our blood. Is that clear, platoon leaders?"

"Yes, Colonel!" all of them answered. Their voices crashed into my helmet in unison. At least they knew how to yell like real marines.

I smiled as I led them into the tunnels of steel. They ran faster now, their short tails flipping high inside the special sock-like appendages we'd built into their nanocloth suits. High tails were a sure sign of high spirits. I felt I'd hit a home run with that quick speech. I'd managed to learn how they thought by now, and I could tell I'd revved them up. Really, it wasn't hard to do.

Very shortly after my speech was over, we met our first obstacle. Our rush forward toward the core of the station was halted by a defensive bulwark thrown up in the primary passage in the center of the structure. Here, the passageway was almost circular, and was about thirty feet across. Depending on your point of view, it resembled a mile-long shaft, or a tall corridor, if you walked on the walls. We'd built it with size in mind in order to let big equipment such as generators and projectors move through the station. I'd envisioned being under siege, and hadn't wanted to have to fly or drag new equipment into place over the surface of the station. Anything outside the armored hull was exposed, and could be vulnerable to bombardment.

Now, the central shaft served us as an odd battleground. The Lobsters had formed up a wall in the central region—a wall made up of rounded humps of some kind. I frowned when I spotted this structure, uncertain where'd they gotten these yard-wide spheroids. Whatever they were, they'd piled them into place and welded them together with a layer of metal. I wasn't sure, but I figured they'd probably taken parts of the station to do it, such as broken boulders from the outer hull and metal from the station itself.

I frowned at the structure and decided I didn't care how they'd built it. The thing was in the way, and it had to come down.

"All beams, concentrate on the—"

"Behind us, sir!" shouted Kwon. His voice boomed in proximity chat, indicating he was very close. A big hand swatted me and I automatically tightened my body.

For perhaps the first time since I'd met Kwon, I stood up to one of his bear-claw blows that were meant to take me down to the ground with him. I watched as he slammed down on the floor of the shaft near me. He was on his belly, turning his projector back the way we'd come.

I lifted my projector. Things were moving in slow motion now, as time always seemed to slow down when a firefight began. Looking forward at the barrier ahead, I realized what its true purpose was. The Lobsters hadn't put it there to stop us, they'd put it there to trap us.

The sizzle and snap of beams began. My body entered that state I think of as full battle-mode. I hadn't experienced my new body in a firefight since I'd undergone fresh microbial baths, new nanite refills and donned the latest in battle armor.

I turned around and saw what was coming. A mass of enemy troops boiled out of the side passages. My Centaurs were running everywhere, spinning around, running up the walls, firing and being shot down. Several had already taken hits and gone tumbling.

I realized in an instant the Centaur species had a critical flaw in their body structures for this kind of fight. They couldn't lie flat and shoot. It just didn't come naturally for them. They could fold up their legs, but their horns and head were still up high, as their arms weren't positioned as close to their heads as was the case for a human body. Worse, they didn't want to throw themselves flat under fire. It was the absolute last thing a herd animal did when in danger. Falling down meant certain death when being chased by a predator.

All around me, my Centaur marines whirled, stood their ground, and fired at the humping horde of enemy that appeared behind us. I was just as bad as the rest of them, burning away while presenting a big fat target.

I was hit almost immediately, then hit again. My body rocked, and my armor smoked. But I didn't feel any pain. I kept firing, taking out an advancing attacker with every strike.

I felt the armor plates on my body moving of their own accord. They were reactive, and as smart as the nanocloth underneath them. When a region was damaged, that region moved out of the line of fire and rolled another plate into position. I kept firing and advancing.

Our weapons were more powerful than the enemy's, I realized. Even better, their armor was like tinfoil. Unfortunately, my Centaurs weren't heavily armored like I was. They were taking a beating.

Kwon had finally given up on getting me to lie on my belly.

"This sucks!" he shouted. "I can't even get a shot, all I see are Centaur legs!"

"Get up and advance," I said.

He did as I ordered, and together we marched toward the Lobsters, burning them. Each one died with a plume of expanding steam, as their suits were at least partly filled with water. Before it was over, they'd managed to hurt me, putting a hole in my left kneecap. It was a small hole fortunately, and the suit resealed itself. I cranked up the exoskeletal setting on that leg and it forced me to walk. My step changed to an uneven one, but I kept moving. I gritted my teeth against the pain and continued advancing.

They broke when about half of them were dead. They'd fought well, and had wiped out most of my platoon. I counted twenty enemy dead, some of them still twisting and writhing in agony. Kwon kicked one of them, and in the low grav the body went twisting down the shaft ahead of us.

"That was bullshit," he said. "They knew we were coming."

"Well, that's their job. These guys are smart, but they aren't the best fighters."

We turned back to the wall that had stopped us. I examined it more closely, snapping on my suit lights.

"Ah," I said, "I get it. These are dead Lobsters. See these rock-like balls? They stacked up their own dead and sprayed constructive nanites over them. The smart metal is acting like a weld to hold the barrier together."

"What killed them all?" Kwon asked.

I shrugged. "Most likely, Welter's people did. They've been fighting down here for quite some time, you know. Maybe Welter killed them all or even built the wall himself during his last stand. There's still no contact from him, is there?"

"No sir. Lots of interference in this big structure. And the central com system is worse than dead. It seems to be jamming all long-range signals."

We blew apart the barrier with grenades and carefully continued past it. I had a grand total of fifteen effective Centaurs, plus Kwon and I. The lieutenant I'd so recently promoted to captain was dead, and I didn't feel like making a new Captain Sky out of the noncoms to replace him. I took personal command and told them Kwon was my second, if I should fall.

We continued up the central shaft until our automaps showed we should take a side route. There, we met up with another platoon—or rather, with their remains.

"They're all dead, sir," Kwon said, stumping around the piles of bodies.

There were Crustaceans, Centaurs and humans everywhere. At least sixty bodies, maybe more, were clustered around a junction of two passages.

"There seem to be more dead Lobsters than anything else."

"That's good!" Kwon said. "Let's make *more* dead ones."

Grim-faced, I pressed on. We were getting close to the generators now. I could see signs of heavy fighting, and I could hear laser fire echoing down the passages from distant fights. I tried my suit radio again, but got nothing other than static. Our com-links didn't synch-up unless we were very close. I realized I could probably shout farther than I could communicate with my headset.

"Let's stay tight," I told my troops. "Anyone who gets lost now is never going to be found."

This was the sort of instruction the Centaurs dreamed of. They were immediately hugging up against one another and bumping their horns into my generator pack. I almost yelled at them, but held back. They'd suffered a lot, and not one of them had broken. I'd asked for their sacrifice, and they'd given it their all. I wasn't going to dishonor any of them by admonishing them now.

For a Centaur, simply being ignored by a superior was a powerful rebuke. Outright confrontation and enduring an angry display was so humiliating that the underling in question often took his own life, or he might become so distraught he could not function properly. I didn't need any of my surviving troops opening their suits in despair. They'd suffered enough, and they didn't deserve a cranky human officer at this point.

"Good job, marines," I said. "You've all done extremely well. The fallen will water the grass with their blood, and will never be forgotten in the song of the winds."

This seemed to make them happy. Tails lifted all along the line. I'd heard the speech from other Centaurs after rough fights, so I figured I might as well give them what they expected.

We made it to Generator Room Three after a few more skirmishes with the Lobsters. I could tell the area had been fought over before. There were bodies here, many of them Fleet crewmen. They were Welter's men, and they'd died putting up a fierce defense.

"Plant the charges, Kwon," I said.

He was already doing it. He hummed as he worked. I marveled at his attitude. All the blood, all the gore, all the bodies strewn everywhere—they never seemed to bother Kwon. As long as he was in a battle zone, he was content and life was good.

"Timer set, sir," he said.

I blinked in my suit. "How long do we have?"

"Ah…oh yeah. Didn't check."

"Out! Out! OUT! Everyone move to the exit, now!"

We ran out of the generator room. Kwon was the last one to the door, and his shadow loomed over me as the explosion bloomed into life. The roar of it was somewhat muted by my helmet and as I'd managed to turn a corner into a side passage. Luckily, I wasn't deafened again. I was, however, smacked from behind and pushed into a pile of squirming Centaurs by Kwon's flying hulk.

We picked ourselves up, with our heads ringing. The corridor had gone black—in fact this entire region of the station had darkened. We turned on our suit lights and beams stabbed into the dusty darkness around us. Centaurs limped and spoke together in their own odd language. I could tell their remarks weren't meant for my ears, as they hadn't engaged my translator. I could well imagine what they were saying.

"Sorry sir," Kwon said. "I have trouble with the timers. I get excited.

"I think you're going back to the explosives training center after we get back home."

"You mean the one back on Andros Island? With all the pits and bunkers?"

"Yeah," I said. "That's exactly what I mean. If we ever get back home, that is."

"Can't do it, sir."

"Why not?"

"Because I've been banned from there, sir. The duty Sergeant said he never wanted to see me again."

I nodded. "All right. But next time, I'm lighting off the charges."

"Very good, Colonel."

-41-

One by one, the generators were taken out. After that, each of the invading companies had their follow-up orders: we were all to hunker down and stay alive until relief came. The gunships and the rest of our infantry were inbound, and with the big guns silenced, they should be able to land as an organized force. We had fifty gunships and about ten thousand men out there, more than enough to sweep aside the surviving Lobster defenders. The only hard part was waiting for them to arrive. I looked at my chronometer, and grimaced. We had about five hours to go. Five hours didn't sound like a lot, but when you were crouching in the dark with a handful of troops, it was an eternity.

"You think squatting here at the gen room is the best idea, Colonel?" Kwon asked me.

I looked at him. My ears had stopped ringing from the grenade attack back on the surface by this time, but they were still sore. A trickle of liquid ran from each ear down my neck. I figured that was a mix of blood and nanites. The worst was the itching. Healing fast always seemed to have its trade-offs. One negative was the horrible itching. As the pressure was low here, I couldn't even afford to take off my helmet and have a good scratch.

"What do you suggest, First Sergeant?"

"Let's go look for Welter. I bet he's holed up around the backup bridge—if he's still alive, that is."

I snorted, catching on. Kwon wasn't worried about the dangers of sitting here beside the blown generator. He was bored and wanted to get back into the action.

"Forget it, Kwon," I said. "We're staying put."

Kwon sat against a wall and pouted. I ignored him and worked on my radio. If I was lucky, the generators were powering the jamming system. The central com system didn't have to work—I could use suit power alone to contact someone.

After a few minutes of fooling with the channels, I managed to get a live conversation to play in my helmet. It was between two officers, and it sounded urgent. I caught something about the bridge, then lost the signal.

We were in a small tool room, about as big as a typical two-car garage back home. Junk was everywhere, and there was a hole in the nearest wall. We used that hole to peer out and listen for approaching enemies. Around me, the Centaurs tensely watched the exits with projectors in their hands. Kwon and I were both resting against walls.

I grumbled and sat there quietly in the dark for perhaps two full minutes. I took those two minutes to think about the Centaurs and how different they were from humans. Right now, I could see another difference on display. If everything was quiet and there was a lull in the battle, human troops tended to relax as much as they could, conserving their energy for the next conflict. The Centaurs didn't seem to operate that way. While they were in a hostile environment, they couldn't rest. Their ears never stopped twitching. Their head swung this way and that, and they paced around, trying to sense approaching danger. I guess it all went back to our racial histories. At some point, they'd spent a lot of time being prey, while we'd become used to the lazy role of the predator.

Finally, I couldn't stand it anymore. I fiddled with the radio again. I thought I heard a squawk, and the name "Major Reza". Kwon came alive and leaned toward me when he noticed what I was doing.

"You got something there?"

"Yeah. Sounds like Reza and her team are in trouble."

"Sure they are. They are supposed to be in trouble. When you paint your butt red and moon the bull, you expect things to become exciting."

I chuckled. "You must have heard that from someone."

"Yeah," Kwon said. "A guy back at the base told me that one. He called himself a redneck, but his neck was as white as a fish belly. Puzzling."

I chuckled again. "I can't take it anymore," I said. "I've got to head back toward the central shaft. From there, we should be able to signal someone. I wouldn't be surprised if we found a nanite stream to plug into."

"Suit power!" Kwon said excitedly. "I'm down to seven hours of juice now."

That wasn't much of an excuse, I realized. This entire battle was supposed to be over in less than seven hours, and moving around wasn't conserving power in any case. But I didn't like the idea of a raging battle going on nearby without even being aware of how the wind was blowing. I guess it was all my own fault. As the overall commander, I could have sat outside on the hull calling shots. But I hadn't, I'd gone into the shit, and now my boots were all dirty and I was tired of being stuck here.

We carefully picked our way through the darkened station back to the central shaft. I cautiously opened my helmet to every channel in sequence. Most of them were silent. But there was some chatter on the general command channel.

"This is Colonel Kyle Riggs," I said, "identify yourselves."

"Colonel Riggs? This is Major Reza. I'm pushing into the interior, sir. The enemy is falling back."

Another voice came on then. "I thought we'd lost you, Kyle!" said Major Sloan. "I'm in the middle of an argument with Reza. She wants to advance, I'm trying to tell her to hold onto the LZ for me. Could you clarify, sir?"

"In my absence Sloan would normally be in command. However, you're over four hours out in space, Sloan. I've been out of contact for over an hour myself. In this case, I would normally defer to the commander on the ground. What do you want to do and why, Reza?"

"I want to break in and follow the enemy, forcing them into a full retreat. They're no longer trying to hold the entire battle station. I think they realize that it's too big for their remaining forces. I want to push into that vacuum they're leaving behind and keep the pressure on. Also, I think there may well be survivors like yourself and Welter's troops in pockets. I want to keep them alive by giving the Lobsters something to worry about."

I nodded to myself. "Sounds pretty good to me. Sloan, you'll have to secure your own LZ. Just pull up some gunships and blast anything that crawls on the exterior hull. Reza, head for the central shaft. I'll meet you there with whatever troops I can gather."

By the time I reached the central shaft again, I'd managed to pull together the remains of five platoons. Sadly, they numbered less than a hundred troops all told. Losses had been grim, and the fighting had been universally heavy. Most of the station was in a vacuum, and my Centaur troops were wearing nanocloth balloons rather than armor. One hit, and they were usually knocked out of the game. Losses among the human marines had only been about a quarter as bad. I attributed this somewhat to their superior experience—but mostly to their armor.

When Major Reza met up with me, she'd lost less than ten percent of her men. Still, they'd definitely been bloodied. She brought a nanite stream down with her, and we powered up on it.

"What's the plan, Colonel?" she asked me.

I could tell she was still in a hard-charging mood. This impressed me. Sloan was a cautious survivor who liked to do things by the book and take his time. This woman had fire in her, and she'd done the job I'd asked her to do and more. Still, I didn't want a crazy person leading my men into doom. That was *my* job. I decided to give her a little test.

"What if I said we're going to advance to the top of the central shaft and retake the bridge?" I asked.

She paused just a moment before saying, "I'd say that was too much to ask, sir. Especially with Sloan's reinforcements on the way. We'd do better waiting for the additional troops before attempting that final assault."

I nodded. It was the right answer.

"What would you do in the meantime?" I asked her.

"I'd spread out, take up defensive positions, and make sure they don't get those generators running again."

"Then that's exactly what we're going to do. Execute the plan, Major."

She stepped away, calling for her captains. I watched her in action. Kwon came over to me.

330

"She's pretty good," he said.

"Yeah, I like her style."

"You think she's hot in there?"

"What?"

"In that suit. It's pretty stuffy you know." He began huffing again, and I realized I'd been the victim of another of Kwon's jokes, which generally involved a weak play on words.

"That's pretty funny, Kwon," I lied. "Let's set up our company on the defensive line."

We'd retaken about half the station by now—the lower half. The generators were on the border, and the Lobsters were showing signs they meant to retake them. I realized there was still time for them to effect repairs and get the main laser batteries operating before Sloan's reinforcements arrived. If they had a decent supply of constructive nanites, all they had to do was retake the generator rooms and pour on a generous layer of the hard-working little bastards. They knew no loyalty, and would patch up the system within an hour or two. I relayed these thoughts to Reza, who agreed immediately.

"We have to hold this line, sir," she said, running a gauntleted finger across the tablet we were both using. Fortunately, the device was built to withstand this sort of treatment and responded with a red line slashed across the map. The line bisected the station neatly, splitting top from bottom.

We organized our troops accordingly, and our numbers swelled by three more companies before the enemy hit us. This time, they didn't come at us via the central shaft. That would give us too great of a range advantage, as they would have to advance into our guns. Instead, they used the smaller side passages, stairways and Jefferies tubes.

"They are even coming up out of the drains, sir!" shouted Kwon, who was taking in contact reports.

"Hold positions. Kwon, let's set up our company as series of relief platoons. If the enemy breaks through, we'll run a fresh platoon to that spot and patch the hole."

It was an old game plan, and we knew the drill well. It wasn't long before our services were needed. "Breakthrough in Generator Room Two, sir!" Kwon reported.

I signaled a platoon and they galloped away. They were all Centaurs in this group. I frowned after them. "Let's follow up with a full squad of humans," I said.

"Good idea, sir," Kwon said.

The good thing about Centaur troops was their fast feet. They made it there much sooner than we could. But they were stunned by the enemy numbers. The Lobsters kept pushing, having burned holes through the walls.

I arrived and began firing immediately. I spotted an enemy gutting a pinned Centaur. I shot a long burst, burning away all eight of its scrabbling feet. The Lobster floated away, arching and flipping. Stabbing down with its claws, it grabbed the Centaur's neck and tried to finish the job. I put a focused beam into its head area, and it finally seized up. I advanced, but the Centaur was already dead.

Heavy fighting went on all around us. Kwon was there, beaming and backing up. Soon we stood with our backs together in the midst of the smoky generator room.

"Sir," he said, "we need more troops."

"No time, we have to pull back."

We retreated as a fresh wave of enemy troops spilled into the room. We'd lost one out of three rooms.

The fighting began then at each of the generators. In each case, the results were a fierce, pitched battle. I contacted Major Reza.

"We're in trouble down here," I told her. "I want you send a full company to each of the three big generator rooms. We have to hold them as isolated pockets. I don't think we have the numbers to maintain a firm line across the entire station."

She didn't like it, but she obeyed. With an additional company at my back, we pressed them back out at Generator Two. It was ours again.

There was a lull in the fighting. I looked around at the mess. There had to be a hundred bodies in sight, and more in every adjacent hallway and storeroom. We were lurking in a smoky haze now, shutting off our suit lights and setting up lanterns here and there to see by. Motion detectors hummed and pinged, waiting.

The next rush was worse than the first. The only generator they'd ever managed to capture was Generator Two, so maybe they thought we were the wimps. In any case, they pushed us hard. After ten minutes of sniping and crawling, I realized they'd won. We'd lost too many men, and my suit had already clamped down on my right arm, taking it off at the elbow. It didn't feel too good, but it went numb at last when the nanites were done.

I switched my projector to my left hand and continued burning swathes into the darkness.

"We have to fall back sir," Kwon said.

He sounded funny, and I looked for him in the darkness and dust. I found him facedown on the floor. He was breathing, but not moving. I grabbed him by an ankle, letting my projector fall and dangle by the power cord.

"Fall back!" I shouted. "Fall back toward the central shaft!"

A close circle of marines came with me. The enemy threw a shower of grenades. The survivors on our side fired and threw some back. There were flashes, booms and flares of brilliant light everywhere. I became confused, uncertain where I was or where I was going. I stuck with the group and kept dragging Kwon.

We backed up into a narrow passage. Every time the squad I was with paused to fire back at the advancing enemy, I let go of Kwon and fired with them.

We had almost reached the central shaft, when I heard a chiming in my helmet.

"Colonel? Are you there, Colonel?"

It was Major Reza. "Yes," I said. "We've taken a lot of casualties and we've been pushed back out of Gen Room Two."

"Roger that," she said. "Sir, the enemy is behaving strangely. They're pulling back here at the central shaft. Are they still attacking you?"

I leaned against a wall and checked Kwon. He was unconscious and had been in that state for some time. He was breathing, but his pulse was thready. He had several wounds, I wasn't sure where all of them were. I wondered if he would make it.

I struggled to make sense of what Reza was saying.

"Major, they aren't hitting us at the moment. But I'm sure they're reorganizing for the next push."

"No sir, I don't think so. The reason I'm asking about your position is I think you're in the last spot they hit. They're quiet or retreating on all other fronts."

I frowned into the gloom. "Send me some relief then," I said. "We'll hold here."

We waited tensely in the dark. I had eighteen men and six Centaurs. The Centaurs had eyes that rolled in their visors. I didn't blame them for being scared. They were becoming an endangered species aboard my battle station.

Finally, after what seemed like a half-century, a fresh platoon showed up. I had them take Kwon and the rest of our severely wounded to the back of the lines. I was surprised to learn that we *had* lines again. The enemy had inexplicably halted their attack and fallen back on every front.

Cautiously, I advanced with my new platoon into Generator Room Two again. It was empty.

Major Reza called me again. I answered, and her next words stunned me.

"Colonel? I have a new contact, sir. It's the Lobsters—they want to talk."

-42-

After talking to the Crustaceans for several minutes, I learned something new about them: they weren't like the machines. They weren't even like the Centaurs or the Worms. They were more like us humans than I'd suspected.

Their commander had carefully calculated his odds, and found them poor. He'd counted our ships, our guns and our men. He knew a relief fleet was on the way. He knew that my force of assault troops had killed a large number of his troops and taken half the battle station. He also knew that he could not hope to hold against the storm that was sure to come in the following hours.

Unlike the Centaurs with their honor, the Worms with their ferocity, or the machines with their vicious fight-to-the-last programming, the Crustacean commander didn't want to die. He contacted me and negotiated terms. By the time Sloan and his men dropped on the exterior, we'd made arrangements to disarm and capture all the alien troops. The commander had asked that he and all his troops be allowed to return home.

I thought about it. There was a lot we could learn from keeping them as prisoners. But then again, if I hoped to weld a peace with this species in the future, keeping them indefinitely would not improve their attitudes toward me. I knew I might be able to give them up later in some sort of a prisoner exchange. But such circumstances were rare in space combat. Usually, the losing side died—all of them.

So, I gave their commander a lecture about biotic solidarity and let him go. He listened, because he didn't have any other choice, then told me I was intellectually inferior and disconnected.

I shook my head and marveled as I pulled off my headset and lay my head back on a pile of nanocloth. I fantasized about the warm shower I planned to take when I got back aboard *Actium* and wondered why the Crustaceans were the way they were. I guessed they couldn't help it. They were cantankerous, huffy intellectuals and there was probably no way to ever change that.

When they'd finally left the battle station, we found Commander Welter. He'd made his last stand with a dozen comrades in the backup-bridge. As far as we could tell, the battle had ended for him and his crewmen hours ago, while we were just entering into the station to retake it. He'd never had a hope of survival, as even if I'd known where he was, I couldn't have fought my way down to his position in time.

Seeing Welter lying there, dead on the floor with his guts burnt out of his open suit, I felt a surge of anger. I regretted letting the Lobsters go free. It took a full minute for me to regain my composure. Just a weeks ago he and I had chased the enemy out of this battle station, but today they'd come back and gotten their revenge.

"I hereby name this structure Welter Station," I told everyone present. I then relayed the message out over the general override channel.

I'd never given the battle station a name up until this point, partly because it was the only such structure we had. But I felt Welter had earned the honor, and I thought it likely we would build more fortifications like this one in the future.

* * *

Three days after the liberation of the battle station, I received a message. These had been tense days, during which we watched and listened at every front. When I heard a message had come in from Kerr via the rings, I hurried to receive it. I requested a hardcopy in my quarters, and rushed down the passageway, bouncing in my haste. The low grav of the ship allowed me to take leaps as high as I felt like, but pushing off too hard with one's feet often resulted in a knock on the head. Today, I was ducking as the ceiling came shockingly close, then pumping my next leg again to take another tremendous stride.

I pulled the message out of the tray in my quarters, and already I was frowning. It was only a single page.

We whooped 'em, Riggs! We took them all, you cagey bastard. I'm sure you thought the Empire would fall, that we couldn't stand up against a Macro fleet without the amazing Kyle Riggs at the helm. Well, you were wrong, boy!

Sure, we've got a few bruises. Who needed Pakistan or Italy, anyway? The fallout over India was the worst, but we're still here! There were plenty of provinces they never touched.

And in case you're considering finishing up what the Macros started with a follow-up attack, I want you to know you won't get through, either. We're ready, and we're still on our feet. Go ahead and give it your best shot.

-General Kerr, Imperial Forces, April 11th

I read the message twice. I put it down, paced around the cabin, then read it again. I shook my head. I hadn't wanted Earth to be hurt. I'd taken a terrible gamble, I realized that now. I should never have let the machine fleet through intact. On the other hand, I knew if I'd chosen to fight the Macros toe-to-toe out here on the frontier, I probably would have lost.

As a human, I owed it to the rest of humanity to defend them against the Macros. Maybe I could have stopped that armada entirely. At the very least, I could have weakened it and saved lives. Possibly millions of lives.

So, why hadn't I done so? Why hadn't I made the ultimate sacrifice, the sacrifice every soldier knows is in the contract when he signs on to defend his people?

It had been too galling, I decided. The idea of fighting for Crow as a patsy, as a chump set up to take the beating his fleet had earned. To die for Crow's Empire, even though I didn't want it to exist. I'd chosen not to do it, and that choice had caused untold damage to my homeworld.

I paced and stressed until Sandra showed up. She read the message, then put it down quietly. I half-expected her to begin scolding me. Maybe this time she would declare me unfit to be her lover.

But she didn't. Instead, she came to me and put her head on my chest. "Crow is a horrible leader, Kyle. Don't feel bad. It's not your fault. Even if the only humans left right now were those out here on the frontier with you, all of us would be better off."

I shook my head. "It doesn't work like that. This is about extinction. The loss of millions hurts us all. We're like a candle flame in this universe, Sandra. When the wind blows, we flicker and dance. A single drop of rain could make us hiss, sputter and waver. A storm would put us out for sure. We're facing a storm right now, and in the end, we're very likely to die out."

She looked up at me, frowning. "What were we supposed to do? Stand in front of that fleet? We would have been mowed, Kyle. Destroyed. Crow wanted that, you realize. He figured he was on the safe side of you. He knew you were closest to the enemy, and expected them to go through you to get to him. Well, you showed him he wasn't so safe. What matters now is Star Force is alive and still strong."

I could hear a tremor in her voice. She wasn't immune to the emotions that this letter would cause in everyone who read it. It was a brave rant by a General who was clearly all but broken after a terrible fight. He sounded to me like a commander who absurdly claims victory while wandering through lifeless streets full of ash.

Sandra hugged me tightly. I patted her with clumsy fingers. When women acted like this, I never knew exactly what to do. I wanted to tell her everything would be all right, and that I would kill the bad man in the morning. But I wasn't sure if I could do it or not. I wasn't even completely sure who the bad man really was. Had Kerr's decisions killed millions? Had mine? Or was it Crow's fault?

Worst of all, I didn't know what the Macros would do next. Possibly, they had another monstrous fleet sailing toward us, only a week behind the last one. In that case, they would soon trash everything we'd built up. Earth had been weakened, and they might not survive another round like the last one. If the Macros did show

338

up, I knew I was going to have to bite the bullet this time and stop them—or die trying.

"I know what you're thinking," Sandra said.

"You do?"

"Yes, and I agree with you. We should do it, Kyle. We should pull together every ship we have, fly to Earth, and take over. Crow must be removed from the throne. He doesn't deserve to sit there."

I stared at her, honestly shocked. "And I do?" I asked.

She blinked back at me. She slowly realized what her words had implied. Then her face hardened.

"Yes," she said, nodding slowly. "Why not?"

I hugged her again and laughed. "Because I'm a soldier, not an emperor. I never wanted to rule anyone. I just wanted Earth to beat the machines. I want peace, and an easy life again."

"I don't know, Kyle," she said. "I don't know if you can ever retire and be a quiet farmer again. I think things have gone too far for that."

I frowned and hugged her, but I didn't answer. I didn't know if any of us would ever see Earth again at all. That thought opened a hole in my heart, one I hadn't known was there.

The End

More Books by B. V. Larson:

STAR FORCE SERIES
Swarm
Extinction
Rebellion
Conquest
Battle Station
Empire
Annihilation

IMPERIUM SERIES
Mech Zero: The Dominant
Mech 1: The Parent
Mech 2: The Savant
Mech 3: The Empress
Five By Five (Mech Novella)

OTHER SF BOOKS
Technomancer
The Bone Triangle
Z-World
Velocity

Visit BVLarson.com for more information.

4712776R00186

Made in the USA
San Bernardino, CA
02 October 2013

P9-DHJ-637

The New Adventures of
MARY-KATE & ASHLEY™

The Case Of The
Rock Star's Secret™

Look for more great books in

~The New Adventures of~
MARY-KATE&ASHLEY™
series:

The Case Of The Great Elephant Escape™
The Case Of The Summer Camp Caper™
The Case Of The Surfing Secret™
The Case Of The Green Ghost™
The Case Of The Big Scare Mountain Mystery™
The Case Of The Slam Dunk Mystery™

and coming soon
The Case Of The Cheerleading Camp Mystery™

ATTENTION: ORGANIZATIONS AND CORPORATIONS
Most HarperEntertainment books are available at special quantity discounts
for bulk purchases for sales promotions, premiums, or fund-raising. For
information, please call or write:
Special Markets Department, HarperCollins Publishers,
10 East 53rd Street, New York, NY 10022–5299
Telephone (212) 207-7528 Fax (212) 207-7222

The Case Of The
Rock Star's Secret™

by Melinda Metz

📘HarperEntertainment
An Imprint of HarperCollins*Publishers*

A PARACHUTE PRESS BOOK

PARACHUTE PRESS

Parachute Publishing, L.L.C.
156 Fifth Avenue
New York, NY 10010

DUALSTAR PUBLICATIONS

Dualstar Publications
c/o Thorne and Company
A Professional Law Corporation
1801 Century Park East
Los Angeles, CA 90067

HarperEntertainment

An Imprint of HarperCollins*Publishers*
10 East 53rd Street, New York, NY 10022–5299

Copyright © 2000 Dualstar Entertainment Group, Inc. All rights reserved.
All photography copyright © 2000 Dualstar Entertainment Group, Inc.
All rights reserved.

THE NEW ADVENTURES OF MARY-KATE & ASHLEY, THE ADVENTURES OF
MARY-KATE & ASHLEY, Mary-Kate + Ashley's Fun Club, Clue and all logos, character
names and other distinctive likenesses thereof are the trademarks of Dualstar
Entertainment Group, Inc. All rights reserved. THE NEW ADVENTURES OF MARY-
KATE & ASHLEY books created and produced by Parachute Publishing, L.L.C., in cooperation with Dualstar Publications, a division of Dualstar Entertainment Group, Inc.,
published by HarperEntertainment, an imprint of HarperCollins*Publishers.*

If you purchased this book without a cover, you should be aware that this book is
stolen property. It was reported as "unsold and destroyed" to the publisher, and
neither the author nor the publisher has received payment for this "stripped book."

No part of this publication may be reproduced in whole or in part, or stored in a
retrieval system, or transmitted in any form or by any means, electronic, mechanical,
photocopying, recording, or otherwise, without written permission of the publisher.

For information, address HarperCollins Publishers Inc.
10 East 53rd Street, New York, NY 10022–5299

ISBN 0-06-106589-7

HarperCollins®, ■®, and HarperEntertainment™ are trademarks of
HarperCollins Publishers Inc.

First printing: March 2000

Printed in the United States of America

Visit HarperEntertainment on the World Wide Web at
http://www.harpercollins.com

10 9 8 7 6 5 4 3 2 1

1

A MUSICAL MYSTERY

"**M**ary-Kate! Ashley!" our mom called. "You're on TV!"

My twin sister and I raced into the living room.

"They're talking about your concert," Dad said.

Ashley and I squeezed onto the sofa between Dad and Mom. We stared at the newscasters on the television screen. It was weird that they were talking about us.

Weird, but cool!

"Soon our town will have its very own music center—with recording studios, rehearsal rooms, video equipment for making music videos, and a concert hall," the woman newscaster said. She smiled straight at the camera.

"That's right," the man newscaster added. "It all happens right after the big Sparkles concert this coming Monday night."

Ashley and I let out a cheer. The Sparkles was our band. We'd been rehearsing for four months, and we were finally going to get a chance to perform.

We cheered even louder when our pictures appeared on the screen, along with photos of Johnny Klause and Andrew Baxter. They were the other two Sparkles.

"The story of how this band was formed is very unusual," the woman newscaster said. "It all started when rock legend

Johnny Sparkle died—and left behind a strange and mysterious will."

"That's right," the other newscaster agreed. "The will said that if a group of ten-year-olds from our town formed a band and played on Johnny Sparkle's birthday, his mansion would be turned into a music center for the community."

"Now, here's the mysterious part," the woman newscaster said. "No one knows why—but Johnny Sparkle's will says the band has to have one red-haired boy with braces, one boy named Johnny, and a pair of blond twin girls."

Ashley and I slapped a high five. "Blond twin girls rule!" I cried.

"If the band doesn't have exactly the right four kids, the town won't get its music center," the first newscaster added. "Instead, Johnny Sparkle's mansion will go to his manager, Sunshine Boyd."

"That isn't the only request in the will.

The band members must also play instruments from Johnny Sparkle's private collection. Sparkle's birthday is Monday night—and so is the concert," the second newscaster continued. He smiled. "All I can say is, it's going to be very interesting. We hope to see you all there!"

"Before the concert you might want to stop by our zoo," the woman jumped in. "Two baby apes were born yesterday—"

Ashley picked up the remote and clicked off the TV. "It *is* totally strange that Johnny Sparkle cared so much about who was in the band," she said. A tiny line appeared between her eyebrows. That happens whenever she's thinking hard.

"Yeah. I can understand why he wanted the band to be named the Sparkles and why he wanted someone named Johnny in the band—since Johnny was his name," I agreed. "And I can even see why he wanted us to use his instruments."

"But why would he care if there were twins in the band? Or someone with red hair and braces?" Ashley asked.

Mom, Dad, Ashley, and I all thought for a minute in silence.

"It makes no sense to me," Dad finally said.

"I guess it will stay Johnny Sparkle's secret forever," Mom said.

I sighed. "Yeah—since he's not around to explain."

Ashley and I are detectives. And detectives hate secrets. We always want to know *everything*.

Ashley suddenly shook her head. "I want to find the answer. I want to know why Johnny Sparkle set up that strange will. I don't know exactly how we're going to do it, but—Mary-Kate, we've got a mystery to solve!"

A new mystery? All right!

"Let's do it," I said. Then I checked my

watch. "But right now we have to go, or we'll be late for rehearsal," I added.

We said good-bye to our parents and hurried out to the garage. In seconds we were on our bikes and pedaling for Johnny Sparkle's mansion. That's where we rehearse.

"I see the mansion!" Ashley called.

"You do not," I answered. "Those trees are in the way."

Ashley and I play spot-the-mansion whenever we're on our bikes. The winner is the person who sees part of Johnny's house first. It's so big that you can spot at least a little piece of it from almost any place in town!

"I do, too," Ashley said. "See that pointy thing sticking up near the top of the pine tree? That's the roof of the second tower. You know, the tower where the library is."

I tried to picture it. Johnny's house is so enormous that there are lots of rooms I still haven't been in. It has an indoor pool, a room with a Ping-Pong table, its very own concert hall, a movie theater, and a mini bowling alley. Plus a ton of bedrooms, a huge kitchen, two dining rooms, a bunch of living rooms, and some storage rooms.

There are rooms for recording music, writing music, and listening to music. Rooms for pretty much anything people ever do. And that includes a library in a tower room with a pointy roof.

"Okay, you win—this time," I told Ashley.

When we turned onto the mansion's street, we both started to pedal faster. That's because we spotted Johnny, Andrew, and Larry McHugh—our band's assistant—standing on the front lawn of the mansion. And they all looked very, very serious.

We sped up the long driveway and stopped in front of them. "What's wrong?" Ashley exclaimed.

"We have a problem. A big problem," Johnny announced.

"Well, tell us!" I demanded.

"It's easier to show you. Go on, Andrew," Johnny said.

Andrew hesitated. Then he pulled off his hat.

Ashley and I both gasped. We couldn't believe our eyes!

2

A SECOND CASE!

I squeezed my eyes shut for a second. Then I opened them and looked at Andrew again.

His red hair—it wasn't red anymore! It was pure black. It looked very weird with his pale, freckled face and red eyebrows.

"What happened?" I asked.

"All I did was wash my hair," Andrew answered. "When I got out of the shower I looked like this." He pointed to his head. "My hands turned black, too," he added. He held them up. His palms were as black as his hair.

"We're sunk! No red-haired kid with braces means no music center for the town," Johnny announced. "That's part of the will, remember?"

"Ahem!" Larry said. He touched his own red hair and grinned, so that his braces glinted in the sunlight.

I tried to ignore him. Sure, he had red hair and braces—but he couldn't sing at all! He tried out for the Sparkles—but he never made it past the first round of auditions.

"Where did you get the shampoo?" I asked Andrew.

"Was it a new bottle or one you'd had for a while?" Ashley asked.

We were both moving into detective mode. Good detectives always ask a lot of questions.

"I bought it at the drugstore just before yesterday's rehearsal," Andrew answered.

He put his hat back on. "It's the kind I always use."

He pulled a bottle out of his backpack and handed it to Ashley. I leaned over her shoulder as she examined it. The label said it would leave hair clean and manageable.

It didn't say anything about turning red hair black!

I glanced at Ashley. She was obviously thinking the same thing I was. The case of Johnny Sparkle's secret would have to wait. We had another mystery to solve first!

Ashley screwed open the bottle and poured a tiny drop of the liquid onto her finger. It instantly stained her skin black.

"We'll need to keep the bottle," Ashley said. She pulled a plastic sandwich bag out of her backpack. She slid the bottle into the bag, then returned the bag to the pack.

"So you had the shampoo with you at rehearsal yesterday?" I asked.

"Was it in your backpack?" Ashley asked.

"Did you put the shampoo away as soon as you got home?" I asked.

Andrew's head was whipping back and forth between me and Ashley. "You two are making me dizzy," he complained.

"Sorry," Ashley said. "But we really need to know everything about the shampoo."

"I had it in my backpack during rehearsal yesterday. And I left my backpack backstage at the mansion's concert hall while we practiced," Andrew said slowly. "I put the shampoo in the bathroom as soon as I got home."

Ashley turned to Larry. "Did you notice anyone in the mansion when we were rehearsing yesterday?" she asked.

"How are my superstars of tomorrow?" a man's voice called before Larry could answer.

I glanced over my shoulder and saw Sunshine Boyd bouncing toward us across the lawn. Sunshine always walks as if he has springs under his feet.

"He was backstage yesterday," Larry whispered.

Sunshine used to be Johnny Sparkle's manager. He was the one who picked us from the auditions. He always comes to watch us practice and jokes about how he wants to manage us someday.

"Wait!" Andrew yelped. "You think someone did this to me on *purpose*?"

That took a long time for Andrew to get! I hope he doesn't plan to become a detective someday.

"Definitely," I told him.

"It's possible," Ashley said at the same time. "Or maybe someone made a mistake at the factory and put dye in the shampoo bottle."

Ashley never jumps to conclusions. But I believe in going on my hunches. And I had a hunch that someone wanted Andrew's hair black.

"Are you kids ready for your first concert ever?" Sunshine asked when he finally reached us. He smoothed down his tie. It was orange with lots of little suns all over it. Sunshine always wears *something* with suns. He says it's his trademark.

"There's not going to be any concert," Johnny moaned. "We have to cancel."

"Andrew's hair got dyed black, and we have to have a redhead in the band, or there's no point in going on," I explained.

"Excuse me, but am I invisible? *I* could take Andrew's place," Larry volunteered. He pointed at his perfectly styled hair. "Red hair—check. Braces—check. Know all the songs—check. Plus you all know I have the moves that will make the fans go wild."

Larry *was* a good dancer. He was going to do some cool dance moves in the concert. If only he didn't keep trying to be a singer!

"Uh—thanks, Larry," I said. "But I bet a

hair salon could get Andrew's hair back to its usual red."

Larry scowled.

"Great idea!" Johnny exclaimed. "Let's cancel rehearsal so Andrew can go to the salon right now."

"You can always tell when people dye their hair red," Larry protested. "Dyed red hair isn't as bright onstage as natural red hair. Don't you agree, Sunshine?"

"Uh—well, it's not an area I have a lot of experience in," Sunshine answered. He ran his hand over his head. It was as hairless and smooth as an egg.

"The will didn't say that the red hair had to be natural," Ashley reminded Larry.

Larry glared at her. "Fine," he snapped. "We'll waste a day while Andrew goes to the beauty shop. Rehearsal tomorrow morning at eleven."

"See you then," Ashley said.

"Bye, guys! Bye, Sunshine!" I called as

Ashley and I headed to our bikes.

We pedaled off slowly so we could talk.

"Did you notice how angry Larry looked when you told Andrew to go to a hair salon?" Ashley asked.

"Yeah," I answered.

"And remember how upset he was when he didn't get picked to be one of the Sparkles?" Ashley said.

I nodded. I saw what Ashley was getting at. "And he wanted to take Andrew's place in the show," I said.

Ashley nodded back at me. "Larry has a very good motive for putting dye in Andrew's shampoo, doesn't he?" she asked.

"Yes!" I said. "A great motive!"

Motive is one of the words our great-grandma Olive taught us. She's a detective, too. She explained to us that a motive is a person's reason for committing a crime.

"Larry really wants to be in the band," I continued. "If Andrew is out, then Larry has a better chance of getting *in*."

"And Larry knows Andrew's hair has to be red for him to be in the band," Ashley added. "Plus, Larry's backstage all the time. So he had opportunity, too."

Opportunity is another word Great-grandma Olive taught us. It means that a suspect was in the right place at the right time to commit the crime.

Ashley frowned. I realized I was frowning, too.

Larry could be sort of annoying sometimes, but he was our friend. Neither of us wanted to think of him as a suspect.

"So what do we do?" I asked.

"We watch—and we wait," Ashley answered. "If Larry really wants to take Andrew's place in the band, he'll try something else. And soon."

THE MYSTERY HEATS UP

"**G**irls, we have a present for you!" a woman's voice cried as Ashley and I rode to rehearsal the next morning.

I glanced over and saw Mrs. Zane, the woman who lived two doors down from the Sparkle mansion. She stood in her front yard with her husband. They were always out there, gardening.

Ashley and I climbed off our bikes and headed over to them. Mr. Zane fumbled around in the pocket of his overalls. His gardening gloves made it hard for him to get a grip on whatever he was looking for.

Finally, he managed to dig out two cassette tapes. He handed one to me and one to Ashley. "It's a duet between a nightingale and a lark," he said proudly.

The plastic case for the tape was sealed with a cute sticker. It showed two birds singing to each other under a smiling sun.

"It really does sound as if they're singing to each other," Mrs. Zane added. She was dressed exactly like Mr. Zane—in overalls with gardening gloves. She had her brown hair in a ponytail, too—just the way he wore his. They were a little weird, but very nice.

"Thanks a lot," Ashley said politely.

"Yeah, thanks," I added. I stuck the tape in my backpack.

"It took us days to get that recording," Mr. Zane told us. "Some kids in the neighborhood have been setting off some kind of explosions—I think they're called cherry bombs—that keep ruining our recordings."

"That's too bad," I said.

"Have you had the chance to listen to the recording of the bumblebees in flight? It's a sound people rarely take the time to appreciate. There's too much noise in our world to hear the beauty around us," Mrs. Zane said. She scratched her nose. Dirt from her glove smeared across her face.

"We haven't gotten a chance to play that tape yet," Ashley admitted.

Mr. and Mrs. Zane were always stopping by our rehearsals and giving everyone in the band their tapes. Ashley and I had a whole stack in our bedroom.

"We will after our concert," I promised as I climbed back on my bike. "We'll have more time then."

Ashley got on her bike, too. "See you tomorrow night at the show," she told the Zanes.

Both their faces turned red.

"Um, we had plans to try and record the courting calls of crickets that night," Mr. Zane said in a rush.

"We wish you the best of luck, though," Mrs. Zane added. She shifted from one foot to the other.

"Well, I'm sure we'll be seeing you all the time when the music center opens," I said. Ashley and I waved and headed off.

We pulled into the driveway of the mansion. Ashley led the way inside. We hurried down the long hallway and through the double doors leading to the concert hall.

We both smiled when we saw Andrew standing on the stage. His hair was gleaming in the stage lights. His *red* hair.

"The hair salon worked!" I cried as we raced up to him.

"Yeah," he answered. "Except even they couldn't get the dye off my hands." He held them up so we could see. They were more gray than black now, at least.

Larry joined us onstage. He studied Andrew's hair. "See, I was right," he said. "The lights don't love dyed red hair the way they love natural color. Maybe I should do a duet with Andrew—just so the crowd gets to see some of the real stuff. We could do a song about all the kinds of food you can get stuck in your braces."

Ashley and I exchanged a quick glance. I knew she was thinking the same thing I was—*I really hope Larry isn't trying to get Andrew out of the band.*

"I don't think we should add anything to the act the day before the concert," Johnny called. He trotted down the left aisle and swung himself up onto the stage.

"I'm just trying to make the show the best it can be," Larry muttered. He checked his clipboard. "I noticed we're out of soda. Can anyone think of anything else we need before tomorrow night?"

Johnny shook his head. "You always think of everything before the rest of us even have a chance to," he said.

"It's true," I jumped in. "You're a great assistant."

"Maybe you'll be a real band manager like Sunshine someday!" Ashley added.

"I guess that might be cool," Larry said. But he didn't sound too happy. "I'll be back in about twenty minutes. I expect to hear some rehearsing when I get back."

He started off the stage, then turned around. "Oh, I almost forgot. Sunshine dropped these off before you guys got here." Larry handed each of us a bright yellow button with a sun drawn on it. "He said they're for good luck tomorrow," Larry added.

"That's so sweet!" Ashley exclaimed.

"He didn't give me one. I guess assistants don't need good luck," Larry grumbled as he stomped off the stage.

"Let's get started," Johnny said.

I strapped on the black-and-red guitar I'd picked out from Johnny's collection. Ashley positioned herself behind the drum set. Johnny sat down at the keyboard. Andrew strapped on his bass guitar and moved up to the mike at the front of the stage.

"Let's start with 'Happy Birthday,'" Johnny suggested.

Ashley counted it off on her drumsticks. "One, and two, and three, and—"

We launched into the song. We planned to play it at the very end of the concert. We figured it would give everyone in the audience time to think about Johnny Sparkle. And we hoped that somehow, someway, Johnny would be able to hear it, too.

"That was pretty good," Andrew called when we finished. "But I think we could use a few more run-throughs."

"Let's go for it," I answered. I wanted the song to be absolutely perfect.

We played it three more times. I kept looking over at Andrew. Just in case somebody—like Larry—had something else planned to get him out of the band.

I caught Ashley doing the same thing.

But the rehearsal was going completely smoothly. Andrew sang and played as well as he ever did.

"Want to move on to 'Alligator Tango' now?" Johnny asked.

"I could use a little more work on that one," Ashley agreed. "One, and two, and—"

KA-BOOM!

4

KABOOM!

*K*A-BOOM! KA-BOOM! KA-BOOM!

"What's that?" I yelled.

"Something's exploding!" Andrew yelled back. "It sounds like it's coming from the backyard!"

I jerked off the guitar and set it on the stage. Then I leaped down to the concert hall floor and flew toward the double doors. Ashley was right behind me.

"Be careful, Mary-Kate!" she cried.

I kept running. Down the long hallway.

Through the stained-glass doors.

And we were outside. The first thing I saw was a small, scorched spot on the cement by the pool. A few scraps of red paper were scattered on top of it.

Ashley picked up one of the scraps and studied it. "Cherry bomb," she announced.

"Mr. and Mrs. Zane—the couple down the street who keep giving us all those tapes—said kids in the neighborhood have been setting off cherry bombs," I added. "The Zanes were upset about it."

"They don't like noise much, do they?" Johnny asked.

"It's because they make those nature tapes," Ashley explained. "They need quiet to do it."

We all headed back inside. We ran into Larry as we reached the concert hall door. He was flushed and breathing hard. His red hair was glued to his forehead with sweat.

"What's going on? Why aren't you guys

practicing?" he asked breathlessly.

"We heard an explosion outside, and we went to check it out," Andrew said. "Some kids set off cherry bombs."

I led the way back into the concert hall. I glanced toward the stage. "Hey, Larry, I don't want to tell you how to do your job—but shouldn't you wait until *after* rehearsal to clean the instruments?" I asked.

"What are you talking about?" Larry demanded.

My stomach turned over.

"You took the instruments backstage to clean them, didn't you?" I asked.

"No. I just got back with the soda," Larry said. He held up the plastic bag in his hand. "It's right here."

My stomach turned over again.

"Well, *someone* did something with them," I cried. I pointed at the stage—the *empty* stage. "Because they're gone!"

MISSION: FIND THE INSTRUMENTS!

"**N**o way!" Andrew exclaimed. "This is horrible!"

"My keyboard was the first instrument Johnny Sparkle ever bought!" Johnny cried. "We have to find it."

"And my guitar was the one he used when he played his first show in Las Vegas. He loved that guitar. And so do I!" I wailed.

"Keep calm," Ashley told us. "Let's check backstage. Maybe Sunshine came by and moved the instruments or something."

"Good idea," I answered. Our footsteps echoed through the empty concert hall as we dashed backstage.

But there were no instruments back there. Just a couple of metal folding chairs and an old microphone stand.

"Now we really are going to have to cancel the concert," Johnny moaned. "The will said we have to use instruments from Johnny Sparkle's collection."

We stared at each other in silence. All our hard work was going to be for nothing. We wouldn't be able to do the special birthday concert for Johnny. The town wasn't going to get the music center.

"Hey, wait!" Ashley exclaimed. "We picked the instruments we wanted when we first started rehearsing, but there are tons more in Johnny's collection."

"Ashley's right! Come on!" I said. I took off through the house. I led the way up the massive marble staircase, then down a hall with a green tile floor and into the room at the very end—the room that held Johnny's huge collection of instruments.

It was completely empty.

Andrew walked into the center of the room and turned in circles. He stared at all the empty shelves and racks. "We're doomed," he burst out.

"He's right," Larry agreed. "You know that saying, 'the show must go on'? Well, it can't. It's totally impossible."

"I guess we should call Sunshine and tell him. And I guess we have to cancel the show," Johnny said. I heard a tiny quiver in his voice.

"We're not canceling!" I cried.

"What other choice do we have?" Johnny shot back.

"Mary-Kate and I will find the instruments," Ashley said firmly.

"But the concert is tomorrow night," Andrew protested.

"We'll get the instruments back in time. We promise," Ashley insisted.

"We can do it. We've solved harder cases than this," I added.

I hoped that turned out to be true!

I scanned the room, searching for some kind of clue. Any kind of clue.

I didn't see even one. Not a scrap of paper. Not a thread. Not a footprint.

"Uh, why don't you guys go home and let me and Ashley work," I said.

"Everyone meet here an hour before show time tomorrow, okay?" Larry asked. He herded Andrew and Johnny out.

"I want to take another look out back where the cherry bombs were set off," Ashley said. "Maybe whoever set off the explosion also took the instruments."

"You mean they used the explosion to get us all out of the way, so they had time to get the instruments out of the mansion," I said. "Good thinking!"

We headed back downstairs. "Maybe whoever took the instruments did it for the money," Ashley said. "Those instruments are valuable. They could be sold for a lot of cash."

"I'm not so sure. Stealing the instruments makes it impossible for us to follow Johnny's will," I said slowly. "And Andrew's black hair would have made it impossible for us to follow Johnny's will, too—except that Andrew dyed it back."

"You're right!" Ashley exclaimed.

"I think there's a connection," I said. I bit my lip. "I think someone definitely wants to stop the concert. And right now, their plan is working!"

MAKING NOTES

"**N**o! Nobody will stop the concert!" Ashley insisted. "Because we're going to find the instruments."

"Let's get started, then." I pulled two evidence bags out of the pocket of my jeans. I handed one to Ashley. I hoped we had more luck finding clues out here in the backyard. If we didn't, we were in big trouble.

I knelt down next to the scorched spot on the cement and studied it. I didn't see anything but the scraps of paper from the cherry bombs. I put a couple in my bag.

Ashley pulled out her detective note-book and a pencil. "Let's list what we know so far," she said. "We know that there was dye in Andrew's shampoo. We know that he had his shampoo in the concert hall where someone could have messed with it."

"We know that Johnny's instruments were stolen. Probably when we came out here after the cherry bombs went off," I said.

"I don't think anyone could have gotten *all* the instruments out of the mansion in the time that we were out here," Ashley pointed out. "There are too many. It would take too long."

"Maybe they just took the ones we were using," I said. "They could have gotten the other instruments before today. None of us have gone in that room for months."

Ashley tapped her pencil against her notebook. "We have to remember that when we think about suspects. We're look-ing for someone who is around the man-sion a lot."

Ashley wrote some more notes. Then she looked up.

"The only clue we have is some paper from a bunch of cherry bombs," she said. "Is there anything else?"

I thought about it. "Larry's hair looked really sweaty right after the instruments were stolen," I said. "And he was out of breath. But that could have been because he was carrying all the soda—not because he was dragging out the instruments."

"Larry seems like less of a suspect now, don't you think?" Ashley asked. "It made sense for him to try and get Andrew out of the band so he could take Andrew's place. But why would Larry want to stop the con-cert from happening?"

"You're right," I said. I felt a wave of relief. "Plus, if the concert doesn't go on,

Larry doesn't even get a chance to do his dance number!"

Ashley nodded. "I'll put him down as a possibility," she said, "but I don't think he should be at the top of our list."

She suddenly leaned over, squinting at the ground. "Mary-Kate, what's that yellow thing sticking out from under your left foot?" she asked.

I looked down and saw that I was standing on a scrap of bright yellow paper. I carefully picked it up and studied it. My eyes widened. "It looks like a piece of a sticker," I told Ashley. "It's got a smiling yellow sun on it."

"A sun?" Ashley repeated. That line appeared on her forehead.

"Sunshine Boyd!" I exclaimed. "But he seems like such a big fan! Why would he want to stop our concert?"

"Hey!" Ashley exclaimed. "Remember that TV show we saw yesterday? The news woman said that if the band doesn't meet the conditions of Johnny Sparkle's will, the mansion goes to—"

"Sunshine Boyd—Johnny Sparkle's former manager!" I interrupted. "So he does have a motive for stopping our concert. *And* he's always around. He had plenty of opportunity to put the dye in the shampoo and steal the instruments."

"I think we have a new number one suspect," Ashley said. She wrote Sunshine's name in her notebook.

I suddenly caught a flash of orange out of the corner of my eye. I turned—and gasped.

Someone in an orange jacket was climbing through one of the windows of the mansion!

"Ashley!" I shouted. I pointed at the window. "Someone's sneaking in! We've got to find out who it is!"

THE SUSPECT LIST GROWS

As Ashley and I stared, a pair of legs in jeans disappeared through the window.

"Let's go!" I yelled.

I bolted into the mansion. Ashley ran right behind me.

"I'll take the second and third floors. You take this floor and the basement," I said.

"Or we could just check the security monitors," Ashley suggested.

Sometimes it really helps to have a twin with a logical mind!

"Good idea," I said. I followed Ashley to the small room across the hall from the auditorium.

Ashley immediately started flipping switches. Images came up on each of the security screens.

There were cameras all over the house. Each camera was connected to a screen, so we could see inside many rooms at the same time.

I moved my eyes from screen to screen. "There. Someone is standing next to the indoor pool. See, by the diving board," I said.

"It's a girl. She doesn't look much older than us," Ashley said.

"What's she doing in there?" I asked.

"Let's find out," Ashley said. "You go through the dressing rooms. I'll go to the emergency exit." She pointed to the door on the screen. Then she checked her watch. "At fourteen after the hour—that's exactly three minutes from now—we'll both go into the pool room. We'll have her trapped."

I nodded. I rushed out of the security room and hurried down a long hallway with white shag carpeting. I turned left into a hallway with tiger-print tile. Then I ducked into one of the changing rooms for the pool.

The smell of chlorine filled my nose. I hoped I wouldn't sneeze. I didn't want to give the girl any warning.

I tiptoed up to the door leading to the pool. I stared at my watch as the second hand went around. At exactly fourteen after, I burst through the door.

"What are you doing in here?" Ashley demanded as she burst through the door on the other side of the pool.

The girl backed up, staring at Ashley. Then she turned to run—and saw me. Her blue eyes widened with alarm, and her face turned so pale it made all her freckles look twice as dark.

"Who are you?" I asked.

The girl sank down onto one of the shiny gold deck chairs. Now that I saw her in person, she looked about eleven or twelve. "My name is Maggie Croft. I live down the street," she answered. She gave one of her dark brown curls a twist.

"That doesn't explain what you're doing in here," Ashley answered. She sat down in the chair next to Maggie's. I hurried over and sat in the chair on Maggie's other side.

"Let me show you something. It will help me explain." Maggie reached into her backpack and pulled out a velvet pouch. Slowly she opened the drawstring at the top.

My heart beat a little faster. What was in there? Ashley and I leaned closer as Maggie removed...a crumpled tissue.

Maggie cradled the tissue in the palm of one hand. She gazed at it lovingly. "Johnny

Sparkle actually blew his nose on this," she whispered.

"Huh?" I exclaimed.

"It's the newest thing in my collection," Maggie said.

She collected used tissues?

"Huh?" Ashley exclaimed.

"I've been collecting Johnny Sparkle memorabilia since I was seven. I have the largest collection in the world," Maggie bragged. She gently replaced the tissue in the velvet bag. "If I could just have something from Johnny's house, that would make my collection absolutely complete."

"So that's why you were here? You were going to steal something?" I demanded.

Maggie jerked her chin up. "I didn't think Johnny would mind. I was his biggest fan. "

"We can't let you take anything from the mansion without permission," Ashley said firmly. "But we'll talk to Sunshine Boyd. He's—"

"I know. Johnny's old manager," Maggie interrupted.

"Right. We'll ask him if there is something of Johnny's you can have—if you promise not to sneak back in again," Ashley continued. "Find us after the concert tomorrow night and we'll let you know what he said."

Maggie leapt to her feet. "I promise a million times! Thanks. Thanks so much!" She started for the door.

"We'll go with you," I said quickly.

Ashley and I followed Maggie through the house and out the front door. We watched as she headed off down the street.

"Do you think we should add her to our list of suspects?" I asked. "The instruments would make a fantastic part of her Sparkle collection."

"If she already took the instruments, she wouldn't need to come back for something else," Ashley said. "And as far as we know, she doesn't have a motive for stopping the concert."

"I guess we could have two mysteries—who put the dye in Andrew's shampoo, *and* who stole the instruments." I frowned.

"Maybe," Ashley said. "Okay, I'm going to put Maggie on the list—but at the very bottom."

We climbed on our bikes. "I keep thinking about our other case—Johnny's secret. You know, the reason he wanted blond twins and a red-haired kid with braces and all that," I told Ashley. "Do you think that could have anything to do with this case?"

"It seems like it is connected," Ashley said slowly. "But I don't see—"

"Ashley!" I interrupted. "I just thought of someone else who's been around the mansion an awful lot. The Zanes."

Ashley squinted at me. "But why would the Zanes want to stop our concert?"

"I don't know," I admitted. "I can't think

of a motive for them. But they have had plenty of opportunity."

"That's true. Okay, let's try to find out where they were during Friday's rehearsal, when Andrew's shampoo got messed up," Ashley said. "But we need to do it without making them suspicious."

I glanced at the Zanes' front yard. They were both out there. Mr. Zane was holding a microphone up to a flower while Mrs. Zane watched. "I have an idea," I said. "Come with me."

We walked our bikes down the block to the Zanes' yard.

"We're helping a friend look for her lost dog," I began. "The last time she saw the dog, he was in this neighborhood. That was on Friday at about four o'clock. Did you see a little black terrier running loose?"

It was a lie, and I don't like to lie. But sometimes, when you're a detective, you need to.

"Friday afternoon?" Mr. Zane shook his head. "No, we were at the museum."

"We watched one of their wonderful documentary films," Mrs. Zane added. She smiled. "But we'll let you know right away if we see the poor little dog."

"Thanks!" Ashley and I said together. We rode off.

"Well, they have an alibi," Ashley said. "They couldn't have fooled with Andrew's shampoo."

"Right," I agreed. "They could still be suspects for stealing the instruments, though."

Ashley shrugged. "I think we should cross the Zanes off our list. They don't have any motive. I still think Sunshine Boyd is our number one suspect. He's the only one with a strong motive *and* opportunity."

"I guess." I felt a sneeze coming, so I reached into my jacket pocket for a tissue.

Huh? I couldn't find my pocket!

"Oh, no!" I exclaimed. "I left my jacket at the mansion."

We turned our bikes around and started pedaling back the way we'd come. In less than a minute we were pulling up the mansion's long driveway. We parked our bikes and headed inside.

Our footsteps echoed on the marble floor of the entryway.

"Wait. What's that?"

Ashley grabbed my shirt and held me in place.

Tap! Tap! Tap! It sounded like footsteps.

Someone else was in the mansion.

And they were moving toward us!

8

THE COPYCAT

It's Maggie! I thought. *She broke her promise not to sneak in again!*

Then Sunshine Boyd appeared in the entry hall. He was followed by a woman in a lime green suit with matching high heels.

"The use of color is fabulous," the woman was saying. She stopped speaking when she saw me and Ashley.

"Oh, hello, girls," Sunshine said. His pants had little suns all over them. I didn't even know they made pants like that!

"This is Dot Garvin," he continued. "She's my interior decorator. I-I always loved the way Johnny had his bedroom decorated. I want Dot to, uh, do mine exactly like it."

I had seen Johnny's bedroom. It was amazingly cool. The bed was a huge swan with the mattress nestled between its wings.

"We just came back to get Mary-Kate's jacket," Ashley said.

"Fine, fine. I'll see you at the concert tomorrow night," Sunshine told us. He and Dot headed out the front door.

"Wow. Now he's our super top suspect," Ashley said. "Maybe he had the decorator in here so she could decorate his room like Johnny's. But maybe he had her here because he wants her to redecorate the mansion."

"Yeah," I agreed. "Maybe he's so sure he'll get the house that he's already planning the changes he wants to make."

"He must be the one. But we need proof," Ashley said. She grinned. "I have an idea where we can get it."

The next day after school, Ashley and I rode to Sunshine's house. It was a one-story building at the end of a quiet block.

"We have a problem," Ashley announced. "Sunshine's here. I just saw him walk past the kitchen window."

We backed our bikes up until we were sure Sunshine couldn't see us. "Now what do we do?" I asked.

"When Sunshine wanted us out of the mansion so he could steal our instruments, he made noise outside. Remember?" Ashley answered. "He set off cherry bombs so we'd all run into the backyard."

"Ashley, I'm shocked!" I teased. "You're acting as if you're sure Sunshine is the one who stole the instruments—and we don't have proof yet!"

"You're right," Ashley said. She sounded a little upset with herself. "I mean *whoever* stole the instruments used the cherry bombs to make a lot of noise."

"How does that help us?" I asked. "We don't have any cherry bombs."

"But we can still make a lot of noise," Ashley explained. "Give me a boost into the tree. I'll make as much noise as I can. When Sunshine comes out to see what's going on, you sneak around to the back of his house and peek into his windows. Maybe you can find some clues."

"Got it." I made a stirrup out of my hands. Ashley put her foot in, and I hoisted her to the bottom branch.

"Ca-caw!" Ashley cried. "Ca-caw! Ca-caw!"

I crept forward and peeked at Sunshine's house. "He's not coming," I told Ashley.

"Meow. Woof. Baaa!" she yelled.

"I would definitely come out to see a cat,

a dog, and a sheep all in my front yard. But Sunshine's still inside," I said.

Ashley let out a long wail. It was amazing. She really did sound like a siren.

Sunshine's front door swung open, and he stepped outside.

Ashley let out another wail, and I raced around to the back of Sunshine's house.

I peeked through the first window. It opened into Sunshine's living room. It was pretty ordinary. There were lots of pictures of Sunshine with Johnny Sparkle on the walls.

I didn't see anything that looked like a clue, so I moved on to the next window.

It was made of frosted glass, so I couldn't see through it.

I moved down to the next window and peeked in.

My breath caught in my chest.

"Oh, no!" I whispered.

9

A SURPRISING CONFESSION

I dashed around to the front of the house. Luckily, Sunshine was nowhere in sight. I didn't stop running until I got to Ashley's tree.

She swung herself down. "What's the matter? Did you find any clues?"

"I found a huge clue!" I answered. "Sunshine's bedroom is in the middle of being redecorated. Half the sun wallpaper is gone. And he has a swan bed in there. It's exactly like Johnny Sparkle's bed."

"Whoa," Ashley gasped. "That means he was telling the truth. He really is decorating his bedroom like Johnny's."

I nodded. "Yep," I said. "And he wouldn't be redecorating his own house if he was planning to move into Johnny's mansion, right?"

Ashley got that line between her eyebrows again. "That wouldn't make sense." She pulled out her detective notebook and flipped it open. "I think we should cross him off our list."

"Me, too," I agreed. "Who do we have left?"

"Everyone on our list is at the very bottom," Ashley complained. "We have Larry. And Maggie. And that's it. We crossed the Zanes off."

"Maggie's motive is pretty strong," I reminded her. "Johnny's instruments would be perfect for her collection."

"I think we should talk to her again. And

right now. We only have a few hours before the concert," Ashley said. She climbed back on her bike.

I climbed back on mine. "Where are we going? We don't know where Maggie lives."

"We can always ask the Zanes," Ashley answered as she started to pedal. "Maggie told us she lives in the neighborhood. Maybe they know her. If they don't, some of Johnny Sparkle's other neighbors must!"

It didn't take us too long to get to the Zanes'. We rushed up to their front door. Ashley knocked, and Mr. and Mrs. Zane answered immediately. They were both still wearing their thick gardening gloves.

"Hi. Listen, we met Maggie Croft yesterday," Ashley told them. "She said she lived in the neighborhood. We wanted to visit her, but we don't know what house."

"The Crofts live in number seventeen, two doors down on the other side of the street," Mr. Zane said.

Mrs. Zane leaned forward. "Shouldn't you two be at a final rehearsal for your concert?" she asked.

"We just have one thing to do first," Ashley said.

Yeah, I thought. *Just one little thing—solve a whole mystery!*

"See you later—and thanks," I said. And then Ashley and I hurried off to Maggie's house.

I knocked.

There was no answer.

I knocked again—louder.

Maggie opened the door. She started biting her lip when she saw me and Ashley.

"I did it!" she burst out. "I'm sorry. I know it was wrong. But I just couldn't help myself!"

COUNTDOWN TO THE CONCERT

So Maggie did steal the instruments. And she confessed! Case closed. Yes!

Ashley grinned at me. I grinned right back at her.

"Come on. I'll give them back to you right now. I really am sorry." Maggie led us up the stairs and over to the first room on the right.

The door of the room was covered with pictures of Johnny Sparkle. Johnny singing. Johnny playing guitar. Johnny as a young boy. Johnny with his pet parakeet. Johnny, Johnny, Johnny.

"I call this the Sparkle room," Maggie told us. She opened the door slowly and flipped on the light.

"Oh, wow," Ashley muttered as we stepped inside.

Six card tables filled the room. Each was covered with a different color felt. On the felt rested all kinds of things.

On the closest table I spotted a guitar pick, a sweat sock, a chewed piece of gum, a tangled knot of hair. Each of the items had its own spotlight shining down on it. I glanced up and saw that the lights were coming from flashlights that had been hung from the ceiling with fishing line.

Maggie pointed to a Popsicle stick in the center of the front table. "I watched Johnny eat that Popsicle," she told us. "That piece of wood actually touched his lips." She closed her eyes and gave a long, loud sigh.

"That's...nice," Ashley said. "But where are the instruments? We have to get them back to the mansion for the concert."

Maggie opened her eyes. "Instruments?" she repeated.

"Yes, instruments!" I said. "Where are they?"

"I didn't take any instruments," Maggie protested.

"You already confessed," Ashley said. "Please, just tell us where they are."

"No, no, no!" Maggie cried. "I did take some things from the mansion—but not the instruments. I found Johnny's toothbrush and a tube of his toothpaste in the little bathroom downstairs. I just had to have them."

This was horrible. Our case had been closed for about two seconds. And now it was open. Wide, wide open!

"I'm sure it will be okay if you keep the toothbrush and toothpaste," I told Maggie.

"We'll ask Sunshine, just in case."

Maggie gave a little hop on her toes. Her brown curls flew around her face. "This means I really do have the most special, most sparkling Johnny Sparkle collection in the whole world!"

"Congratulations," Ashley told her. "We have to go now. We have a case to solve."

"Good luck," Maggie said. She reached down and stroked the felt of the card table.

I grabbed Ashley's arm, and we tiptoed out of the house.

"Do you think Maggie was telling us the truth?" Ashley asked when we had shut the front door behind us.

I nodded. "As soon as she saw us, she admitted she took the toothbrush and toothpaste. If she was lying about the instruments, why not lie about the toothbrush, too? That way she could have kept everything."

We started our bikes across the street

and slowly headed down the block to the mansion. "I don't know who should be on the top of our suspect list now," Ashley said.

"Well, Sunshine is off. And the Zanes are off. And now Maggie is off...." I didn't want to say what I was about to say. But I had to.

"Maybe we should talk about Larry again," I blurted out. "Do you think he could have been angrier than we thought about not getting into the band?"

"So angry he would want to stop the concert?" Ashley asked. "Maybe. Except he was out getting soda when the cherry bombs went off, remember?"

"He *said* he was out getting soda," I answered.

"I guess he could have bought the soda on his way to the mansion. He could have hidden it backstage. That way he would have the perfect alibi."

"Right," I agreed. "His alibi would be that

he was at the store when the instruments were stolen."

We wheeled our bikes up the driveway and parked them. Andrew and Johnny's bikes were already there.

"He would have had just enough time to set off the cherry bombs, run back to the auditorium, and stash the instruments somewhere in the mansion. We didn't search every room," Ashley added.

I glanced at my watch. "We're running out of time," I said nervously. "The concert is supposed to start in one hour and five minutes."

Ashley tapped her chin with her finger. "I think I have a plan," she told me. "A plan that will tell us for sure if Larry is the thief."

WILL THE SHOW GO ON?

Johnny peeked out the door of the green room. That's the place where performers wait to go onstage. "Larry's coming," he whispered.

"You know the plan, right?" Ashley asked Andrew.

He gave a fast nod.

"Hi," Larry said as he stepped into the room. "No instruments?"

"Ashley and I talked to all of the suspects today," I told him.

"We told each of them, if they took the instruments, all they had to do was put them back onstage before the concert," Ashley added. "We promised there would be no questions asked."

"But it's getting really late," Larry said. "If someone was going to return the instruments, wouldn't they have done it already?"

"Maybe not," Ashley said. "Sometimes it takes a long time for someone to realize they've done a wrong thing."

She stared at him. I stared at him, too.

He didn't turn red or look at all guilty. But that didn't mean he *wasn't* guilty.

I glanced at Andrew. Did he remember what *his* part of the plan was? Ashley and I had done what we were supposed to do. Now it was Andrew's turn.

I leaned over and nudged him with my elbow. He gave a little squeak. Then he sat up straighter and cleared his throat.

"Larry, even if someone does bring back

the instruments, you might have to sing for me," Andrew said. His voice came out in a loud croak. He sounded like a frog with a cold. "I have a sore throat. There's no way I can sing tonight."

A smile started to form on Larry's face. But he quickly turned it into a frown.

"Of course I'll sing for you. No problem!" Larry told Andrew. "Uh—it's too bad you're sick, though."

Larry sat down next to Johnny on the violet leather sofa.

Ashley and I exchanged nervous looks. This wasn't how the plan was supposed to work.

Here's how the plan *was* supposed to work. Larry would be so excited about having the chance to sing that he would run out and get the instruments from wherever he'd hidden them.

But Larry was just sitting on the sofa. Just *sitting* there.

Maybe he thought it would look suspicious if he left the room as soon as he heard that he had the chance to perform tonight. Maybe he was trying to think of a good excuse to go out.

I checked my watch: Seven-twenty.

The concert was supposed to start in forty minutes. In ten minutes the audience would start coming into the auditorium.

Come on, Larry, I thought. *There's not much time left!*

But Larry just sat there.

Sat, and sat, and sat, and sat.

And sat.

I checked my watch again: Seven-thirty.

"Ashley, maybe we should go check the stage. Maybe the instruments are back," I blurted out.

"Good idea," Ashley answered.

We rushed out of the room and over to the stage. We peeked out from the wings.

Of course the instruments weren't

onstage. We never really told any suspects to return them to the auditorium. That was just a story for Larry.

But it was starting to look as if we were wrong about Larry. Which meant we had no suspects at all!

"What do we do now?" I asked Ashley.

"I don't know," she admitted.

We both stood there. Staring at the empty stage. I could hear people out in the auditorium.

I headed over to the thick red curtain. I pulled it open a teeny, tiny bit and peeked out.

Our whole family was in the front row. I saw Maggie Croft, too. And Sunshine Boyd. And a bunch of kids from school. And a bunch of people I didn't know.

"They're all waiting to hear us play," I said.

Ashley moved up behind me and peered out. "All the people are going to be so disappointed if the show doesn't go on," she answered. "Especially because if there's no show, there's no music center."

"Maybe we should tell them all to go home now," a voice said from behind us.

I looked over my shoulder and saw Johnny standing there.

"What's the point of them staying?" he continued. "All they're going to hear tonight is a big concert of silence."

My heart gave a hard double thump.

"That's it!" I exclaimed.

12

THE INCREDIBLE ANSWER

"**W**hat do you mean, that's it?" Ashley asked.

"I know who did it. The Zanes!" I said.

"The Zanes?" Ashley repeated. "But we crossed them off our list. They don't have any motive for stopping the concert."

"Yes, they do. I just figured out what it is!" I said. "They hate noise. A music center in the neighborhood means lots of noise."

"And that would mess up their tapes," Johnny burst out. "Way to go, Mary-Kate!"

"But the Zanes have an alibi for the day the dye was put in Andrew's shampoo," Ashley reminded me. "They were at the museum."

"Maybe," I answered. "Or maybe they weren't. We didn't bother to check. But now we need to find out if they really went there!"

We hurried back to the green room. Ashley grabbed her backpack. One of the Zanes' tapes fell out as she removed her detective notebook. I picked it up—and gasped as I noticed the sticker on the tape's plastic case. It showed two birds, singing to each other under a smiling yellow sun.

A smiling sun! I ripped open my backpack and pulled out the evidence bag with the scrap of sticker on it.

"Look!" I cried. I held up the tape case and the scrap of paper. "They're exactly the same! This proves that the Zanes set off the cherry bombs!"

"Well, it proves that they were there," Ashley said. "But that isn't enough. They could have been there anytime. We need to prove they lied about where they were on Friday."

"But how?" I moaned. "No one will remember whether the Zanes were at the museum or not. I bet hundreds of people went there last Friday."

"What kind of detectives are you?" Andrew demanded, coming over to Ashley and me. "The concert starts in twenty minutes, we have no instruments, I told Larry he could sing in my place—and you guys are talking about the museum?"

Ashley quickly explained what we were trying to figure out.

Andrew stared at us. "That's easy," he said. "No one was at the museum last Friday. It's closed on Fridays."

"What?" I grabbed his shoulders. "Are you sure?"

"Sure, I'm sure," Andrew said. "My mom works there."

"I can't believe it!" I cried. "Andrew, you just solved our case!"

"I did?" Andrew looked shocked.

"Come on, Mary-Kate. Let's get over to the Zanes' house. We have instruments to find—and I've got a plan!" Ashley said.

We tore out of the mansion and down the block to the Zanes'. As we ran, Ashley told me her plan. It was perfect!

We rang the Zanes' doorbell. Mr. Zane opened the door. When he saw us, he quickly put his hands in his pockets.

"Hi. We know you weren't planning to come to the concert," Ashley said. "But just in case, we wanted you to know that it's been canceled."

"Oh, too bad," Mr. Zane said. But he sounded kind of happy.

"Now the town won't get its music center," I told them.

"It is too bad," Ashley agreed. "Our band was hoping we could record a song using some of the stuff you taped."

"We were going to write a song about a nightingale and a lark to go with the recording you gave us," I added.

"That sounds wonderful!" Mrs. Zane exclaimed.

"It would have been great," Ashley agreed. "But without the recording studio at the music center, we won't be able to record any songs at all."

Mr. and Mrs. Zane exchanged a look. Mr. Zane cleared his throat. Mrs. Zane gave a little cough. Mr. Zane cleared his throat again. It was as if they were having some kind of coded conversation.

"Come with us," Mrs. Zane said at last.

"This is it," Ashley whispered in my ear as we followed the Zanes into the house.

She was right. When we walked into the living room all I saw was instruments. On the sofa. On the chairs. On the coffee table. On the floor.

I spotted my guitar propped against the wall. I raced over and hugged it.

"We're sorry we took the instruments," Mr. Zane said. "We would have given them back. We just wanted to stop the music center from being built."

"The noise makes it so hard for us to make our tapes," Mrs. Zane jumped in. "And we want people to hear the amazing sounds they are missing every day."

"When the music center opens, you'll be able to use the recording studios," Ashley told them. "They have machines that can take out background noise."

"And we really would like to do a song with your sounds," I added. "Like the sound of bees in flight. Please come to the concert. I bet it will give you a ton of ideas for what we can all do together."

"We would be delighted," Mr. Zane said.

He hurried over to Ashley's drum set. "Let us help you get your instruments back to the mansion."

As he pulled his hands out of his pockets, I noticed that the skin on his palms was dark gray.

"Hair dye?" Ashley asked. She held up her finger and showed them the gray spot where she'd tested the dye from Andrew's shampoo bottle.

It hit me. "Is that why you were always wearing your gardening gloves?" I asked. "So we wouldn't see the dye?"

Both Mr. and Mrs. Zane looked embarrassed.

"That's right," Mr. Zane admitted.

"The dye is harmless," Mrs. Zane added. "We didn't want to hurt anyone."

I smiled at them. "We know that," I answered. "Now let's go." I checked my watch. "It's ten minutes to concert time!"

THE SPARKLE SECRET

"**E**verybody! Everybody! Ev-ery-bo-dy! Do the alligator tango!"

I played the last chord of the song. The audience went wild, cheering and whistling and clapping.

Then Sunshine Boyd walked onto the stage. Andrew moved away from the microphone and Sunshine stepped up to it.

"I just wanted to let you know that all the rules in Johnny Sparkle's will have been followed," he announced. "This town now owns the Sparkle mansion—the finest music center in the country!"

The audience began to cheer again. Ashley, Johnny, Andrew, and I cheered, too.

"This never would have happened without you two," Andrew called to me and Ashley.

"Yeah. You rock!" Johnny told us.

I hurried over to Ashley's drum set. She jumped up and we slapped a high five.

"There's just one other mystery I wish we'd been able to solve," Ashley said.

"I know," I answered. "If only we'd been able to find out Johnny Sparkle's secret."

"Yeah, I—" Ashley began.

Then Sunshine waved a hand for the crowd to quiet down. It took a minute, but the auditorium became completely silent.

"I want you all to hear a letter from Johnny Sparkle," he said. "Johnny's will said that if this concert happened, this letter should be read."

Sunshine cleared his throat and began to read. His voice came out a little quivery.

"Dear Everyone,

I hope you're enjoying the concert. I wish I could be there with you. And who knows, maybe in some way I am.

I've been thinking about my life a lot lately. Especially about the happy times. I've had a lot of those.

You want to know what the happiest ones were? Playing with my very first band, the Sparkles. We had more fun playing concerts in my little backyard than I've ever had playing anywhere else.

I wanted four other kids to have the same fun I did. That's why I put it in my will that kids from the town had to form a band.

I thought it would be cool if the new Sparkles were at least a little like the old Sparkles. So I asked for one red-haired kid with braces, two blond twin girls, and someone named Johnny.

I'm sure you'd rather be listening to them play than listening to me go on. So peace, love, and all that.

I'm out of here.

Johnny"

I looked over at Ashley. We both smiled.

Now we knew the rock star's secret. And it was a great one.

Sunshine folded the letter and put it in his pocket. When I looked at his face, I saw one tear running down his cheek.

I walked over and took the microphone. "Now we'd like all of you to join us in singing 'Happy Birthday' to Johnny Sparkle," I announced.

I glanced offstage and saw Larry watching from the wings. "That means you, too,"

I called to him. "Get out here!"

Larry bounded out and stood next to Andrew. "This totally makes up for you getting your voice back," he told Andrew with a grin.

I took Sunshine by the arm and backed up until we were both standing next to Ashley. Johnny held his hands ready over his keyboard.

"One, and two, and three, and—"

We all started singing "Happy Birthday." All of us—everyone in the whole place. It sounded awesome.

Even the Zanes were singing.

Ashley and I watched them. We both started to giggle.

The Zanes were singing as loud as everyone else. But they had their fingers in their ears!

Hi from both of us,

Ashley and I were having the best time at cheerleading camp. Ashley was even good enough to try out for captain! But someone wanted to make sure she lost the vote—no matter what.

It all started when Ashley's lucky pom-poms were stolen. Then she was threatened in a scary cheer! Was someone trying to get rid of the competition? Or was there another motive behind this cheerleading caper? That's what we had to find out!

Do you want to find out more? Take a look at the next page for a sneak peek at The New Adventures of Mary-Kate & Ashley: *The Case of the Cheerleading Camp Mystery.*

See you next time!

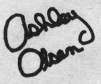

The Case Of The
CHEERLEADING CAMP MYSTERY

Ashley and I sat on the grass with Marla, Wendy, and the other girls from our cheer squad, the Panthers. Princess Patty and her squad, the Tigers, were next to us.

The junior counselors all lined up. They did a special Welcome cheer for us. At the end, two of the counselors lifted our counselor, Kim—and threw her into the air!

"Wow!" Ashley breathed. "That's a basket toss."

Kim tucked her legs close to her body as she came down. The other counselors caught her. It was totally cool!

I turned to Marla. Kim is her big sister. "Kim is really great!" I said.

Marla nodded. "She's the best. That's why the Panthers have won the All-Camp competition for the last five years—because she's been squad captain every year."

"Not this year," Patty reminded us in a snippy tone. "This year she's a counselor—so she can't compete. That's why we Tigers are going to cream you guys this year!"

"I don't think so," Wendy said with a smile. "I'm going to be captain of the Panthers. And I am not going to let my squad lose the title!"

Kim came over to us, carrying some folders. "Listen up, Panthers," she called. We gathered around her.

"You're going to divide into three groups," Kim told us. "Ashley, Wendy, Marla—since you three are competing for squad captain, you're each going to lead a group." She handed each of them a folder. "Here are copies of a cheer for your group to learn. It's your job to organize your

group and prepare the cheer. You'll perform it for Coach Bradshaw in half an hour.
I'm here to help anyone who needs help."

"All right!" I said.

I was in Ashley's group, along with two
other Panthers, Katie and Trisha.

Ashley opened her folder and handed
each of us a copy of the new cheer. "Let's
just read it out loud so we can hear what it
sounds like," she said. "Ready? Hit it!"

We all began to shout out the cheer:

*"Two, four, six, eight, Ashley Olsen,
don't you wait! If you don't want major
trouble—"*

I broke off as I read the rest of the cheer.
So did Katie and Trisha. But Ashley
frowned and read the last line aloud.

"Quit the tryouts on the double!"

Ashley and I stared at each other.

This wasn't a cheer. It was a threat!

Someone was trying to stop Ashley from
becoming squad captain!

Take a Peek Inside our Diaries!

3 Very Special Books in the Two of a Kind Series

Dear Diary,

When Mary-Kate and I packed up to come to White Oak Academy, I thought boarding school would be like regular school. But it's totally strange! The principal is called a head-mistress, seventh grade is called first form, and my roommate is called – well, I call her weird. And the worst thing is, there's this huge dance coming up.

I know, I know. I, Ashley Burke, don't want to go to a dance? But here's the deal – the girls have to ask the boys. And I don't know any!

– Ashley

TWO of a Kind Diaries

First in a Special Three-Part Series!

Calling All Boys

The Diaries of Mary-Kate & Ashley

OUT NOW!

–look for *Winner Take All* coming in April 2000 and –*P.S. Wish You Were Here* coming in June 2000

ALL-NEW STORIES, SETTINGS, AND DIARY FORMAT—SAME AWESOME SERIES!

www.maryandashley.com

DUALSTAR PUBLICATIONS

™ HarperEntertainment

TWO OF A KIND TM & ©2000 Warner Bros.

IT'S YOUR FIRST CLASS
TICKET TO ADVENTURE!

Free
movie Poster *
in every Video.

Own it only on Video!

TM & © 2000 Dualstar Entertainment Group, Inc. Distributed by Warner Home Video, A Time Warner Entertainment Company, 4000 Warner Blvd., Burbank, CA 91522. All rights reserved. *Passport to Paris* and all logos, character names and other distinctive likenesses there of are the trademarks of Dualstar Entertainment Group, Inc. *While supplies last.

ADVERTISEMENT

GAME GiRLS

SOLVE ANY CRIME BY
DINNER TIME™

PARTY DOWN WITH THE
HOTTEST DANCES AND
COOLEST FASHIONS

The New Adventures of
MARY-KATE & ASHLEY™

DANCE PARTY of the CENTURY™

GAME BOY
COLOR

PC
CD-ROM

www.marykateandashley.com

DUALSTAR
INTERACTIVE   www.acclaim.net

Licensed by Nintendo. Game Boy Color is a trademark of Nintendo of America Inc. © 1996 Nintendo of America Inc.
© & TM 2000 Dualstar Entertainment Group, Inc. Acclaim® © 2000 Acclaim Entertainment, Inc. All Rights Reserved.

Mary-Kate & Ashley Olsen Invite You

To Russia, With Love

SUMMER CRUISE: JUNE 25 - JULY 2, 2000

Welcome aboard an awesome cruise vacation to parts
of the world you've only read about. Join Mary-Kate & Ashley
as they explore Finland, Sweden, Estonia and even Russia!

It all begins with a visit to our website at **www.sailwiththestars.com** or
have your parents call Sail With The Stars at **805-778-1611**.

Adventures for a Summer. Memories for a Lifetime.

Reservations must be made exclusively through Sail With The Stars®. Reservation deadline: March 15, 2000 based on availability.

CST#2002736-10

Check it out!

Mary-Kate & Ashley are on the web at

www.marykateandashley.com